DRAGON'S LORE

15 May 2013

Sami —
I'm so glad I got
to meet you at MRMS!
Best,
S L Roth

S.L. Rottman

Published by AFterwords
©2012 S.L. Rottman

Cover art ©2012 Teresa Jacoby
Cover design by Art Wickberg

All rights reserved. No part of this book may be reproduced or transmitted in any form or any means, electronic or mechanical—except by a reviewer who may quote brief passages in a review to be published in a magazine, newspaper, or on-line—without permission in writing from the publisher. Your support of the author's rights is appreciated.

Summary: Maeya Daceae must bond with a reluctant Dragon and together they journey to join Rider Saeb and her rebel Clan.

ISBN 978-0-9799812-8-9

S.L. Rottman is the award-winning author of many books for teens. A teacher, football fan, and avid reader, Rottman calls Colorado home. Visit **www.slrottman.net** for more information.

Other books by S.L. Rottman:

DRAGON'S LUCK

SINCERELY

HERO

ROUGH WATERS

HEAD ABOVE WATER

STETSON

SHADOW OF A DOUBT

SLALOM

OUT OF THE BLUE

With special thanks to all who have been harassing—I mean, asking—for the sequel. Your enthusiasm made it easy for me to go back to Saeb's world.

PROLOGUE

SAEB

A black shadow covered the ground and filled my heart with joy.

Galanth! I cried in my mind.

A whirr of happiness filled me, and I felt the Orb's warmth along his back even though I was sitting in the shade of a large Trident tree. Tare Adonso, Rider Amso, Rider Hord and Frist were scowling at me, Jessen looked impatient and even Mom and Naela were very somber, so I carefully kept the smile off my face. I wanted to be riding my Dragon, I wanted to be talking to my sister, I wanted to be learning my herbs, I wanted to be doing anything other than listening to their grievances. I already knew what they had to say; I had heard all their concerns too many times.

"This will not work."

"We cannot stay."

"We are too vulnerable."

"Saeb, are you listening?"

"Aye, Tare," I said with a sigh.

"Listening is not enough," Frist said. "Listening is not doing."

"If you are not happy, you may leave," Adonso said sharply.

"As you may," Frist snapped back.

I closed my eyes and felt Galanth soaring. I had not realized that being fought over could be so exhausting. In the Lore mother told me as a child, there were princesses who were desired and wanted and lived in luxury.

Being a Leader was a far cry from being a princess, I had learned. Although I had tried to get my "council" to meet and make decisions without me, I had not been successful. Nor was I good at avoiding daily meetings. Sleeping next to Galanth did not deter them from tracking me down. Leaving camp before the Orb had lightened the sky didn't work; staying in my bedrolls only meant they all crammed into my small room. I had even tried hiding in the privacy bushes, but Mom and Saraiva were not embarrassed to follow me, and soon the men barged in, too. So I quit trying to hide, and simply waited at the Trident tree as soon as I had finished first meal each day.

Tare Adonso and Rider Amso always joined me, as did Frist. Riders Hord and Pedso seemed to have an alternating pattern, and Mom and Saraiva usually did the same, though sometimes both healers came. Often Paben or Stram would come to discuss hunting or guarding concerns, and Reena had even come a few times to complain about the difficulty of gardening.

Often I found myself stuck under the tree until mid-day meal, giving suggestions and trying to find compromises. I had discovered that as a Leader, if my opinion matched the petitioner's, my approval was sought. If my opinion was different, then my approval did not matter—

"Saeb?"

Reluctantly, I opened my eyes. "I know. You're right."

"What?"

"About what?"

"All." I rubbed my face. "We cannot stay. In spite of all the work we have done, this is not where Speare Clan will stay. I know that."

Everyone began speaking at once, and I didn't even try to listen to them. I waited until the outburst was over.

"The Sparks will be ready to move in two days time," Frist said, "Though it would have been easier had you agreed with this when we first told you."

"I do not care about the Sparks." I tried not to enjoy the look of shock on Frist's face. "No more than I care about the Riders," it was harder to remain passive at Tare Adonso's look of confusion, "or the healers, or the hunters. You all still see yourselves separately. I see this as part of our problem. Until the Speare Clan is ready to move as one, we are not going anywhere."

Tare Adonso and Frist turned to look at each other. We had been at the butte for almost one full cycle of Sister Orb, and yet it was the first time that I had seen them look at each other without distrust and hatred plain on their faces.

"The Speare Clan is ready to move," they said together, sounding as if they had rehearsed it.

Now I did smile. "Not yet. But already we are closer." I stood and stretched. "We need to be a true Clan—a true extended family—that trusts and depends upon each other. I have tried to show that I value all who are here, but until you—my council leaders—show that you value each other, the others will continue to distrust and dislike each other."

Mom, Saraiva, Hord, and Rider Amso nodded. After a moment,

Tare Adonso and Frist did, too.

"And now, I believe Rider Saeb has somewhere to be," Mom said.

"Aye."

"But—"

I looked at Rider Amso. "Next meeting?"

He frowned and I feared he would argue, but he said, "Aye."

"Until then," I said to the group at large. There was a general murmuring as I left, but I was aware of the heavy footsteps at my side. I was not leaving alone, but I did not look to see whether it was Tare Adonso or Frist who had come with me.

"How is your arm?" After our travels, I knew the sound of Tare Adonso's voice better than anyone's, except, of course, Galanth's.

"It heals slowly."

"But it heals?"

"Aye." I did not want to elaborate. My mother was a gifted healer, and she was the only one I allowed to tend to my strange wound.

When I had grabbed the Wyzard's stick, it had taken me to the Cave of the Dead, and there were times that I thought my wrist and palm were still there. My arm from my elbow to my finger joints had been red, swollen, and painful, except for my wrist and palm, which had been black. My wrist and palm had faded to a deep bruise purple, with the exception of white symbols that seemed to be seared into my skin. The rest of my arm, however, was perfectly fine. Although it seemed right to have a scar on my wrist that almost mirrored the scarring my Dragon had on all four of his legs, I had taken to wrapping my wrist with a bulky scarf, simply to hide it. It was scary enough for me to look at; I didn't want to scare my Troupe, too.

"Rider Saeb, I know that you feel you must look strong to be a good leader, but a true leader will also acknowledge their mistakes."

"Isn't that what I just did, Tare Adonso? Do you think it was easy to admit that I picked a bad place for us to begin building?"

Tare Adonso inclined his head toward me. "It was a very important first step. But why must we wait? Now that you have recognized your mistake, why don't we begin to fix it immediately?"

"Because we must be able to work together before we try to travel together. Because we must wait for Dirk, Noss, and Paben to return. Because I am waiting to see where the Dragons that Riders Pedso and Amso have spotted are going. Because, although this is not where we will settle our Troupe for good, this is where we need to be right now."

Tare Adonso was quiet, and I had begun to hope that perhaps he would allow me to go when he said in a musing tone, "It was a wise idea to send the pages out, looking for eggs."

"Aye," I said cautiously. He had said as much when we sent the pages out when the Sister Orb was still full. It was not his style to repeat himself.

"But we have no idea how long they will be gone."

"I told Noss to be back before a full cycle of the Sister Orb." She was hiding now, so the pages should be either already heading back or getting ready to do so.

"A task such as that can not always be dictated. It may take them longer."

"Or they may be back before the Orb sets," I countered. "We will wait for the pages to return."

"We could move now—"

"We will wait."

"—and leave two or three pages behind, to help with the eggs if they found any."

"You would leave them to track us?"

"We will not hide. We will be easy to track."

"For Wyzards as well?"

"Pages are trained in tracking and—"

"Tare Adonso, I am not leaving my page behind. Noss is my friend as well, and I care about him." It was only with great difficulty that I did not yell at the Tare. I knew that Tare Adonso was Noss' father, but no one else knew it. For some reason, Noss and Tare Adonso kept it secret, so I kept it, too.

"Aye, Rider Saeb, then we will wait for the pages to return. What do you think of sending a scouting party out ahead to find a promising location?"

I took a deep breath. "Tare Adonso, these are concerns for the council, not for just the two of us to decide."

"But—"

I stopped and finally turned to look at the Tare. "You asked me to be Leader. You were the one who suggested that I be led by a council. Yet you seem to want me to make decisions based solely on what you have said and without input from others. I have decided to stay here. If you wish to challenge that decision, bring it up at our next meeting."

"Aye, Leader."

His patronizing was better than criticism, at least for the moment. "Good."

"But—"

"Tare, do you remember being a Rider?"

A strange look crossed his face, and I regretted being so blunt. Riders became Tares only when their Dragon died, and the emotional pain often took the Tares, too. Tare Adonso had been strong enough to survive his Dragon's death and had also proven himself to be a wise and good leader. However, things were changing. Not only was Galanth the Dragon of Prophecy, but Tare Pedso had become a Rider again when a young Dragon had lost its Rider and had accepted him. As far as anyone knew, that had never happened before.

"I need to spend time with Galanth," I said. "As it is, I get less training time with him than the other Riders."

"As it is, you and Galanth are beyond any training that Pedso or I could give you. It is hard to remember that he is only a hatchling, and that you and he have not been together for a full set of seasons. He is a remarkable Dragon. And," he added, sounding begrudging, "you are a remarkable Rider and Leader. The Power That Is has provided well for our Troupe, and I should not question it as much as I do."

"The Power That Is provided good counsel for our Troupe as well, and I am grateful for it, Tare, I truly am. But I would like—"

"—to go be with Galanth," Tare Adonso finished with me. "And you should," he added with a nod. "As you suggested, we will discuss options at our next meeting."

I smiled. "Aye."

I did not rush my climb to the top of the butte. I grabbed a hard roll and an apple as I went past the central hearth. I could have called to Galanth and had him fly down to me, but two more small groups had joined us recently. Though they had specifically come looking for the Dragon of Prophecy, two of the children and one of the adults were terrified of all of the Dragons.

The wild Gyphanna spread across the butte, long green leaves bending with the breeze. Mom said it was almost ready to bloom, and she and the healer apprentices were watching it carefully. They wanted to catch it just before the buds opened, to catch them at their full potency. Tyleen was sitting in the Gyphanna, and I don't think she would have known I had arrived had not Tam pricked up his ears and then come bounding over to me.

Tyleen had found the wolf pup and saved his life. He, in turn, had saved us several times. Though we had carried him for much of our travels, no one would carry him when we moved again. Instead, perhaps a small child would ride him like a pony.

"Greetings, Tam," I said with a laugh as he shoved his muzzle under my hand, demanding attention. "Did Tyleen not feed you?"

"Of course I fed him," my sister said indignantly, "and he was perfectly content until he saw you." At the sound of her voice, the young wolf turned and bolted back to her side, graceful and fierce all at once. "Do you seek Galanth? I saw him land not too long ago."

"Aye."

"Will you have time to talk after evening meal?"

"Aye," I said, though not with the joy that I should have felt. Even my family had to make requests of my time. I waved to her and continued across the top of the butte.

We had eight Dragons with our Troupe, but only six were lounging in the thick grasses: two green, two red, one gold, and of course one black. Because both our blue ones were missing, I knew that it was Riders Pedso and Pand who were out scouting, watching for approaching groups. Having Dragons that could travel so far was very beneficial.

Tare Adonso had warned me that others would seek to join us, but until the first group found us, I had not believed him. Already, our Troupe of twenty-four had grown to thirty-three, and there were four more groups that were moving towards us. How many peep—peasants, laborers, farmers—would seek us out for protection? How could we help all of them?

The council had spent several meetings arguing whether we should approach the groups or if we should leave them be. So far, we had agreed to keep our distance and let them come to us, but I feared that it was only a matter of time before Stram and Frist brought it up again. I knew Tare Adonso agreed with Frist but didn't want to say it; knowing there was another group with a Dragon approaching so slowly bothered him, but he wouldn't explain why.

Galanth's black head popped up amongst the green and gold, his silver scar shining like a necklace. Treeva, Landin's golden Dragon, and Amso's green Graena were his two favorite companions and were stretched out on either side of him. So far, we only had one other male Dragon, but Galanth was several times bigger than he was, and all of the Dragons seemed to recognize that he was Dragon of Prophecy as well as a natural leader.

Galanth yawned, showing his ever-growing fangs. *Are you done with the meeting?*

Aye.

And done counting Dragons?

I like to know where everyone is, I thought as I began to work my way toward him.

You cannot be responsible for all.

I know.

And yet you still worry about everyone, he teased. *Even now, you wonder why Treeva is here and Landin is not.*

That—

Has less to do with Treeva and more to do with Landin, he said slyly.

"Let's fly," I said sharply.

I am sorry, Rider, he thought to me, standing and stretching. *I promised to stop picking on you.*

"So stop!"

He lowered his head so we were eye to eye. Crimson specks reflected back to me as he said, *You worry too much. You used to smile more.*

There is much to worry about, I thought, tracing the ridgeline above his left eye. Life with my Dragon was amazing, and it scared me to think about how close I came to destroying not only my time with him but taking his life as well, but that was nothing to the suffocating panic I experienced every time I realized that peep and folks were leaving Clans and towns to find the Dragon of Prophecy and me, that we were expected to do great and amazing things, that they were looking to us to change the way the world—

Breathe.

I exhaled and leaned my forehead against Galanth's. See? I thought, I can't even do that without your help.

Are we flying today?

Aye.

Do you want a rig? he asked. Riders Pedso and Landin had been working together to create a rig that helped Riders stay on their Dragons. They said that it was for all Riders, that it would be helpful when we were in battle in case we were injured. But I knew that they were worried about me. Twice my mind had gone to the Cave of the Dead, and they feared what would happen if I were flying on Galanth and it happened again.

Nay, I thought, moving around to his side. He bent his leg so I could use his knee like a step. As I settled myself on his back, he stretched his wings, so thin and delicate they looked like they would tear easily, yet they were blacker than the sky when Sister Orb hid.

Should we scout?

I frowned. It was tempting. I would like to find the Rider I was waiting for, the one Meegan's spirit had told me to expect when I last went to the Cave of the Dead. I wanted to meet Maeya, I wanted to learn what she knew and start learning to work together as a team. But I felt that it was more important that Maeya find me. If I found her, if I brought her to me—

It would not be her destiny. It would be yours.

Aye.

But you believe her destiny lies with ours.

Aye.

It troubles me to have a Prophecy from the Cave of the Dead, Galanth said.

Meegan will not lead us to harm.

She looked like Meegan, Galanth said, echoing both my mother and Tare Adonso. *That does not mean she was Meegan.*

"I believe it was Meegan. And I believe Maeya will come to us."

So where will we fly today?

"Anywhere," I said, resting along his neck. "Everywhere." His scales were radiating heat and felt good. "Let us enjoy time in the clouds and on the ground together, for I fear we will not have much of it in the coming days."

CHAPTER ONE

Maeya turned a slow circle. Nothing was moving, except the wisps of smoke from the still-hot ashes. Nothing sounded, except the wind moaning above the Spike.

She allowed her eyes to look down and was blinded by her own tears. What little was left of her Dragon's egg was at her feet. Maeya was afraid to move, for fear that it would disintegrate, leaving her nothing to bury. She didn't know if it was appropriate to bury a Dragon's egg, but she was beyond caring. She would bury the egg, bury her page, and bury her dreams of being a Dragon Rider.

"Rider Maeya!"

Maeya nearly screamed as she spun around.

"Rider Maeya, I need your help!" Maeya tried not to cringe at being called a Rider. She could feel the hole deep inside her, the hole that insisted she would never be a Rider.

Maeya stared in disbelief at Quoran. She thought all had perished. How had he survived? He was bouncing on the balls of his feet, clearly agitated. The old scars across his flushed face stood out in vivid detail.

"Please, Rider Maeya!"

She took one step toward him and he turned and trotted away. There was no choice but to follow him.

Maeya rounded the far side of the mountain, outside the view of their Cave. Quoran was kneeling next to a prone figure. Cyr Sajen.

Dropping to her knees on the other side of the Cyr, Maeya stared at his bruised and bleeding body. Quoran had done a fair job of staunching the blood, but she could tell that the wound along the wrist and hand, at least, would need stitching—possibly the wound on his lower leg as well.

Maeya began to reach for the small rag next to Quoran when Cyr Sajen's uninjured hand shot up, grasping her wrist with incredible strength. Maeya stared down into his intense bright blue eyes.

"Rider Maeya. Where is your egg?" From the day they were given the egg, Riders-in-training were never to leave it unattended.

Maeya wanted to bow her head and look away, but she could not pull her gaze from his. "My egg is gone, Cyr Sajen. It was destroyed in the attack."

He took a raspy breath as his grip on her wrist tightened painfully. "Are you sure?"

"Aye. I felt it." And that was all she could say. Maeya had been bathing in the creek, with her egg wrapped carefully in the carrying sling, when the attack had come. She had seen the blue streaks of fire, and had been unable to move. She hadn't even ducked under water. But the blue flame did not come charging across the water. Something seemed to stop it. Maeya could feel the heat, but it all stayed on the bank, incinerating her egg.

"We have lost them all," Quoran whispered.

"One Dragon escaped."

With difficulty Maeya turned her focus back to Cyr Sajen. "Cyr?"

He took another raspy breath. "I saw it. The Cave, the fields—everything and everyone—were in flame. Including Veet." Quoran made a strange noise in the back of his throat while the Cyr continued, "But not his Dragon. Veet's Dragon got away. You must go after it."

Maeya started. "What?"

"You have lost your Dragon—" now Maeya was the one making a strange noise— "and it has lost a Rider. You must help each other survive."

"Cyr—"

"I may only be a Cyr," he choked, "I may have never had a Dragon to ride, but I understand the pain and grief that are felt by both Rider and Dragon. You have lost two different halves, but together you may be able to help each other."

"Cyr—"

"Go now!"

"But you need—"

"Whatever I need, I feel certain page Quoran can give."

Maeya blinked.

"Aye, Rider Maeya," Quoran said suddenly, "I can help Cyr Sajen."

"He needs stitches," she began.

"Aye," Quoran agreed, "And I have seen your stitching. I will do it whether you are here or not."

Maeya stared at Quoran. Even when they had been pages together, he had never been snippy before.

"Cyr," she tried again. "I don't think I'm—"

"Rider Maeya, you're wasting time!"

"I'm not a Rider," she cried out. "My egg never hatched!" She had carried the egg with her everywhere for the last year, just like the other twelve Riders-in-training had done. Ten of the eggs had hatched while Sister Orb had been full. Sister Orb was almost in hiding now, and Swald and Maeya had been the only two still holding eggs of the newest clutch, while all the other Riders were spending time with their Dragon hatchlings.

"You have been trained," Cyr Sajen wheezed. "And now you both have holes that the other can fill. Go. Go now." His voice was getting weaker, but his eyes were almost painfully intense.

"Please, Rider Maeya," Quoran said softly. "I will tend to him. We will wait here."

"It is time to meet your destiny," Cyr Sajen said.

Maeya took his hand. "That Dragon is not my destiny," she said. "It was Veet's destiny."

"Not even the Power That Is has control over destiny. Destiny, Rider Maeya, can be of your own making. And that is a lesson you learn now."

"Where is Veet's Dragon?" Maeya asked.

"*Your* Dragon fled," Cyr Sajen said with emphasis.

"Then how shall I find it?"

"You shall look. You shall find it." He squeezed her hand. "And you shall bring it back."

"What if I don't?"

"You will," he wheezed. "You will because it is your heart's desire. Your desire is to meet your destiny, to be a Rider."

"I have no food," Maeya said. "I have no blankets."

"Make your destiny," he said weakly. "Prove your worth to all."

Prove her worth by finding a Dragon who might not want to be found. Prove her worth by leaving a wounded Cyr. Prove her worth by staying out in the open without supplies. Prove her worth.

Maeya didn't know her worth.

Cyr Sajen relaxed his grip on her. Maeya nodded as she gently set his hand against his chest. "Aye. I will find Veet's Dragon. And we will return to the Cave." And then, she thought, we shall see what destiny looks like.

Maeya stood up quickly and walked away. She wouldn't look back. Because if she did, she feared wouldn't be able to leave.

***   ********   ***

Maeya had been born an aristocrat's daughter, then served as a page. Then she became a Rider-in-training. Now the Cyr insisted she was a Rider, but she didn't have a Dragon. What was a Dragon Rider worth if she didn't have a Dragon?

She began walking through the Trident trees, enjoying their fresh scent, especially after the acrid, smoke filled air in the Cave. It was also nice to have time to herself, time that wasn't crowded with a need for cooking, sewing, or training. Maeya was supposed to be looking for Veet's Dragon, but she felt like she was merely wandering.

The area around the Cave was bountiful. Squirrels, rabbits, snakes, birds, Quan bugs, crickets, vines and flowers were teeming throughout the forest. The Trident trees spread a thick canopy over her, and only once in a while did Maeya find patches of light from the Orb.

As she moved through the forest, she paid careful attention to the wildlife. It was easy to scare up a small animal every few paces. What she wanted to find was an area where the animals weren't everywhere, where everything, down to the smallest insect, was quiet. Even as hatchlings, Dragons instilled fear in most animals.

Maeya wandered long past the time that she would have gone to the central hearth to find soup or jerky, or flat bread. But everywhere she went, she was greeted by the warbling of a crimson rush or startled by the sudden streak of a frightened hare. The Dragon must not be in this section of the Trident trees. Maeya would have to expand her search.

She stopped briefly to catch her breath and strengthen her resolve before leaving the safe Trident boundary behind her and entering the valley.

The valley spooked her. It was wide open with very few bushes big enough to conceal anyone. Maeya could see a few trees, mostly ash and oak, looking forlorn, as if the Trident trees had personally rejected them. She knew it would be difficult for anyone to ambush her, but she was still spooked by the strange feeling that hung in the air.

The Orb sank behind the precipice with unusual speed. The precipice stood guard over their valley, casting its impressive shadow. It was the Spike for which their Cave was named. Sometimes Riders would circle the top, but the rocky crags were impossible even for Dragons to land on.

In the heat of the growing season, the shadow brought welcome shade. At the moment, though, the shadow felt as if it was ice inside Maeya. She knew, logically, that it wasn't icy, that it was just a shadow, but she also knew that the darkness followed the shadow. Sister Orb's sliver of light would not be much help tonight. And she would be alone.

Alone in the Trident forest, without food or shelter.

Yes, the shadow felt cold.

The world did not scare her. She was of noble blood and she knew the respect she was due. She was from a poor noble family so she knew the meaning of work, but she also knew the importance of comportment and image. She was a Rider-in-training and understood responsibility and teamwork.

Maeya wanted to be a Rider and she felt the duty and honor lurking out of her reach.

She knew the only way to conquer a problem was to face it. But how did you face a problem you couldn't find?

As the last reaching rays of the Orb traced the edges of the Valley, Maeya knew she had to act quickly. Either she would return to the Cave or camp here. Continuing to look for the Dragon would do nothing more than lead her to injury. Once she crossed the valley and was back in the cover of the trees, she felt much better.

Wolves and pumas hunted at night. Quan Bugs tried to evade the owls in the darkness. Snakes were common. Japon bushes grew close to the Trident trees, and the Japon thorns were poisonous.

There was a cluster of Trident trees, and she decided it would be the best place to bed down even though Sister Orb was almost in hiding, which meant it was the time when Trident trees would be the most active, according to stories. Maeya was not afraid of the trees; she believed they could move at will, but she had done nothing to incur their wrath.

Old Lore told of an entire forest moving from the perimeter of a pasture and re-establishing itself outside the opening of one of the Caves, trapping one of the Clans inside for days before they were able to cut their way out. Nani used to terrify Maeya with stories of the greedy bounty hunters and dishonest Riders who were torn to bits in the Trident trees during the dark of Sister Orb.

There was no way she would be able to get back to the Cave, she decided. She was better off digging in until the Orb returned to the sky.

Maeya found a sturdy branch and began digging at the base of the largest Trident trunk. The very last of the lingering light was fading when she finished. Although Maeya had outgrown most of her childish fears, she had never been alone quite like this. As she dragged a few branches over, she realized that her small scratched-out bed more closely resembled a shallow grave.

Pushing the thought away, Maeya lay down. Cradled in the ground, blanketed by the branches, she hoped to stay warm—and unscented by the hunters around her.

     ***   *******   ***

In spite of her jitters, Maeya slept heavily. The Orb had already painted the sky and the colors were fading by the time she opened her eyes. She was slightly stiff from the hard ground, but overall she had been warm and cozy. Sitting up, Maeya rubbed her eyes and yawned.

And then she froze.

Maeya had dug out her bed at the base of a Trident trunk. She knew that as well as she knew her own name.

Yet now she was lying in the middle of an open clearing almost twice as wide as she was long.

Before her stomach completed its first roll, she looked down at the dusty ground.

Wolf prints.

Wolf prints everywhere.

Wolf prints circling, pacing, surrounding her. At least three piles of wolf scat, one of them still steaming, in the brisk early air.

Maeya tried not to scream, and she succeeded.

Until she took a full breath.

She screamed. She screamed so loud and hard that her throat hurt until the next time the Orb rose.

She screamed and the Trident forest swallowed the sound. There was no echo, no gradual fading of her scream. It was swallowed whole.

Her scream served to convince her that she had survived a night alone among the Trident trees. The Trident trees had moved away from her. But what of the wolves? Had they been turned back by the trees? Or were they protecting her as well?

She wished there was someone with her, someone to ask, someone to share this confusion. Maeya didn't know who she would like to have with her, but she knew she didn't like being alone.

Then she realized that nothing was moving. Birds weren't taking wing, rabbits weren't scurrying, squirrels weren't scampering. Her scream hadn't scared anything.

Because there wasn't anything around to scare.

The Dragon must be close.

Maeya threw the branches off of her and scrambled out of her small bed. As soon as she got to her feet, she realized that she had to quickly relieve herself. She tried to ignore the wolf prints she covered with her own. It was harder to ignore the fact that she was entering the forest, going into a place where wolves might be waiting for her.

Once Maeya had finished, she began circling outward from her clearing, looking and listening for signs of the Dragon. When she found blackberry bushes, she stopped and collected handfuls; she couldn't remember her last meal. She needed to listen for the Dragon and the wolves, not her growling belly.

Maeya lost track of everything. Where she was, how long she had been walking, what types of berries she had eaten, how many sets of wolf and puma prints she passed, everything. She had not found any fresh water, and while the juice from the berries helped, her mouth and lips were parched.

At first the silence of the trees had been exciting. Maeya had been positive that she would enter the next clearing or round the next boulder and find the green Dragon. After a while, though, the silence became unnerving. Forests were supposed to be full of sound.

Today, even the wind held its breath.

The Trident trees were so still they looked like carvings instead of living beings. Maeya tried to match the silence around her, but her steps seemed overly loud. She winced when she stepped on a dry leaf; flinched when she broke a twig. Her breathing rasped in her ears, drowning out the small sounds that she strained to hear.

It came as quite a shock, then, to suddenly realize that she was approaching a creek. Maeya could hear the running water, and she had been listening to the softly hinted whisper build for several moments without noticing it. The sound had snuck up on her.

She hurried through the bushes and undergrowth, not caring that she was snapping branches and rustling leaves. She needed water.

Charging out of the last bushes, she scrambled over the river rock and small boulders, splashed into the water, and as soon as she was in up to her waist, she let herself sink under. Maeya opened her mouth and let the water flow in. She didn't care that she still had her clothes on; this was the best washing they were likely to get for a while.

The cool water ran through her curly red hair, lifting and separating it with the current. The gurgling sloshing noise of the creek filled her ears before they were plugged with water. Maeya surfaced, shaking her head and clearing her ears. She choked a little, having tried to drink a bit too much too fast.

She leaned her head back again and let herself float downstream for a moment. The crystalline blue above her contrasted sharply with the dark trees all around. Standing up, Maeya slicked her hair back from her forehead, and then she wiped the water from her face before finally looking around.

Here the creek was very gentle and not too wide. Its deepest point only seemed shoulder high, and the bottom was relatively free of the large rocks that bordered the creek.

Maeya cupped her hands and took another drink. This time she tasted a metallic hint, but it was still cool and soft on her lips and mouth.

Aside from the soft splashes where the water cascaded over a sharp rock, there was no sound, no movement. The creek was the only thing that seemed to be normal in this Trident forest.

She sighed and looked upstream, then downstream. Walking in increasing circles outward from her tiny camp had not been successful, so she felt no need to continue the pattern. It would make more sense to follow the creek. She needed fresh water. So did all creatures, including the Dragon.

The question, then, was whether to go up or downstream. Downstream, the Trident trees seemed to be closer to the stream, almost in the stream, choking it with their roots. The trees hadn't hurt her last night. Did that mean she should trust them? Upstream, for a way at least, the Trident trees seemed to be back away from the creek, as if they were giving it room.

Maeya began floating downstream, staying in the middle of the creek, enjoying the very gentle push the current gave her.

Downstream she discovered that the creek spread out, forming a large pool. Maeya was now wading in knee-deep water. The current eddied out from the center of the stream to the banks, and all the river rocks were polished, smooth and flat. Some of the rocks were golden or brown, but most were onyx. One was almost a pale green.

Maeya stopped and stared.

The pale green boulder on the edge of the creek wasn't polished smooth.

Clumsily she splashed over, tripping and almost falling on her face. She barely caught herself, and landed hard on her hands and knees, sending water spraying over the boulder.

The scaly, pale green boulder twitched.

"Greetings, Dragon," Maeya said.

The hatchling flinched at the sound of her voice. Maeya heard it hiss even though she couldn't see its head. The Dragon was lying on its side, curled in a ball, facing the bank.

"Greetings," Maeya said again, circling around it so she could see the head. The once emerald scales looked like a washed-out moss. Maeya could see its side rise and fall as it struggled for breath. Its head was half underwater and its eyes were closed.

Maeya reached toward it, intending to lift the head up and at least rest it gently on the nearby rock.

Without opening its eyes, the Dragon snapped at Maeya's hand, just missing her.

She got the feeling it didn't mean to hurt her. It was just a warning.

"You can't stay in the water," Maeya muttered, lifting the Dragon's head and gently setting it on a rock out of the water, "You're already too cold and too weak."

It wanted her to leave it alone.

"I have to help you, Dragon," Maeya said. Something whispered, just tickling her ear, but Maeya stood up straight.

She had a sudden image of fire, a feeling of sadness.

"I'm sorry, Dragon. Veet is gone."

Grief, thick enough to choke on, deep enough to drown everything else.

"But you live. As do I." There was another tickle, just inside Maeya's ear. "Pharla," she said, realizing that the Dragon had just told her its name, "I have to help you."

The Dragon raised her head off the rock and turned to the other side before lowering it into the water again.

Once more Maeya reached for her, ignored her hiss, and lifted her head back onto the rock.

The Dragon glared at her. *Leave. Leave. Leave.*

"I'm staying here, Pharla," Maeya said calmly. "I won't leave until you do. We will be leaving together."

Alone.

"I will protect you," Maeya said.

No protection.

Maeya was getting frustrated. Talking with Dragons was not as easy as she had thought. She had thought that their minds would work together, that they would understand each other from the beginning. But all she was getting from Pharla were phrases and feelings and contrary ideas. She was beginning to get a headache.

The Dragon took a deep breath, and Maeya could hear the air rasping in her. She had to get her out of the water.

Stay.

Even though Pharla didn't want to move, she had to. She wasn't safe. She needed warmth and food.

No. Stay. Maeya got a sense of the water caressing the Dragon's sides. It hadn't fallen in the water; it was there by choice.

Maeya took a deep breath against the headache and surveyed the Dragon critically. Pharla wasn't that big, but it would be difficult to get a good hold on her. And she would probably be heavy.

Maeya was strong, for her size, but she was rather small. Moving the Dragon would be difficult.

Leave. Maeya saw an image of herself. *Stay.* She saw an image of the Dragon. *Alone.*

"No," Maeya said softly. She reached out and put her hand on the top of Pharla's head. The Dragon twitched away from her, and she let her go. "It would be better if you would help me, Pharla. I might hurt you if I try to carry you."

Leave.

"I can't. You are hurt." Maeya stroked her wing, tracing from where it joined her back down to the first joint in the wing. The thin membrane was so pale her wing looked almost white.

Veet.

Maeya sighed. Veet had been a thorough Rider-in-training. He always carried his egg with him, he talked to it all the time, and Maeya had even seen him fall asleep with his hand still caressing it. He had bonded well with Pharla. And once she had hatched, he never left her side. He had been totally devoted. Now she was reciprocating.

And it could kill her.

She got an image of Pharla and Veet and a sense of contentment.

Maeya was tired of going in circles this way. "You and me," Maeya told her. "You and me." She stood up and moved around so she was standing behind Pharla again. "You and me," Maeya grunted as she wriggled her hands under the hatchling and began to lift. Maeyas guess had been right. Pharla was heavy. But Maeya was going to move her.

An image of her fighting, struggling, flashed through Maeya's mind. But Pharla was too weak, and she only managed to kick her back feet once. Still, it was enough to make Maeya stumble.

Maeya's ankle twisted underneath her, but she clenched her teeth and stayed upright, shifting Pharla slightly in her arms.

Down.

"You and me," Maeya repeated. "I'm going to take care of you."

Down. This time she got an image of Pharla splashing through the water next to her, walking out of the river.

"Promise?" Maeya panted. She managed two more steps and she wasn't sure she'd be able to carry Pharla to the bank after all. At least, not all at once. She'd have to set her down, catch her breath, and get a better hold on her before Maeya could continue.

Down. Me.

Maeya's ankle was throbbing and her headache was getting progressively worse. She set Pharla down, trying to be gentle, and the Dragon walked out from under Maeya's arms.

Pharla wobbled and stumbled a little, but Maeya couldn't tell if it was because she was weak, or if the water and uneven surface was causing her problems. Once the Dragon got out of the creek, however, it became obvious. She was so weak her belly barely cleared the ground. She continued until she was about a body length away from the creek, and then she collapsed.

Leave.

Maeya looked up at the Orb. It was almost directly overhead. She nodded. "Aye," Maeya said to her, and set off across the creek and into the trees on the other side.

Pharla needed food, and Maeya was pretty sure she was going to have to travel a ways before she found any prey. Most of the animals had left the area because of Pharla. But maybe they hadn't gotten her scent across the creek yet.

Maeya stopped suddenly. Pharla needed food, but Maeya didn't have any weapons. She had her knife, but she didn't have a spear, or bow, or even her bolo. How was she going to provide for Pharla?

Maeya looked back over her shoulder, and saw the still form lying in the light of the Orb next to the sparkling creek, and she began to smile.

CHAPTER TWO

When Maeya returned to Pharla's side, the Trident shadows had just begun to cover her. She was relieved to see that Pharla's scales were beginning to darken up a little. Her wings looked more green than white now.

Maeya set the three large fish down in front of her. She had learned to tickle fish as a child, but she had only tickled little minnows before. These trout had been more work. Not to tickle, but when grabbing and throwing them out of the water, they had strength she hadn't expected. Two got away from her before she learned to grab them the right way.

Pharla didn't move. She didn't even open her eyes.

"I brought fish," Maeya told her.

Not hungry.

"You have to eat."

No.

"Pharla, please."

Nothing.

Deciding to follow her lead, Maeya ignored her. Maeya picked up one of the fish and began to clean it. She cut the head off and then gutted it. She discovered she was glad it was such a big fish; it was much easier to pick the bones out. Maeya didn't enjoy raw fish, no matter how often her page Tygan had insisted it was a delicacy when served by his peep at his home. But she was hungry. In truth, she was beginning to think her headache was the result of her hunger. And more than that, she knew she would need to keep her strength up to care for Pharla.

Maeya made quick work of the fish, and then buried the remains. It was bad enough she was leaving the two remaining fish out in the open, waiting for Pharla. Any wolf or puma in the area would be drawn to them because of the scent.

She glanced at Pharla and saw that her eyes were still closed, and the fish in front of her was already drawing flies. A fire would be necessary tonight, to keep both predators and bad dreams away.

Maeya began collecting as much dry kindling as she could, and then started finding larger dry sticks. Some were big enough to be logs. She was not skilled at making fires without firestone, but she knew how. And she would have to succeed, because failure was unthinkable.

Piling everything a body length away from Pharla, Maeya scratched out a small bowl in the ground before she arranged her kindling just so.

Watching Pharla sleep, Maeya spun a sharpened stick against the dry grass stacked on top of a knotted log. Her anger helped her spin it fiercely. How dare Pharla shut down like this? She was completely ignoring Maeya, not allowing Maeya to help her. Worse than that, Pharla wasn't helping Maeya, either.

Pharla had been the biggest of the hatchlings. The Cyrs and Tares had been impressed with how agile she was, and how well she had bonded with Veet. Tare Cret had been especially impressed and had declared that he believed Veet's Dragon would be able to ingest the firestone and breathe fire before the end of Harvest. He had watched the Dragon's breathing with interest. But Pharla wasn't breathing fire now.

She wasn't breathing at all.

Maeya dropped the stick and scrambled over to her on hands and knees. Pharla didn't raise her head to snap or hiss. Maeya placed the palm of her hand as close to her nostrils as she could without touching her snout. She held her own breath as she felt for Pharla's. Finally, just before Maeya began to sob, she felt a faint warm brush of air. Pharla was still alive. Barely.

Gently, Maeya placed her hand on the side of Pharla's neck. Her pale scales were hot to the touch. Tears streamed down Maeya's face. She didn't know what to do. She had to save Pharla, but how? She didn't know how to stop a Dragon's fever, she didn't know how to make her eat, she didn't know how to get her back to the Cave, SHE DIDN'T KNOW!

It was hard for Maeya to breathe. Her chest had constricted with fear and anger, and she could only gulp in air.

No, she told herself fiercely. *No. This is not how it's going to end. I'm not going to be named a Dragon Rider twice and then let them both die. I'm NOT.*

With a little bit more clarity after making that promise to herself, Maeya was able to think. She needed to keep Pharla warm, in spite of the fever. If Maeya let her get cold again, she'd never come back. The fire was more important than ever.

Maeya returned to the kindling, where she had succeeded in blackening one blade of dry grass before she had stopped. She wasn't stopping this time. Not until she had a healthy fire. She set to work.

She focused so much on the stick and the kindling that she was aware of nothing else until she saw a small yellow flame. Then she began carefully feeding that flame, one thin blade of dry grass at a time until it could accept two, then three, then four at a time. Slowly Maeya began adding small twigs, letting each one catch fire before adding another. When the fire was about the size of a bird's egg, she added larger sticks. Not until the fire was merrily consuming three large sticks at a time did Maeya look up again.

Fear had stopped her from looking. Maeya was afraid that the Power That Is was going to take Pharla in spite of her efforts; she was afraid that nothing she could do would stop it.

But Pharla did not look any worse. Once again Maeya had to hold her hand over Pharla's nostrils to assure that she was still breathing. Maeya felt the panic and loss threaten to sweep over her again. Building the fire had taken her mind away, however briefly. Now she needed something else to do, another purpose to occupy her.

Maeya picked up the fish, and found a crook in a branch to set them in. Hopefully it would keep the predators at bay, although the owls may think they were being handed a treat.

What else? Running her hand through her hair, Maeya tried to think of what else she could do.

Maeya had not often been sick as a child. She tried to remember how Nani had treated her ailments. A very sour paste, mashed something, stood out in her mind. But she didn't remember what Nani had used to make it.

Japon roots.

The answer flashed into Maeya's mind as if someone else had said it. But she knew, instantly, that it was right. She had even questioned old Nani when she learned the name.

"Japon thorns are poisonous," Maeya had said, leaning away from Nani and the small cup.

Nani looked at her with an eager and concerned expression. "That's right, child, the Japon *thorns* are poisonous. This is made of the *roots*. It will help you."

"How?" Maeya asked suspiciously.

"Trust me," Nani had soothed. "I would never let harm come to you."

And because Maeya did trust her, and because she was only five, she had allowed Nani to tip the cup up to her lips. Soon, she had been feeling much better.

Maeya needed to go find Japon roots, and she would have to hope that Pharla would be all right without her. Running her hand over Pharla's head one more time, she said, "I'll return shortly. Wait here for me," she added, trying to sound commanding. It came out as more of a plea.

An image of Pharla lying there without any legs flashed through her mind, but Maeya ignored it as she patted her one more time and then headed into the woods. Maeya knew Pharla couldn't get up and walk away from her right now. That wasn't why she had told Pharla to wait for her.

For the first time in days, Maeya finally had a bit of luck. She located a Japon bush almost within shouting distance of Pharla. Kneeling gingerly in front of the bush, she looked at it carefully.

The bush knew how to protect itself. The branches spread both low and high, reaching wide. Black thorns were visible under each leaf. Anyone wanting to get to the roots would have to move the branches away in order to get to the bottom of the plant, and by moving the branches, exposure to the thorns was almost guaranteed.

But it looked like something had gotten too close to this bush recently. Three of the lower branches were broken. Maeya hoped that one of the wolves or pumas had managed to get a thorn or two lodged under their skin.

She pulled her knife and cautiously grasped a broken branch with the tips of her fingers, making sure she wasn't in contact with a thorn. Then she cut the branch the rest of the way, tossing it to the side.

The other two branches were just as easily removed, and soon Maeya had a clear spot in which to dig for the roots. She dug quickly, reminding herself to be aware of the branches that were on either side and above her, too. The soft black soil soon gave way to milky white roots. Maeya cut them and then covered the hole. No sense damaging the bush any more than she already had. It was a dangerous plant, but it had some good uses.

When Maeya returned, Pharla hadn't moved. Her scales were still a pale green, but she didn't look any worse—or better—than she had before.

Maeya found a flattened rock and a hollowed-out piece of log, and began crushing the root in the improvised bowl. She added water and then she was stuck.

How could she make a Dragon drink?

Maeya looked over at Pharla and was surprised to see the Dragon watching her. Her amber eyes were almost obscured by the enlarged black center, making Pharla look absolutely helpless.

"I have a healing draught for you," Maeya told her.

Pharla closed her eyes.

"You must drink it," Maeya said, standing and carrying it toward her.

Pharla shifted her head away from Maeya. She didn't move far or very fast, but she was turning away from her.

"It will help you feel better."

No.

"Pharla, you must get better."

No.

"Please, Pharla!"

Turning her head back to Maeya, moving faster than Maeya thought she could, Pharla opened her eyes and glared. *No. You don't want me,* she said.

"Yes, I do!"

You want a Dragon, she snuffed. *You don't want* me.

"Pharla, I want you!"

No. And she shut her eyes again.

Maeya knelt in front of her, once again ignoring the rocks that dug into her knees, ignoring the throbbing pain behind her eyes. "Pharla, please. I want to be your Rider. I want to help you." Maeya's voice dropped to a whisper. "And I want you to help me."

You need help?

"I lost a Dragon," Maeya said simply. "There is a hole. Much like the one you feel, I think."

And there was. She hadn't really let herself think about it before, but ever since she had seen that terrible blue flash, seen her beautiful Dragon's egg smolder and char, there had been a nagging ache in the back of her mind, like she had forgotten something and the lost memory hurt.

You need a Dragon, Pharla repeated. *You don't need me.*

"I need a Dragon," Maeya acknowledged, "And you need a Rider. We both lost...someone. We can be someone to each other now."

Pharla surveyed her, and Maeya knew she did not like what she saw—or perhaps she was looking for something that she did not see.

No.

"Please, Pharla, I just want to help you get better."

Maeya sensed exasperation from Pharla, but at least there wasn't any anger or disappointment.

I do not want you.

"Aye," Maeya said, refusing to burst into tears. Pharla's words cut her more than her teeth could, but Maeya would not let her know that. "I just want to help you get better. You may find another Rider."

She continued to look at Maeya, not blinking. The black center of Pharla's eyes expanded and contracted, and Maeya knew Pharla had sensed more of the hurt than she had intended. *It is not for you to give me away,* Pharla said.

"I will take you to Cyr Sajen. He can find you—"

I will choose my Rider, she hissed suddenly, and Maeya leaned back, afraid that she might attack her. Even in her weakened state, Pharla could kill her while Maeya was kneeling unarmed in front of her.

Maeya swallowed. "Yes. It is for you to choose your Rider. But first you must heal. Gain strength."

Aye. And then you'll take me to the Cave?

"Aye."

And then you will leave.

It was a command, and there was nothing further to say. Maeya left the bowl of crushed root in front of her and went to retrieve the fish.

*** ******** ***

In the following days, Pharla was a bit more receptive to Maeya's help. She ate fish, rabbit, and squirrel. Maeya guessed that the smaller forest animals returned because they had to; they were too small to forage far from their homes.

Although Pharla ate well, and asked for help the first time she got a drink from the creek, she still excluded Maeya. Maeya talked to Pharla all the time, about the sunset, the Trident trees, the creek, the Kollarian Clan, Spike Cave, River Reed Cave, Tare Cret, and eventually the volcano eruption. The Wyzard attack was too recent to bear thinking. In four days, the only images Pharla sent to her were of two squirrels, a big trout, and a fleeting thought of the creek somehow being dry. That was it. She didn't bother to hiss, let alone snap at her when Maeya approached, and she certainly didn't miss Maeya when she vanished into the dark wood to hunt.

Tickling fish was the easiest way to get food, but Maeya wanted Pharla to get her strength back and that meant red meat. Three doses of Japon roots seemed to have beaten the fever, and Maeya had been using the remainders to reduce her own headaches. Now Pharla just needed her stamina back.

The hatchling was growing rapidly. She was too big for Maeya to even think about picking up now, let alone trying to carry, but she was still too weak to travel back to Spike Cave.

The squirrels, rabbits and foxes were relatively easy prey with the spear Maeya had made. She was better with a bolo, two rocks sewn into pockets at either end of a leather band. Swinging the bolo above her head made noise, but her distance and accuracy made up for that. Unfortunately, her bolo, hunting knife, spices and bowls were all back at the Cave, and probably nothing but ashes.

Maeya saw plenty of puma and wolf tracks, but she never saw the creatures themselves. She was eager to return to the Cave, eager to show Cyr Sajen that she had accomplished his task, but it no longer felt like a matter of pride or accomplishment. It no longer felt urgent. It felt like they had nothing but time.

But forever didn't feel like enough time to get Pharla to accept her.

*** ******* ***

Maeya had three rabbits slung over her shoulders. She was singing softly to herself, because after the last kill, the trees seemed to have shut out all of the Orb's light.

Suddenly she pulled up short. Something was crashing through the trees behind her, making more noise than speed. She dropped behind a Gyphanna bush. There was no time to warn Pharla. Maeya would have to stop whatever was charging toward her; she couldn't let it go on to Pharla. She hefted her spear, glad that the sharpened stone had not chosen today to break.

Her legs began trembling from crouching so long. It sounded like the creature must almost be upon her, but sound travelled strangely in this Trident forest. Peering through the trees, it was difficult to say if the trees were being shaken by whatever approached or if the trees were trying to block it.

The trembling shifted suddenly to a sharp cramp in her lower leg. Maeya stood, almost involuntarily. Just as she left the safety of the Gyphanna bush, the crashing was upon her. She hefted her spear and watched as the last saplings parted in front of her.

Maeya had already begun to throw the spear, but she was able to slightly alter her aim just as she released. That, combined with Quoran's quick duck, allowed the spear to sail harmlessly past his left shoulder.

Quoran sank to his knees, sobbing.

Maeya grabbed both his shoulders and shook him. She raised her hand to slap him, but then lowered it instead. His clothes were dirty and tattered as if he'd been sleeping in the dirt. Scratches covered his arms and face and one foot was bare and bloody. His face was pale and his hitching breaths rasped angrily. He could not talk now; nothing she did would make a difference.

Instead, she stood, gathered the three hares, and reached down to pull him to his feet. She almost fell under his weight as he clung to her and continued to cry. This frightened Maeya even more. Quoran was always calm, almost stoic. What had happened?

Together they staggered back toward Pharla. Even bearing his weight and hearing his ragged breath, Maeya was aware of how clear the path had become. There was not a twig or leaf to step on, not a shrub or tree in their way. Other than Quoran's moaning sobs, they made not a sound.

Pharla, of course, heard them.

The hatchling had, for the last three days, been curled up in a hollow crater, only moving to the river to drink.

When they reached the riverbank camp, it was deserted. Maeya let go of Quoran, terrified that Pharla had left.

Quoran sank into a heap and Maeya dropped the rabbits in a pile next to him. She set off to find Pharla. Fortunately, she didn't have to go far. Pharla had curled up near a bush. Her dark green scales helped her hide.

"Are you well?" Maeya asked her.

Aye. But Pharla's eyes were so big the golden ring was barely visible around the black center. *What is amiss?*

"I do not know," Maeya said truthfully.

The Cave—

"I do not know," she repeated. "But I hope to find out." Maeya turned to Quoran.

Caution.

Maeya looked back over her shoulder. "Pardon?"

Caution. Things are...teetering.

Maeya stared at Pharla until she heard Quoran moaning again. She didn't know what Pharla meant, but she knew that it felt right. Something had happened. Something had caused their world to teeter.

"Quoran," Maeya said when he took two quivering breaths in a row without sobbing, "What is it?"

"A page from River Reed Cave came. He said...he said..."

Maeya waited, but Quoran seemed stuck. He continued to stare past her. Just as she opened her mouth to ask him again, Maeya heard movement. Pharla was walking toward them. There was no hobbling, hesitation, or other sign that she had been on the brink of death only days ago. When she reached them, she gracefully folded her legs beneath her, reposing in a very regal position. Her eyes were liquid gold as she stared back at Quoran.

Maeya was left out of the conversation; that's what it felt like. And how could she be sure that Pharla wasn't talking to him? Dragons communicated telepathically with their Riders, and she had made it plain that Maeya was not going to be her Rider. Perhaps she had chosen Quoran instead.

Why does he need to find me?

Maeya watched Quoran watching Pharla with such a look of adoration that it almost made her ache. An unexpected wave of irritation slid through her mind.

Why does he need me?

Maeya started as she realized the irritation she felt was not her own, but rather Pharla's. Maeya had not answered her question, and Pharla was annoyed.

WHY?

Maeya winced against a sudden pain that seared through her head. "What did the page say?" she asked Quoran.

"He came seeking refuge. He said that Cave River Reed had been destroyed."

Maeya felt energy seep out of her. "What do you mean?"

"All. All is gone," Quoran gasped for breath. "All is gone!" he wailed.

"No," she said, because it was the only thing she could say. "No."

"Cyr Sajen has left."

"What?"

"Cyr Sajen believed you and the Dragon dead."

"Why? I have not been gone so long as that, have I?"

"Nay," Quoran said quickly, "He knew when he sent you that you would be gone a season or two if you were successful. But he had a dream that you had been attacked by a wolf." Maeya felt a chill dance down her spine and tired to ignore it. "I *told* him you were alive, that you needed him..." Quoran trailed off, shaking his head.

"How did you know we were alive?" Maeya asked him.

"I believed," he said simply.

"But Cyr Sajen didn't," Maeya said, more to herself than to Quoran.

"He wouldn't wait. He and Jael—the page from River Reed—fled, hoping to find safety at Salt Cave. What if it's not there?" his voice rose frantically. "What if Kollarian Clan is wiped out and we're all that's left?"

"Why do you need Pharla?" Maeya asked Quoran.

He took a great, hitching breath. He looked up, and Maeya involuntarily followed his gaze before she realized that his eyes were rolling back in his head. He slumped over in a faint.

Scrambling over to him, Maeya managed to get her hand between his head and the rock it almost landed on. It softened the blow a little, but her hand felt nearly crushed.

Gently she straightened him out, so he was lying down in a more natural position. She wished she had a blanket to cover him, but since she didn't, she turned to stoke the fire.

We must talk to him!
"He is exhausted."
Wake him!
 "I will let him sleep."
I need to know—
"He is exhausted. He will sleep and be able to tell us more when he wakes himself."

Pharla drew herself up. Her golden eyes were snapping with anger. *I—*

"This is not about you! For once, I do not care about making you happy!" Maeya hadn't meant to say that, hadn't really realized that she was so tired of trying to reach Pharla. But as soon as the words were out, she had no desire to take them back. In fact, she plunged on. "Veet always tried to make you happy. I have tried to make you happy. But just this once, it's not about you. You are not the only egg, Dragon, or being that matters. Quoran is hurt. Others have died. Your happiness is not important right now."

Holding her head and tail high, Pharla stalked back to her hollow and curled up again. Maeya knew she had lost any chance of bonding with the green Dragon, but she told herself it didn't matter.

Quoran slept. The Orb sank and Maeya cooked one hare while Pharla ate the others. Quoran slept. Sister Orb climbed, washing out the light of the stars. Pharla, lying cozily on the other side of the camp, rested her chin on her tail and watched Maeya sleep. The only sounds were the occasional snaps of twigs as the hunters of the dark and their prey moved through the woods. Pharla closed her eyes. Quoran slept on. The Orb rose again, splaying warm colors across the sky. Pharla rose and walked to Maeya.

It is time to wake him.

"Aye." But Maeya still didn't want to. In the early light, with the scared side of his face turned away, he looked peaceful. She felt sure that once he opened his eyes and finished the tale, none of them would feel peace again.

Quoran deserved peace, she thought. The memory of the volcanic eruption washed over and through her, so vivid she could almost feel the heat and taste the ashes again.

     ***   *******   ***

It was only by Dragon's Luck that she had been at the creek that day two years ago, refilling a water skin. A giant hand of air pushed Maeya under, and she felt the sudden frightening rise in water temperature as the flames skittered across it, casting light on the river bottom rocks.

A body plunged into the water next to her, and when it began to float to the surface, Maeya held it under water. Better to drown than burn, she had thought.

As soon as the water above them lost the ginger glow, she pushed the body above her to the surface, even as her own body fought to keep from inhaling the water.

The air was hot and dry, and Maeya's throat protested as she gasped it in. The world around her—rocks, ground, and few remaining tree trunks—was black as pitch. The body floating next to her tried to slip below the water again. Determinedly, Maeya pulled it toward the bank, choking on the water even as it cooled her burning throat.

When she finally reached the shore, she allowed herself to look at the page she had pulled under with her. It was Quoran, and the left half of his face was red and black with burns. The burns had traveled down his neck too, and covered most of his left shoulder. But he would consider himself lucky when they found the charred remains of four pages, three Riders-in-training, a Cyr and two Tares. There was little Maeya could do to tend to Quoran; she was not trained as a healer. Maeya stood and almost fell again due to the light feeling in her head. For a frightening second, the black of the ground and the blue of above swirled and she was not sure which way to go. When she was steady again, she ran for the Cave.

But the healers at the Cave were overwhelmed. Three other pages and two Riders-in-training were burned worse than Quoran, scarred on the face, chest, and arms, and in two cases, burned so badly they were unable to survive, but lived in agony, alternately moaning and screaming for two passes of the Orb before becoming forever silent.

Maeya took what salve she could and hurried back to him.

Quoran wasn't where Maeya left him. She panicked, fearing that he had died and she had only imagined saving him. "Quoran?" she called, "Quoran!" Maeya calmed down enough to realize that she was staring at drag tracks through the singed ground. She followed them and found Quoran, propped up against a large boulder and panting.

"Easy," Maeya said to him. "You must rest."

"Nay," he said, "I must leave."

"Leave?" she repeated in confusion. "Why?"

Tears leaked out of his right eye. "Why? Why? Do you really not understand?"

"I understand that you are hurt, and that you must see the Healer."

"I must leave," he said adamantly. "No Rider will want me now."

"You are a valued page."

He began struggling again, trying to get to his feet. Maeya tried to push him down, and inadvertently touched his wounded shoulder. He howled in pain.

"My apologies!" she said quickly. "Quoran, please, you must stay still, until we're ready to walk you back to the Cave."

"Haven't you been listening? I can't go back!"

"You must," Maeya said firmly, drawing on her mother's way of commanding the peep at the estate. "I have said you will go back and that is that."

He shook his head. "I do not care what you say."

Her noble blood didn't matter. She was merely a page here; she was his equal. "I will see to it that you get a Rider's Honor."

The naked hope and longing that showed on the unburned right side of his face almost made her want to cry. "Truly?"

"Truly," Maeya had said, relieved to see that he had relaxed back against the boulder and didn't appear as agitated. "You will serve as a great page for a great Rider someday."

*** ******** ***

A sudden sense of understanding went through Maeya.

Startled, she turned to Pharla, but the Dragon was watching Quoran, not interested in Maeya in the slightest. *Please. We need to wake him now.*

It didn't matter. Pharla wasn't interested in her as a Rider, Maeya reminded herself. She had lost that opportunity. No, she had chosen to refuse that opportunity; she had not lost it.

Maeya walked over to Quoran and Pharla was there. No matter what she did, Pharla was always just a breath ahead of her.

As Maeya knelt down beside Quoran, he stirred, sensing their presence. Still half-asleep, he tried to twist away from them, tried to avoid what he knew he would be returning to when he awoke.

"Quoran," Maeya said, reaching for his shoulder. He turned to face her, eyes open and clear.

"Rider," he said. Maeya almost looked behind her to see the Rider he was talking to. He sat up, clasping his arms around his knees. "I really did find you."

We need to know.

"Aye. That you did."

"Cyr Sajen wanted me to find you."

"Why? Why was it important for you to find the Dragon and me?"

Quoran opened his mouth, but then shut it again, so fast Maeya was afraid he would break his teeth. His eyes glazed over in a very strange way. "I don't know."

"Quoran!"

"I can't remember."

"You must try!"

He remembers. He lies.

"Please, Quoran. Try!"

He shook his head. "I don't remember."

Beside her, Pharla hissed.

Maeya took a deep breath, trying to calm herself and get Pharla to settle down as well. "Start at the beginning," she said. "Start with what you do remember."

"I already told you everything!"

He hasn't said anything!

"Quoran, tell me—"

"I told you last night!" he said, his voice rising almost to a squeak. "I told you everything!"

Pharla butted Maeya's arm with her head.

"Why were you looking for Veet's Dragon?"

He stared reverently at Pharla. "She may be the last Kollarian Dragon," he said.

Now what?

"What?" Maeya said.

You were going to take me to Cyr Sajen!

"You're sure Cyr Sajen left?" Maeya asked Quoran. Cyr Sajen had been so hurt, so weak when she had left—but how long had she been tracking Pharla, healing her, trying to get her to accept her? It seemed so very long.

"Aye. He and the page."

Now what are we going to do?

"Did they take anything from the Cave?"

"Aye. Eggs."

It was a blow. "Cyr Sajen took Dragon eggs?"

"Aye."

"How many were there?" outside of her and Swald's unhatched eggs, Maeya didn't know of any.

"Fewer and fewer eggs have been hatching," Quoran said, "The Tares didn't know why. They kept the eggs. There were many. Perhaps a dozen or more."

"Did he take them all?"

His head bobbed twice more before he could get it to stop. "I do not know, Rider! I could not go back into the Cave!"

Maeya sank back on her heels. He had not seen everything. Some eggs could still be there.

She pushed herself to her feet again, grabbed her spear and sharpened rocks that she had gathered.

What are you doing?

"Where are you going, Rider Maeya?" Fear made Quoran's voice sound childish.

"To the Cave," she said. She turned and looked directly at Pharla. "To see what remains. Then we will find another Cave."

Maeya had been walking only a few moments before she heard them behind her. It was easy to distinguish that there were two. Quoran moved with an inherent clumsiness; Pharla moved with the eagerness of the very young.

Maeya felt a flush rising from deep within her, almost from her belly. Was Pharla following her? Or coming with Quoran? Or was she merely following the same path?

Quoran came bumbling up to her side. "Rider Maeya, they are all gone."

Because of the constriction in her throat, Maeya didn't trust herself to speak. She nodded, just one firm nod.

"Rider Maeya—"

"I know, Quoran," Maeya made herself say. "But I must see."

"Rider?"

"Aye?"

"Rider Maeya, I ask page's honor."

"If I ever become a Rider, you shall have it," Maeya said humbly. She had promised, so long ago, that Quoran would be a great page to a great Rider. He had stayed at the Cave at her urging, though none of the Riders had been accepting of him. He had been page to Cyr Sajen, which while a great responsibility, was usually saved for older pages who couldn't keep up with Riders. She knew sweet Quoran hadn't given up on his quest to be a great page, but she wasn't so sure she'd be a good Rider.

Quoran put a hand out, whether to steady Maeya or to draw comfort, she didn't know. All she knew is that they ended up walking the rest of the way with their arms around each other's waists, and not a root or branch touched them. Maeya couldn't hear Pharla behind them, nor did she dare look, but all the same, she knew the Dragon was there.

*** ******* ***

Even without the smoke that still clung to the Cave and its surroundings, it looked wrong. It was too still, too quiet, too empty. Quoran had been right. They were all gone.

He stopped as soon as they crossed the river. "I can't," he whimpered. "Please, I can't."

Maeya released his waist even as he dropped his arm from her. She kept walking. She could not condemn him for staying, but neither could she tell him it was all right. "Stay with the hatchling," she said and sensed his surprise as well as Pharla's.

The Spike Cave had always been a warm and welcoming place for Maeya. True, her family's modest estate offered many more luxuries, and the villages they had passed while traveling to the Cave had been quaint and appealing, but the Cave seemed even more. It was cozy without being constricting; protective without being restraining; rife with tradition while open to newcomers like herself. It had felt more like home than the house in which she had been raised. The Cave had had a sense of permanence, of community.

No longer.

Maeya took six steps into the Cave before she had to retreat and empty her stomach. But she had to go back in. Even if the chance of recovering useful items was small, she still had to know. She had to know how many had died.

The heat emanating off the rock walls was enough to be suffocating. Why was the smoke and heat still lingering? Had the Wyzards returned for a second attack? Camp supplies and bodies were strewn everywhere. The once neat paths that wound through the individual rooms were hard to follow because there was so much debris. Maeya had to throw up again, but she refused to leave the Cave. She stepped into the nearest room and added more to the mess.

Maeya decided she would be best served if she were to locate usable supplies and take them outside to Quoran. He needed something to do, and everything brought from the Cave would need to be scrubbed. If she got a little more fresh air while taking items out of the Cave, well, that was just an added benefit.

It didn't take her long to determine there wasn't much that could still be used. Very little clothing had been left unburned. She did find three hide blankets that had minimal singeing, although she was dubious about ever getting the smoke smell out of them. Four knives were in good shape; the fire seemed to have tempered them instead of melting them. Amazingly enough, Maeya found one intact bolo, though it was not her own. She also recovered polished stone ammunition.

All of the bowls and flasks in the main hearth were broken, but Maeya found a few undamaged ones in other rooms. Likewise, the fire had consumed the herbs, dried fruits and meat. She and Quoran would have to hunt and gather on their own.

After three trips out to Quoran and Pharla, Maeya was sure she had salvaged everything worth saving in the Cave. But she made herself go one more time. The idea of leaving Dragon eggs haunted her. She couldn't just give up.

As she passed the kitchen hearth, a glimmer on the far side caught her eye. Maeya walked over to it. It was a medallion, one she recognized as being page Wilad's. It was smeared with blood, and drops of blood trailed away from it. She followed the blood trail, going closer to the cave wall, ducking as the ceiling dropped lower.

There, in the very back, were two bodies. Wilad had died, but he had taken one of the Wyzard Faithful with him. Maeya knelt by Wilad and placed the medallion in his hand. She rose to a crouch so she could walk back out to the main part of the cave. Then she stopped. That wasn't a rock near Wilad's foot.

That was a Dragon's egg.

Holding her breath, Maeya crawled over to the egg and picked it up. Turning it over in her hands, she could not find any cracks or signs of trauma. Maeya thought she recognized the slightly speckled pattern on the leathery egg; it had been Swald's.

The Orb was just above the Spike when Maeya left the Cave for the last time. Pharla was lazing in the light, stretched out and almost oozing contentment. Quoran had not been idle. He had fashioned an over-sized pack from of the hides, and had loaded everything into it.

When he saw her approaching, he jumped to his feet. "Rider Maeya!" He saw the egg and his jaw dropped. "Is it whole?"

Pharla raised her head and hissed.

"Aye," Maeya said. "Page Wilad gave his life to keep it so."

"Rider-in-training Wilad," Quoran corrected, staring at the egg. "Tare Gerand gave him the egg."

"This poor egg is in need of a Rider who can stay alive."

Quoran was eyeing the egg warily. "Perhaps that Dragon would be better off without a Rider."

"What do you mean?"

"Perhaps the egg carries Dragon's Luck."

Maeya laughed. "It carries a Dragon, Quoran. Not luck."

But Pharla hissed again, and this time some of her darker neck spines rose, sending a chill down Maeya's back.

Dragon's Luck. Maeya had been promoted to Rider-in-training, but her egg had never hatched. Her egg and almost everyone in her Cave had been killed, yet she hadn't been hurt. Cyr Sajen had given her a second chance and sent her after a powerful Dragon hatchling, but the hatchling didn't want her. Some would call that Dragon's Luck. Maeya merely called it her life.

"I see you have prepared for travel," Maeya said.

"Aye."

"Where is your pack?" she asked him.

"It is here," he said, hefting the large bag.

"Then where is mine?"

He looked at her with utter confusion. "Rider Maeya?"

"My pack," she repeated. "Where is it?"

"I will carry your pack," he said. "That is my honor."

"Quoran, I'm not letting you carry all of our supplies like a pack horse."

"You have other duties to tend to, Rider," he said gravely. "That load will be lighter if you let me carry this one."

"You're being difficult."

He raised one eyebrow at her, since the scarring prevented both eyebrows from going up. "I am trying to help you," he said.

"You won't be any help if you work yourself into the ground."

You won't be any good if you waste your energy on useless arguments.

Maeya turned in surprise. Pharla was staring at her. Quoran didn't seem to notice.

"I will not work myself too hard," Quoran continued solemnly.

"Is that a promise?" Maeya asked.

"Nay, Rider. It is my vow to you. I must always be able to help you."

She studied him for a moment, and then said, "You must also work on your sense of humor."

"Aye, Rider, if you say so."

Exasperated, Maeya said, "Quoran, would you please smile?"

"Beg pardon," he said meekly. "But this does not seem the best place for laughter." He gestured to the Cave behind them.

"Perhaps not," she said, although she preferred to remember the Cave as a place of laughter rather than a place of slaughter. "But even when you were Cyr Sajen's page, you did not smile enough."

This is pointless.

Maeya did not spare Pharla a glance. She needed Quoran to relax and trust her. She needed him to help her relieve tension, not add more. Pharla could criticize everything—indeed it seemed that she would—but Maeya would not let Pharla ride her. She was the Rider. She was, at least temporarily, in charge.

You said you would take me to another Cave. Pharla was unbelievably petulant.

"We will go to another Cave," Maeya muttered under her breath, before adding for Quoran to hear, "In truth, I would like to begin traveling now." It wasn't so much that she was in a hurry to leave as it was that she did not want to sleep in the shadow of the Spike tonight. If they left now, they could be well on the other side of the valley before the Orb sank behind the Spike. "I need one of the hides," Maeya said.

Quoran quickly retrieved it from the pack. "A sling?" he asked, even as he deftly began cutting the hide in half.

"Aye." A sling would make it easier and safer to carry the egg. In short order, Quoran was helping her slide the sling over one shoulder and under the other, nestling the egg close to her body.

"Which Cave will we go to?" Quoran asked, shouldering the large pack.

Maeya began leading the way down the trader's path. It was the fastest route out of the valley. It would take them to the nearest village, and from there they could travel the trading road with relative ease.

"We're going home," Maeya said.

"Rider?" Quoran asked uncertainly, glancing back at the Cave.

"My home," she clarified. "My family estate."

Why?

"Are you sure that's…" Quoran trailed off.

"What?"

Maeya stopped and turned to stare at him. He stopped several paces from her, shifting nervously on his feet. Pharla kept walking, pushing past him toward Maeya. The Dragon didn't stop, either, but stepped determinedly around her. Her tail lashed dangerously close to the egg before she continued on the path. Quoran started, but when Maeya didn't move, he stayed where he was, looking miserable.

"What, Quoran?"

"Are you sure that's wise, Rider?" he mumbled, without looking at her. "Should we not be looking for a Cave?"

Aye! Listen to the great page!

"We will look for a Cave," Maeya said to both of them, "But my home is closer than the nearest Cave, and we shall be given provisions there."

Relief showed plainly on Quoran's face. "Of course, Rider Maeya. We're merely stopping for provisions. I should know better than to question your decisions, Rider."

"Please call me Maeya," she said. She had enough to worry about without him calling her Rider every other word. She wasn't a Rider. She didn't have a Dragon.

"Pardon, Ri—Maeya."

You've got a new egg. Maybe you will get a Dragon.

Maeya sighed. At the moment, she wasn't sure she wanted a Dragon at all.

CHAPTER THREE

When they made first camp, they had, in fact, travelled far enough to get out of the Spike's shadow, but not by much. Quoran's panting and red face made her fear he was going to pass out. Yet when she suggested that he divide the pack and allow her to carry some, he managed to increase his pace for a few steps. So she had stopped twice, feigning a need for water or rest, because she could see no other way to get him to slow down. Each time, Pharla stopped well beyond them, curled up in the shade of a bush, surveying Maeya through slitted eyes.

"This will be good for the night," Maeya said, when they came to a small creek that turned just before a small hill. Pharla stalked to a bush, tail lashing angrily.

"The Orb will not set for a while yet," Quoran puffed, looking up at the sky.

"Aye, but Pharla's shorter legs are not used to traveling so far and so fast."

Indignation laced with anger smothered Maeya. Pharla turned so her back was to Quoran and Maeya. She flopped down, dirt and dry leaves flying out from under her. Maeya, however, found Pharla's irritation reassuring. After being ignored all day, she was pleased to have provoked any kind of reaction.

She turned back to Quoran to find him staring at her with wide eyes. "Rider Maeya? Who is Pharla?"

Maeya gestured carelessly toward the green lump in front of the bush.

Quoran was shaking his head. "Dragons are not pets," he said, glancing over at Pharla. He pitched his voice lower, "You do not get to name them as if they were a cat or a dog."

Maeya could sense Pharla's approval. "Trust me, Quoran, had I named her, it would have been something simple, such as Honey or Flower." The approval reverted to disgust.

"Then why do you call the Dragon Fa...."

"Pharla," she said clearly. "Because that's what her name is."

"But how did—"

"Quoran," she said in exasperation, "Is there something wrong with her name?"

"N-n-nay," he stuttered.

"Then what's the problem?"

"Who told you her name?"

"She did."

Quoran sat down so fast it appeared his legs must have given out under him. "The Dragon has spoken to you?"

Maeya shrugged. Pharla didn't speak to her in the strictest sense; it was more a series of ideas and feelings that Maeya knew were not her own.

"But she hatched less than a season ago!"

Maeya felt her brow rise. "Less than a full cycle of Sister Orb," she said.

Quoran wrapped his arms around his legs and rested his head on his knees. "By the Power That Is, we must find Cyr Sajen."

"But first I must find dinner," Maeya said, removing the sling and setting the Dragon's egg on the ground by Quoran's feet. "We will be traveling for many more days, and will need to keep our strength up."

As she stood up, she caught Pharla looking at her. As Pharla put her head back down, Maeya got a fleeting image of a rabbit.

"Aye," she mumbled under her breath as she pulled her bolo from her belt and began to climb the hill. "You prefer rabbit."

Hunting did not take Maeya long, and she was heading back to the camp as the Orb kissed the sky farewell. She had set out hoping to get two rabbits, but they had been so plentiful and easy to hit that she had gotten four. They would need to eat tomorrow, after all, and the hunting might not be so easy.

She watched her footing and moved quietly through the dusk. Having Quoran with her was a source of comfort, but he hardly made her feel secure. As pages, they had practiced with both bow and spear before the volcano erupted, and there was a reason why none of the Riders or Riders-in-training—including herself—had clamored to have him as a page. He was gentle and kind and wise—and clumsy and soft. Beyond acting as a guard, he would not be much help in keeping their camp secure. The Wyzard Faithful could be anywhere.

As Maeya walked back up the hill with the rabbits she caught sight of movement. She dropped to a crouch and froze. The light breeze was enough to lift her hair back and away from her face, but not enough to do more. The Trident leaves hung still, not swinging and rustling.

Maeya tried to throw her senses out, to hear or see or feel what was nearby, and met a wall of grumpiness.

"Pharla," she whispered, "Is all well?"

Aye. There was a moment's hesitation and Maeya sensed that Pharla was looking around the camp. *All is well. Why?*

Maeya crawled to the crest of the hill, still not convinced. She had seen something move and that meant—

She was almost on top of the wolf before either of them knew it. The wolf had been watching the small camp at the bottom of the hill. It spun, snarling and baring angry teeth, as it realized that Maeya was right behind it. The wolf was close enough for Maeya to feel the warmth of its breath. She braced herself for the pain of the bite, for there was no way she could get her knife between her and the beast in time. Perhaps the wolf would miss her throat; perhaps she would get the chance to defend against the second bite....

The wolf cocked its head to the side and stopped snarling. Maeya's hand stayed at her belt, lightly resting on the knife's hilt.

The brown eyes surveyed Maeya and she felt naked and helpless, but unafraid. The wolf dipped its head—nodded—and turned to trot away. She watched it as it moved easily and silently around the camp, glancing over its shoulder to Maeya twice. Suddenly another shadow rose, and a second wolf sat up as the first wolf stopped in front of it. Both of them looked over at Maeya, and a weird last bit of light reflected off their eyes. The first wolf continued around the camp, until it was on the opposite side from Maeya, and there it blended back into the shadows. The second wolf was gone from sight as well, but Maeya had no doubt it was still there.

Maeya looked back down on the camp, and realized there was a third pair of golden eyes watching her. Pharla was still curled up by the bush, but her head was raised and her luminous eyes crackled with more light than the fire did. Quoran was kneeling by the campfire, and both bedrolls were spread out. It looked very cozy.

All is well. No need to stay up there.

Maeya wasn't so sure.

What is amiss?

But Maeya didn't want to worry her.

Too late for that now, Pharla thought tartly. *What worries you should also worry me.*

You do not sense danger?

From the wolves? Nay.

You know about the wolves?

They have been with you since you found me.

"'Tis nothing," Maeya said out loud, trying to drown her self-recrimination for allowing Pharla to sense her fear and make light of it. "You want dinner," Maeya said, scrambling to her feet and making her way down the hill.

Pharla sniffed and closed her eyes.

Quoran made short work of dinner preparation, and Maeya complimented him on the creative seasoning he used. He apologized for the lack of bread and vegetables, and no amount of reassurance seemed to cheer him up. Maeya kept looking for signs of the wolves but did not say anything. She did not want to scare Quoran, and bizarre as it was, it seemed that the wolves were keeping watch over them.

Pharla raised her head and looked at her, and Maeya knew that the Dragon was more aware of her thoughts than she wanted her to be. Out of desperation, Maeya asked Quoran about his training with the Cyr.

"Why did Cyr Sajen take you as his own page? I thought the Tares and Cyrs just used whatever pages were nearby."

Quoran bobbed his head. "Aye, but Cyr Sajen had many specific duties and needs as the Lore Keeper."

"The what?"

Quoran looked her with something akin to disapproval. "Lore Keeper," he repeated as if that cleared everything up.

"What kind of specific duties and needs?" Maeya asked, hoping he would give her enough information for her to understand the Lore Keeper's role without her having to ask again.

"Why, the ability to remember specific details from stories exactly, to remember everything word for word, and to be able to tell the stories word for word, for individuals or for entire Caves if the time calls for it."

"O."

"Cyr Sajen would be most intrigued by your Dragon's progression," Quoran said, gazing across the fire to Pharla. She had eaten a whole rabbit with a few quick bites, but had not been interested in the second one. Although she was once again curled up with her head resting on her tail and facing away from them, Maeya could tell that Pharla was listening to all that was being said. In fact, she was listening rather intently.

"What's so unusual about Pharla's name?" Maeya asked, remembering the conversation from when they first stopped at camp.

"Don't you remember you Lore?"

"No, Tare Terce sent me hunting during Lore teaching. In truth, most Tares and Cyrs found reasons to send me out during training." Except Cyr Sajen, and he did not often work with the Riders-in-training.

"It's not that her name is interesting," Quoran said leaning forward, "It's that she's already told you! Most Dragons don't start communicating with their Riders until they've seen all the seasons, and it's not unusual for them to see the seasons twice before the can communicate clearly enough to tell the Rider their name. It's true that female Riders often get the communication bond earlier than males, but in all the Lore Cyr Sajen ever told me, he never mentioned a Dragon that revealed its name before it saw its third season." Quoran shook his head and looked at Pharla. "And then, of course, there's the transfer."

Maeya waited, but when he didn't continue, she asked, "The transfer?"

"She had bonded with Veet first. It's difficult for Dragons to successfully transfer their bond."

"Difficult?" Maeya asked. "How difficult? Cyr Sajen made it sound like it was something that could be done."

"O, he wanted it done. He told me after you left to find the Dragon that he thought the hatchling could grow to become a Dragon of stories, if it could bond with you. But he expected it to take a full set of seasons."

"Why?"

"That's how long it took Eleena to get Naria."

Maeya didn't need to look over to Pharla to know that her eyes were open and the hatchling was hanging on Quoran's every word.

"Naria? The great Naria?"

"Aye."

"But—" Maeya shook her head, trying to clear it. "Eleena always had the great Naria."

"Nay," Quoran said softly. "She did not."

"But—"

"Rider Maeya, I can tell you the Lore, but I must tell it correctly. Will you listen?"

"Aye."

"Without interrupting?"

"I will do my best," Maeya answered, trying to ignore the sense of doubt coming from Pharla.

Quoran cleared his throat, and told Maeya the story of Eleena and Naria in a way she had never heard it before.

"Wysleck Zardina was guaranteed a Dragon's egg; the line of Zardina Riders was long and powerful, though they had not had a great Rider in several generations. Eleena, his younger sister, wished to be a Rider more than anything, but she was only second born. So she came with Wysleck as a page. She was a great page, but Wysleck was not a good Rider-in-training, in spite of all her help."

Maeya watched the fire and lost herself in Quoran's gentle tones as he told the story of Wysleck and Eleena.

***   ********   ***

Tare Cal, the Rider Trainer, came along the path.

"Ah, Wysleck, there you are. And…" he broke off, searching.

"Eleena," she said helpfully.

"Yes. You're here too."

She bobbed her head and smiled, pretending not to notice the disapproval she heard in his voice, pretending not to be disappointed that after two years at the Cave, she was still a nobody in the eyes of the Tares. Eleena wished that Wysleck had at least thought to move a little closer to the egg while playing with the stick.

"We need everyone back to the caves," Tare Cal said abruptly.

"Why?" Wysleck asked as Eleena quickly stood up and moved toward the egg. Tare Cal frowned at her, and she stopped just short of picking it up.

"Why?" Wysleck repeated. "We're supposed to have the afternoon with the eggs."

"Tinom's egg just hatched," Tare Cal said.

"Really?" Eleena squealed. She couldn't help it. The idea of baby Dragons appealed to her.

The clutches of eggs usually hatched within three days of each other. Although she had grown used to seeing the full-grown Dragons and their Riders during their time at the Training Cave, Eleena had not seen any young Dragons or hatchlings.

Tare Cal merely raised an eyebrow at Eleena.

She quickly looked at the ground and tried to remember to be a page, one who was seen and heard only when needed.

"So we're to be sequestered in the Cave now?" Wysleck sighed, tucking the carved Trident stick away in his tunic. "What luck."

He took three steps back toward the cave. Eleena burst into a loud coughing fit. He looked back at her, irritated, and she glared at him before looking pointedly at the egg.

Wysleck had the grace to blush slightly as he turned on his heel to retrieve the egg. Eleena tried not to groan out loud at the cavalier way he grabbed the egg and carried it on his hip.

Tare Cal cleared his throat and she hurried to follow Wysleck up the path back to the Cave.

There was a large crowd around Tinom, of course, and all the pages were expected to be working, so it wasn't until nearly midnight that Eleena was able to catch a glimpse of the first hatchling.

Since she was one of the last to see the newest Dragon, she had already heard that it was green. The Dragon was curled up on a pillow next to Tinom's mat, much like a cat would. It was the size of a large cat, too. Tinom, of course, was sleeping, but his page, Matew, was busy repairing Tinom's vest.

Eleena smiled and nodded at Matew, who smiled back but didn't slow his stitching.

As tired as she was, her feet felt light as she went back to her fire. Soon, they would have a hatchling curled up on the pillow that Wysleck had made and that Eleena had improved. Or so she thought.

Several times the Orb passed. One by one, the Riders-in-training became Riders as their eggs hatched. All but three hatched within three days. The three who remained Riders-in-training were good friends, and not well liked outside of their own group.

Wysleck was saying, "Try it, Elmrond! I bet you can."

Elmrond grimaced in concentration. The small flask in front of him began to tremble and then rose off the ground a few inches.

"Oh, come on!" Brind snorted. "You must be able to do better than that!"

Brind must have broken Elmrond's concentration, because the flask dropped back to the ground, tipping over and splattering water across the dirt floor.

Eleena was wishing she had chosen to go with Noll and Jens, Brind and Elmrond's pages. They had decided to go watch the other hatchlings. Eleena looked at the three eggs resting on her sleeping mat.

She didn't try to eavesdrop, but it wasn't hard to tell that Tare Cal and the other cave members were growing nervous. There had never been an egg that didn't hatch; now there were three. No one knew what it meant, but it felt ominous.

"Eleena, fetch us some wine," Wysleck said while never looking away from his staff.

"I think I—"

"I'll do the thinking for my page!" Wysleck snapped. "Now go!"

She turned to go, hating the laughter she heard at her expense, but hating even more that Wysleck had changed so much in the last years that he no longer seemed her brother. Indeed, it often was hard for her to remember that they shared blood and a last name.

As Eleena headed for the wine stock, she tried to think of what she'd say if anyone questioned her on the way back. Once the eggs had hatched, all Dragon Riders-in-training had been forbidden any spirits.

"Eleena."

She just barely stopped short of running into Tare Cal's broad chest. Confused and frightened to see him wearing his great cape, she stepped aside on the path to get out of his way. Behind him were four more Tares, all leaders of different Caves and all wearing the capes of their Caves, most of them carrying impressive staffs, too. The leaders had shown up before the eggs hatched, and now they were busy surveying the new Riders and Dragons, pitching the advantages of their own Caves. It was rare to see them together without any bickering.

"Eleena?"

"Y-y-yes, Tare Cal?" she stuttered.

"Is Wysleck at his fire?"

"Yes."

"Who else is with him?"

"Elmrond and Brind."

"Anyone else?"

Eleena shook her head. "Just them. And their eggs," she felt compelled to add.

He gave her a strange look then, and paused before saying, "You aren't just a peep from the estate, are you? You are also of the Zardina family?"

She made herself stand straight and look him in the eye. "Second born to Wysleck."

"And you chose to come with him? Surely Stavs Zardina didn't order you to come."

"It was my choice."

"Zardina Riders have always been strong," said another elder behind Tare Cal.

"And there has always been a Rider from the family," added another, while Tare Cal continued to study Eleena.

"We're going to speak to Wysleck," he said finally. "'Tis no matter for a page to hear. But I wish to talk to you later."

"But Tare—"

"Go elsewhere," he said, sounding almost gentle. "This is no reflection upon you."

One of the other elders leaned forward and murmured something in Tare Cal's ear. He hesitated as he studied her again before he nodded. "Stay close. We will have a task for you before the Orb begins to sink."

Eleena watched as they swept importantly past her. The fear in her stomach was multiplying like the rats that hid in the dark recesses of the caves.

A few moments later, a bellowed curse echoed through the giant cave. "Banished from the Dragon Riders!" There was no mistaking Wysleck's furious voice.

Eleena began to trot back to their fire. She had made it perhaps twenty paces before she heard another raised voice.

"We refuse to go!" Eleena was pretty sure that was Brind.

On another path, she saw Dragon Riders and Riders-in-training also moving toward Wysleck's room. Eleena increased her speed. Perhaps she could once again undo whatever damage Wysleck had done.

When she reached their site, Wysleck, Brind, and Elmrond were all standing opposite of the Tares. Tare Cal and the others all stood with their arms relaxed at their sides, but there was an air of suppressed violence. Wysleck's friends had their arms crossed over their chests, but Wy was clenching and unclenching one fist, and gripping his carved half-staff with the other.

"It is time for you to leave," Tare Cal said, a quiet steel underlying his words. "Now."

Elmrond took a step toward the edge of our campsite, but when he saw the others weren't moving, he stopped. He looked angry, but more than that, he looked scared.

The staring contest, it seemed, would go on forever. But then Wysleck growled, "Fine. Who wants to play with overgrown lizards, anyway?" He gestured at the eggs and Eleena felt her heart stop. "Eleena, gather our gear. I'll meet you at the mouth of the Cave."

She opened her mouth to protest, to tell him she didn't want to go, but Tare Cal beat her to it.

"Eleena stays."

"She's my sister," Wysleck said, taking a few menacing steps toward the Tares. "She's coming home with me."

"No, son, she's not."

"I'm not your son!" Wysleck roared.

There seemed to be a strange sadness in Cal's eyes as he said, "No, you most certainly are not. I'd give much to know whose son you really are. Nonetheless, Eleena stays."

Wysleck opened his mouth and she quickly cut in, afraid of what he might say.

"I'm your sister, Wysleck, not your ward. It was my choice to come as your page; it is now my choice whether or not to go," Eleena faltered as he turned his glare to her, "and...and I choose to stay with Tare Cal."

His lip drew back in a frightening scowl, and she wished she were standing closer to the Tares, or perhaps Tinom and his Dragon.

"For that?" He demanded in a sneer, pointing at the Dragon's eggs that were nestled on her mat, wrapped in her blanket.

"Yes," Eleena said simply.

He seemed about to say something else then stopped. "Let's go," he said instead to Elmrond and Brind.

Brind immediately turned to step out of their site, but Elmrond hesitated. "I need to get my things," he began.

For some reason, this was what pushed Wysleck over the edge. "You don't need anything," he roared. "We have everything right here!"

He raised his small staff, and the Trident wand began to glow the eerie blue Eleena had seen too many times before. "This is ALL! Those are nothing!"

He swung the small staff violently, and a giant red ball burst forward, striking one of the eggs.

The egg— Eleena was pretty sure it was Elmrond's—turned black and began to smoke as an ear-splitting wail filled the entire cavern. She felt in her soul that it was the death cry of the unborn hatchling.

Eleena flung herself in between Wysleck and the remaining two eggs. Tinom's green Dragon made a strange keening sound that changed to an angry hiss. Tinom charged Wysleck, his shoulder lowered for a full tackle.

From under his shirt, Brind pulled a staff similar to Wysleck's and aimed it at Tinom. One of the Tares stepped in Eleena's line of vision, and she was unable to see what happened. But Tinom dropped heavily to the floor of the cave.

"No!" she heard Matew wail.

There was another blinding flash as Eleena scrambled backward from Wysleck toward the two eggs. One of them was cracked. The Tare who had blocked her sight now fell in a heap, partly covering Tinom.

The cave was full of shouts and stamping of feet as people from all over tried to come to their small fire.

Elmrond, Brind, and Wysleck stood back to back in a small triangle, each holding a glowing Trident stick. Wysleck was facing Eleena.

"Move."

To terrified to speak, she shook her head.

He began to swing the stick, and Eleena watched the blue glow begin to travel through the carvings from the handle up to the tip.

Suddenly Brind shrieked in pain, and Wysleck turned in confusion.

Tinom's Dragon, already the size of a small dog, had launched itself at Brind. And though its teeth and claws were small, they were all razor sharp. It was shredding his skin, laying it open in small ribbons, but Brind was covering his neck and face, preventing a fatal slice.

Wysleck turned the staff on the Dragon and his friend.

Somehow, the Dragon jumped off Brind a fraction of a breath before the ball of fire hit. Brind's agonized shriek was short, but Eleena would never forget it. The small green beast landed beside her and the remaining eggs.

When Wysleck aimed the staff back toward Eleena, she knew that she was facing her last seconds. He would kill her, sister or not, for standing in his way.

As he raised the staff, all the anger Eleena had held in check boiled over. She could feel her skin tingling, and a powerful surge drove her to her feet. Eleena would not die cowering at Wysleck's feet.

It seemed as if time slowed down as she saw the ball of fire leave the tip of the stick, and she wondered why the stick would glow blue but fire red heat. Instinctively, Eleena threw her hand up, and watched in shock as the fireball exploded a mere pace away from her.

Once again, silence descended upon the cave. Tare Cal turned a very strange shade of white.

Wysleck grabbed Elmrond's elbow, and dragged him from their room. Those who had been charging up to meet them parted in silence, not even turning to watch as they passed through the mouth of the cave.

All eyes were on Eleena.

She didn't know what to say, or what to do. But then a noise from behind her made her turn. The egg that had cracked was now hatching. Eleena dropped to her knees as a blood-covered Dragon weakly pushed the shell away from itself.

Its eyes were closed, but as the last of the shell fell away from it, it opened both eyes and stared at Eleena. It began to speak in a powerful bass that didn't seem to match the helpless body.

> *In time of need and time of fire*
> *You protected your heart's desire.*
> *In the coming years of woe*
> *All will fall 'neath evil glow.*
> *But in the future lies our dreams*
> *Of power once ripped at seams*
> *By descendent true of witch*
> *And a Dragon dark as pitch.*

The voice reverberated through Eleena's skull, down her spine, and shook her smallest toes. Her teeth rattled. She bowed her head down, and when she looked up again, the hatchling's eyes had closed.

A hand grabbed her shoulder.

"Eleena."

Her whole body wanted to heave, to throw up everything from the last days. But she couldn't move.

"Eleena," Tare Cal said gently. "It is always hard when a Rider loses their Dragon."

She stared at him, uncomprehending.

"But when a Dragon loses its Rider, it is just as hard." He gestured. Several pages were lifting Tinom's body. Two more pages were trying to console the grieving Matew. A circle of Tares was standing guard around the fallen Tare. The young Dragon's emerald green scales looked bleached out as it hissed at everyone who came within reach.

"It will need your help to recover."

"Shouldn't it be paired with a new Rider?"

"It has been. You."

"I'm to be its Rider?" Eleena asked in disbelief.

He nodded. "The Dragon that chose you has passed," he said, gesturing to the small hatchling still mostly in its shell. "At least we now know why it chose not to hatch," he murmured to himself. "But we have one more to foster."

Eleena turned back to the hatchling. "He chose me?"

"It seems so."

Desperately she fought down the knot in her throat. "I was going to have a red Dragon."

"Your Dragon was white," Tare Cal said gently. "See? The membrane had not yet separated."

With a shaking hand, Eleena reached out and pulled part of the membrane from its head. Underneath, small pearl white scales would never grow larger. She had never seen or heard of a white Dragon.

"But what did it mean?" Eleena asked.

"It spoke to you?" Tare Cal asked sharply.

"He spoke to all of us!"

"Tare Trallen, Tare Jalso!" The Tares came quickly toward them. "What did he say?" Tare Cal demanded. "Exactly how did he say it?"

Eleena recited what she had heard; what she thought the entire cavern must have heard.

Tare Cal and Tare Trallen exchanged significant looks.

"You will need to come see the FullTare," Tare Jalso said. "This must be—"

"Later," Tare Cal said. "Now she must spend time with Tinom's Dragon, before it's too late."

"What do you mean?" Eleena asked.

Tare Cal turned her, and kept his hand on her shoulder as he guided her farther into the Cave. "It will take a long time for you to bond with the Dragon, but it can be done."

"But I need to go home," Eleena said. "My parents need to know about Wy."

"The Dragon needs you," Tare Cal said. "You will discover that you need it, too, but it needs you even more."

"We need you, Eleena," Tare Jalso added in a heavy tone. "We will get word to your parents, but we need you. May the Power That Is see to it that you never have to know how much we really need you."

*** ******** ***

"But she did," Maeya said, when Quoran paused and she realized that he was done with the Lore. "She did know how much we needed her—and Naria."

"Aye," Quoran agreed. "In time, she came to know just how much the Clan needed her. She and Naria were able to help the Clan rebuild. The power of female Riders was recognized, and the Dragons began breeding again. For many generations, the Clan grew stronger. But as tends to happen, there came times of disagreement, and the strong Clan Rider Eleena built broke into four separate, weaker Clans. Rider Eleena, luckily, did not live to see her great-grandchildren break what she had built."

There was a sense of sorrow and confusion from the bush where Pharla was curled.

"She and Naria," Maeya mused, "A Dragon that Eleena was not trained to bond with."

"The Tares may not have intended Eleena and Naria to bond, Maeya, but the Power That Is surely did."

Before crawling into her bedroll, Maeya made a circuit of the camp. She carefully stayed away from the wolves, but she saw three. As she drifted off to sleep, she wasn't sure what she found more reassuring, the fact that the wolves were standing guard or that Eleena had successfully bonded with a Dragon meant for another.

CHAPTER FOUR

Dragons were part of Maeya's life. They had been for almost three years. Though Spike Cave was the training Cave for Kollarian Clan, there were always Riders and their Dragons flying in and out. Once the hatchlings and Riders-in-training were deemed ready, they would leave and go to one of the battle Caves, ready to fly and defend against any attacking Clans or Wyzards, but they often came back to visit the Tares and Cyrs who had mentored them, or to check in on the pages and encourage the new Riders.

Pharla was only a hatchling, but she was still a Dragon. In spite of being ill, she had grown rapidly and now, as she saw her second cycle of Sister Orb, she was the size of a new-born calf, and just as solid. Her green scales could get lost in the growing season fields, but it was still Awakening, so her emerald sheen contrasted with the newly green fields. The only color other than green was in her golden eyes. They had gotten darker too, and were more of an amber than a yellow. The spines that ran the length of her neck and along the sides of her tail were such a dark green as to almost look black from a distance, matching her teeth with their sharp edges.

Other than making sure that Pharla was with them and had enough food and drink, Maeya didn't pay much attention to her. She was part of who Maeya was, though. Every once in a while, Maeya felt one of Pharla's thoughts rip through her. Her thoughts seemed to match her teeth and spines in their sharpness.

It was on their fourth day of travelling that they approached the first village. They were still moving slowly because Quoran refused to allow Maeya to carry anything other than the Dragon's egg. As they approached, Maeya was trying to construct new arguments, determined to split the load when the Orb next rose. At their current pace, it would be another end of Sister Orb's cycle before they got to the Daceae Estate. They did not try to avoid the village for two reasons. The first was that Maeya was trying to travel quickly. The second was because Maeya had forgotten the awe she felt the first time she had seen a Dragon.

Before they got to the first house, Quoran pulled a tunic from the pack and wrapped it awkwardly around his scarred face. He knew from experience that strangers did not respond well to his scars at first sight.

This time, however, he was hardly noticed.

The village peep were not used to Dragons. The traveling trio was mobbed from the moment they walked between the first two houses. When they passed the third house, Pharla was walking directly in front of Maeya. By the time they had passed the sixth house, Pharla dropped back to walk next to Maeya, almost stepping on her feet as the hatchling tried to stay as close to her as she could. Maeya was surprised that Pharla wasn't trying to stay close to Quoran. He walked in front of them, attempting to clear a path.

Hands. All that Maeya would remember later from that village was hands. All those hands reaching for her, reaching for Pharla. Peep reaching to touch a part of Lore.

Maeya remembered voices, too. A constant babble of voices, sometimes rising, sometimes falling, but so layered it was impossible to hear anything except one word: Dragon.

The peep were fascinated, but not frightened; they had probably never seen a Dragon so young. Pharla was too little to command the reverence she should have been given. The peep reached for her as if she were a barnyard cow who had given birth to triplets. Rare, and therefore deserving attention, but nothing to be feared or respected.

Throw something at them.

"What?"

Throw the egg at them.

"Pharla!"

Then throw something else at them. Just get rid of them!

Maeya finally sensed Pharla's fear under the anger. "We'll be out in a moment. We won't stay."

In the center of the village, where the healer's, the inn, the baker's, and the butcher's formed a small square, they were almost forced to stop because there were so many people around them. Pharla's fear turned to panic and became difficult to separate from Maeya's own thoughts. Quoran looked back over his shoulder at Maeya, and she lifted her chin forward.

He nodded and as he turned back to face the peep, he pulled the tunic off his face. Most of the crowd parted in front of him. Pharla and Maeya stayed close on his heels. The peep didn't stop following them until they were well out of their village. Quoran didn't stop walking until they couldn't see the village when they looked back.

By the Power That Is, I hope I never feel like that again.

"I'm taking you to a Cave. There you will be well cared for."

Pharla didn't say anything else, and Maeya was surprised to feel bitter disappointment.

After the town, Maeya was able to fell two quail and one rabbit with the bolo. The village road didn't have enough traffic to scare many animals away.

Quoran and Maeya were both quiet as they set up camp. Pharla curled up close to the fire instead of under a tree. She hadn't said anything to Maeya since leaving the last of the peep behind.

Maeya had tried to pet Pharla's neck, but the Dragon sidled out from under her hand, and then increased her speed, getting distance between herself and Maeya.

While Quoran saw to the quail (Pharla had snapped up the hare as soon as they had stopped), Maeya cleared the bigger rocks from the site, and gathered some loose pine needles for bedding. Then she checked on the egg.

The first day of travel from the Cave, Maeya had been convinced that she had felt movement under the leathery shell. But as they were approaching the village, she had confessed to Quoran that she must have been imagining it.

The egg was still intact, but that was her only comfort. It should have hatched weeks ago, at the same time that Pharla and the other eggs had hatched. How long could a Dragon's egg last? Maeya's family had a chicken coop at the estate, and although she had never collected the eggs, she had overheard the cooks talking about eggs going bad. Maeya sat down to watch Quoran cook, absently cradling the egg against her body.

"All is well?"

"I do not know," Maeya said, "I fear it should have hatched by now."

"The Power That Is will determine when the egg shall hatch," Quoran said, sprinkling a few more spice leaves onto the quail breast.

"What happened to the other eggs that didn't hatch?"

"I do not know."

Pharla made a strange coughing sound, then she got up and walked away from both the fire and the bedding Maeya had set out. She flopped down on the ground, hard, head pointing away from them.

Quoran glanced at her and then at Maeya. "Why have you not been caring for her?" he asked in an undertone.

Maeya did not bother to lower her voice to match his. "She does not wish for me to care for her," Maeya said shortly.

"She is your Dragon," Quoran whispered.

"No," Maeya said, "She does not want me. She has been very clear about that."

"Rider Maeya, you must try."

She stared at him. "I have tried," she managed to growl.

Quoran glanced over at Pharla and then again at Maeya. "Forgive me, Rider, but I have not seen it."

Maeya opened her mouth to argue, but she realized that he was right. Since he had joined them, she had been too busy examining the remains of the Cave and then leading their journey to pay much attention to Pharla. Maeya nestled the egg in the swirled pile of the sling, and set it close to the fire for warmth but not close enough to get singed.

It's impossible to harm a Dragon egg, Pharla said scornfully as she approached.

"Really?" Maeya asked, stopping just a few paces from her. "I saw eggs destroyed not very long ago."

There's a difference between singeing and destroying.

"Aye," Maeya said as she hunkered down. "That there is. Do you know? Can Dragon eggs go bad?"

A Dragon may go bad, she said, *the egg will not.*

"I don't understand."

The egg will not hatch until there is a worthy Rider, she said with a sniff, turning her head away from Maeya.

An image of the egg she had carried with her flashed through her head. It had not hatched. She was not a worthy Rider. No wonder Pharla didn't want her.

"Are you well?" Maeya asked her after a few moments. She did not want to break the silence, but did not she want to leave Pharla, either. She wanted Pharla to talk to her. She wanted Pharla to want her.

All is well.

"I am sorry about the village," Maeya said awkwardly. "The peep should have known better."

You should have told them.

"They would not have listened to me."

Affairs are sad indeed if the peep no longer listen to Riders.

"I'm not a Rider."

Pharla turned her head to look at Maeya. Her amber eyes almost glowed in the firelight. *You want to be a Rider.*

There was something Maeya was missing. Pharla's words meant more; she was looking for more than a response to the statement. Maeya was quiet, searching for what she might be looking for. She looked around the camp, finally resting her gaze on the Dragon egg.

Go back to the precious egg, Pharla snapped, swinging her head away from Maeya again.

Jealous! The knowledge rushed through Maeya. Pharla was

jealous of the egg! When she said that Maeya wanted to be a Rider, she was looking for confirmation of something more.

"Pharla, I want to be your Rider," Maeya said urgently. "I want to protect the egg because all Dragons are important, but I want to be *your* Rider. If you don't want me," the burning sensation in the back of her throat took her by surprise but Maeya forged ahead, "If you don't want me, then when we get to another Cave, I will find you another Rider. But I won't look for another Dragon. I will leave the Dragon's egg for another Rider-in-training."

Maeya waited, watching the fire dance in the reflection of Pharla's scales. Her back rose and fell with each breath. The spines were lying flat against her neck. Slowly she lifted her muzzle from the ground and once again turned her head to look at Maeya.

How do I know that you want me?

"How do I know that you want me?" Maeya countered. "You are in mourning for Veet, and he was a good Rider, and an even better person. Why would you want me?"

I have gotten to know you, she said slowly. *You take your responsibilities seriously. You are kind. And you like to laugh.*

"I have not laughed much lately."

Let us hope that will change, Pharla said, laying her head on the ground once again, but this time close to Maeya's leg. *Let us be done with being sad.*

"Aye, it is time to be done being sad," Maeya agreed. She closed her eyes, and felt her headache start to evaporate.

***   *******   ***

That night, Maeya finally convinced Quoran to fashion a second pack for her and divide their supplies. She probably would not have been successful, except that she asked him to carry the Dragon egg as well.

"You want me to carry it?" he had asked in disbelief.

"Aye." Something stopped Maeya from explaining that Pharla was jealous of the unhatched babe.

"But...but that is not....is not a page's...It should be a Rider's duty!" He had finally spluttered.

"Perhaps you shall be its Rider," Maeya said.

Quoran's eyes were huge. "Nay, Rider Maeya. Being your page is all the honor I wish."

"I hope you continue to feel that way," she said sincerely. "But I feel it would be better if you carry the egg. It will allow me more time to attend to Pharla."

Quoran's brow smoothed. "O. Of course, Rider Maeya. You cannot care for Pharla while burdened with the egg."

It is not always kind to give false hope. Pharla said later as they walked.

"It is not false hope," Maeya argued, dropping her voice to a whisper so Quoran wouldn't overhear.

You do not have to speak, she said tartly.

Maeya blinked. O, she thought, You can hear my thoughts as I hear yours?

Of course.

Perhaps he will be a Rider someday, Maeya thought. After all, I started as a page.

Quoran will not become a Rider.

Why? Maeya thought to her. Pharla sounded so final that she did not bother to ask if she was sure.

All Riders have certain qualities. Quoran does not.

Glancing at Quoran, Maeya thought, What qualities?

Pharla looked at her and then snorted. *Intelligence is usually one.*

"Quoran is intelligent," Maeya tried to sound confident, but even to herself, she didn't sound convincing.

Pharla snorted again. *I wasn't referring to Quoran.*

"O. You think that I should already know the qualities that all Riders have?"

Riders have different qualities, because each Dragon is different and seeks a match. But there are general qualities that Riders share.

Maeya could tell that Pharla was annoyed with her, but she couldn't tell why. And she really wanted to know what separated Dragon Riders from others. "Such as?"

Must you fish for compliments?

"I'm not—" O. That was why Pharla was annoyed. She thought Maeya wanted to hear about herself. Maeya tried another tact. "What qualities is Quoran missing?"

But Pharla shook her head and refused to answer.

After that, Pharla traveled next to Maeya. Sometimes Quoran walked with them, but more often he ranged ahead, a meek scout. Maeya told him to keep a watch for villages and homesteads; they gave those wide berth. And they made much better time.

Three nights later, Maeya felt nauseous. The hills they were traveling through were familiar and they would reach the Daceae estate before the Orb reached its next zenith.

"Is the squirrel foul?" Quoran asked anxiously.

"Nay," Maeya said, tossing the rest of it toward Pharla. "Your cooking, as always, was good."

"Then what is amiss?"

"I will be home tomorrow."

"What is your home like?"

Maeya shrugged. "It is a modest estate," she said, repeating what her mother had always said. "There are three floors, and eight bedrooms, a small ballroom, and of course a large dining room. The kitchen itself is the largest room, because cook has to make enough for everyone."

"And how many are in your family?"

"Just my parents and me."

"And you required so much space?" Quoran marveled. "It does not sound modest to me."

"We did not have as much as we used to," Maeya said, again hearing her mother's voice within her own. "There was not enough money in recent years, so much of what we had was sold."

"Do you not like your home?"

Maeya made herself smile. "I love my home," she said, "But I am bringing bad news. I fear it will all be different."

"The Power That Is will give you strength," Quoran decreed, "You have not traveled this far to find sorrow at the end of the trail."

We have spent too much time in sorrow, Pharla echoed.

"Where is your home?" Maeya asked Quoran, looking for a change in subject.

"I do not have one," he said.

Neither do I.

Maeya glanced at Pharla, but her head was turned and she did not want to mention the hatchling's sorrow to Quoran. Pharla's home was with Maeya, and she would be sure to let her know that. "What do you mean?"

"My father was a peddler," he replied. "We never had a home. The path of the Orb was all I knew."

"Why then become a page?"

"My father died when I was seven," he said. "We were in a village called Kallir. The Tares had come to recruit pages and Riders. I was lucky enough to be chosen as a page."

"You had to be chosen to become a page?"

"Aye, Rider Maeya. Those of us who do not have Rider lineage are not immediately accepted into the ranks."

"O." Maeya felt badly for not knowing this before. She had decided to become a page, had traveled to the Cave, and had never given it another thought. She didn't realize that others who wanted to be pages could be turned away.

Quoran looked over at Pharla. "She is growing fast," he said.

Maeya accepted the chance in topic eagerly. "Aye. She is nearly as tall as a young bull," she said.

"But she is much better looking."

Aye. Never compare a Dragon with a bull.

Maeya grinned. "She doesn't like to be called cattle," she told Quoran.

His brow went up. "How much of her thoughts can you understand?" he asked excitedly, "Are you getting single or multiple images from her?"

"I—" Maeya began.

"Riders usually do not start to get their Dragon's thoughts until after a full set of seasons! O, how I wish Cyr Sajen was here! He would know what to do."

Caution.

Maeya glanced at Pharla. She had raised her head and was staring at her. *Things are teetering. Do not reveal all you know.*

Quoran hadn't noticed. "Does she understand what you say to her?"

Maeya shrugged so that she wouldn't have to lie. She liked Quoran and trusted him, but she also trusted Pharla's instinct to keep her uniqueness quiet. "What other Lore can you tell me?" she asked instead.

"What Lore do you wish to know?" he asked, the unscarred side of his face lifting with a smile.

It dawned on Maeya that Quoran was perhaps the most valuable thing that had survived the attack. Pharla growled in her mind. *Other than you, of course,* Maeya thought to her impatiently.

"Well, we'll be travelling for a while," she said. "Why don't you start at the beginning?"

"The very beginning?" Quoran asked skeptically. "But you know all about the beginning and Lenzupra."

"No," Maeya said, shaking her head. "I have never heard of Prenzupa."

"Lenzupra," Quoran corrected. "How is it a Rider knows so little of our history?"

"Remember, I was a page for two sets of seasons," Maeya said, "And a Rider-in-training for only three seasons."

Quoran nodded. "I forgot your training was so short," he said.

Why was your training short?

We kept losing Riders-in-training. Some quit because their eggs wouldn't hatch, some quit because they wanted families, and some—

Were killed in attacks.

Aye, Maeya thought, reaching up to pat Pharla's neck.

"Does it help that I'd like to learn about it now?" Maeya asked.

Something snapped in the trees and Quoran jumped. "What was that?"

Maeya grabbed her knife and stood up. "I'll go check, if you promise to tell me Pren—"

"Lenzupra's story. As soon as you get back."

She slipped into the trees, smiling. Each night she had checked the perimeter of their camp, and each night she had found two, three, or four wolves. They no longer bolted as soon as they saw her, but they didn't allow her to get close to them, either.

Tonight, however, Maeya could not find what she had come to consider her friends. She lost her smile. She made three wide circuits of the camp, and saw no sign of them. Maeya was nervous, but she didn't know what to do about it. If the wolves were no longer traveling with them, or if they simply did not want her to find them, there was little she could do about it. Still, it bothered her more than she wanted to admit.

When she returned to the fire, Quoran was pacing around it, clearly agitated.

"Rider! Are you well?"

"Aye."

"You were gone a long time."

"I wanted to be sure there wasn't anything nearby. All is well."

"Truly?"

"Truly. Though it will be even better if you have some tea ready for us."

As Maeya planned, the request distracted Quoran. He began pouring water from the skins into the simple bowls he had whittled over the last two nights. It was not the same as true tea, he had fretted, for the leaves did not steep as well as they did when the water was hot. But it was more pleasant than simple water, and it gave Quoran something to do.

Maeya sat on her bedroll, knowing better than to offer to help. She was surprised when Pharla came over and stretched out on the ground next to her.

"Are you all right?" she asked, tentatively reaching out to stroke the dark-scaled neck.

Aye. What were you looking for?

"The wolves have left us," Maeya said softly. "I am not sure why."

Since we do not know their purpose, perhaps it is good that they are gone.

Perhaps, Maeya thought, but I rather miss them.

Quoran turned to hand her the bowl of tea, and slopped much of it over the edge when he realized that Pharla was next to her.

"O, pardon, Rider—"

"Quoran, it's fine. Sit and tell me about Leprunzal."

Quoran groaned. "Her name was Lenzupra," he said, drawing out each syllable, "Though her friends called her Zupra."

Maeya grinned. "O Zupra! I know her story! She is the mother of all Dragons!"

Scorn emanated from Pharla. *A human cannot be the mother of any Dragon, let alone all of them!*

"Hardly," Quoran said with a chuckle. "I suppose she could be considered the mother of all Dragon Riders, but she did not birth any Dragons."

He is a fit keeper of Lore.

"I guess I don't know her story after all. Which means you need to tell me."

"Aye." Quoran settled himself on his bedroll. Maeya watched as he took off his shoes, set them just so next to his blankets, adjusted his vest, and slicked his brown hair back from his forehead. It was part of his evening routine and she had already learned not to interrupt it. He fixed his eyes on the flames in front of him, and she could tell that he was remembering another fire and the words that Cyr Sajen had taught him.

"Lenzupra," he finally began, "Lived before the Clans had Caves, before the crops had a sleeping season, before the Orb had a Sister."

"That was a very long time ago," Maeya observed.

"Rider—"

"Apologies. I'm not supposed to interrupt."

"Lenzupra was a beautiful maiden—"

"Why are they always beautiful?" Maeya asked. "Why are the women of Lore never plain or even ugly?"

Pharla snorted.

Quoran simply stared at her.

"Apologies," Maeya said again.

Quoran took a sip of his cold tea from his bowl and regarded her in silence.

"Truly," Maeya said in as serious a tone as she could, "I will be good."

Pharla snorted again.

"I will. I will be absolutely quiet."

Quoran took a deep breath and began again.

*** ******* ***

Before the Clans had Caves, before the crops had a sleeping season, before Dragons had Riders, before the Orb had a Sister, there was a beautiful maiden named Lenzupra.

And there was a terrible Dragon named Milistin.

Milistin had terrorized and destroyed more villages than he had left intact, until the day he saw Lenzupra. Upon seeing her warm smile and long golden hair, he had been smitten. Her hair seemed to glow like the light of the Orb. So he swooped in, grabbed her, and took her to the Spike. And he set her on top of the highest crag and left her there.

Every day, he brought her a kill and some vegetation. He would drop entire deer and cow carcasses, branches from apple and orange trees, and even an occasional bear.

Lenzupra was beautiful, but she had been raised by a very practical mother. So while she was stranded on the crag for seasons upon end, she made use of every scrap Milistin brought her. The animal teeth became needles and knives, which she used to make the skins into new clothing. She used the large bones and branches to build first a platform, then a room, then a whole house upon the top of the crag.

Time passed and as Milistin continued to bring her materials, she continued to make her house larger, more comfortable, and taller—always taller. For though she was on top of the Spike, she longed to soar with Milistin.

Her blonde hair had been down to her waist when Milistin grabbed her, and by the end of the first year it had been to her knees. Then it was as long as she was tall. Soon she was doubling it over, just to keep from tripping over it.

Seasons continued to pass. Her hair seemed to grow faster with each pass of the Orb, and Milistin loved to see it glow.

But Lenzupra's smile was not as warm, for she was lonely. She tried, everyday, to speak to Milistin, to get him to take her in the sky with him. But she could not make him understand.

One day, as she moved about her house on the crag, the bit of sinew she had used to tie up her hair broke, and her hair cascaded down the crag, forming a golden waterfall that caught and reflected the Orb's light. Milistin dropped down on the far side of the crag, and watched her hair sparkle and shimmer. He stayed until the Orb kissed the sky farewell, and then he flew off. And left Lenzupra with an idea.

Carefully she cut off her hair and then began braiding. When she was done, she had a long, thick coil of braided hair.

The next morning, Lenzupra was waiting for Milistin's delivery. He appeared over the horizon, flying low, and she was pleased. He was bringing her a large beast, which meant he would have to come in close to drop it off.

She waited, coil in hand, until he opened his claws to drop the elk. And then she threw her coils of hair.

The loop settled neatly over Milistin's head. With a roar, he took off for the clouds, not realizing that Lenzupra was dangling from the rope of hair beneath him.

As soon as he felt the rope tightened, he looked down, and saw the bald maiden dangling below him. He did not recognize her, and screamed with fury.

The golden braid, as it tightened around the scales of Milistin's neck, turned crimson. The crimson traveled down the braid to where Lenzupra swung, staring in delight at the world below her. When her hair turned crimson where her hands were gripping it, something amazing happened. She could hear Milistin's thoughts. And he could hear hers, and realized who his Rider was.

He dropped gently to the hills below them, and set her on the ground. And there they stayed until the Orb sank. When it rose again, she grabbed hold of her crimson braid and climbed upon his back. He flew away with her and they lived a long and very happy life together.

***   ********   ***

Maeya waited until she was sure that Quoran was done with the Lore. "None of that makes any sense," she complained. "How did she get water? And fire—she would need fire for cooking! And it would take more than a few seasons for her hair to grow that long! And why did it turn red after she cut it off?"

Quoran sighed. "Maeya, it is Lore. It is an old, old story."

"Aye, but that doesn't mean it should be so unbelievable."

"It is meant to explain the beginning of the Riders."

"It gives more questions than answers."

That is because you have lived with Dragons, Pharla said. *Those who have only heard of Dragons like to believe in more magic than we have.*

"So you know that the Lore is not always true," Maeya said.

A sense of doubt came to Maeya.

"Lore has many purposes," Quoran was saying, "And we know that as the Lore is passed down, it sometimes may lose the details of truth, but the heart of the truth remains. That is why we must protect the Lore, to keep the heart safe."

"But when we know the details are faulty—"

"It was *before*, Rider, before the Sister Orb and before the sleeping season. How do you know the details were faulty? Could there not be things from that before that do not exist now?"

"Aye," Maeya said, still watching Pharla. "Does that mean that there may be things that exist now that will not in the future?"

"Aye," Quoran said simply. "And there will also be things that do not exist now that will exist then. There have always been times of change. Things must change."

He is right, Pharla thought suddenly. Maeya could feel her distress, and it made her stomach hurt.

What do you know? she asked the Dragon.

I do not know, she replied, *but I can feel it.*

Are you reading my mind? Maeya thought at her.

Can't you feel it? Pharla asked in way of answer. *Can you not feel everything shifting?*

Maeya could. She didn't know what it was, or how it was. But things were wrong. Caution would be needed for a long time to come.

CHAPTER FIVE

As the Orb rose in the morning, Maeya was tending to the fire. Quoran jumped up. "Rider Maeya, why did you not wake me?"

"All is well," Maeya told him. "I am capable of cooking."

"Did you not sleep?"

"All is well," she repeated.

There is a difference between caution and deceit.

Maeya looked over to where Pharla was in the middle of a yawn. "I am anxious," she said to both of them. "I have not been home for a long time."

"Our early meal will be fast," Quoran promised.

"Nay," Maeya said, "Our early meal will be while we walk."

Pharla bobbed her head up and down. Maeya took it to be agreement, although she wasn't getting any direct thoughts from her.

Quoran quickly repacked their meager supplies and doused the fire. Maeya helped him arrange the sling and settle the egg against his chest. The egg was close to his heart. If there were any chance of a Dragon choosing Quoran, it would be this egg.

It won't happen.

"Nothing is set," Maeya muttered, hefting her rucksack to her back, "The Power That Is is fluid."

Some things are certain, Pharla said, walking away from the camp without Maeya for the first time in days. *Your tendency to challenge everything being one of them.*

"I don't challenge everything," Maeya called after her. "You've got me confused with you!"

Pharla didn't even look back at her. Quoran, however, stared. "She talks to you," he marveled.

"Sometimes," Maeya said. "Let us be on our way."

"Aye."

Although she rose early and didn't let them have a fireside meal, Maeya was not eager to see her old home. It was more of a need to get it over with.

She had realized, after talking to Quoran about their homes, that she had lied. She didn't have a home, either. True, she had been born and raised in one house. The first time she had ever spent more than three nights outside of the Daceae roof had been when she reached the Cave to begin training as a page.

Maeya had called it her home all her life, but looking back now, she could see that it had never been a true home. It had been a house. People who shared her bloodlines lived in that house with her. But it was not a home.

The Cave, with its dirt floors and rooms designated simply by rocks on the ground, was her home. The pages, Cyrs, Tares, and Riders, whether blonde, brunette, red-haired, dark or light, were her family. She belonged with them. And now they were gone.

The house Maeya was returning to was not her home. She could not return to the Cave that was. She would have to find a new home. She would have to make one.

And it will be with me.

Aye, that it will, Maeya thought back to Pharla.

*** ******* ***

They saw the smoke long before they could see the cause. Maeya's stomach clenched in fear. This was the smoke of a wildfire or battle. How many more had died?

We should go to another Cave, Pharla said.

"I thought you had agreed to stay with me," Maeya said. "I thought I was your Rider."

Pharla butted Maeya's arm with her head. *Aye. But you need to talk to Cyrs and Tares.*

"Aye, but first I must face this."

Why?

"I need to know what's happened. I need to know about my mother and father and Nani and our peep."

You are no longer a Daceae.

"I am too!"

You are Maeya, Rider of Pharla.

"Aye. But I am still a Daceae. I always will be."

Why? You do not feel it is your home.

Maeya kept walking in silence. It was not something she could explain, but it was something she felt deep within her. It was important that she was a Daceae. She could not forget that. Nor could she let others forget.

Quoran hesitated as he reached the crest of the hill. He turned and looked back at them. Maeya waved him on.

"We will not stop," she called.

Yet when she reached the top of the hill, she had to. Only a small section of field was causing the smoke. The rest of it had burned so hot and so far down that there was nothing left to smolder.

From this hill, Maeya should have been able to see cottages, barns, and sheds dotting the field all the way up to the main house. The house, a full three stories with a barn behind it, should have dwarfed the cottages around it.

But the house was gone. The only things still standing were the four outer support pillars, nearly as tall as five men standing on each other's shoulders. Of the barn, there was nothing upright. A large blackened square showed where it once had been.

In spite of the smoke and evidence of destruction, what upset Maeya most was the stillness of it all. Nothing moved. The few trees that had not disintegrated were charred poles; the grasses that once formed a lush covering were ashes. The wind wasn't blowing, the clouds weren't moving, and all was still. The entire landscape was void of life.

You have seen, Pharla said. Her thought was a soothing breeze through Maeya's head. *It is time to move on.*

"Nay," Maeya said, forcing her feet to continue walking. "I must finish this."

Finish what?

"Saying good-bye to the life I knew." For she would never go back. As a page, she had always believed that someday she would return to her house, that she would look for a husband, perhaps have children, perhaps even please her mother. But even if the house was still standing, even if her mother and father were now at the front steps, waiting for her return, she would not have been coming back.

Maeya was a Rider.

Her life belonged to her Dragon.

Then heed me, Pharla urged. *Let us move on.*

"My life belongs to you," Maeya said over her shoulder, "But the decisions remain mine."

Pharla huffed.

As they crossed the blackened valley, single file and very exposed, Pharla's word came back to her: caution.

Maeya felt an inexplicable need to hurry, to run. But there was nowhere to go. The only cover was high on the hillside, in the trees that grew on the other side of the creek. She felt a driving need to get to the house, but there would be no better cover there. She realized her error, but it was too late to do what she should have done: leave Pharla and Quoran in the copse of trees at the top of the hill. There was nothing for them to do here, and they would have been safer in the cover of the trees. Maeya vowed that she would remember this mistake, and never repeat it.

Quoran's pace had slowed, but as Maeya moved to pass him, he matched his stride to hers. "O, Rider Maeya. I share your sorrow."

She reached over and squeezed his arm.

Where the first three cottages had been, there was nothing but ash. When they got to the fourth cottage, however, there were bodies. Every cottage and shed after that had charred corpses, some of them cattle and sheep, but many were peep. Too many.

It was strange. Maeya didn't remember so many peep at their estate.

Pharla was almost on her heels. It was comforting.

When they were close to the main house, Maeya stopped. "You should wait here with Pharla."

Quoran nodded.

Why?

This is about me, Maeya thought to her. It is not about you.

Pharla didn't feel satisfied with that response, but she folded her legs underneath her and lay down. Quoran stepped almost gingerly over to her and then sat down beside her, cradling the egg, and trying to look around himself all at once.

"I'll be right back," she said, more for her benefit than theirs.

The estate house had been built on the only rise in the flat of the valley. Maeya climbed the gentle slope, trying to remember happier times: playing hide-and-boo with the other estate children, running to ask if this time one of the new ponies could be for her, walking and daydreaming about having her own estate to run, coming home when Nani called her in for meal time or lessons.

Maeya stopped trying to remember happier times. In truth, she didn't have many.

At the perimeter of the house, she paused. The pillars and few beams that had been thick enough to maintain some of their shape were daunting. Did she really think she could find anything here? Exactly what was it she was looking for? She didn't know, but that strange inner force pushed her on, insisting there was something here to do.

Maeya took a deep breath and stepped into the ashes. They swirled up and around her, making her sneeze and cough, which in turn swirled more ashes. She told herself that she was imagining that they still felt warm. There weren't any glowing embers—this fire had been out for some time.

A glint reflected from the Orb caught her eye. She waded carefully through the ashes and reached down.

It was a silver platter. Maeya remembered it as a gorgeous oval platter with intricate flowers and thorns around the border and the name Daceae in beautiful script in the center. The flowers and script were melted away. The flat oval shape had warped and stretched. But through the blackened soot, the silver had somehow caught the Orb's light.

Clasping the platter to her chest, Maeya continued to wade through the debris. Although she was sure she wouldn't find anything else of recognizable worth, she kept looking. She realized that this was what she had come for: tangible memories, mementos she could carry with her as proof of the Daceaes and who they were.

Maeya made a zigzag path through the ashes. Her legs were black from the knees down. Close to one of the outer stone pillars, she made another find: several spoons and one dinner knife. They would require much cleaning, but they were both sentimental and useful. She walked a straight line to the next pillar. Mother used to keep her jewelry behind a false stone in the pillar. Perhaps the stones had protected her valuables.

When Maeya reached the far pillar, she realized that she would have to climb it if she wanted to look for the gems, for her parents' room had been on the second floor.

A breeze stirred, and the top layer of ashes began sifting away, dancing over the blackened ground. She heard a moaning, and remembered how the house had always been so noisy when it was windy. She had thought it was because of the shingles, but apparently it was the supporting pillars that had made the wind sound so sad. There was another moan, long, low, and full of sorrow.

It wasn't coming from the pillar.

It was coming from behind the pillar.

Awkwardly Maeya shifted the platter and all the spoons to one hand, grimacing when they clanked together. The moaning stopped. She had a very sooty dinner knife in her hand and she no longer had the element of surprise.

Taking a deep breath, Maeya stepped around the pillar.

There was a small hollow on the side of the pillar, and curled up in it was a disheveled and ash-covered peep. With hands up over their head, and only a few strands of ash-gray hair visible, the peep was cowering in fear. Maeya was struck dumb. Had she not heard the moaning, she would have assumed this was just another corpse. Maeya did not know what to say.

"Greet—" she cleared her throat and tried again. "Greetings. May I assist you?"

The peep merely shuddered and pulled their knees up. Clearly he (she?) was afraid of anyone who was moving around the estate.

Maeya tried again. "May I assist you?"

Another low moan, really more of a whimper. Two steps and Maeya was towering over him. He pulled his knees even tighter to his chest.

"Leave me. I beg of you. Leave me to die!"

The words alone would have given her pause, but the voice sent shivers down her neck.

"Nani?"

The hands dropped down from the blackened face. Even having heard her voice, Maeya wasn't positive it was Nani. Her wrinkled weathered skin was stretched tight because of the swelling on the entire left side of her face. The purple bruises would turn blue in a few days, if she lived that long.

"O, Nani," Maeya whispered as she sank to her knees next to her.

Nani had been old when Maeya left home. She was surprised the intervening years had been so unkind to her. Without her troublesome charge, Maeya thought Nani would find time to relax, maybe even do more of the knitting she had tried so desperately to teach Maeya.

Her left eye stared unfocused past Maeya's shoulder. Her right eye, while focused on Maeya, reflected only confusion and no recognition. Nani's right hand gripped her arm convulsively.

"It's me, Nani. It's Maeya. I came home."

Nani said something but it was unintelligible.

Maeya looked around, but there was nothing to help her. She needed water, a blanket, a fire to keep Nani warm, she needed a roof overhead—but there was nothing. Nothing but the pillar against which she huddled.

We're coming.

"What?"

We're coming!

Nani tried again. "Bab...Babsh hoe."

"Yes," Maeya said, trying to stem her tears. "Baby's home."

Nani smiled, or tried to, but it just twisted her face.

What baby?

Pharla, Maeya began, then shook her head, trying to dislodge the headache that was coming on again. *Pharla, bring water!*

Aye. And fire and blanket and a roof. What baby?

There's no— Maeya stopped. Pharla had been listening to her thoughts the whole time. She knew as well as Maeya did what she thought she needed. *I'm the baby,* Maeya told her. *I was always baby to Nani.*

O. When will you grow?

DRAGON'S LORE 73

Maeya smiled sadly at Nani as she thought to Pharla, I think I just did.

***   ********   ***

Pharla arrived before Quoran did, almost materializing in front of Maeya. She was sitting with her back against the pillar, cradling Nani's head in her lap. Nani had tried to speak twice more, but Maeya had not understood her. Her eyes closed, and Maeya listened to her rasping breathing.

What is wrong?

"I don't know," Maeya said softly. The only visible mark was the large bruise on her face. She didn't appear to be burned or cut.

She is old, Pharla said. *Injuries take a greater toll.*

"Aye."

Quoran came huffing up. "My apologies, Rider Maeya," he panted. "Pharla just got up and left! I didn't know what to do! I wanted to stay as you had instructed, but—"

Maeya cut him off. "I'm glad you followed her. I need your water skin."

He lifted the strap off his neck and handed it to her. As she gently tipped it up and let the water dribble into Nani's partly open mouth, she asked, "Do we have any means of shelter? Or fire?" Nani shuddered in her lap.

Quoran looked around dubiously. "I will find a way," he said.

"Leave the egg and pack here," Maeya said. "If you need help—"

"Nay, Rider. I shall get the fire first."

Nani shuddered and moaned again. Maeya looked down at her. Her eyes were open, staring straight ahead. "Nani," she said softly, "We have need of a fire." Nani trembled. "You are cold. And we will want light when the Orb sinks."

"Sooner than that," Quoran said as he carefully set the egg next to Maeya. "There is a storm coming."

"Truly?" This was news that she did not appreciate.

He is correct, Pharla told her with some surprise. *A storm comes this way.*

"Make haste," Maeya told Quoran, "But don't take risks. There is still a feeling of danger here."

"Aye," he bobbed his head. "That there is."

"I cannot nurse both of you. Use caution."

Aye. Advise others to do what you will not, Pharla said with a sniff.

***   ********   ***

Nani languished. For the first pass of the Orb, Maeya was wishing desperately that she would recover, but by the second time Sister Orb rose, she recognized that the Power That Is would be kinder indeed to take Nani from this place of pain.

She was feverish, and, Maeya was convinced, delirious. She spoke in low whispers of the "changed one." She spoke in moderate, not quite sad, tones of a "happy day of return." And she screamed in terror when the "blue lightening" destroyed the house.

Nani's screams, beside hurting Maeya's ears and causing gooseflesh on her arms, brought worry as well. If the danger that Nani feared was present, it certainly knew where they were.

The storm that Quoran had predicted crashed over them before the Orb completely went down. It obliterated Sister Orb, and sent waves of icy drops cascading down upon them.

"My apologies," Quoran chattered to Maeya as he shivered.

"For what?"

"For not finding enough to make an adequate shelter."

"Nay, Quoran, no apologies. You did bring us shelter—" a few logs were crossed above them with a small worn hide stretched between them, "—and it is not your fault we linger here," Maeya added as Nani moaned between them. The rain fell upon them only slightly less than it would have if they had been in the middle of the field, but Maeya felt the illusion of partially increased safety. Pharla was nestled between the stone pillar and their backs.

I am not a cushion, she had snapped irritably when Maeya first leaned against her.

"You are not," Maeya agreed, resting her hand upon Pharla's scales, "But you have just recovered. I do not want you catching chill again."

Then let us travel and generate heat.

"We will stay and conserve heat together," Maeya told her.

She could sense Pharla grumbling, but she subsided quietly and stayed still for the rest of the storm.

"She relives her terror," Quoran now observed, wiping Nani's face with a slightly dry cloth.

"She dreams," Maeya said.

Quoran stared at her in disbelief. "Nay, Rider. These are the nightmares of one who lived through it."

"Aye? So what did she live through?"

"A Wyzard attack," he replied promptly.

"But why would the Wyzards attack? There were no Dragons here."

But Quoran had no answer for that, and they waited out the rest of the storm in a cold silence.

*** ******** ***

Nani was tenacious; Maeya had learned that as a child. Now she clung to life in such a way that Maeya was sure Nani would win the battle, whether it was a desirable win or not.

Pharla left the stone pillar on the third day. She burrowed out a warm spot under the opposite pillar, on the side that got the most warmth from the Orb and the least bite from the wind. She didn't respond when Maeya spoke to her, nor did she eat the two hares she brought. Maeya left it to Quoran to see to the Dragon while she tended to Nani.

Shortly after mid-meal on the fourth day, Nani opened her eyes. Her left eye still stared unseeing past Maeya, but her right eye was clear and focused.

"Taena," she said.

"Nay, Nani," Maeya swallowed the lump hearing her mother's name created. "It's Maeya."

She blinked and stared at her. "Maeya? You've come home?"

"Aye, Nani," Maeya said, feeling her throat constrict. She had been waiting for Nani to die; she never thought she'd recognize her again. "I have. What happened?"

"You look so like your mother."

"Where is Mother? And Father?"

Nani's eyes filled with tears. "Gone, child. I'm sorry, but they are both gone. The Power That Is works in such strange ways," Nani murmured. "You have returned to find me thus."

"All is well," Maeya assured her. "I will take care of you."

"Child, there is no caring for me now. My time is done."

"Nay, Nani. You will travel with us."

Nani managed to lift her head less than the length of Maeya's little finger as she tried to look behind her. "Who are you with?"

"Quoran, my page."

She smiled slightly. "I'm glad you made friends as a page."

"Are you hungry, Nani? I have some broth—"

"Nay. I have no need of food."

"You need to get your strength back, so that—"

"My strength is leaving me now, Taena. I can feel it. Soon I shall sleep, and find what secrets the Power That Is hides behind the Orb."

"Nani—" Maeya tried to argue, but Nani thought she was talking to Maeya's mother, and there was nothing for it but to listen.

"Aye, Taena, she has the Rider's blood, but she has the witch's blood as well. You cannot let her go to the Cave just because you're tired of being a mother. It is too dangerous for her! It is too dangerous for all!"

"Nani, please," Maeya begged. She had to stop talking. Nani's breath was becoming ragged. Tears streamed down Maeya's face. She wished she knew if this was a remembered conversation or a dreamt one.

"Maeya is so good." Nani was rasping now, almost panting. "How can you let her go? How can you not love her?"

Maeya closed her eyes and turned away. She had always known her mother didn't love her, but hearing it from Nani's voice ripped her inside.

Those were the last intelligible words Nani said. She continued to fight for breath, though, long after she stopped talking. Long after the Orb had sank, she rasped and panted as if she had just quit running the longest race of her life.

But as Sister Orb rose the fifth time, her gasps came farther and farther apart. It hurt to watch her, hurt to listen, hurt to know that she was hurting and there was nothing Maeya could do. Maeya could only wait, holding her hand and wiping the sweat off her face, hoping that the Power That Is would make it easier for her.

Finally, shortly before the Orb rose again, Nani surrendered her body.

And Maeya gave in to her tears.

*** ******** ***

Maeya was too overcome to be of much help as Quoran dug a grave for Nani. Pharla kept her distance from Maeya, too, curling up several paces away with her back to her. Maeya could not remember ever feeling so alone. She cradled the Dragon's egg, pretending she did it for the egg, not for her own need.

While Quoran was occupied digging Nani's grave, Maeya gritted her teeth and climbed the stone pillar, wrapping her arms and legs around it as if it were a tree.

Maeya knocked on the stones, trying to find the loose one that hid her mother's jewelry box. For a few moments, she wondered if she had forgotten how the house had looked and had climbed the wrong pillar. She slid down and tried to climb a different pillar, but her arms were shaking, and Maeya still couldn't climb high enough to find the hidden rock. She cried as she fell down to the rock foundation.

When Quoran had laid Nani in the shallow pit, Maeya forced

herself to stand, and joined in the final appeal:

> "The Power That Is took care of what was, is, and will be.
> The Power That Is takes care of what was, is, and will be.
> The Power That Is will take care of what was, is, and will be.
> This body was, is, and will be because of the Power That Is."

Their voices stopped together. Quoran had not known Nani. Maeya could not find the strength to keen for her. She was tired of death. All burials have sorrow, but Nani's was simply awful.

Quoran cleared his throat.

"Aye, we're leaving," Maeya said. "Right now."

A relieved smile flashed across his face before he could stop it. "How long will it take to load the packs?"

He took four steps over to the pillar and lifted the packs he had set behind it.

"We'll be following the Orb," Maeya said as she hefted the pack onto her back and he picked up the Dragon's egg.

Quoran frowned. "Arc Side Cave is on the other side of the pass."

"We're not going to Arc Side," Maeya said. Kollarian Clan had five Caves. Spike, the training Cave where she and Quoran had been, Arc Side Cave, River Reed Cave, Salt Cave, and Father Cave. "I don't think there will be a Clan Kollarian Cave that is still whole," Maeya said bitterly.

You said you'd take me to a Cave!

"We're going to a Cave," Maeya snapped. Poor Quoran stared at her. Maeya forced herself to moderate her tone. "I promised Pharla I'd take her to a Cave, and I will honor my promise."

"Salt Cave is—"

"We're not going to Salt Cave," Maeya cut him off. "We're not going to a Kollarian Cave."

"Where shall we go, Rider?"

An excellent question.

"We're going to Clan Uture. Meadow Spear Cave."

"But that's several days ride from here, and we're walking."

"I know," Maeya said, settling her pack a bit more comfortably. "That's why we'd better get moving now."

She suited action to words and Quoran wasted no time following.

At the top of the rise, wolves began to howl. Maeya paused and took one last look at the Daceae estate. She did not think she would ever see it again. Looking at the blackened land, she did not wish to.

"Rider? I don't remember the trees being that close to the house."

Maeya surveyed the valley. "That's because they weren't," she said flatly.

"They moved?"

"Aye."

"I thought moving Trident trees were only part of Lore," Quoran whispered.

As Maeya gazed at the four standing pillars, she felt a stab of remorse. As a child, she had wished to see the trees move. Now they were blocking her view of what remained of her house, and part of her was grateful to not see the charred remains. But part of her wished for one last look. From this distance, the stone that hid her mother's jewels would be just a part of the whole. How she wished she had been able to retrieve them!

They would have been a perfect reminder of her mother: glittering and cold.

CHAPTER SIX

What is wrong? Pharla was walking next to her. Maeya's home valley was out of sight, yet no one had spoken.

Too many things, Maeya thought back to her.

What?

But Maeya's thoughts were no more than a jumbled mess. Cyr Sajen, sending her to find and bond with Pharla even though he knew the chances were slim and then abandoning her; their Cave and her family estate not much more than a pile of ash; reports that River Reed was ash as well; Nani confirming her worst fears of her mother; the total loss of everything she had called home; a nagging feeling that she should have tried harder to get her mother's jewel box; the rejection from both an unhatched Dragon and then a Dragon—

I have accepted you!

"Quoran?"

"Aye, Maeya?" He was puffing behind her, but Maeya could hear him hurrying to catch up a little more.

"Do you recall any Lore about Riders blocking their Dragon's thoughts?"

"Pardon?"

"Nothing," Maeya said. She could sense that Pharla was insulted, but she didn't care. She couldn't live with a Dragon pulling all of her thoughts out of her head.

Only the ones that matter.

Maeya glared at her, but Pharla didn't so much as turn her head to look at her.

"Rider?"

Maeya sighed and refused to answer him.

"Maeya?" he said timidly.

"Aye?"

"How long will it take for us to reach Meadow Spear?"

"Many days."

"What if we had horses?"

Maeya snorted. "Horses cost money, Quoran." *Yet another reason I should have tried harder to get Mother's jewels,* she thought.

Why? Could you ride them?

I could have traded or sold them, Maeya thought, though she knew she wouldn't have.

"Aye, Rider."

"Do you have any?" she asked, stopping to turn and look at him. Pharla continued on. Maeya was surprised to see a flush creeping up under Quoran's scars.

"Aye, Maeya. I do."

"Enough for a horse?"

"I think so."

Maeya's hands were on her hips. "Where did a page acquire enough to buy a horse?"

Quoran was quite red but he looked her in the eye. "Cyr Sajen was in a hurry to leave. He did not take all his possessions."

"You took his money?"

"Aye." He shifted from one foot to another, and then said, "Your Dragon's getting stronger. She's put a fair bit of distance between us."

Maeya refused to be distracted, although she did turn to start walking again. She grabbed Quoran's arm, forcing him to keep step with her instead of dropping back again. "What else did you take from Cyr Sajen?"

"Nothing!" He glanced sideways at her and must have seen her doubt. "In truth!"

"May I see the money?"

Instantly he shifted the Dragon's egg slightly to one side, pulled a small pouch from inside his trousers, and handed it to Maeya.

Her breath caught as she spilled the coins from the pouch to her open palm. Not just a few pieces of silver; there were at least a dozen. And almost as many gold. This was more money than Maeya had ever seen, let alone held.

"Quoran—" she began.

"The money is good, aye?"

"This is—"

"I didn't take it from Cyr Sajen," he repeated quickly. "He left it behind. Besides, it belongs to the whole Clan, and…and now…" he faltered for a moment. "It will help our journey."

"Our journey where?" Maeya mused.

We won't get anywhere if we move this slowly.

"We won't get anywhere if we move too quickly and exhaust ourselves," Maeya retorted. "You, especially, need to take care to recover."

"I'm fine," Quoran said, puzzled.

As am I, Pharla said while Maeya scolded herself for speaking out loud.

"We will travel at a steady pace," Maeya said firmly. "There is no dire need for speed, but we will not linger, either." She replaced the coins into the pouch and held it out to Quoran.

He actually took a step away from her. "You keep it."

"It is yours."

"It is for the Clan," he said. "I did not take it for myself. If there were a Tare or a Cyr with us, then…but since there's not…." Quoran kept both hands on the Dragon's egg, saying, "It is for you, Rider. A page should not have that."

And that was one reason why Maeya didn't want to keep it, either. She still felt a page. But she was a Rider now, and beyond that, she was leader of their small group, perhaps the leader of the last of the Clan Kollarian. "We will need to watch for the next town," she said, sliding the pouch in her pocket. "We don't wish to draw attention, so I will take the egg and lead Pharla around the town while you go and find good mounts—"

Quoran exclaimed, "Nay!"

Maeya blinked at him. "What?"

He flushed again, but said doggedly, "I will lead Pharla and take the egg, and you will go into town. I know nothing of horseflesh, and even less of dickering."

Maeya knew little of horseflesh and dickering, too, but she didn't think that would change his mind. Then he spoke the final reason in a quietly embarrassed tone.

"I do not know how to count money. I cannot do sums."

"We will have to fix that," Maeya sighed.

"Cyr Sajen tried to teach me, but—" Quoran shrugged. "He got quite frustrated with me."

"I will still try, but I doubt we will have time before we reach the next town."

That is certain. For it is over the next hill.

Maeya opened her mouth and just barely managed to snap it shut in time. What do you mean, Maeya asked Pharla in her head.

I can smell it. Pharla shook her head. *There are many people and animals. It must be a town.*

Maeya did not remember a town so close to the Daceae estate, but she had been gone a long time. Perhaps a new settlement had come in.

"Let's be cautious," Maeya said. "I do not want to be seen until we decide to be seen."

***   *******   ***

The decision to backtrack half a day to make camp was not popular, but Maeya insisted.

"If we stop here, we run the risk of being seen."

"Then let us continue around the town," Quoran argued. "That way we won't lose any ground."

"Someone could see us and follow us."

Quoran gave her a look that matched Pharla's incredulity. *You're being stubborn*, Pharla said flatly.

"Look, we know there's a good place to camp back there and it's not far. There might not be a good spot on the other side."

Quoran raised his brow but simply nodded his head. "Aye, Rider, it is possible."

So they retraced their steps to where the trader's road crossed the creek, and then followed the creek to a pleasant Trident copse. Maeya ignored Quoran's mutterings about the trees. Until they harmed her, she would trust them. She set out to hunt, and found wolf prints further upstream. She felt much better about their camping decision, especially when she was able to get a yearling deer with her bolo.

Quoran's eyes lit up at the sight of the deer, but he didn't go so far as to say he had been wrong.

I'm sure there are deer on the other side of the town, was Pharla's reaction, though she made short work of the haunch Maeya brought to her.

While the venison cooked, Maeya sat against a Trident tree watching Quoran break the deer's teeth out of the jawbone and wash them in the creek.

"What are you going to do with them?" Maeya asked, but Quoran merely shook his head.

Pharla was lounging in the lingering light of the Orb, clearly enjoying the lazy warmth. *I would be happier if we were still traveling*, she said. *It is not good to be on our own for too long.*

Why not? Maeya thought to her, but Pharla didn't answer.

"Why do Dragons need Riders?" Maeya asked Quoran.

"Pardon?"

"Does the Lore explain why Dragons need Riders?"

Quoran shot a glance at Pharla before looking at Maeya. "I thought Tare Terce had covered that with all the Riders-in-training."

"Nay."

"Are you positive?"

"If he did, it was when he had kicked me out."

Quoran didn't say anything, but his unscarred brow lifted in doubt.

"Quoran, I may not have been the best Rider-in-training when it came to our lessons, but I was far from the worst. I listened to the Tares and was never put on the spot for daydreaming. When Tare Terce or Tare Jin explained why the Clan needs the Dragons, I listened. If they had ever talked about why the Dragons need us, I would remember."

And why does the Clan need Dragons?

"I remember Tare Terce telling us that if we did not have the bond with the Dragons, then we would be in danger from their attacks," Maeya went on, answering Pharla's question while showing Quoran that she had, in fact, listened to her lessons. "And of course, that makes perfect sense. We wouldn't be able to defend ourselves against a Dragon attack."

"There are ways," Quoran said, throwing a nervous glance toward Pharla, "At least according to Lore."

"Is there Lore from before Lenzupra? About peep defeating Dragons that wanted to attack?"

"Aye, but this is perhaps not a good time to talk about it." Again Quoran looked nervously at Pharla.

As if I don't know what I'm capable of, she thought in disgust. *I could rip you both to shreds if I so chose.*

But you don't, Maeya thought to her.

No.

Why not?

Pharla merely turned her head away from Maeya.

"Tell me why the Dragons need Riders," Maeya said to Quoran.

"Lenzupra—"

"You told me this one."

Quoran stood, put his hands on his hips, and glared at Maeya in such a way that she knew she had pushed too far. "When you ask for Lore, you must listen!"

"Quoran—"

But he was stomping off into the forest and ignored her.

"Do you know, Pharla?"

Pharla stood, stretched, yawned, and walked away.

"By the Power That Is," Maeya muttered, "I can't wait to find a Cave to call home."

When Quoran returned, Maeya was turning the venison and Pharla was dozing between the bedrolls.

"Apologies—" they both began at the same time.

"Nay, Quoran," Maeya overrode him when he tried to apologize again, "You were in the right to scold me."

Quoran flushed. "A page never has a right to scold a Rider."

You will not win this. Accept his apology now or hear it repeatedly over the next several days.

Maeya grinned because she realized Pharla was right. "If you will tell me the Lore of Dragons, I will accept your apology."

Quoran opened his mouth and then snapped it shut again. Maeya did not need to hear Pharla's observation, *He is afraid he will snap at you again when you interrupt him.*

Perhaps I will not interrupt him this time, Maeya thought.

Pharla snorted.

"After we eat?" Quoran half-suggested, half-asked.

"Of course."

*** ******** ***

When Lenzupra lassoed Milistin, she used her hair. By doing so, she created a bond that had never been experienced before. Dragons, though highly intelligent and powerful creatures, do not have a soul. Milistin had taken her to the Spike crag simply because he found the sparkle of her hair fascinating, not because he loved her or wanted to be with her. With the bond of feeling coursing through the braid, he experienced happiness for the first time, and sorrow as well.

Though Lenzupra had lassoed Milistin out of necessity—there had been no other way to catch him—once she had flown with him, he never tried to throw her off his back. On the contrary, when the Orb rose, he would kneel down and lower a wing, making it easy for her to climb up. Lenzupra left the braid around his neck, not because she was afraid he'd leave her, but because it made it easier for her to hold on.

Lenzupra was happier than she had ever been, soaring on Milistin's back. She smiled up at the Orb, relishing the warmth and the light, feeling the breeze tickle the back of her neck, enjoying every moment. After Milistin landed at night, whether on a hillside or near a riverbank, Lenzupra would gather her food and find a place to bed down. And that's when the loneliness came.

She did not talk to Milistin or ask him questions. She went through each day silently, smiling when happy or crying when sad, and she thought that was what her life would be. Milistin didn't speak to her, for he didn't know how. But the more they flew together, the stronger his emotions became—emotions he had never experienced until she had entwined him in her hair.

They had been traveling together for almost a season and all had been going well. And then Milistin flew over a village.

The villagers, of course, screamed and ran in terror. Like any predator, the movement drew Milistin's eye, and he banked sharply, swooping back over the village. Three children were running for the safety of a small house. The smallest tripped and fell; the oldest turned back to help. Milistin extended his talons, ready to snatch the child.

"No!" Lenzupra cried from his back, and for the first time ever, she struck him. "No! No!"

Startled, Milistin shifted abruptly. One of his wingtips caught a rooftop and that threw him off balance even more. It also threw Lenzupra from his back.

It took Milistin a few moments to get his balance, and by the time he turned back to the village, the adults had swept the small children and Lenzupra to safety. The village square was empty; nothing stirred.

Milistin landed in the middle of the square, feeling abandoned for the first time ever. The feeling overwhelmed him, and he roared in sorrow. But when he roared, he also blew flame, for his heart didn't know what to do with the pain.

Then he heard screaming. He turned to the sound. He had never heard Lenzupra scream before and he didn't know her voice, but the braid still tied around his neck fairly sparked with the energy of her fear and confusion. For though the villagers thought they were keeping Lenzupra safe, she thought they were harming Milistin; and they did not speak the same language to make the other understand.

Milistin began to knock over walls and houses, looking for Lenzupra.

Lenzupra began knocking over villagers, trying to get to Milistin.

And then she broke through to him: Stop! Stop! Stop!

And he understood. She had screamed it in her mind and he understood. And because it was coming from her, he stopped.

The villagers were tired of trying to keep her safe inside, and they let her go. She ran to Milistin. As soon as she touched the braid, all of his thoughts and feelings flooded into her. His fear of losing her, his anger at not seeing her, his distress for not keeping her happy.

Lenzupra hugged him, telling of her love of him, and her fear of his power, and her sorrow of his confusion.

And through the braid the emotions became words, and the words became understanding.

*** ******* ***

"I don't understand," Maeya said. "All we give Dragons is emotion?"

"Aye."

"But...that...that...doesn't seem too...doesn't seem fair," Maeya said.

"Fair?" Quoran asked.

"They give us protection and strength and fire," Maeya said slowly, "And we give them emotions?"

"Aye."

"That's all?"

All? Isn't that everything?

Maeya looked at Pharla in surprise.

From our Riders we gain the capacity to feel sympathy, and happiness, and jealousy, and anger, and fear....

"But why would Dragons want emotions? Don't emotions cause humans enough trouble?"

"But life with emotions is so much richer! Life without emotions is not really living," Quoran said earnestly.

"So a Dragon without a Rider will not feel emotions?"

Quoran cocked his head at her. "I do not know. We bond Riders with the Dragons as soon as they hatch. I do not know what a Dragon without a Rider would do."

"Is that the only reason Cyr Sajen sent me after Pharla? So she could have emotions?"

Quoran looked troubled. "Truly Rider, I do not know. She had already bonded with Veet, so I think...."

"She could already feel," Maeya said. She knew it was true. Pharla already had strong emotions when Maeya found her; she had not needed a new Rider.

Love.

What? Maeya thought to Pharla.

Riders give us love. And what value is there in life if there isn't love?

CHAPTER SEVEN

Quoran's refusal to go into town was, Maeya knew, the best decision. She could not teach him figures and money in the span of one night, and they certainly could not afford to spend all the money on a pair of horses. In truth, Maeya was nervous about trying to haggle, for she had never been involved in purchasing anything bigger than a honeycomb. When the traveling gypsies had stopped in their fields, Nani never let her go trade with them. And when she was a page, the Tares and Cyrs had kept pages away from the peddlers who came to the Cave.

In spite of Quoran's assurance that she looked fine, Maeya was nervous. Clad in a tan tunic and brown leggings that had multiple patches, she wasn't sure she would be able to make herself walk down the town streets. How could she possibly avoid attracting attention? It would be painfully clear that she was not one of the town girls, and her curly red hair was too long to try to pretend she was a young boy. She didn't look like an eccentric wealthy heir, either.

Maeya walked the main street first, hoping to determine which of the stables seemed clean and honest. But this was not a normal town.

The town was large in a rather strange way. She did not see any taverns or inns, or any pillow houses. For a small town, there seemed to be an inordinate number of apothecaries and jewel shops. In spite of all the storefronts, the main street was virtually empty.

Odder still, there was only one stable. True, it was a good-sized barn, with an open loft and fresh scents of alfalfa hay and warm oats, but a town this size should have two or three stables. It would be harder to haggle if there was only one place to do business, but she didn't have a choice.

No one answered her call of "Greetings!" She began to walk the stalls, looking at the horses. A glossy chestnut with a light dappling on the rump caught her eye, as did a sleek gray mare with cream colored mane and tail, but she feared either one of them would empty the small purse.

A rather sad-looking dun, who had either been neglected or was approaching the end of his life, was one Maeya thought she could afford. But the rest of the stable had good bloodlines. She began to despair that she would find two suitable mounts. Perhaps taking turns on a horse would be enough to speed up their trip. Assuming, of course, that the dun would actually be able to carry them.

Maeya had just opened the stall door when a beefy man appeared in the stable doorway. His curly hair was shot equally with gray and pieces of hay, and although his clothes looked clean, there was the unmistakable aroma of manure clinging to him. His heavy brow furrowed as he looked down at her.

"What are you doing here?"

"Your pardon," Maeya said, "I was interested in buying a horse."

He snorted. "That ain't a horse. That there's a nag."

She tried not to agree as she eased her way into the stall. The dun flicked an ear at her, but otherwise gave no indication that he knew Maeya was there. He suffered her to check his legs and hooves, and even lifted his head a fraction as she opened his mouth to check his teeth. She did this last because it was expected of her, not because she had any illusion of being able to determine his age. But when Maeya held his head between her hands and he looked at her, she felt reassured. His eyes were tired, but not rheumy. She ran a hand along his sides, and could easily have counted his ribs had she the inclination.

"He's not bad, for a nag."

Maeya glanced over. The stableman was leaning against the stall, watching her. It was clear that he was regretting his classification of the dun; it put him at a disadvantage for the haggling. Or it would have, if she had any idea how much a horse should cost.

Once again, he helped her without meaning to. "I can let Spiker go for eight pieces of silver."

"Spiker?" Maeya asked in what she hoped was an idle tone. Inside, her heart was thumping. Spike Cave was done, but perhaps Spiker would help them survive. "What kind of name is that?"

The stableman shrugged. "A name is all. Can be changed easily enough. Just eight pieces of silver."

"How did a nag such as Spiker end up in this fine stable?"

"Old man Trad didn't have any means for keepin' him. Gave him to me last half Sister Orb, and I gave him a bag of flour, a cask of mead, a side of lamb, and a hot meal."

Maeya sighed loudly as she ran her hands down Spiker's hocks. "Bit of swelling."

"Still a high stepper."

Spiker snorted for Maeya and she laughed.

"Might be able to go to seven if you can overlook the hocks."

"Perhaps I should come back next full Sister Orb to see if you can put some meat on him and make it a smoother ride."

"Perhaps then I'll be asking twelve."

"Perhaps I'll offer five."

"Perhaps I'll accept six."

Maeya patted Spiker's neck, liking the way his head arched just over her shoulder. In a year or two, she might be too big for him. He was compact, in a good way. "Five is all I've got."

His eyes narrowed. "Only a fool would offer all they have."

Maeya shrugged, and gave Spiker one final pat. "Five is all I've got for him," she said, letting herself out of the stall.

Half a smile tugged at the corner of his mouth. "Perhaps if you find another for a price that pleases me, I'll be able to let him go for five."

"Mmm." Deliberately Maeya walked in the middle of the row, glancing at the horses. Most had come to their doors, sticking their heads out. It was a good sign. The stableman may drive a hard bargain, but the horses were not afraid of him. Perhaps Spiker really had been starved by his former owner's situation.

"See any that please ye?"

"The gray, and perhaps the chestnut."

His brow rose. "You're lookin' for three?"

"I'm looking for good horses at a fair price," Maeya said. "I have not yet decided how many."

"M' name's Hoart," he said.

She nodded. "Master Hoart, you run a clean stable."

"Aye," he said, politely ignoring the fact that she had not given her name. "That I do."

"If I were looking for three," Maeya said, stopping in front of the gray's stall. "What would it cost me?"

"This gray, the chestnut, and Spiker?"

"Aye." He wasn't giving a price for any three horses, and she had to respect him for that.

He leaned against the mare's stall, assessing her. When he turned to look at her, his slate eyes showed no hint of emotion. "Ten pieces."

"For all three?"

"Aye."

"Gold?"

He made a face. "I'm not talking about silver."

Maeya tried to figure in her head. Five pieces of silver had been agreed for Spiker. Perhaps five pieces silver equaled one gold now; but it used to be nine. The chestnut would be the preferred mount for most; he probably would fetch five or even six pieces of gold, which would leave three or four for the mare.

Acting more confident than she felt, Maeya said, "Four pieces. For Spiker and the mare."

Those slate eyes turned flinty. "I run a good stable. I don't take kindly to bein' mocked."

Maeya tried to breathe evenly as she met his eyes. "You run a good stable, Master Hoart. I offer four pieces of gold for the mare and the nag."

Hoart turned and walked away from her. The gray mare nudged her, looking for a treat. Absently Maeya pushed her creamy forelock back. She had a black mark on her forehead, but she wouldn't stand still long enough for Maeya to examine it. Tossing her head, the mare pulled away from her.

Maeya took a deep breath. She had driven the bargain too hard, it seemed. And now, feeling the weight of the gold and silver in her pocket, it seemed foolish to have been stingy about the price. The question was whether Master Hoart had been insulted past the opportunity to apologize and appease.

Pushing off the gray's wall, she turned to go after him and instead found a girl a bit older than herself bringing two halters. "Hoart says you bought the gray and the dun."

Maeya blinked. "Aye."

The girl walked down the row of stalls, her golden skirts kicking up dust and straw. Her dark red hair lay neatly down her back in a way Maeya's never could, and her slate eyes were devoid of all emotion.

Recovering as quickly as she could, Maeya cleared her throat and said, "Master Hoart left before I could ask if he has saddles for sale as well."

She cocked a brow at her. "Aye. Three pieces of silver will buy two."

Maeya nodded, feeling that to bargain again would be rude. "Does she have a name?" she asked, indicating the mare.

"Lark."

"A pretty name," Maeya said as she took a halter from her.

"Aye. She's a pretty mare, but she's too jittery. You'll find a better ride on Spiker." The girl looked at Maeya.

Maeya followed as the girl led Lark between the rows of stalls. When they reached Spiker's stall, Maeya held out her hand, expecting the girl to give her the halter. Instead, Maeya found Lark's lead in her hand while the other girl slipped into Spiker's stall.

Once they were in the paddock, the girl quickly tied off Spiker's lead. Maeya tied off Lark's, doing her clumsy best to imitate her knot.

"What's your name?"

"Daegny Hoart," the girl replied. "Who are you?"

"Maeya."

She stopped to look at Maeya. Before Daegny could ask further, Maeya asked, "How long have you lived here?"

"Nigh on a full set of seasons," Daegny said, tossing her a brush. "As soon as Hoart heard of Tiburn, we moved here."

"What drew him to Tiburn?" Maeya asked, tasting the strange name on her lips for the first time.

"Freedom from Clans and useless Dragons," Daegny said, setting to work grooming Spiker. As the dust rose in the air, his coat gained the tiniest bit of sheen.

"You think Dragons are useless?" Maeya asked. Her voice sounded strangled, and she hoped Daegny would think it from the dust.

"Hoart does."

"Do you agree with your father?"

Rolling her eyes, Daegny said, "He is not my father."

"O. Apologies."

She waved that away. "He is my uncle. He took us in when my mother died, before she revealed my father's name."

"O." Maeya said again, uncomfortable. "Do you agree with your uncle?"

She snorted. "What have the Clans done but attack each other with the Dragons?"

"What about the Wyzards?"

Daegny waved the brush again, causing Lark to toss her head. Absently, Daegny caught her muzzle, patting and soothing the mare. "The Wyzards used to leave the villages alone."

Maeya sensed something. "Used to?"

Daegny glanced over her shoulder. A few men were sitting on logs just outside of the nearest building. They appeared to just be gossiping; yet there was an air of something strange about them.

"Just after the last time of the full Sister Orb, blue evil came."

"Blue evil?"

"Aye. It killed a few. And many in our village were taken."

"Taken where?"

A cough from one of the men behind them made Daegny look over her shoulder. "No matter," she said, bending over to lift Spiker's hoof. "Where are you bound, Maeya?"

"I follow the Orb."

"Who travels with you?"

Maeya shrugged.

"'Tis not safe to travel alone."

"I shall be fine."

"May I give you some advice?"

Again Maeya shrugged. It seemed safer than saying anything.

"Stop at the tailor's. There will be a dress or two that are ready-made, and she will not take long to get one on you."

"I do not need a dress."

"I fear you do. You draw attention dressed as you are."

Involuntarily, Maeya glanced at the gossiping group of men. The hairs on the back of her neck rose as she met the stare of one. He was a contemporary of Hoart, but where the stableman's lined face spoke of tough decisions honorably made, this man's lines spoke only of anger.

"You look like a Dragon Rider."

Maeya flinched before she could stop herself. She forced a laugh, but it felt and sounded strained. "I am merely a traveler."

"You are not a traveler," Daegny said calmly, using long brush strokes on Spiker. "You are a Rider."

Lark bumped Maeya's arm with her muzzle; she didn't like it when Maeya stopped brushing. She began running the brush across her hide again.

"There are many villages like Tiburn along the path of the Orb," Daegny said, "And many peep who would as soon kill a Rider as let them spend their gold or silver. You would be best served if you bought a dress. Perhaps two."

"Thank you for the advice," Maeya said, trying to get her swirling thoughts together. There was widespread hatred of the Dragons? Why had she never heard of this? "But I do not have the time, silver, or need for a dress. The horses are what I need. As soon as they are saddled, I will be on my way."

Maeya couldn't figure out how peep could hate Riders. At the Cave, Tares and Cyrs lectured about how honorable and desired their positions as Riders and pages were, told stories of how beloved their heroes were, explained why Tares and Cyrs were revered for their age and wisdom. They were filled with their own glory, with the glory of their past deeds.

Daegny dropped the brush and turned on her heel. Maeya tried to quash the fear she felt settle in her stomach. She tossed her brush to land with a clatter next to Daegny's. Lark danced, tugging on her lead, but not straining it too hard. Quickly Maeya checked Lark's hooves. They were clean except for one small pebble in her left fore. She dug it out and as she was straightening again, Daegny rounded the corner, struggling to carry two saddles.

Maeya stepped over and relieved her of one saddle. Daegny moved to toss hers on Spiker's back.

"Wait," Maeya said. "These are both sidesaddles."

"Aye."

"I need two saddles for riding astride."

Deagny raised her brows. "It would not be seemly for you to ride astride in town."

"Then I will lead the animals out of Tiburn," Maeya said, fighting her impatience. She needed to get out of the town quickly. She could not tell if the sense of urgency was all hers, or if Pharla was creeping into her thoughts again. "I don't want sidesaddles."

Shaking her head, Daegny stalked off, carrying the saddle, and leaving Maeya holding the other.

When Daegny returned, she had one astride saddle.

"Daegny—" Maeya began.

"Do not argue," she said in a low tone. "You must take one sidesaddle. It is the best I can do for you."

Daegny moved to lift the saddle onto Spiker.

"I will not pay for a sidesaddle," Maeya said, dropping it in the dirt. "If all you will sell me is one saddle, then I will only pay for one."

"You are lucky to be getting this one," she hissed. "Please, do not—"

"Is there a problem, Daegny?"

Maeya spun to find Hoart and another heavy-set man frowning behind them.

"Nay," Daegny said quickly, pulling so hard on the cinch that Spiker danced and tossed his head. "I've nearly finished the sale."

Maeya looked at Hoart as he continued to stare at his niece. The man with him stared at Maeya, and she did her best to avoid looking at him. Maeya felt that she should speak up, that she should demand a second astride saddle, but fear congealed her throat.

"The gray will be a good ride for you, m'dear," Hoart said, picking up the sidesaddle and swinging it lightly on to Lark's back.

"Do you have need of anything else?" Daegny asked her. "Bridles?"

Maeya blinked. "Aren't they included with the saddles?"

Hoart chuckled. "Only if you asked for them."

Maeya raised her chin. "For three pieces of silver, bridles should come with the saddles."

"Three pieces—" the man with Hoart swallowed the rest of what he was going to say when Hoart elbowed him in the gut.

Feeling a bit vindicated although angry that she was, in fact, being taken advantage of, Maeya said, "Aye. Three pieces of silver should cover the bridles as well."

"Aye," Daegny agreed. "Perhaps it should."

The men—the ones across the street as well as the two beside them in the barnyard—watched silently while Daegny went to fetch the bridles. Maeya said nothing as she waited.

Shortly after Daegny returned, the horses were ready to leave. Maeya paid for them and the tack, and she was ready to mount. She took a small step toward Spiker, but Daegny shook her head forcefully. Gritting her teeth, Maeya turned to Lark, led her to a block, and swung up, feeling ridiculous on a sidesaddle while wearing leggings.

Daegny handed Maeya Spiker's reins, and she thought Daegny might be trying to convey a message to her with a serious look, but she could not interpret it.

Nodding curtly at all of them, it was the best she could do to grind out, "Much thanks for your help. May the Power That Is assure you good fortune."

The men nodded, but did not return her wishes.

"May the Power That Is assure you safe journey," Daegny said, earning a glare from Master Hoart.

Maeya tried to relax and let her body sway with Lark's rhythm on the way out of town. She did not want to look as anxious as she felt. The main street was not comforting in its quiet. Now it seemed waiting for an ambush. Or perhaps waiting *to* ambush.

Maeya did not pause to look around as she left town. She knew exactly where she was going; without effort she could point directly to where Pharla was. Maeya knew the hatchling was curled up and enjoying the warmth of the Orb, and knew that she was impatient to be on their way. She wanted to join a Cave.

The Dragon was becoming a heavy presence in the back of Maeya's skull, a thick blanket through which all her thoughts seemed to pass.

It was important to get to a Cave soon. Maeya had to get Pharla out of her head.

Lark's gait was smooth and almost lulled Maeya to sleep. Spiker followed sedately behind, not requiring any additional attention. Her mind drifted.

Nani thought Maeya had witch's blood. Did that affect her claim to becoming a Rider?

Heritage is less important than aptitude.

Then why can't Quoran be a Rider? Maeya asked Pharla. He learns quickly enough.

He learns, but he does not excel.

He could.

Pharla sighed in disgust, and Maeya could almost see her turning her head away. *At least he learns,* she conceded. *You seem unable to.*

Maeya felt Pharla's presence shift away, tucking herself further into her brain, leaving Maeya alone with her thoughts for a moment.

Maeya was Pharla's Rider now, she knew that, but Pharla didn't like her very much. This thought hurt. She had done everything she could to help Pharla, to ease the passing of Veet, and yet she still pushed her away. They were supposed to help each other recover from their losses. But Maeya still felt a hole next to where Pharla was in her mind, a hole left by the Dragon who had never emerged from the egg that she had carried for many cycles of the Sister Orb.

Did Maeya want to be a Rider? Yes. Did she want to be Pharla's Rider? Yes. The answer was almost surprising in its conviction. Somehow, she would make Pharla like her. She just didn't know how.

Suddenly Maeya noticed that Lark was stepping high, her ears were pricked forward, and she was tossing her head, pulling against the bit.

The mare could smell Pharla.

Maeya was torn between riding right up to camp—there was a chance Lark could bolt or throw her—or leading both animals, with the chance that one or both of them could hurt each other or Maeya while fighting the lead.

But when she looked back, she discovered that Spiker was still plodding along almost placidly. His ears were up, true, but he hadn't broken out in a nervous froth like Lark.

Lark gave a sideways hop, and Maeya decided she would be safer on the ground. Quickly she slid off, feeling more secure with both feet on the ground. Spiker almost walked over Maeya, pushing his whole head right into her chest, bobbing his head up and down.

"Bridle itches?" She asked, reaching up to scratch where the band crossed behind his ears. Lark pulled away from Maeya until the reins were taut. The mare was quivering all over.

Maeya took another step, and Spiker moved with her. Lark stayed put, stretching her neck out and leaning back against the reins. Maeya turned and tried to pull her forward.

"Rider Maeya?"

"I was successful," Maeya said over her shoulder.

"Aye," Quoran said, eyeing Spiker dubiously. When he looked at Lark, he brightened considerably. "I bet she's a sweet stepper."

Maeya handed him her reins. "Glad you approve of your mount. Her name's Lark."

"Isn't she yours? She looks...." He trailed off.

"She looks terrified. She fears Pharla. Spiker isn't affected yet. I would prefer a horse that can get close to Dragons."

Quoran's face cleared. "Of course, Rider. But I'm afraid few horses ever accept Dragons."

"We will—" Maeya began.

Instinctively she dropped to one knee when she heard twigs snapping. Someone had followed her from Tiburn. She cursed herself for daydreaming while riding instead of paying attention to her back.

A bit of satisfaction oozed through Maeya's mind, satisfaction that wasn't hers. But she didn't have time to explore it.

Quoran had followed her example and was crouching close to Lark. Maeya was glad he hadn't let go of the mare's reins, but as frightened as Lark was, she feared that the horse might strike out with a forefoot and split his skull.

It was silent in the small clearing, except for Lark's heavy breathing. Maeya felt exposed, kneeling on the ground without any weapons nearby. The long moments stretched out, and she began to wonder if she had really heard the snap at all.

"You do like to make things difficult," Daegny announced as she calmly strode into clearing. She was leading two horses, one the handsome chestnut, the other a sleek roan.

"I don't recall inviting you."

"If you had invited her, she wouldn't have come," a new voice said from behind the horses.

He was tall, and looked the same age as Daegny. Ember curls escaped from the band at the base of his neck. With the addition of the two horses he was leading, the clearing was feeling very cramped. And although his face was handsome, he looked very stern.

He sketched a bow in Maeya's general direction. "Darvo Hoart."

"Maeya."

"Quoran."

Daegny was surveying the clearing, ignoring the fact that her two horses were tossing their heads nervously. "Not much of a camp."

"This isn't our camp," Quoran said with a quick grin.

Maeya glared at him.

"Then why are we waiting here?" Daegny raised a casual hand to the chestnut's muzzle, and the animal settled instantly.

All the animals began to calm down. It was as if a peaceful wind had caressed them. Even Lark ceased her nervous stamping.

"Why are you here?" Maeya snapped.

"Because you're leaving Tiburn," Darvo said, "And Daegny will do anything to leave Tiburn."

"Well you've left," Maeya said. "Why don't you keep going?"

Quoran looked shocked. "Ri—"

She cut him off before he could call her 'Rider' in front of them, "Quoran and I prefer to travel alone."

"'Tis not safe to travel alone," Darvo observed.

"'Tis romantic," Maeya said, grasping for the only excuse she thought Daegny would believe.

Poor Quoran's eyes suddenly took up half his extremely pale face.

Daegny looked askance. "You are not wed," she said as she peered beyond them, looking beyond Quoran's shoulder.

"Daegny," Darvo said in the tone of one who is much used to arguments. "You do not know that."

She rolled her eyes. Quoran opened and closed his mouth a few times, and Maeya was grateful he stopped any sound from coming out.

There was a very awkward silence as they all just stood there. Maeya was determined not to speak first. She wanted Darvo to talk Daegny into leaving.

You are not leading.

Maeya blinked.

Riders are leaders.

She clamped her jaw shut.

Riders must lead!

I am leading, Maeya thought to Pharla. But I do not wish to lead them.

Why not? They are strong. They can speed our travels.

Two can travel faster than four.

Four can make and break camp faster. And have better luck with hunts. And have more rest while posting guards for camp. And—

"Fine!" Maeya blurted out. "They may come!"

Smug satisfaction from Pharla, the same Maeya had felt when she had first heard Daegny and Darvo approaching.

Darvo's eyes widened slightly. Quoran smiled, but did not look entirely comfortable. Daegny merely nodded.

Irritated that she had responded to Pharla out loud, Maeya snapped at Quoran. "See to the horses. Hobble them here."

"Don't be daft," Daegny said, "We cannot leave the horses unattended." She began leading her horses forward. Neither of them, Maeya noted, had sidesaddles on. "They will be safer in camp with us."

"We will post guards tonight," Maeya said. "They stay here."

"But—"

"Daegny," Darvo said in a deep rumble. "Do not push your good fortune further. If the Power That Is truly sent her as your guide, then surely the Power That Is would prefer that you to listen to her."

The Power That Is sent me as a guide? Maeya thought, bewildered. Daegny flushed, but she raised her chin as she turned to face Darvo. How could the Power use Maeya as a guide?

Nonsense. She is a fanciful girl. Strong, but given to much daydreaming.

Maeya closed her eyes, wishing she could close Pharla out as well.

Beware your wishes. They will not always lead you to happiness.

A sudden spike of pain bolted through Maeya's head, and she almost missed what Daegny was saying. "—something foolish, than I certainly will say so."

"There are reasons you do not always see," Darvo said. "Uncle was right about that."

"Uncle doesn't—" Daegny flared up but then cut herself short. "What reason do you sense?" she asked him.

He shrugged, looking at Maeya instead of at his sister. Those flinty Hoart eyes were piercing regardless who owned them, it seemed.

Maeya turned back to Quoran, fighting back her headache. "See to the horses," she said again. "I will see to our other needs."

"Aye, Ri—Maeya," he caught himself.

Daegny moved to hand her reins to Quoran, but Darvo seemed to materialize in front of her, handing her his reins instead.

"But—"

"You were ever better at calming the beasts," he said, "And it seems they need your presence. I will assist Maeya."

"I don't need any assistance," Maeya snapped.

"Then I will have time to hunt," he said, unperturbed. "While you see to your 'other needs.'"

Maeya's stomach dropped. Those flint eyes were unreadable, but she realized that he knew far more than she wanted him to.

Darvo half-smiled as he half-bowed at her.

Aye, he knew more than Maeya wanted him to. And she didn't have half an idea what to do about it.

An idea wouldn't be enough. Maeya could almost sense Pharla watching him through her eyes. *There is more to him than two halves.*

Maeya followed Pharla's presence toward the camp. Quoran had picked a good spot. A small creek elbowed next to a gentle hill but Pharla was not swimming in it. The grass around the hill was thick and lush, spotted with wild roses and strawberries. Clouds wisped by above them, but the wind wasn't stirring the leafy trees.

Their packs were tucked in next to a large boulder, and Maeya could just see a strap of the leather carrier sticking out between their packs. Quoran had collected a fair amount of firewood and cleared an area for the fire. But otherwise, the campsite was empty.

"Are you hiding?"

Darvo's hand dropped to the stout knife he wore at his waist. "Who's hiding?"

Pharla's irritation almost felt sticky in Maeya's mind. *When will you learn?*

Maeya looked to the hill. *Why are you hiding behind the hill?* She thought to Pharla. *You are the one who told me to lead and let them join us.*

'Tis not leading when you give in to pressure.

Maeya could have screamed in frustration.

That would hardly show leadership.

"Maeya?" Darvo said in a low voice. "What's amiss?"

"Naught," she ground out between her teeth. "Perhaps you should begin your hunt, while the light is still good."

Darvo looked at her. "And leave you with someone who is hiding?"

Maeya arched an eyebrow at him. "They are hiding from you."

"O." He dropped his hand from his knife, and his stance relaxed. "How long will they hide?"

"Longer than you will hunt, I am sure."

He smiled, slightly crookedly, and it made his almost handsome face simply gorgeous. "I criticize Daegny for not taking polite hints, and yet here I stand, doing the same." He sketched another bow. "Do you prefer hare or venison tonight?"

"Venison, with thanks."

Another smile; he knew Maeya sent him after the harder hunt to be rid of him longer. But did he also know they needed more meat than an extra hare or two? Her mind insisted that he did.

Pharla agreed.

CHAPTER EIGHT

By the time Maeya had the fire built up enough for cooking, Quoran and Daegny had joined her. She heard them talking, and Daegny giggling, long before she saw them. But as soon as they joined her in the clearing, they got quiet.

Daegny surveyed the campsite and sniffed. "There is plenty of room for the horses," she said.

"Did you calm them?" Darvo asked, coming from the other side of the clearing with a mid-size doe slung over his shoulder. He did not sound out of breath, and Maeya realized that she had not considered his strength before. Should he try to overpower them, she and Quoran didn't stand a chance.

There is more than one kind of strength.

"Aye," Daegny said. "They are settled."

Quoran looked doubtfully at her, but said nothing.

Darvo seemed to know what he was thinking, though. "'Twas difficult, aye?"

"Aye," she grumbled.

"Then I believe Maeya knows what is best for the horses." He dropped the doe to the ground, and Quoran scuttled over to begin skinning it. "I'll tend to my own kill," Darvo said in a mild tone that nonetheless stopped Quoran cold. "You'll have the cuts to cook shortly."

"Very well," Quoran bobbed his head.

Daegny was staring at Darvo. He ignored her and began deftly skinning the deer. After a moment, she stalked off, heading back to the horses.

"Quoran," Maeya said in a low tone, "I'm going—"

"Aye," he said, cutting her off. It was a measure of how jumpy he was that interrupted her like that. "I'll make sure they help with the meal."

Maeya smiled to herself as she picked up her pack and then egg, keeping the egg hidden behind the pack. Quoran was full of surprises.

He is protecting his Rider. That is his honor. That is not a surprise.

Where are you? Maeya thought to her as she left the light of the fire.

You know where I am.

"Pharla, I'm too tired to play games." Exhaustion was so deep in her, she was sure it would never get out of her bones. A strong headache made her want to close her eyes even more.

Here, Pharla was walking toward Maeya, her green body blending nearly perfectly with the lush grass. *I am here.*

"Please don't hide from me."

She dipped her head. *Don't hide from me.*

Maeya blinked. "I'm unable to hide from you!"

Pharla cocked her head to one side, and Maeya could sense her weighing what she had said. But then Pharla merely turned and walked back to a small copse of trees, thick with bushes. *I need to hide from the others.*

"Why? You wanted them to travel with us. We cannot keep you secret the whole way to Meadow Spear."

Pharla snorted in irritation. *They cannot just see me. You will have to explain things first.* She curled up under a bush, and the green leaves tickled the tops of her scales, brushing along her back, along the wing joints. Maeya could feel it!

She set her pack and the egg down. Pharla shifted ever so slightly away from the egg.

"Daegny is a pretty girl," Maeya said, feeling a need to talk. "Darvo is handsome as well. He seems much more amiable than she."

For the moment, Pharla said. *But don't count on it always being so.*

"Daegny has a way with the horses," Maeya continued, "And I think she will make our trip easier because of it."

Few horses can tolerate Dragons, Pharla said. She sounded troubled. *It is something that has been unchanged. The wolves and some of the cats have begun to tolerate us, but never the horses.*

"Why?"

Melancholy filled Maeya.

"Can you sense wolves?" Maeya asked. "Can you talk to them?"

I can sense if they're near, as I can with any being that makes sound or scent. But I cannot talk to them, nor can they talk to me. I cannot talk with anyone, other than my Rider.

"But you get a sense of others," Maeya said, "You have a clear sense and opinion of Quoran."

That is observation. You could do as well, if you tried.

"Maeya!" She flinched. Darvo's voice sounded as if he was close. *Haste! He'll be in sight soon.*

Maeya scrambled out of the brush, pulling the egg and carrier after her, and was on her feet when Darvo rounded the edge of the hill.

"I thought I might find you here."

Quoran was supposed to keep them away.

Stay there, Maeya thought to Pharla, I'll come back after we eat. Maeya sensed Pharla's resentment. *I may wish to stretch my legs.*

Stay there, Maeya told her again.

"It won't do any good to travel in a group if we continually split up," Darvo said with an easy smile.

Maeya smiled back. "It will take me a while to get used to traveling in a group," she said, just stopping herself from adding 'again.' Maeya held the leather-wrapped egg casually in front of her. "I thought you were going to help Quoran with the meal."

"Quoran has begun cooking. Supper will be ready soon."

"I am surprised how quick your hunt was."

"I do not linger when I hunt," he said. "I find it best to keep Daegny busy. She is helping Quoran as we speak."

"I would have thought she'd still be sulking."

"She is pretty, and used to getting her way," Darvo said. He hesitated and added, "As are you."

He turned to climb back over the hill before Maeya could analyze his comment. Did he think that she was pretty? Or used to getting her way? Thinking about it did her no good at all. And Pharla's sense of amusement didn't help, either.

*** ******** ***

The venison was excellent, but conversation was sparse. Quoran took the compliments from Daegny and Darvo in good stride, but when Maeya tried to ask what herbs he had used, he turned the conversation to the horses. He much admired the chestnut Daegny had brought.

"Aye, my sister knows horseflesh."

"How many years separate you?" Quoran asked them.

"None," Darvo said.

Daegny fairly twinkled across the fire at Quoran. "We are twins."

"In truth?" Quoran asked. "I've never met twins."

"In truth, we are less alike than most siblings."

"In truth," Darvo said, looking at Daegny, "We are more opposites born together than we are twins."

"Nay," Maeya said. "You have the same look."

"Aye," he agreed morosely. "All the boys say so."

They laughed, and much of the tension left their group.

When Maeya finished her second helping, she set her plate on the ground and took a long swallow from her water skin. The egg was wrapped in its carrier, looking like a small pack by her feet. She cleared her throat, and was startled to find all three staring at her as if they had been waiting for a speech.

You are their leader. They look for leadership.

Will you follow my lead? Maeya asked her.

Aye, Rider. That I must.

She would have liked to have the opportunity to pursue that more, but with six eyes turned her way and a dull ache at the back of her head, Maeya had to focus on what she was going to say. Quoran nodded encouragingly at her.

"You have chosen to travel with us," Maeya began, "Our journey will be a dangerous one, I fear. And so I give you leave now to decide that you don't wish to travel with us."

Daegny crossed her arms. "We've made our decision."

"But we didn't know it would be dangerous," Darvo said, and somehow Maeya got the sense that he was mocking her. "It is most kind of Maeya to give us a chance to leave now."

"As if we can't leave whenever we want!" she snorted. It occurred to Maeya that perhaps Daegny spent too much time with the horses.

"Nay," Maeya said softly. "You must choose now. Either you will leave or you will stay with us until we reach our destination."

"Which is?" Darvo asked.

Maeya shook her head. "You must choose now. One or the other."

Daegny glared at her while Darvo continued to watch her with a half-smile quirking his lips.

"'Tis not a choice," Daegny objected. "Not if we do not even know where you are bound."

"There is danger," Maeya repeated. "And once I tell you why, I will not let you leave."

The two Hoarts stared at each other over the fire. The fire snapped and popped merrily while the Orb painted the sky coral and peach and tension returned to their camp.

"There is danger whether we travel with you or not," Daegny said finally, and one of the horses whickered. "We will travel with you to your destination, and perhaps beyond."

Maeya looked at Darvo. He merely nodded his head once. "Aye."

"A vow."

Daegny tossed her head and looked up at the sky. "By the Power That Is, I vow to stay with you until you reach your destination."

Darvo looked straight at Maeya. "I vow to stay with you, by the Power That Is."

Her stomach flopped, which Maeya attributed to what she now needed to tell them. "We travel to Meadow Spear." She had been expecting a reaction, but neither of them so much as flinched, so she clarified, "Clan Uture's Meadow Spear Cave."

"You go to join the Riders," Daegny said. "That hardly requires a vow."

"She is a Rider," Quoran said.

Daegny blinked. "In truth?"

"In truth."

"Then how did you get so far from the Cave and Tares? They do not let their Riders out for trips."

"We are from Spike Cave." Again, Maeya expected an outburst, but they stayed calm.

"Spike Cave was destroyed, almost two full Sister Orbs past," Daegny said, glancing at Darvo. He nodded in agreement.

"Aye," Quoran whispered. "That it was."

"You did not sustain those injuries recently," Darvo said.

"Nay. I was burned years ago, when a volcano erupted and took half of Spike Cave with it."

"You said Tiburn is against the Riders," Maeya said.

Daegny laughed. "You cannot think Tiburn attacked your Cave! They are just tired old men. They don't want to pay portions to the Clans for protection when they feel they can protect themselves."

"You did not know Tiburn's philosophy, yet Daegny said you were cautious when you stopped at the stable," Darvo observed, "What is it you fear?"

Maeya leaned down and lifted the carrier. Quoran frowned, but said nothing. She set it on her lap, and let the leather fall off the egg.

Daegny looked puzzled, but Darvo's mouth gaped open. "The Power That Is," he murmured in awe. "I will protect you, Rider, and ensure that you reach Clan Meadow Spear safely."

"What is it?" Daegny asked, reaching forward as if to touch it.

Quoran slapped her hand away. "Don't! It is a Dragon's egg."

"I wasn't going to hurt it," Daegny snapped, rubbing her hand. Quoran had struck soundly and a red spot was already forming.

"Only the Rider may handle the egg," Darvo said.

"This is not my egg," Maeya said, handing the egg over to Quoran.

A strange expression crossed Darvo's face. "Your pardon, Rider," he said to Quoran. "I did not realize—"

"I carry Rider Maeya's honor," Quoran said calmly, stroking the egg while Daegny glared at him.

Darvo looked confused. "You're a page?"

"Aye."

"Then whose egg is it?" he asked.

"We do not know," Maeya said. "It has not been willing to hatch."

"If it is not your egg, then—" Darvo broke off suddenly, and his eyes widened. "The horses!"

"They're fine," Daegny said, still staring at the egg Quoran held on his lap. "Do not worry about—"

"That's why they're so nervous!" Darvo exclaimed, talking over his sister as if he had not even heard her.

"What?" Daegny pulled her attention from the egg. "Why?"

"They do not like the Dragon."

"What Dragon?"

"Maeya's Dragon," Darvo said, a new respect in his voice.

"Rider Maeya," Quoran corrected.

"Quoran," Maeya began.

"'Tis your honor I carry," he said stubbornly, "And it is past time you accept it."

Maeya sighed as the coral sky gave way to amethyst.

He is correct.

"Your timing is perfect," she said to Pharla as she appeared at the edge of the fire's light.

She waited patiently as Maeya walked to her. There were ruby and golden spots from the fire reflected in her emerald scales, making her look vibrant even though she stood still as a statue. Gracefully she extended her neck, resting her chin lightly in the palm of Maeya's hand.

"This is Pharla," she said. When Maeya turned to look back at her small group, she was stunned to find both Darvo and Daegny on their knees. Daegny looked shocked, but Darvo looked reverent.

"We thank you for allowing us to travel with you," Darvo said, bowing his head.

"We will carry your honor well," Daegny added breathlessly.

Quoran opened his mouth but closed it again when Maeya shook her head at him. He frowned at her, and Maeya knew that Daegny was going to hear about the history of pages serving Rider's honor whether she wanted it or not.

"There is one thing more I must tell you. Coming from Clan Kollarian, there is no promise that Pharla and I will be accepted at Uture's Meadow Spear. Nor can I promise that there will be a place for you."

Darvo nodded. "We accept that fact."

"Our path may be dangerous—"

"You already mentioned that," Darvo said with a grin. Then the color drained from his face. "Your pardon, Rider."

Maeya waved her hand in dismissal of his perceived insult. "The Wyzards may be after us, may be tracking us as we speak."

"Some Faithful came in to Tiburn and discovered the town's

dislike of Dragons," Daegny said. "For several days, all was well, but then they began demanding and ordering…fights broke out…and…."

"They took people away," Darvo said grimly.

"Be grateful they left Tiburn standing," Maeya said, just as grim. "They destroyed my home, and killed all inside."

"And they did worse at Spike Cave," Quoran added.

He does not realize the Cave was your true home, Pharla said in a soothing voice.

Daegny asked, "How could they do worse?"

"They killed people and Dragons," he said.

"And eggs," Maeya whispered.

Daegny covered her mouth with one hand and her eyes welled with tears. "Dragons? Then they are powerful indeed. Why do they destroy so? What do they want?"

Maeya shrugged. "I think they want power. They want to annihilate the Dragons. They want to rule all."

Daegny faltered, "If…if…if they truly killed Dragons at Spike Cave—we will never be able to stop them."

"We can stop them," Darvo said, though he sounded uncertain.

"No. I will stop them." They stared at Maeya.

We will stop them. Pharla whirred and satisfaction washed over Maeya.

***   ********   ***

Pharla and Maeya slept near the hearth fire. Quoran kept the egg with him. Daegny and Darvo went to guard the horses. Maeya was nervous about leaving the twins unguarded, but she would have to trust their vows.

Leaders must learn to trust others to do their work.

Aye. Maeya rolled over on her bed of pine needles. At the base of her skull a throbbing pain threatened to keep her awake.

You are a leader.

"Pharla, it is time to go to sleep."

In the morning, things took a while to sort themselves out. Daegny oversaw the packing and loading of the horses. She saddled Lark for Quoran, and left Spiker to be a packhorse. When Maeya went to console him for this slight, he lifted his black-trimmed ears and rumbled deep in his chest as she scratched behind his ears.

Darvo went on another short hunt, and brought back yet another deer. He offered half of it to Pharla, which she devoured.

Quoran and the twins traveled ahead of Pharla and Maeya. It had taken a near fight to get them all to ride together in front. Both Quoran and Darvo wanted to ride as tail guard.

Daegny sniffed. "Fine, leave me to ride alone out front, encountering who knows what dangers around every bend."

"You need only smile to conquer any man," Quoran said gallantly.

"And glare to terrify all others," Darvo added.

"I have Pharla to guard me," Maeya snapped. "Daegny will need help from both of you to keep the horses in line."

Daegny favored Maeya with one of her glares, and Maeya realized Darvo was right. Daegny was scary! "I can care for the horses," she began hotly.

"Of course you can," Darvo interrupted. "Rider Maeya was just trying to get rid of Quoran and me."

"Will you carry the egg?" Quoran asked.

"Nay," Maeya said. "You have cared for it well."

When he looked at her dubiously, Darvo said, "I'd be happy to help carry the load."

Quoran's glare was almost equal to Daegny's.

It took them longer to break that first camp, but Maeya was confident that they would find a rhythm and learn to work together.

During the morning, it was easy for Maeya to keep up with Pharla and the others, but she did not realize how quickly she had been walking. At mid-meal, her legs felt like jelly. The others had finished eating and were obviously waiting for her, but she was loath to stand again.

Pharla had plunged into the water as soon as everyone else had stopped. Now she was on one side of the brook while the rest of them, including the horses, were on the other. Most of the horses were nervously grazing; they were facing Pharla and keeping an eye on her, looking ready to fight their leads if they thought they needed to run. Lark, however, had pulled the full extent of her lead away from Pharla, and stood staring at her, occasionally blowing through her nostrils in fear. She did not graze nor relax her stance at all while they were stopped.

Spiker, meanwhile, was grazing almost at the brook's bank, his lead extended toward Pharla.

Impulsively, Maeya stood and untied Spiker's lead. He walked deliberately to the water and took a few steps into it before lowering his head for a long drink. Maeya followed, letting the lead hang limp.

When he was finished, he stood watching Pharla, water dripping from his muzzle.

Pharla raised her head. Maeya crossed the brook and stopped on the other bank, just a few strides from Pharla.

Spiker didn't hesitate when he followed her across. Once Maeya stopped, he dropped his head and began grazing again.

He is not afraid, Pharla said. *Why is it the broken beast who is not afraid?*

He is not a broken beast, Maeya thought to her. He is Spiker!

"Daegny," Maeya called over her shoulder. "Would you bring me a saddle? Not the sidesaddle!"

Daegny was nearly as skittish as the other horses while she was changing the tack on Spiker, but she refused to let Maeya help. "You are a Dragon Rider," she said almost breathlessly. "I will hold your honor."

"Daegny," Maeya said, "I have a page. I would like a friend."

Daegny gave her an enigmatic look as she finished pulling Spiker's cinch tight. Without another word, Daegny put his packsaddle—still loaded!—on her shoulder and splashed across to the other horses.

Maeya's afternoon was much more pleasant. Spiker traveled next to Pharla as if she were an old gray mare.

I think I'm insulted.

I think I'm happy, Maeya thought back to her.

Spiker may look like a nag, but he had no trouble keep up with Lark, Storm, and the other horses. And though Pharla's legs were shorter than the horses, she easily kept pace with them.

Because they had two camps to guard, they were no better rested than they had been before. Darvo was worried about the wolves around the camp. But they traveled much faster. Maeya had despaired of reaching Meadow Spear before the early harvest; now she knew they'd be in time to help tend the plants if allowed.

The thought should have made her happy.

Instead, Maeya found herself the last one ready to leave after first and mid-meals, and she was calling a halt at camps long before the Orb was ready to sink.

Camp Meadow Spear was ahead. And she did not know what it held for them.

*** ******* ***

Maeya's fellow travelers had various skills of their own, but watching them work together was impressive indeed.

In the first pass of the Orb, they divided the camp duties. Quoran was in charge of the hearth, bedding, and meals. Daegny saw to the horses, all six of them, by herself, and usually was done before either of the boys. Darvo procured and dressed the meat. It was a bad end-of-day meal if they only had three hares for the four of them, and three more for Pharla.

They wouldn't let Maeya do anything. No matter how she tried to point out that she was just as much a member of the group, they wouldn't hear it.

"You're not a member of the group," Quoran said flatly. "You're a Rider."

You are a leader. Lead. That is all the work you are to do.

Worse, Darvo and Daegny agreed. Maeya would no sooner stand up to get another helping of stewed carrots and quail than Daegny would take her bowl and fill it for her. When she moved to add a log to the dwindling fire, Darvo took it from her hand, as if she lacked the strength to set it on the flames.

All Maeya was allowed to do was tend to Pharla and the egg. Now that they were no longer walking, Quoran refused to carry the egg. He insisted that a page was not worthy. Maeya could sense that Darvo wanted to take it, but after Quoran's initial reaction, he knew better than to mention it.

Quoran had quickly summed up the roles of page and Rider: a Rider cared for and rode the Dragon; the chosen page did all else for the Rider. And Maeya had chosen Quoran as her page. No one else could have that honor.

While the human members of the group did not question the pace Maeya set, her Dragon certainly did.

Why are we stopping? We could travel beyond the next ridge before the Orb sinks if we hurry just a bit, Pharla groused.

I am tired, Maeya thought at her. She rubbed her forehead. *And I am not feeling well,* she added.

Maeya sensed concern, quickly followed by determination.

Then we must travel faster. There will be a healer at Meadow Spear.

"I don't need a healer," Maeya muttered out loud.

"A healer?" Darvo asked from across the fire. "Why do you need a healer?"

Quoran looked up. "Rider? What's wrong?"

"Naught," Maeya snapped.

You said you were ill!

She groaned as her headache throbbed even stronger. Quoran was at Maeya's side in an instant, hands on her face, peering into her eyes.

"Do you have pain?"

She swatted Quoran's hands away. "I will be fine."

Perhaps he knows herbs!

Quoran clearly didn't believe Maeya. "Is it your head? Your stomach? Your ears?"

"Quoran, please."

"Maeya, he only wants to help," Daegny said.

Yes, let him help you. Another bolt of pain shot through her head.

"Rider Maeya," Darvo said, shooting a look at Daegny, "surely knows what's best for her."

"Clearly she is not feeling well," Daegny said stubbornly. "I don't know why she won't take our help when it is offered."

"I do not—"

"Do not meddle, Daegny," Darvo said patiently. "Let the Rider and her page handle it."

"Please let me help," Quoran begged, looking at Maeya anxiously.

Let him help!

It was evident she would not get any rest. "I have a headache," Maeya said. Even to her own ears she sounded surly.

Maeya could sense Pharla as if she were hovering above her instead of standing a few paces away.

What is that? she asked abruptly.

Maeya realized that Pharla had seen her mental image of Pharla being a humming-bird sized Nani, wringing her taloned hands, flitting right above her head.

"Is it in the front of your head?" Quoran asked. "In the back? Between your ears?"

"All over," Maeya said, leaning her head back and closing her eyes. She heard Quoran leave.

That isn't me! I'm not a...a...an annoying little buzz!

I see I've insulted you again, Maeya thought to her.

Pharla withdrew from her mind, at least as much as she had of late. Maeya could feel her curled up, an infinitesimal itch just behind her right ear. She wished she could scratch her out.

Maeya stayed still, listening to the others move about the camp. They spoke to each other, but in lowered voices as if afraid they would disturb her further. They had no idea how disturbed she really was. This was not how her life was supposed to be.

Children were supposed to be loved.

Caves were supposed to be secure and safe.

Leaders were supposed to be followed, not pushed.

Riders were supposed to be in charge of their Dragons, not bullied by them.

Maeya heard footsteps approaching, and she forced her eyes open.

Quoran knelt next to her, with a steaming mug. "This should help," he said. "It tastes bitter, though. We do not have honey to sweeten it."

Maeya smiled, or tried to. "You have done all you can, Quoran, and I thank you. I will drink it as is."

"In truth?"

She sighed, but raised the mug to her lips. Even knowing it would be bitter, Maeya almost spit it out in his face. She forced herself to swallow. "Are you sure?" she croaked out. "I must drink this?"

Aye. You must be well.

"Aye," Quoran said miserably. "I do wish I had the honey."

"I wish it more," Maeya said, eyeing the mug. She had promised Quoran, but she was not sure she could make herself take another sip, let alone finish all of it.

"Wish what?" Darvo said, appearing out of the shadows. Maeya stared at him. The boy had the ears of a hound.

"Wish we had honey," Quoran said, still watching Maeya. "The boiled Japon roots are unpleasant." He hesitated, then added, "But you must drink it, Rider."

"I feel sure my headache will pass," she protested. "I will do better with rest than with drinking this."

"Daegny," Darvo looked across the fire. "Quoran needs honey."

She arched an eyebrow at Quoran. "I could be a honey."

Quoran flushed in the fading light, but Darvo merely looked exasperated. "Quoran needs honey for the Rider's potion."

"O." That was all she said as she turned on her heel and left camp.

"Wait!" Quoran called, but it was too late. He turned to Darvo. "It's getting dark. Go with her!"

"She does not need my help."

"It could be dangerous! There have been wolves around!"

"She will be fine," Darvo assured.

"But—"

"If you must argue," Maeya interrupted petulantly, "could you do it elsewhere?"

Quoran immediately bowed and scurried away, admonishing over his shoulder, "Please, Rider, drink the Japon root!"

Darvo favored her with his crooked smile again. "Wait," he advised. "Daegny will bring honey for you shortly."

He winked before turning away, and Maeya was positive her headache abetted slightly.

The pain seemed to mute the activities around her. Vaguely she was aware of Quoran's return to the fire, his short words with Darvo. They went about camp duties while she lay on her blankets, alternately hoping for death or a reprieve.

Darvo had just spitted the venison flank and was setting it to cook when Daegny returned, bearing a dripping honeycomb. Quoran jumped to his feet and fetched one of the many bowls that Daegny and Darvo had brought on the packhorses. He murmured his startled thanks.

Pharla observed, *She has more surprises than most.* The fog in Maeya's head cleared enough to realize she was right.

"How did you do that?" Maeya asked Daegny.

Daegny looked at her, the picture of innocence.

"How did you find the hive and retrieve the honey so quickly?"

"It is easy if you follow the bees," she said, tossing her hair.

"I doubt a magician could do it so quickly," Quoran joked, smiling as he brought the honey to Maeya.

Quoran had his back to Daegny, so he missed her flush.

Maeya sat up straight, in spite of the bolt of pain that threatened to split her skill. "What kind of magic do you practice?" she demanded. "Are you a good witch or a bad one?"

Quoran's grin faltered. Daegny glared at her.

"I'm helping you," she said tartly. "That should answer all of your questions."

"You're a witch?" Quoran asked in disbelief.

"We are not magic," Darvo said. He was sitting just out of the firelight, and it was difficult to see his face.

"You aren't?" Maeya asked, trying to keep her tone mild.

"We are gifted," he said. He sounded unbelievably tired.

O.... O, yes, I see. Of course.

What do you see? Maeya asked Pharla, but she was gone from Maeya's mind as quickly as she came, and Pharla had not even lifted her head from where she lay. Maeya turned her attention back to Darvo. "Gifted?"

Silence stretched between them, till finally Daegny sighed. "They won't let us leave," she said to Darvo, "Nor will they leave us. We might as well tell them."

"Yes, please," Maeya said, fighting her impatience, "Tell us. How are you gifted?"

"I am a Speaker," Daegny said.

"A Speaker?" Quoran asked. He was mixing honey into the foul concoction. Maeya was not sure she'd be able to make herself try it again.

"Aye," Daegny said softly, "I can speak to animals."

She had been able to calm the horses faster than anyone else. Saddling and grooming, unsaddling and hobbling, the horses had never balked. Of course. "What about Pharla?" Maeya asked.

Don't be foolish, Pharla said. *She is not my Rider.*

Daegny was shaking her head. "I get no sense of her. I did not even know she—" Daegny paused and tilted her head. A smile slowly crept across her face. "No, that's not true. I do get a sense of her. It's a void. I didn't realize it before, but it's as if an animal is there, but I cannot feel it at all. There is a presence, but nothing else. Hmm," she said to herself. "I should have noted that before."

"So you asked the bees where their honey was and they told you?" Quoran asked.

"No, it doesn't work that way," Daegny said. "I can Speak to them, tell them what I want. But they do not Speak back to me. They can respond to what I tell them, but they do not talk. Sometimes I can tell what they're experiencing—extreme fear or pain. Tonight I just told a hare I needed to find the beehive. The hare led me there."

"Is that all?" Maeya asked, feeling weak. Following a hare through the trees to a beehive, but Daegny did not consider herself a witch.

She is not, Pharla said calmly. *She is gifted. They both are.*

Maeya looked at Darvo. "And what is your gift?"

He looked troubled as he said, "I can sense the animals as well."

"You are also a Speaker?"

He shook his head. "I sense them, but they do not sense me. I can find the injured, weak, and old animals around me. They do not sense me, so it is easy for me to approach them."

"That's why you hunt!" Quoran exclaimed. "Why you are so fast!"

"Aye," Darvo said grimly. "And why I have to dress my own animals. Finding one injured beast during a journey is good luck. Finding one each night," he shrugged. "Peep will think you are a witch."

"You only find the injured animals?"

"Or old," he nodded. "And when there aren't any, I can sense which is the weakest in a herd."

"'Tis a good gift."

Darvo shrugged again. "Like any gift, goodness is in the eye of the beholder." He smiled, but even in the darkness Maeya could see that it was not a fully happy smile.

"What of Pharla? Do you sense her?"

"Nay. I do not think she is an animal in that sense of the word."

"We are happy you have such gifts," Maeya said. "You have made our travels easier."

"Aye," Quoran said. He smiled shyly at Daegny, then looked at the mug sitting by Maeya's foot and his smile faded. "Rider, please, you must drink."

Maeya sighed and closed her eyes. When she opened them, Quoran was holding the mug up to her. Steeling herself, she lifted it to her lips and took the tiniest possible sip. It now tasted like thick, strong ale. Maeya smiled at Daegny and then Quoran.

"You have made our journey much better indeed."

CHAPTER NINE

While Quoran's potion did help alleviate Maeya's headache, it also made her sleepy. She slept soundly that night, for the first time since the Wyzards had destroyed Spike Cave and torn her world apart. Maeya slept so soundly, in fact, that she did not wake when the others began moving around the camp and preparing breakfast. She did not wake until they woke her, and then it was with difficulty.

"Rider?" Quoran leaned down, peering at her with concern.

Maeya barely managed to open an eye.

"How do you feel?"

She wanted to tell him that other than being sleepy, she felt fine, but her tongue was so thick in her mouth that she could not make any words. Instead, she grunted.

"I think you gave her too much," Darvo said. Maeya felt helpless and embarrassed as he surveyed her.

"I prepared it as Cyr Sajen taught me," Quoran fretted. "In truth, the honey should have made it even weaker."

"Where is Pharla?" Daegny asked.

Maeya tried to snap her eyes open. They did open, but slowly. Fighting the weight of sluggishness, she tried to sit up, but could not. Instead, she cast out with her mind. *Pharla?*

Aye, a sigh drifted slowly through her mind. It was muted, as if it were far away.

Are you well? Maeya asked her.

For a long moment there was no response. *Too tired.*

The potion, Maeya sent to her.

What?

It drugged us, she tried to explain. *It got to both of us.*

What potion? Feeling her exhaustion made Maeya's eyes drift shut again.

"Rider!" Quoran was lightly slapping the sides of her face. "We do not see Pharla."

"Fine."

"Maeya!" Someone was lifting her. Maeya felt her head drop forward, chin resting on her chest. She tried to raise her head. She settled for opening her eyes slightly. She saw feet gathered in front of her.

Taking a deep breath, Maeya tried again, "She's fine. Pharla," she took another breath, "is fine."

"Good," Quoran sighed.

"Are you sure?" Darvo asked sharply.

"She's a Rider," Quoran snapped. "If she says—"

"She's drugged," Daegny interrupted. "Perhaps she's just having a dream. She may not be aware of what she's saying to us."

"Pharla," Maeya struggled to get her lips and tongue to cooperate. "Pharla is tired. Tired but fine."

"Where is she?" Daegny asked.

But it had taken too much to get that out. Maeya didn't know where Pharla was, and she could no longer feel the Dragon in her mind. Sleepiness erased any concern Maeya might have felt. Sleepiness was the only thing she knew.

When Maeya woke next, the Orb was past mid-point. Her bedroll had been moved; instead of being next to the large log, she was under an ash tree that was casting pleasant shade. Quoran and the twins were seated on the log. They appeared to be talking although she could not make out the words. Maeya could see the horses grazing on the other side of the camp.

She took a deep breath and pushed herself up to rest on her elbows. Her head rocked inside, and her stomach rolled. After a few deep breaths, Maeya felt certain she would not cast up what she had eaten at last meal. She felt something at her side and looked down. Quoran had evidently nestled the Dragon egg in the blanket next to her.

Pharla? Maeya waited, but there was no response.
Pharla? She tried to shout with her mind.
Too tired.
Still? Maeya's mind was rapidly feeling clearer.
Just sleep.
Of course, Maeya soothed. Where are you?
Tired.
I know, Maeya said. But where are you?
On the wall.
Where?
On the wall.
Pharla, there—
Tired. Sleep.
And she was gone again.

Maeya struggled to a sitting position. She could not see any wall.

"She's awake!" Darvo exclaimed.

Quoran leapt off the log and hurried to Maeya. "Are you well?"

"Aye."

"My apologies, Rider."

"For what, Quoran?"

"For the potion. For drugging you," he faltered.

"You were trying to help me, correct?"

"Aye."

"And you had learned this from Cyr Sajen?"

"Aye. He had many headaches."

"Then you had no way of knowing that it would not be helpful to me. It did get rid of my headache."

"Truly?"

"Aye."

Quoran looked so relieved, it made her smile. "All is well, Quoran," but as the words left her lips, she realized that she lied. "Where is the wall?"

"Wall, Rider?"

"Is there a wall nearby?"

"Nay," he said, looking confused.

"Darvo, in your hunting, did you find a wall?"

"Nay, Rider. No wall."

Maeya frowned. If Pharla had said she were in a cave or tree, Maeya would not have worried. She would have left the Dragon to sleep it off as she had. But Pharla had said she was on the wall. And a wall meant a farm or village or town. It meant peep.

"Daegny, do you sense Pharla?"

"I told you that I cannot—"

"You said you sensed a void. Do you sense that void?"

"Nay," she said, throwing her shoulders back. "If I did, I would have told you."

"You said Pharla was fine," Quoran said.

"She is," Maeya agreed. "But she says she is on a wall, and that worries me."

"Can you not speak to her?" Daegny asked.

Maeya glared at her. "That is how I know she is on a wall."

"Ask her where the wall is," Daegny said in a patronizing tone.

"She is feeling the affects of the Japon root," Maeya explained. "She was unable to tell me more than that she is on a wall, and very, very tired."

"The root affected her?" Quoran wailed.

"All will be well," she said, patting Quoran's hand.

"We can find the wall," Darvo assured Quoran. He slung his bow over his shoulder and stood. "We can find the wall faster if we begin looking now."

"Wait," Daegny and Maeya said at the same time.

"I will try to reach Pharla again."

"I will Speak to the animals," Daegny said right over her.

Daegny ignored Maeya as she turned to leave and both the boys tried to stop her. *Pharla?* Maeya shouted in her head. *Pharla, wake up!*

Why? She sounded tired but not as groggy as before.

Where are you?

Irritably, she said, *I told you I'm on the wall.*

Where is the wall? Maeya asked her. *From the camp, which way is the wall?*

You know, she said, and Maeya realized that she did. Pharla was awake enough now that Maeya could once again sense her.

"That way," Maeya pointed. "Just on the other side of those Trident trees. There's an old wall. She is probably safe. I don't think anyone has used it for a while."

It certainly hasn't been tended to, Pharla grumbled, and Maeya got images of stones falling from the ivy-covered wall.

"Should we just stay here?" Quoran asked doubtfully.

"Nay," Maeya said. "We might as well move. We will not travel far today, but at least it won't waste a full day."

Darvo smiled at Maeya before he began clearing camp. Her stomach made that strange and unpleasant flip again, until she caught Daegny staring at her.

"You can saddle Spiker," Daegny told her.

Maeya blinked but didn't say anything. She had been asking to help around camp, but now Daegny made it sound like a punishment.

Spiker moved toward her awkwardly, his head bobbing with excitement. Maeya unhobbled him and led him to a tree where the saddles and packs were spread. Even in just a few days, his coat had gained more sheen, and his hips and ribs were not quite as visible. By the time Sister Orb was full again, Maeya was sure he'd be better looking than Lark.

Maeya saddled him as quickly as she could, but Daegny was already working on saddling a third horse by the time Spiker was ready to go.

Quoran was frowning, whether at Maeya or Daegny she could not quite decide, until it finally occurred to her that he was frowning at both of them. In his eyes, Daegny was not treating Maeya as befit her station, but Maeya was not requiring it, and therefore they were both guilty.

As Maeya swung up on Spiker, her head spun with sudden

sleepiness. She could sense Pharla yawning, fighting to stay awake.

Peep.

"What?"

There are peep here, for all they ignore their wall. I am not alone.

Have they seen you?

Disgust seeped in. *I know better than to be seen.*

You are not feeling yourself, Maeya chided her, yawning even as she did so. You are not in complete control.

I am always in control, Pharla insisted.

Maeya knew better than to waste her time in arguing.

Use caution.

"Aye." Carefully Maeya accepted the egg that Quoran handed up to her.

In your travels, Pharla sniffed, and Maeya wondered if she would ever be able to get a thought from her Dragon without feeling irritation.

Maeya turned her attention to their camp. Though she was not worried about being followed, it made her feel better to know that their camp did not reflect usage. "We need to ride with care," Maeya said. "Pharla says there are peep in the area."

"I will take the lead," Darvo said, pulling an arrow from his quiver. "Daegny, you take the rear."

"I will ride rear guard," Quoran objected. "We will put the girls in the middle."

"I am better suited as rear guard," Daegny said, likewise readying her bow. "I will Speak to the animals. They can give us warning."

"You said they don't speak to you!"

Daegny smiled at him, when Maeya knew she would have skewered her with a look for that blind comment. "All animals Speak to everyone. We just have to listen."

Exhaustion swept through Maeya again. It felt like they were back to the first day, with everyone bickering.

So they moved out for their short trip, Darvo in the lead, then Maeya and Daegny, each leading a packhorse, and Quoran bringing up the rear.

Maeya fought to stay awake for the ride, but Spiker's easy gait soon lulled her into a lazy doze, just on the outskirts of being aware. And then suddenly, she was falling.

The jolt of landing on the ground was bad because she tensed up so much on the way down, but that was not what hurt the most. What hurt was the realization that she no longer had the egg in her hands. She had dropped it.

Practically bouncing up from the ground, Maeya spun wildly,

trying to spot the egg. Dimly, she heard the others around her, shouting and looking for an attack.

What's amiss?

I fell asleep! Maeya thought at her furiously.

Good idea, Pharla sighed.

Still searching for the egg, Maeya let her Dragon fade out again.

"Rider!" Quoran's face was pale around the angry red scars. "Were you hit?"

"Nay," Maeya said, "I fell off."

"You were thrown off Spiker?" Daegny sounded incredulous.

Maeya glared at her. "Nay. I fell."

"You mean you just slid off? He didn't take an extra step or anything?"

"I fell!" Maeya snapped. "And I dropped the egg."

Quoran immediately scrambled off Lark and joined her in the frantic search for the egg.

"Here," Darvo said. Maeya looked up to see him sitting calmly astride his roan, pointing to a grassy spot near the road. "It is here."

Quoran scurried to fetch it as Maeya sank weakly to her knees. She watched as Quoran scooped up the egg, and Darvo continued to follow the egg with his eyes. He seemed drawn to it, but out of respect for Quoran, he had made no move to pick it up when he would have been perfectly justified to do so.

Bringing Maeya the egg, Quoran panted, "I don't think it has been harmed."

She turned the egg over in her hands, checking carefully, but did not find any cracks.

Maeya tried to hand the egg back to Quoran. He put his hands behind his back and shook his head.

"I am not as recovered as I thought," Maeya said, "Please carry it to our next camp."

"You will not drop it again," he assured her.

Maeya glanced over at Darvo. She thought he shook his head, but it was so slight it might have just been the wind lifting a lock of his hair.

"Perhaps you should walk," Daegny said tartly. "That would guarantee that you not drift off to sleep."

Maeya stepped next to Spiker and Quoran took the egg while she swung herself up. He handed her the egg and went back to Lark. "Ride with me, Quoran," Maeya said. "We will talk, and that will help."

Maeya tried not to smile at Daegny's sudden pout.

***   *******   ***

When the rock wall came into view, Maeya pulled up under a large pine. The boughs spread out far and wide, but the lowest one was well above her head, even while seated on Spiker. Although Maeya couldn't see her, she could sense that Pharla was close, and safe, and that was enough.

Trying to hide her distress over how far Pharla had traveled while she slept, Maeya dismounted smoothly, egg in hand. She set the egg carefully in a V created by the tree's roots and turned to begin unsaddling Spiker before Daegny could say anything.

Darvo completed a circuit around the clearing and then dismounted next to Maeya. Without saying anything, they quickly worked together to unsaddle the horses. It felt comfortable. It felt good.

Quoran kept sending glances their way every few moments, even as he gathered wood for the fire and set out our plates and bowls. Daegny so carefully did not look at them that Maeya could almost feel her need to stare.

Darvo dipped his head slightly as he turned to leave the clearing. *Caution!*

Maeya froze, as did Darvo. Every bird in the trees had been calling, filling the forest with song. The birds fell silent, as if some unseen hunter had slain them all with one true arrow. Daegny crouched, making Quoran flinch as the knife appeared in her hand. And through the sudden silence of the forest, the approaching footsteps sounded like thunder.

"Peace," Maeya murmured, gesturing to Daegny and Darvo to put down their weapons. It took her only two steps to reach the egg. Maeya picked it up and handed it to Darvo before stepping directly in front of him. "Use care," she said over her shoulder.

Thus they were all facing the bushes even before the small blond man plowed through it. At first glance, Maeya thought he was a child, for he stood no higher than her nose. Then she saw the dark stubble on his face, and the well-defined muscles, and she realized that although he was short, he was a man grown. He carried with him a bolo, and the hilt of a sword was just visible behind his back.

He scanned their group, and for a moment, seemed at a loss. Then he chose to address Daegny. "Who are you and where are you bound?"

Daegny drew herself up, looking almost regal. "By what right do you barge into our camp?"

"Who are you?" He snapped. Maeya realized that his eyes reflected fear, not anger.

"We mean no harm," Maeya said. She could feel Pharla in the back of her mind. "We are merely passing by."

"To where?"

For some reason, Maeya felt more comfortable disclosing their identities than she did their destination. Pharla agreed. "My name is Maeya. This is Darvo and Daegny, and that is Quoran. We are traveling together, and mean to do so in peace."

"Why are youngsters traveling alone?"

"We are young but capable," Maeya said, trying to impart a light warning in her tone. "And who are you?"

"T—Igny."

"Tigny?" She asked, letting him know she had heard the slip.

He is hiding something!

"Igny," he repeated, sounded much more sure of himself. "I come on behalf of my peep, to ensure our safety."

"We mean no harm," Maeya said again. "You may tell your peep we will not linger."

"What do you fear so?" Daegny asked. She was still standing with her head high and shoulders back, looking completely composed. Her split riding skirt fell gracefully to her ankles, and if the lavender jacket was smudged, it did not detract much.

"M'lady," Igny said with a slight bow, "The Wyzard Faithful attacked a few passes of the Orb ago. We are wary of strangers in ways we never were before."

"Our peep were attacked as well," Daegny said grimly. "We have no wish to meet up with Wyzard Faithful again."

"Did you lose many?" Maeya asked.

"We lost several peep, and…" Igny hesitated, as if unsure of what to say, "…and much more."

He is hiding something! Pharla said again, sounding more distressed. *Caution!*

Pharla, sometimes we have to trust, Maeya told her, sending her as much soothing feeling as she could. "May the Power That Is help your village recover quickly."

A strange look crossed his face.

"What is the name of your village?" Maeya pressed. "We are not entirely sure where we are."

"We serve a Clan."

Remembering Tiburn, Maeya said, "We are friends of the Clans."

He cocked an eyebrow at her. "You can serve a Clan," he said, "You cannot be friends with several."

"I fear things are changing, Igny," Maeya said. Nodding toward Daegny, she added, "My friends are from a town that serves no Clan."

He made a face. "They are fools."

"Aye," said Daegny, making a face back at him. "But fools are often the hardest to stop."

Igny had to grin slightly at that. Then he nodded at Quoran. "Were you friends with the Dragons who did that to you?"

Quoran whimpered but made no sound.

"You are lucky to be alive," Igny continued, still studying Quoran's scarred and puckered face. "The Power That Is has marked you, and that mark is a heavy one to bear."

Maeya sensed Pharla, closer to them now, almost directly behind Igny. Suddenly his smile faded. He turned and looked over his shoulder. Then looked back at them.

"Are you sure you travel alone?" he asked.

He feels me! Pharla nearly squeaked.

Maeya burst out, "You're not from a village at all, are you? You don't *serve* a Clan—you are *from* a Clan!"

"You are a Tare," Quoran said suddenly.

Maeya blinked, but looked at Igny again. "T—Tare Igny, that's you, isn't it?"

He stood straight, and although Daegny had looked regal before, Igny looked imperious. He was a Tare. There was no doubt.

A new Rider.

I'm not ready to tell him I'm a Rider, Maeya told Pharla, trying to get her to settle down.

New Dragon. Pharla wasn't making any sense.

"Why do you hide your status?" Maeya asked as Quoran bowed low to the Tare. He reached up to grab Daegny's sleeve, tugging it until she bowed as well.

"After the attack, we did not feel safe."

"You have Dragons and Riders to protect you," Maeya pointed out.

Dragon— Pharla fretted in Maeya's mind.

"No longer. We lost all."

The world spun before her eyes.

"We had ten Dragons and Riders," he paused, visibly collecting himself. "We had six Tares and two Cyrs, and many pages. They are all gone. Dragon's Luck let me live." His face was so pale, and his eyes were so haunted, that Maeya knew that he told the truth.

Quoran made a strange noise in the back of his throat. He seemed to be trying to communicate something with Maeya, raising his eyebrows and twitching his head.

"We have not been courteous, Tare," she said smoothly, and could see the tension slide off Quoran's face. "Will you join us at our fire?"

"With pleasure," he said. "I feel we have much to discuss."

"More than you know," Maeya heard Darvo say quietly behind

her. Maeya had almost forgotten he was there.

Maeya turned and stared.

Darvo was cradling a Dragon egg that was missing the top half. A pale green Dragon blinked up at him from within.

Darvo raised his eyes and a powerful emotion shone through them. "I am a Rider, too, Maeya."

CHAPTER TEN

The Power That Is watched over their fire that day. Maeya had not helped with the hatching of any Dragons. Quoran had—with Pharla, in truth—but he seemed too stunned to be able to function. He sat right where he stood, not moving to a boulder or log, just dropping onto the slightly damp earth.

Tare Igny's wide eyes made him look even more childish for a moment. Then he turned to Daegny. "Quickly! Bring a hare or squirrel."

Daegny's perfect mouth opened in an O, and wordlessly she shook her head, backing away. Maeya thought of her Speaking to the animals, and suddenly realized that Daegny had never hunted with Darvo; that she ate little meat, if any, at each meal.

Daegny sank down next to Quoran. But while he hung his head, she stared in fascination at her brother and the hatchling.

"I'll go," Maeya said. She pulled her bolo from the Spiker's saddlebag and crossed the clearing toward Pharla.

Maeya let the feeling in her mind pull her to where the Dragon was.

Pharla was lying down, front legs tucked under her, no longer on the wall but next to it. Her back was nearly level with the top of the wall, Maeya noted.

I'm growing, she preened.

Aye, and your attitude keeps perfect pace.

Pharla raised her snout sharply, reminding Maeya forcibly of the way Daegny was always tossing her head. *I was trying to help.* Maeya heard the pout clearly.

Maeya looked again and saw two hares lying just in front of Pharla's front legs.

"You are hunting for yourself?"

For the hatchling.

Maeya bowed her head toward Pharla. "My pardon. And my gratitude."

Pharla inclined her head ever so slightly toward Maeya. *They will be good for the new Dragon,* she said, whirring with a satisfaction that Maeya did not understand. There was none of the previous jealousy that had colored everything before.

Maeya should have taken the hares to Darvo and the hatchling then, but she hesitated. "Did you eat?"

Aye.

"Will you stay here? So I can bring my bedroll?"

Aye.

"Are you feeling better?"

The Dragon hatchling yawned, exposing her teeth, which, in addition to getting longer were also getting more numerous. *I slept well.* She blinked, long and slow. *Go. Feed the hatchling.*

Maeya hurried off to do just that.

"The hatchling will eat in spurts," Tare Igny was saying to Darvo. "It will be ravenous for days, and then not eat for days. Force nothing. The hatchling knows what it needs."

Darvo was staring at his Dragon, cradled in his arms. Contentment radiated from him.

"Here," Maeya whispered.

The hatchling's eyes popped open as Darvo nodded, taking the hares from her.

His Dragon hatchling barely gave him time to get a grip on the legs before it was lunging at the little animals.

Tare Igny gave Maeya a look she had received many times as a page. She ducked her head and turned to help Quoran and Daegny with evening meal.

"Do we have enough dried meat put aside, Quoran? Or should I go hunt for our evening meal?"

"We have plenty, Ri—Maeya," he said quickly, seeing her raised brow. "And Daegny has found a cache of nuts."

"Perhaps I should go look for berries?"

"Nay. Sit and relax."

"Relaxing is what I did all day," Maeya grumbled. "I feel it now. I will not be able to sleep well under the Sister Orb, I fear."

Quoran gave her a sly grin. "I could offer some more Japon root."

Maeya rolled her eyes and he laughed. It felt good to once again be treated as an equal.

There was a sudden cry and a loud laugh from the other side of the camp. They turned and watched Darvo shaking his hand, spots of blood evident.

Daegny drifted away from the fire, but stopped well away from Tare Igny and her brother. She sat on a large rock, drew up her knees, and rested her chin upon them, watching her twin go where she could not.

"Even as newborns they can be quick," Quoran murmured. His

eyes held pain.

Maeya put her hand on his arm. "I'm sorry, Quoran. This must be painful for you."

He shrugged and shook his head. "Tare Terce made sure that Veet knew what he was doing. He didn't let me near Pharla for almost a day." He smiled sadly and continued, "Veet had that same awed-yet-wistful look that Darvo has now. I imagine that is how they will look when they hold their own babes for the first time as well." He coughed. "That's how Darvo will look, at least."

Sorrow filtered through Maeya's head. Pharla was remembering, too.

"I did not get to see Pharla till she was a day old," Maeya said softly. "I came to see her as soon as I could."

Maeya felt Pharla trying to remember that, but she could not.

He looked up at her. "It brings back sorrow for us both."

"Aye."

"But where there is sorrow, greater happiness may be felt later," Quoran said a few moments later.

Maeya cocked an eyebrow at him. "If the Power That Is grants happiness after the sorrow."

"There is always happiness that follows sorrow, and sorrow that follows happiness. 'Tis the way the Power works." He put a pinch of herbs into a pan, followed by the nuts that Daegny had found. "I have much happiness in being your page," he said. "The Tares and other Riders were good, but they were always distant. You…" he trailed off, unsure how to finish.

"I was a page first," Maeya told him, "And now I am your friend who just happens to be a Rider."

He smiled, a true smile, and she knew that he was happier to have her as his friend than he was to be her page.

The meal was soon ready, and Quoran and Maeya dished out three plates. They knew better than to disturb the Tare and Darvo. When they were ready to eat, they would ask for food. Quoran went to Daegny, and helped her rise from her seat. She looked back over her shoulder several times as she approached the fire, and when she sat again, she sat facing Darvo.

Daegny was quiet as Quoran and Maeya joked through the meal. She did not eat much, but neither Quoran nor Maeya called her on it. At least she ate some.

Finally, when Quoran and Maeya had just finished washing their dishes, Darvo and Tare Igny came to the fire. Darvo strode past his sister as if he didn't see her, and came straight to Maeya.

"Did you see?" he asked, taking both her hands in his. "Isn't it glorious?"

"Aye," she said, smiling. "The Power That Is granted your wish."

His smile faltered just a little. "How did you know that was my wish?"

"I have eyes," Maeya said, trying to release her hands from his grip, "I saw how you looked at the egg."

Tare Igny cleared his throat behind Darvo. "It is most important the hatchling get to the Cave and begin bonding with the other Dragons, so it will not be mistaken for an enemy. With the loss of Eagle Cave and Meadow Speare Cave," he shrugged and missed Quoran's involuntary start, "Perhaps a Kollarian Clan Cave such as River Reed Cave will take us in. Once we reach a Cave, you won't see much of Darvo for a while. His duties as a Rider will be onerous."

"But he can choose a page," Daegny said suddenly. "A page to do his honor, a page who will spend time with him."

"Aye," Tare Igny said, chewing on a tough piece of jerky. "He has the right to give his honor to a page, but it would be best if he choose one from the Cave. One who knows the Cave and can help him with the rules."

"But he gets to choose," Daegny pressed. "It is his decision."

"Aye," the Tare began, but Daegny cut him off.

"Give me your honor," she said to Darvo, "We share blood; let us share the work of a Dragon Rider."

"That is not how a page works, Daegny," Quoran scolded. He sounded embarrassed that his pupil could know so little.

Tare Igny gave Quoran a strange look, but he spoke to Darvo. "If you feel you must choose one of your companions, it should be Quoran. We do not allow female pages or Riders."

Quoran threw his shoulders back and actually stared Tare Igny in the eye. "I serve my Rider's honor, and will never release it."

Tare Igny blinked. "You are indeed a well-trained page," he murmured, "But I do not see your Rider with you."

Maeya sighed and stood. "Tare Igny, I am Rider Maeya, late of the Spike Cave of Kollarian Clan. Our Cave did not survive the Wyzard's attack, and we are all that is left. If you are willing to accept our new hatchling and Rider to mentor, I ask that you take me as well."

And me!

Patience, Pharla, Maeya sent to her. *Not yet.*

Tare Igny sighed and rubbed his face. "Kollarian Clan was always so rebellious. I heard that they still allowed female Riders, but I did not wish to believe it. 'Tis much too dangerous to allow female Riders."

Maeya knew that the Kollarian Clan had only had three female Riders in the last generation, but she sensed that sharing that information would not help her case.

"I am sorry, Rider Maeya, truly I am," Tare Igny continued, "But I do not feel you will be accepted as a Tare at any Panir or Uture Cave."

You are a Rider! Indignation reverberated through her mind.

"Why didn't you have female Riders at Meadow Spear?" Maeya asked, cutting off what she sensed was going to be a scathing remark from Quoran.

"It is too dangerous," Tare Igny said simply. "Many of our best female Riders were driven insane by their Dragons."

"But the most powerful Rider of all Clans was Eleena!" Quoran burst out.

"Aye, there were a few early female Riders from times of Lore—Eleena and, of course, Lenzupra. But through the generations, the Clans learned the painful truth. It's true that female Riders who survive the first two full Sister Orbs with a hatchling often become the most gifted Riders, but the Uture council of the distant past decided that the risk was not worth the potential gain."

"The female Riders go insane?" Daegny asked, looking at Maeya.

"Aye. Or they just…die. As do their Dragons."

Darvo flinched.

No, Pharla whispered.

"But you said if they survive the first cycles of the Sister Orb—" Quoran prodded.

I have seen my third full Sister Orb! Pharla perked up.

Come to me, Maeya urged her. *Be quick but be quiet.*

"Aye. But it is rare." Tare Igny looked at Maeya with somber eyes. "As a Rider, I grieve for your loss, but you were probably lucky. You still live."

"We thrive together." Maeya raised her chin. "And we will continue to do so. Which Cave we call home matters little to me, so long as we are together."

Pharla stepped out of the trees. Maeya did not need to turn to see her; she felt Pharla's presence fill her more than she thought she could bear. Pharla stopped just behind Maeya. Lowering her head, she rested her chin lightly on Maeya's shoulder.

"Rider, your pardon," Tare Igny said hoarsely. "I did not realize your Dragon survived. Our reports said all at Spike Cave had perished."

"Your reports are faulty," Maeya said, reaching up to stroke Pharla's neck. "Perhaps you ought to check the source carefully."

"We did," he said, still watching Pharla with awe. "Rider Ret was most clear."

"Rider Ret?" Maeya repeated in disbelief.

"Aye. He came to our Cave immediately after the attack on Spike

Cave." Tare Igny appraised Pharla. "Of course, Teglin already has the strength of flight, and Pharla does not. Is she in her third Sister Orb?"

Maeya nodded, but she was distracted. "Rider Ret lives?"

"Aye," the Tare sighed deeply and studied the young Dragon and Rider. "Rider Ret was looking for something. He did not find it at Meadow Spear and left after two days. The Wyzards attacked three days after that, in the dark of the Sister Orb."

"Rider Ret had nothing to do with that," Maeya said sharply. Darvo stared at her.

"Nay, Rider, I did not mean to imply that," Tare Igny said quickly. "He was looking for...someone to fight with him. None of our Tares wanted to attack the Wyzards—"

"What about the Riders?"

"We didn't let him talk to them," Tare Igny said. "Ret left, looking for those who would fight a war with him, a war he plans to start."

"You don't think the Wyzards have already started it?" Darvo asked.

Tare Igny stared through Darvo. "We should push toward the Baza Clan."

"Where is the nearest Baza Cave?" Daegny asked.

"Where shall we go?" Quoran asked Maeya, but it was Tare Igny who answered.

"We will probably have to travel until the Sister Orb is full again," Tare Igny said, "But it would not be hard travelling."

"We shall try the Panir Clan," Maeya said promptly. "Camp Lythe is the closest Cave to us now."

"How many more days of travel will that take?"

Maeya shook her head. "I do not know. But it doesn't matter—we will travel until we find a Cave to join, whether it is Camp Lythe or beyond."

"Aye," Quoran agreed.

Tare Igny's mouth tightened. "Who is the leader here?"

Everyone stared at him.

"Do you challenge everything that the leader says?"

Quoran looked at Maeya and then back at the Tare. She could tell that he didn't know how to answer. He was a page, trained to listen to the Tares. But she was his Rider, and he had been following her.

Darvo and Daegny, however, didn't have that conflict.

"Rider Maeya is our leader," Daegny said, giving Maeya a pleasant surprise.

"We follow our leader; we do not need another one," Darvo added.

Tare Igny arched an eyebrow at him. "Indeed?" he said, steel behind his soft tone.

Darvo inclined his head, the picture of courtesy. "Aye, Tare. While we welcome your company and would like to hear your suggestions, especially about my Dragon, it is Rider Maeya who we follow."

Quoran's eyes were huge and his mouth was clamped shut as if he were afraid of what it might say.

Tare Igny stared at Darvo, who calmly returned it.

And suddenly, Tare Igny seemed to deflate. "Aye, we will follow Rider Maeya, and perhaps the old Tare may occasionally be of use."

"I am sure you will be of great help," Maeya said, "We have learned to travel well together, but there is no doubt we have more to learn. We will travel to Camp Lythe, with your guidance. Do you have other peep to travel with us?"

"Nay," he said, a sad look crossing his face.

Daegny opened her mouth to say something, but Darvo shook his head. She tossed her head in return and stomped off toward the horses.

That seemed to be a signal, and Quoran and Darvo began to move away as well, heading for camp chores.

"Rider Maeya, may I have a word?" Tare Igny asked.

"Aye," she said, trying to keep suspicion from her tone. Had he given in easily with the plan of bullying her in private?

He will find you a tough target, Pharla thought, startling her. Maeya had not realized she had been following the group's discussion.

"You have earned respect and trust from your troupe," he said, "and you have successfully bonded with a Dragon, both unusual feats for a female."

He paused and Maeya nodded her head, simply because it seemed to be the thing to do.

"I want to assure you that I am willing to follow you as part of your troupe. I will not fight you for leadership."

Maeya blinked. "With thanks, Tare, that will make things easier."

"But I wish to be able to talk to you openly, and give you advice. It is my experience that if advice is given before it is needed, it is easier to heed. Trying to give advice during a battle is not nearly as effective as practicing for one, as an example."

"Aye," she said cautiously. "What advice do you feel I need now?"

"I do not know you, and that makes this hard to say, but it must be said."

Perhaps not, Pharla said. *Perhaps you ought to tell him not to make this any more difficult than it already is.*

But before Maeya could open her mouth, Tare Igny was talking again, in a low, rushed tone. "Not much information about female Riders was passed on in the Uture Clan. Most of the information about female Riders wasn't so much information as bad jokes that got told among the Tares." He cleared his throat. "Mating is a very complicated thing, for both peep and Dragons."

Had he told Maeya that Sister Orb was going to have three brothers next to her in the sky, he could not have surprised her more. "I do not need it explained," Maeya said to him in a rush. Her cheeks felt burned.

"Nay, but you need to know that your Dragon will affect your mate."

I will?

"How?"

He shrugged, clearly uncomfortable. "Again, we have not had a female Rider in Uture Clan for generations, so much of our knowledge has been lost. But I do know that there is…a correlation between the Dragon and Rider when either mates. As a result," he cleared his throat again, "It would be best if you do not choose a Rider for a mate. But if you do, choose one that has a mate for your Dragon."

"A male Rider who has a male Dragon," Maeya said slowly.

"Aye."

Can I choose the Dragon?

Maeya tried to fight the flush but could not as she stammered, "What if my Dragon chooses a mate first? Will I—will he—will we—"

"I do not know," he said, and Maeya could only assume her cheeks matched his for brightness. "In truth, I do not. But it is best to choose carefully. And wait," he added. "Wait till you are both…grown."

But I will be grown before you!

May the Power That Is grant me strength, Maeya groaned.

*** ******* ***

True to his word, Tare Igny did not try to take over their small troupe. They all got up and completed their chores, and the Tare's helping hands seemed everywhere, dousing the fire, loading the saddlebags, filling water skins. They were moving out of the camp before the Orb had begun to climb above the horizon.

Darvo and Maeya traveled together. They took turns riding Spiker, who was still the only mount to allow the Dragons close to him.

Even he was a little skittish that day, though, until he had the opportunity to meet Darvo's new Dragon. Once he saw that Pharla accepted the hatchling, he settled down.

Tare Igny and Quoran led the group, talking as they went. Quoran was soaking up every bit of information he could get from Tare Igny. He was a great page.

Daegny rode in the middle, leading the two packhorses by herself. When they set off, she was looking back over her shoulder at Maeya and Darvo every few moments. By the time they finished mid-day meal, however, she refused to look at Darvo at all. And when they resumed travels, she rode straight and stiff in her saddle, looking neither right nor left.

Maeya was fascinated with Darvo's Dragon. *You were that little,* she thought to Pharla.

Not any more, she thought smugly.

"What color do you think it will be?" Maeya asked Darvo.

He made a face at her. "It is green, of course."

Maeya shook her head. Gesturing but not getting too close to the hatchling, she said, "Look at the edges of its scales. They're lined with yellow."

"It's green."

She, Pharla thought to Maeya. *Please tell him the hatchling is a girl, not an it.*

Maeya cleared her throat. "Pharla wishes me to tell you that your Dragon is a girl."

"In truth?" Darvo looked delighted. "Tell her thanks. I did not like calling her an it."

Maeya grinned. "That is why she wanted you to know."

They traveled quickly, but not hard. They stopped for midday meals, and if they found a pleasing campsite before the Orb was quite down, they stopped. None of them, not even Pharla, felt the need to hurry.

We have a Cave of our own now.

Not quite, Maeya said.

Tare Igny, especially, seemed to enjoy traveling with purpose but no fear. He loved to talk. He told stories of Dragons and Riders past, of events at Meadow Spear Cave (their Awakening fest seemed no more than drunken revelry to Maeya, but he made it sound poetic in his lilting voice), and of the rare breeds of horses and cattle Meadow Spear had raised. But he didn't speak of the attack on Meadow Spear, or of the Wyzards.

No one else noticed that, or at least no one spoke of it. Quoran and Daegny listened with obvious delight to the Tare's stories. Darvo listened when he could pull his attention away from his little hatchling. She did not often want to be far from him, sometimes clinging to his tunic like an overgrown kitten.

Maeya found herself pulled in two directions. Pharla rarely slept close to the fire, and Maeya wished to be with her. Several times Maeya settled herself on a log or in a hollow just outside the firelight, listening but not joining the stories and discussions. When the others at last turned to their sleeping blankets, Maeya would slip quietly to the bush or hill where Pharla had curled up.

"Why are there four Clans?" Quoran asked the Tare as the Orb sank below the horizon.

Tare Igny grunted. "Because men disagree."

"Perhaps if female Riders hadn't been banned, that wouldn't be a problem," Daegny pointed out with false sweetness.

Tare Igny had already learned not to rise to her baiting. "That was part of it, of course. We must assume that originally there were as many female as male Riders—"

"Zuprenzle being the first Rider ever," Maeya added, earning a pained frown from Quoran.

"Lenzupra," he groaned. "Lenzupra! Rider Maeya, you must pay attention!"

"I do," she retorted, "But it's a great way to make sure you're listening!"

"I'm the one who asked! Of course I'm listening!"

"Are you both done?" Tare Igny asked mildly.

"Apologies, Tare," they said together and grinned.

"Our first Clan was never named, and there is much debate as to which one left or which one stayed, but the two oldest Clans of record are Kollarian and Panir. Each claims to have been the home of the great Eleena, which of course is not possible, but the Lore is unclear. She brought them together for a time, but then they split apart again. Then each of them split, and Baza came from the Panir Clan and the Uture from Kollarian."

"Clearly the Kollarian Clan is the original," Daegny said, "For they still allow female Riders."

"As far as I know, each Clan has had a female Rider at least once. But I did not think any of the Clans actively recruited females anymore, either."

Maeya squirmed uncomfortably. "Spike Cave did not actively recruit females," she admitted, "But they were the only Cave that did not turn us away."

Tare Igny grinned. "I thought as much."

"Maeya put up with much as a female page," Quoran said. "Many of our male pages quit for less harassment than she received."

"Aye, it takes a strong person to do what they have been told not to do," Tare Igny said mildly. Maeya was certain that had he been with a group of males, he would have added stupid to the description as well. "It also takes a strong person to survive the loss of a Dragon, which is why we honor Tares."

"And Cyrs," Quoran added.

"Cyrs?" Tare Igny asked.

Quoran's face reflected the surprise Maeya was feeling. "Does Uture not have Cyrs? Riders-in-training who never flew with their Dragon?"

Tare Igny made a distasteful face. "Why would we honor them?"

"For all the training they went through. For the egg that didn't hatch."

"The egg did not hatch because the Rider-in-training was not worthy; that is hardly anything to celebrate."

"The Dragon inside the egg died before hatching," Quoran said.

Tare Igny sat up. "What did Clan Kollarian do with unhatched eggs? By the Power That Is, please do not tell me the eggs were destroyed!"

"We....I...I do not know what was done with eggs that did not hatch for Riders-in-training. But I do know Cyrs were wise, and had earned respect."

Igny snorted but said nothing else.

"Cyr Sajen was very wise," Quoran insisted, his voice rising sharply. "He was Lore Keeper of Spike Cave."

"Lore Keepers are respected at all Caves," Tare Igny said, "Though Uture Lore Keepers are not failed Riders-in-training."

"Cyr Sajen was not a failure!"

"He was lacking something the Dragon needed," Tare Igny said.

"But—"

"Perhaps each egg seeks something specific," Maeya suggested, "So it is not as much a failure of a Rider-in-training as much as a missing quality...a mismatch of Rider-in-training with the wrong egg."

"Perhaps," Tare Igny said grudgingly.

"So the four Clans are Baza, Kollarian, Panir, and Uture?" Darvo asked, steering the conversation back.

"Aye."

"How many Caves does each Clan have?"

Tare Igny looked troubled. "I do not know. Uture used to have five: Meadow Spear, Awakening, Eagle, Training, and Trident Caves. But after the recent attacks—" He shrugged. "I do not know who is left."

"Why now?" Maeya asked. "Why are the Wyzards attacking *now*?"

"What do you mean?" Darvo asked when Tare Igny merely shook his head and stared at the fire.

"The Clans have been split for generations," Maeya said, "And we have quarreled with each other more than with the Wyzards. Yet suddenly, the Wyzards are attacking. And they're attacking all the

Clans, not just one that is close or infringing upon their land."

"Maeya, do you remember the Lore that I told you of Eleena?" Quoran asked.

"Aye."

"Do you really remember it? Or is it as silly as Zenplura to you?"

"Lenzupra," Maeya said firmly.

Quoran smiled, but it was a sad smile. "Tare Igny says the pitch Dragon has hatched."

"How do you know?"

Tare Igny said, "Rider Ret left Meadow Spear when the messengers came from Clan Panir, telling us the Prophecy was true."

"O." That was all Maeya could say. Suddenly her mind was full of confusion, fear, resentment, anger, relief, and anticipation—and none of it was her own.

"Who?" Darvo asked.

Maeya stood. She swayed for a moment, but no one noticed. "I need to go...to go check on my Dragon."

Daegny demanded, "Who hatched?"

"Tell them Eleena's Lore, Quoran," Maeya said as she turned to leave the fire. "They both need to know."

Maeya stumbled twice on her way back to Pharla, and virtually collapsed on top of her Dragon instead of by her side. It was a measure of Pharla's state of mind that she did not snap at her.

Nearby, a wolf howled, and Maeya found a measure of reassurance.

"Why do you fear the pitch Dragon?"

Things are teetering. And Pharla would say no more.

CHAPTER ELEVEN

Maeya woke with a headache, but resolved not to say anything. A minor headache seemed a small price to pay for the joy of being a Rider.

The hole from the destroyed egg was gone, for Pharla had opened up and filled Maeya's heart. She was a constant voice in Maeya's head, sharing observations of the land they traveled through and the beings they traveled with. While Pharla still thought of Tare Igny with a coating of distrust, she seemed genuinely fond of Quoran and Darvo now, and more accepting of Daegny than Maeya herself was. The horses meant nothing to Pharla, with the exception of Spiker, who had gone from being tolerant of the Dragons to actively seeking them out. Though they would hobble him with the other horses when then made camp, come morning he would invariably be found closer to where Pharla and Maeya had bed down.

The only one in their group that Pharla did not volunteer opinions about was Darvo's hatchling.

"Is she progressing as you did?" Maeya asked Pharla the fourth morning they were breaking camp.

Aye. She has bonded well with her Rider.

"Aye," Maeya said dryly. Darvo's Dragon had spent so much time crawling about his chest and shoulders that both of his shirts had multiple holes and tears in them. "Can you speak with other Dragons?"

She is young. It will take time, Pharla answered, but there was a sense of concern and unease.

"But when we get to a Cave, you will be able to speak with the other Dragons?"

"Aye," Tare Igny said from behind Maeya, causing her to jump. "When she's older, she'll be able to speak to both you and other Dragons. The Dragons speak to each other just as we do. It is helpful, especially during battle, for them to relay information to their Riders that can then be passed to everyone else. By the time awakening season comes again, perhaps even sooner, your Dragon will begin communicating with you, first through images than through words. The first time you hear your Dragon's name...." He sat down on a log and smiled, clearly enjoying a memory. "'Tis a marvelous thing."

Maeya took a deep breath. Though she had asked the rest of their small troupe to keep Pharla's secret, she realized now that there was little harm in telling Tare Igny, and that perhaps there was great harm in keeping it.

"Tare Igny, does it always take so long for a Dragon to begin speaking to their Rider?"

Maeya did not look at Pharla, but she could tell that the Dragon had just rolled her eyes.

"All young take a while to speak, Maeya," he said in a very condescending tone. "We do not expect babes to start speaking after birth; why should Dragons be any different?"

"And a full set of seasons passed before your Dragon told you its name?"

"We were through our second growing season before Palth told me his name, aye."

"I would have had a hard time waiting that long to know Pharla's name," Maeya said.

Tare Igny stared at her for a few moments. "Whose name?"

"Pharla," Maeya said. "And I feel certain she would have been insulted if I had just called her Dragon or hatchling."

My Rider knows me well.

"You do not get to name your Dragon, Rider Maeya."

"I did not, Tare Igny. She told me her name on the same day she told me to leave her to die."

Maeya found it difficult to ignore the remorse that Pharla suddenly felt. *I'm glad that you're such a wise Rider.*

More stubborn than wise.

Aye, but wise to know when to be stubborn.

That almost sounds like a compliment, Maeya grinned.

Pharla raised her head and stared at Maeya, giving her one slow blink.

"Rider Maeya, I think you are confused. That is to say, I think you want to hear your Dragon so much that perhaps you are making it up."

Maeya glared at him. "I most certainly am not!"

"Maeya—"

"I can prove it. What would you like me to ask her?"

"Maeya—"

"I can have her leave," Maeya said. Pharla stood immediately.

"No—" Igny said, though he was staring at Pharla with big eyes.

Nay, Pharla said, walking directly to the Tare. *Tell him I will bite him the next time he calls you a liar!*

"Pharla!" Maeya said sharply as Pharla snarled in Tare Igny's face.

"He did not call me a liar."

Yes he did!

"Nay," Tare Igny said quickly, "I merely thought you might be imagining or dreaming what you want to hear."

"Pharla," Maeya said again, "Leave Tare Igny. It will be hard enough to be accepted into a Cave if you haven't attacked a Tare. If you bite him, I do not think any Cave will take us."

Pharla lowered her head so she was eye to eye with Tare Igny. *Make him take it back.*

"He did not mean it as an insult. There is no need for an apology."

"Apologies, Pharla," Tare Igny said immediately. "Truly I meant no disrespect. But I have never heard of a hatc—such a young Dragon speaking to their Rider."

I am not the one he called a liar!

"Pharla," Maeya said in exasperation. "He didn't call either of us liars! He was making sure that—"

"Apologies, Rider Maeya, for not immediately believing what you said," Tare Igny whispered.

Pharla snorted in the Tare's face, and then walked back over to Maeya. She lowered her head again and stared into Maeya's eyes. *We have already done too much together to be disrespected.*

Maeya reached up and put her hands around the back of Pharla's neck and pulled her forward, so their foreheads were touching. Going around bullying Tares will earn us nothing but disrespect, she thought sternly. The Tare did not know. Things are changing. Things are teetering, remember?

Aye, Pharla said, closing her eyes and leaning into Maeya. *I forgot, but you remembered.*

We must both remember, Maeya thought to her. Always.

*** ******** ***

They broke camp, and Maeya tried not to laugh when Tare Igny decided to ride ahead as a scout.

"It will make me feel better to know we're not going to ride into a Faithful camp without knowing it," he said.

It would also keep the most distance between him and Pharla.

"How much longer do you think we will have to travel?" Darvo asked as he swung up on Spiker.

"At least a few more passes of the Orb," Tare Igny called over his shoulder. "Once we get to the town of Sundee, we will be three days out."

"Sundee?" Quoran asked.

"That's what he said," Daegny answered since Tare Igny was out of earshot. She looked up and Maeya followed her gaze. Two owls were flying away.

"Sundee is pledged to the Panir Clan," Quoran muttered.

"Aye, and we're going to Camp Lythe, which is a Panir Camp," Maeya said. "All will be well."

Quoran looked troubled.

"All will be well," Maeya repeated.

"Rider, Clan Panir has many different traditions and beliefs. It may not be easy to join their ways."

"It may not be easy, Quoran, but we will do what needs to be done."

"What if they are like Uture, and will not take a female Rider? What if they ask you to give Pharla up?"

They could never ask that!

Maeya knew they could. "I will say no."

"But what if—"

"If we can not join them, then we will move on. We will find a place, Quoran. Together."

He is a wise page, to be cautious.

Aye, Maeya thought. He is a better page than I deserve.

***   ********   ***

They traveled with purpose, though Maeya knew Quoran was tired. In truth, she was, too. She had felt the sharp pain of losing everyone at Spike Cave and the Daceae estate; now she felt the wearing pain of not having a home, not having a bed to call her own. They did not travel hard, but they traveled far, and that was not easy.

Tare Igny was waiting for them when the Orb reached its zenith, and they sat together to share dried venison, fresh razenberries, and tea. Quoran offered to ride ahead, and Maeya was surprised when Igny agreed.

Quoran set off on Lark.

"Your turn, Maeya," Darvo said, leading Spiker to her.

Maeya smiled weakly. "My legs and feet agree; my backside, however, would rather I keep walking."

"Perhaps we should take a longer rest," Darvo said. "We do not have to travel every day, do we?"

Maeya expected Pharla to criticize Darvo for being lazy or insist that they keep moving, but Pharla didn't say anything. Maeya glanced over to where she was curled up next to a tree. Pharla was watching Maeya but still stayed quiet.

"There isn't a need to hurry," Tare Igny answered, "However it would be better for both Dragons to get them to a Cave."

"Why?" Darvo asked the question for Maeya, and though Pharla made no comment, she could sense her interest, too.

"Like most creatures, Dragons are social. They need to learn their social behaviors early."

Maeya felt Pharla lose interest. *I know how to behave.*

You threatened a Tare.

But I didn't hurt him. And I haven't hurt anyone else, either.

Don't you want to be around other Dragons? Maeya asked her.

But Pharla was in a quiet mood.

"Riders?" Daegny called. "Are we moving on?"

Both Tare Igny and Darvo looked to Maeya. And it was tempting to say nay, tempting to say let's make camp for a day or two, but Maeya knew it would be the wrong decision.

"Aye," she called back. She swung herself up on Spiker's back. Ready Pharla? She thought.

Aye, and Maeya realized that Pharla was already moving and was almost next to Daegny. Unfortunately, Daegny's mount realized that Pharla was there a split second before Daegny did. Storm reared, throwing Daegny to the ground, and then bolted.

O, Pharla thought, *by the Power That Is, I did not mean to—*

I know, Maeya sighed. But perhaps there are some things about social behavior that you still need to work on.

Darvo hurried toward his sister. Maeya was stroking Spiker's neck, assuring him that he was the best horse they had, when suddenly Daegny's mount came charging back to them. Quoran and Lark were hard on its heels.

"Get down!" Tare Igny wheeled his horse over to Maeya's side, and pulled her off Spiker. They landed in a tangle on the ground, but before Maeya could do much more than gasp, Igny had pulled her up again and was half-dragging, half-carrying her to a large boulder.

Pharla? Maeya called in her mind.

Hiding.

"What—"

Before Maeya could finish her question, three men on horseback came thundering into the clearing. There was a terrifying flash of blue, and Maeya felt a scream in the back of her head that dropped her to her knees.

Tare Igny was on his knees beside her, but he was notching an arrow in his bow and taking aim. He loosed two arrows in rapid succession and then paused with a third arrow, surveying the scene.

One of the horsemen was on the ground, almost directly in front of Maeya, one arrow protruding through his neck. The second man was also on the ground, but his foot had caught in the stirrup, and his mount was dragging him back the way they had come. He yelled, but as Maeya watched, his head bounced hard on a rock, and the only sound after was that of the horse's hooves.

Maeya heard a scream, this time with her ears, from the other side of the clearing. She felt certain that it must be Daegny.

As she looked, though, her view was blocked by the third horseman. He wore a shiny covering such as she had never seen, stiff and bright, and when Igny loosed his third arrow, it merely bounced off the man's chest with a strange thunking sound. The man turned toward their boulder, and as Maeya dropped behind it again, she caught sight of the strange stick he held, caught sight of the blue light that came arcing out of it.

The blue light was blinding over her head; the tree branches beyond her burst into flame. Tare Igny was kneeling beside her, another arrow notched. She did not see any more in the quiver on his back. Suddenly she realized how truly foolish they all had been, travelling so openly without guards or even weapons.

"Maeya," Tare Igny rasped, "I am going to run. Hopefully, he will follow me. Get Darvo and the Dragons and go. Find a place to hide if you must, but get the Dragons to a Cave. Protect them and protect yourselves."

"Nay! We stay and fight together!" Maeya looked at the small hunting knife in her hand. Darvo had leant it to her at their last camp and she had forgotten to return it to him. It was the closest thing to a weapon that she had.

"Rider M—O, Quan dung!" Maeya looked up sharply at Tare Igny's sudden moan.

Loping toward them were two huge wolves.

Maeya pushed back against the boulder, bracing for the attack. But at the last possible moment, one of the wolves swerved to the right of the boulder, and the other one leapt over it. Maeya spun in time to see the wolves attack the Wyzard.

Neither wolf could get a grip on the horseman's shiny clothing, but both kept jumping up at him, snapping and growling. The horse was jumping and prancing, trying to bolt away from the wolves, but the rider had such a powerful grip on the reins that the horse's head was bowed down. With his other hand, the Wyzard flailed about with his strange stick, but nothing seemed to happen.

Then one of the wolves wrenched itself around in the middle of a lunge, and instead of going for the Wyzard's face or chest, went for the hand holding the stick. The powerful jaws clamped down, and the horseman yelled in pain. He dropped the reins, pulled a dagger from his waist, and then buried the dagger in the wolf's side.

The wolf yelped and dropped to the ground. The horse, freed from the iron hold, took hold of the bit and ran full-tilt from the clearing. Its rider clung to the saddle, bouncing awkwardly. The second wolf was hot on the horse's heels.

Pharla? Maeya asked.

I am well.

Where are you?

Safe.

"Quoran! Maeya? Tare Igny? Where are you?"

"Here," she said, as she and Tare Igny emerged from either side of the boulder.

"Help him! Please help him!" Daegny was sitting up, cradling Darvo's head. It had all happened so fast that neither Hoart had had time to get out of the way. Darvo had merely protected his twin and his hatchling by covering them with his own body. The hatchling was sitting on Darvo's chest, making strange mewling noises.

"What happened?" Tare Igny asked. "Did one of the Faithful stab him?"

"Nay. I think he got kicked," Daegny said.

"Kicked?"

"Aye, by one of the horses."

Tare Igny's fingers began gently exploring Darvo's scalp. "Maeya, where is Quoran?"

Maeya looked up to find Daegny's troubled grey eyes piercing her own. "I have not seen him since Lark—"

We need him!

"I will go find him," Maeya said.

"Do you think the Faithful—"

"I will find him, Daegny."

We need Quoran.

Do you know where he is? Maeya asked. All she got in response was an image of Lark running while Quoran clung desperately to her saddle.

She stood, dusted her knees off, and turned to go seek her page. A whimper stopped her.

The wolf had fallen and had not gotten up, but had it not died. Blood was soaking the ground around it, and its breathing was labored, but it looked at Maeya with clear eyes. Maeya approached it slowly, waiting for it to snarl or growl at her. She had learned at a young age to be cautious of wounded animals. Often times it was the dying beast that was the most deadly.

Rider—Maeya glanced to her left and saw Pharla emerging from under some low-spread Gyphanna branches. *Is this why they travel with us? To protect us? Why?*

But Maeya had no answer.

Maeya drew to within a pace of the wolf and she dropped to her knees again. The wolf lifted its head slightly, but still did not show any aggression. It was holding something in its jaws. Behind her, Maeya could hear Tare Igny and Daegny speaking, but she could not make out the words.

Slowly, Maeya reached out her hand and placed it on the wolf's neck. The wolf whined and lay its head down. She moved her hand slowly up towards the wolf's face, the thick bushy fur sliding smoothly beneath her skin. Maeya swallowed hard, and moved her hand directly to the wolf's mouth, grasping the stick it held.

Careful, Pharla's warning breezed through her mind.

The wolf released the stick. Slowly Maeya began to pull her hand away. The wolf turned its head sharply toward her hand. It opened those powerful jaws once more—and licked her hand. Then it lay its head back down and expelled its last breath. Unexpected tears burned in Maeya's eyes.

She turned the stick over in her hands, and realized that stick was a poor term. It was polished smooth, intricately carved with multiple designs running the entire length, and about as long as Maeya's forearm. It was as big as her thumb at its thickest, and tapered to the size of her little finger.

Gingerly, Maeya gave the stick a little wave, what she thought she had seen the Wyzard doing with it. Nothing happened. She waved it a little harder, and heard a snap! Turning it over in her hands, she discovered a crack about a third of the way down the stick.

The clopping of horse hooves caused Maeya to raise her head, hoping to see Quoran and Lark. Instead, Spiker stood in front of her. He lowered his head and bumped her shoulder with his muzzle.

Maeya pushed herself upright and tucked the stick in his saddle bag. "Want to help me find our friends?"

He rumbled deep in his chest and she smiled. As she swung herself up on Spiker, Daegny was standing up.

"Why are you still here?" Daegny demanded, hands on her hips. "You're supposed to be looking for Quoran!"

"Aye," Maeya said, picking up the reins even though Spiker was already turning and walking away.

"We need Japon roots for Darvo," Daegny called after her. "Make haste!"

Maeya pulled up and turned in her saddle, intending to scold

Daegny for making so much noise, but Tare Igny had grabbed her arm and drawn Daegny back down next to him and Darvo.

Trusting the Tare to impress upon Daegny the importance of caution and stealth, Maeya turned back in her saddle, and let Spiker have his head. Though he did not break into a trot, Spiker moved at more than his usual plodding pace, and Maeya was certain he was taking her to Quoran. Still, she kept her eyes and ears open. The Faithful had left, but that did not mean they would not return.

Spiker did not take her far. She saw Lark first, in her usual wild-eyed stance pulling against the reins, trying to get away. Her reins were wrapped around one of Quoran's wrists, and his dead weight was all that was keeping her there.

"Quoran!"

He did not move or respond in any way.

Sliding off Spiker, Maeya hurried over to Quoran. He was slumped against a log. She intended to unwrap the rein, but when she saw that it was actually cutting into his flesh, she whipped out Darvo's hunting knife, and sliced Lark free.

The horse stumbled from her unexpected release, and she fell awkwardly on her hind end. She scrambled up quickly though, and turned to run. Spiker moved directly in front of her. When she turned to move around him, he blocked her with his body again. Spiker nickered to her, and Lark seemed to quit.

Maeya put her hand under Quoran's chin and lifted his head. His face was pale, but not bloody. She could not see any blood on him, other than his left wrist. Carefully, she imitated Tare Igny, and ran her fingers through his hair. She didn't find any blood or lumps.

She patted his cheek. "Quoran? Quoran!"

His eyes fluttered.

"O, thank the Power That Is," Maeya breathed. "You're all right."

"Am I?" Quoran lifted his hand. "I'm not certain my head should still be attached."

"Do you think you can get on Lark?" Maeya asked.

"I probably can," he said, "But I really do not wish to. She has a head of her own and a frightening tendency to bolt at the least cause."

"I would not push you, but I will feel better when we are all together again. Tare Igny can see to your wrist then."

Quoran looked at his hand and blinked in surprise at the leather strap embedded in his skin. "O." His face lost what little color it had regained.

"Steady, Quoran, steady. I want to move, but only if you can do so without falling down again."

"Aye," Quoran said, using the log as leverage to stand up. "But I did not fall. I was thrown." He took a tentative step toward Lark. She immediately tossed her head and took a few steps.

"Why don't you take Spiker?" Maeya suggested, feeling a twinge when the horse pricked his ears forward at the sound of his name. "I will take Lark."

"Aye, Rider." Quoran reached for the saddle and swayed.

Maeya put a hand out to steady him. "Are you sure?"

Quoran grunted as he swung himself up on Spiker. The only reason he didn't pitch headlong over the other side was Maeya's firm grip on his ankle. "Aye," he said as he straightened himself, "I believe I will feel better when we are together some distance from here."

CHAPTER TWELVE

Maeya was relieved to find their other four horses waiting with Tare Igny and the Hoarts. Daegny took her to task for not stopping for the Japon root, but the ever-prepared Quoran had some in his bedroll. While Tare Igny tended to Darvo, Maeya tried to assist Quoran, and Daegny flitted between both pairs.

Quoran reassured Maeya that she had done the right thing by leaving the rein wrapped around his wrist. He gave her step-by-step instructions on how to mash a bit of dried Trident blossom into a paste with the Gyphanna leaves.

"Shouldn't we soak your arm in the creek?" she asked.

"This will help numb my skin," he said through gritted teeth. "It hurts enough as 'tis without being yanked back out."

Listen to the page, Pharla advised.

Maeya bit her lip and tried not to think about the fact that she, too, had been a page and was not completely worthless, and that, as a Rider, some of her opinions ought to carry weight as well.

Of course, Pharla soothed, *but Quoran knows his herbs and healing.*

And Lore.

Aye.

And how to talk to Tares.

Aye.

And pretty much everything else.

Pharla snorted and the conversation ended.

After Quoran's arm was free of the rein and wrapped in large soft maple leaves, they both turned to help Darvo. Tare Igny had stopped the bleeding, but Darvo still had not woken. Darvo's hatchling continued to mewl on his chest.

When Maeya sat down at Darvo's side, Pharla got up and walked over, curling up behind her. Maeya reached towards the hatchling, but she immediately hissed, and dug her talons further into Darvo's shirt and, Maeya feared, the flesh below it.

You are not her Rider.

She is not helping her Rider sitting there, Maeya thought to Pharla. Indeed, I believe she is causing more harm. Can you speak to her?

I will try again. Maeya sensed a shifting in the pressure that she recognized as Pharla's presence in her mind.

The hatchling closed her mouth and turned to look at Pharla. She cocked her head. Tare Igny moved Darvo's arm, causing his shirt to shift across his chest. The hatchling snapped at the Tare.

Maeya sensed growing frustration from Pharla. Tell her we all want to help, Maeya thought. Tell her we're all upset that he's hurt.

I'm trying!

"I know, I'm sorry," Maeya said.

"'Twas not your fault, Rider," Tare said absently. "We were all foolish to think that just because we were not in a Cave we would not be targeted by the Wyzards."

Maeya did not bother to respond; she was watching the hatchling climb awkwardly off Darvo's chest and crawl to Pharla. Pharla shifted slightly, and the hatchling climbed up her leg, and nestled there. In spite of Darvo's insistence that his Dragon was green, Maeya was once again struck by how pale—nearly yellow—his hatchling's scales were.

"Thank you, Pharla," Tare Igny said, "Now let's move him to the base of that tree."

Quoran moved to take Darvo's feet. Daegny shoved him out of the way. "You're hurt," she said.

Maeya steadied Quoran. "If you weren't before," she muttered under her breath, earning a weak grin from Quoran.

Tare Igny and Daegny carried Darvo to the tree. Maeya and Quoran gathered the horses, and tied them off by some bushes. Pharla and the hatchling stayed where they were. That made Maeya nervous, for they were in the path that the Faithful had used.

Could you move back to your bush? Maeya asked Pharla.

She fell asleep.

But—

She is young and terrified and asleep. I do not think waking her is a good thing.

Maeya turned to Tare Igny. Quoran had gone to sit on a nearby fallen tree, and Daegny followed him.

"Should we not move?" Maeya asked the Tare. "What if the Faithful come back?"

The Tare shrugged. "If they come back, chances are they will not be expecting to find us here. They would expect us to move away from the scene of the attack. Perhaps hiding in plain sight is our best option."

"But—"

"We are out of sight of the traveling road," the Tare continued, "And we will keep watch. They will not catch us by surprise again."

"Besides," Daegny said from Maeya's shoulder, making her jump, "we do not have any means to fight. We are better off staying here. They probably think that they killed—" she swallowed hard "—killed a few of us."

Rest Rider, Pharla said. *You will need it. I will get the hatchling to move soon, but for now we all need to rest.*

***   ********   ***

They stayed there that night, though none of them truly slept. Darvo, though he didn't wake, thrashed and muttered a lot. Quoran finally gave in to the shock and the pain, and sobbed for a while. Daegny held him, offering him the comfort her twin could not take.

Eventually, when Quoran had calmed down, he and the Tare spent much time conferring about how to best treat Darvo's injury.

"We need more Japon root," Tare Igny said.

"Aye," Quoran agreed, "But I have not seen any Japon bushes since we left Tiburn." At Igny's inquisitive look, he added, "I knew my supply was running low and have been watching for it. I need more hazelwood, as well, and would prefer to find some sweet onion bulbs, but where I will find those before the end of growing season, I do not know."

"We need an apothecary," Tare Igny said.

"Sundee is ahead of us, aye?" Maeya asked.

"Aye. Though I do not know how far. Nor do I know how we could pay for the supplies we ought to have."

Quoran shot a nervous look at Maeya.

"Let us get to Sundee and then we will determine what we can afford and what will we have to do without," she said to the Tare.

"You have money?"

"Some."

If Tare Igny was bothered by her vague answer, he did not show it. "You and Quoran will go to Sundee and bring back the necessary herbs and treatments."

"But that will waste much time!"

"Darvo is not ready to travel, Maeya."

"We will take him to Sundee," Maeya insisted. "We will carry Darvo if we must."

"I can rig a travois," Quoran said.

"I will help," Daegny added, "and I will walk next to my brother. We will bring him to Sundee."

"It is not wise to rush—" Tare Igny began, but he stopped when Maeya looked at him. "Aye, we will take Darvo to Sundee. We will get him the attention he needs."

She nodded toward Quoran. "Darvo is not the only one who needs attention, Tare. Have you seen to Quoran's wound?"

Quoran submitted to the Tare's inspection, and to his credit did not smirk too much at Maeya when the Tare pronounced the wrist to have been well tended.

Quoran left Darvo with Tare Igny long enough to put together a small meal for them. Maeya did not want to venture far from the camp, so she did not seek more than the three squirrels she was able to fell with the bolo.

Pharla was lying with her legs tucked under her, watching over Darvo and his hatchling.

"Will these do?" Maeya asked Pharla.

Aye, Pharla said with a trace of amusement as the hatchling slid off Darvo's chest and hurried to the squirrel. Without hesitation, the hatchling began tearing into the nearest carcass.

"Are you sure?" The hatchling was already moving on to the next squirrel, though she had not finished all of the first one.

I am not hungry today.

"Are you well?"

Aye, Pharla shifted slightly, rolling to her side and curling her tail around her. *I am simply tired. And not hungry.*

Maeya could understand both feelings, but still—You must keep your strength up, she said. We may not always be able to hunt.

Aye, Rider, Pharla said almost meekly. She grabbed the last squirrel by the tail, tossed her head to fling it up in the air, and swallowed it whole.

Maeya moved over to the wolf. She could not bring herself to skin it, or to offer it to the Dragons.

We do not wish to eat our allies.

I do not wish to leave it lying here, either, Maeya thought to Pharla.

A burial?

"Aye," Maeya answered out loud and she set to work. At first no one noticed what she was doing; they were too wrapped up in caring for Darvo and discussing best way to make the travois. But as she was dragging the wolf's body to the grave, she caught Quoran's quizzical look. Then he simply nodded and went back to talking to Daegny. And as she began scooping the dirt back into the grave, Tare Igny came over.

"Would you like some assistance, Rider?"

"Nay," Maeya said, for it felt right to be the one burying the wolf.

"I have never seen wolves behave that way," the Tare said thoughtfully. "What drove them to attack the Faithful?"

"Perhaps they were protecting the Dragon," Maeya suggested.

We hardly need protection, Pharla thought.

We certainly did, Maeya retorted.

Pharla grumbled in her mind.

Tare Igny shrugged, "Either amounts to the other, I suppose, and both are strange. After all, Clans have never kept dogs in the Cave."

"We had two at our Cave," Maeya said. "One was a very old dog who belonged to our Healer, the other was a young pup a new page brought with him at the beginning of awakening season."

"'Tis so odd, how the Clans have changed from each other," the Tare mused. "For in Uture Clan, none of the Clans allowed dogs. And no one ever argued."

"Why not?" Maeya remembered longing for a puppy as a child.

"The dogs of Wysleck, of course," Tare Igny said. "Shortly after Eleena became Leader, Wysleck asked for a meeting. They worked out a 'truce,' and as a peace offering, Wysleck gave her three puppies, puppies that grew into dogs and attacked the next clutch of hatchlings and killed them all."

No dogs, Pharla said firmly. *No dogs allowed at the Cave.*

He turned and began walking back to Darvo. "These wolves never looked at our Dragons, though. Or at us."

I rather like having the wolves around, Maeya thought to Pharla. I wish this one had not died.

Aye, Pharla agreed, but she sounded troubled. *And I wish we knew where the others had gone.*

Maeya put the last bit of dirt on the grave and packed it down. Thank you, she thought. Thank you for helping us.

She stood and saw an owl taking wing. Impulsively, she swung her bolo and dropped the owl. She walked over to the others, feeling better for some reason.

"I will take first guard duty," Maeya said and no one argued. But she did not seek relief as Sister Orb traveled the dark sky. Daegny and Quoran stayed up late, building a travois. The Tare was in continual motion caring for Darvo.

When the Orb rose, none of them were well rested, but all were ready to move on. Darvo was strapped into the travois, and though they originally intended to have Lark pull him, they quickly realized their mistake: with the hatchling clinging to Darvo's shirt, Lark was unwilling to get close to him. They harnessed Spiker instead.

"Maeya, why don't you ride Lark?"

"I'm fine."

Quoran frowned. "You're swaying on your feet. Did you sleep at all?"

"No more than you."

Tare Igny quirked an eyebrow. "I should hope not, since you were on guard."

Maeya felt herself flush. "My point was that none of us have slept."

"My point is that we may not have slept much, but the rest of us slept *some*. You did not. Up you go," Tare Igny bent down next to Lark and made ready to help her in the saddle.

"I will walk," she said.

"You are wasting time," Daegny snapped from her horse. "Get in the saddle!"

Please, Rider. I will stay with the group.

Startled, Maeya glanced at Pharla. Maeya hadn't realized that she had been worried about her, but Pharla was right. *Truly?* Maeya asked. *You will not falter or wander away?*

I will stay as close as Lark will let me, she said.

Maeya accepted Quoran's help into the saddle. "Daegny, keep an eye on Darvo. Let us know if we need to stop."

"Just go!"

They went, Lark and Maeya in the lead, Tare Igny, Quoran and the other horses in the middle, and Spiker pulling Darvo at the end. Maeya would have to trust that Daegny would be able to keep her mount calm enough to stay within view of her brother. Maeya could not see Pharla, but she could sense the Dragon, and knew she was close, and for now, that was enough.

*** ******** ***

Peep.

Where?

Close.

Have I already passed them?

Nay. I think it's the town.

Maeya sat up straighter in the stirrups, straining to see. And there, just barely in the distance, she could make out wisps of smoke. *Aye*, Maeya thought to Pharla. *Thank you. I'll find a good place to camp soon.*

Aye.

Are you well?

Tired. Pharla paused. *As we all are.*

How is Darvo's Dragon?

She paused so long Maeya wasn't sure Pharla was going to answer her. *She is exhausted. The fear has worn her out.*

We are safe now.

Her Rider is not.

But—

"Maeya! Hold!"

She pulled Lark to a stop and waited while Tare Igny caught up. "Sundee will be close."

"It's just there," she said, pointing to the smoke.

"Aye," he said, sounding relieved. "We will need—"

"To find a place to camp," she said. "And then we will discuss who will go into town."

"There is not much to discuss. Darvo must be taken in, to see a healer. Daegny will certainly not leave him. Quoran must go to replenish herbs. And you must go to make sure that he is not cheated."

"Why don't you do that?"

"It is not my money."

"I can give you—"

"It is better if I stay with the Dragons, Maeya," Tare Igny said firmly. "I will guard the camp and keep them safe. You will guide the twins and Quoran through the negotiations of Sundee."

"But—"

"Please, Rider," Tare interrupted, "I beg of you, do not give me money. Do not make me go into town." He wheeled his horse around and trotted back to the others before Maeya could say anything more.

When Maeya found a likely camp, Tare Igny managed to keep Daegny or Quoran between them, so she could not challenge him again. Quoran, of course, thought it only right that Maeya be the one going into town, and as Igny had said, Daegny was not about to leave her twin. Nor, it would seem, was Darvo's Dragon going to leave him.

Pharla, could you—? Maeya began.

I will not ask a Dragon to leave her Rider, Pharla said from under the bush she had claimed.

Igny foolishly tried to forcibly remove the small hatchling from Dravo's side, and it took several minutes to slow the bleeding.

"Good thing you're going to replenish your healer supplies," Igny said to Quoran.

Quoran frowned as he peered under the bloody cloth. "This should be stitched."

"Too bad we have no mead," Daegny said. "It would help with the sting."

"I will be fine," Igny said. "No stitches. How are we going to get the hatchling to move?"

Maeya knelt in front of the travois, putting her neck and face uncomfortably close to the sharp teeth and talons of the small but quick Dragon. "Please," she said, "We seek help for your Rider. We must take him to town, but we don't want to harm you." The hatchling cocked her head. Though her scales were a washed out yellow-green, her eyes were dark jade, alert and inquisitive. Maeya felt reassured that she was listening, and though she wasn't sure the hatchling could understand what she meant, Maeya pressed on. "We need you to stay here with Pharla and the Tare. We will return your Rider, hopefully in better shape than he is in now."

Truly, you will be safe with me, and my Rider will keep yours safe.

The hatchling blinked twice before nodding her head. Maeya held out her hand, but the small Dragon turned her back, and climbed up Darvo's shoulder. She nuzzled under his chin, and rested her cheek against his for a moment before stepping lightly off Darvo and jumping from the travois. She walked quickly toward Pharla, and curled up in the crook of her foreleg.

Thank you, Maeya thought to Pharla, *Though it would have been less painful for Igny if you had just started with that.*

I didn't realize that she was afraid, Pharla replied. *I thought she had just been showing loyalty to her Rider.*

"Let's go," Daegny said, already climbing back in the saddle. Quoran was also mounting, and Tare Igny was handing him Spiker's lead.

Be good, Maeya thought as she swung up into Lark's saddle.

Be careful, Pharla returned, lowering her head and closing her eyes. *The peep are restless and things are—*

—teetering, aye. Maeya sighed.

CHAPTER THIRTEEN

"And I thought Tiburn was an unfriendly place," Daegny muttered. She and Maeya were leading the way into Sundee, Quoran just behind them with Spiker placidly pulling Darvo's travois. Quoran had wrapped his face again, but even that did not explain the averted faces and hostile stares that they had been encountering since the outskirts of town. Twice they had asked for directions to the apothecary and been ignored. Once they had been spat at. Maybe the man had just been spitting, but he had seemed to spit in their general direction.

"Do you feel peep?"

Daegny rolled her eyes. "Only when I want to be slapped."

"I meant—"

"I know what you meant," she snapped. "I sense the anger in this town." She took a breath. "And fear," she added more quietly, "there is much fear." Daegny drew up, and waited while Quoran and Spiker passed her, then followed next to her twin.

Usually, the center of a town was where the bustle of activity was found, where all the bartering and loitering happened. Yet as they made their way to the center of town, peep seemed to evaporate. The dirt road was empty; not a horse, wagon, dog, or person in sight. The wooden buildings were coated with dust, and looked old and tired. Had they not passed so many peep on the outskirts of town, Maeya would have thought the town deserted. She began to despair of finding an herb seller, let alone an apothecary.

"Hssst!"

Startled, Maeya pulled too hard on Lark's reins. The temperamental mare reared, and had Maeya not already been anxiously gripping the saddle, she surely would have fallen.

A dark shadow emerged from an alley; at least that's what Maeya thought she saw.

"Seek ye aide?" a girl's voice asked.

"Aye," Quoran said. "We seek a heal—"

"Follow me quickly," the shadow said, disappearing back in the alley.

"How?" Maeya asked, but Quoran was already dismounting and tying his horse's reins to a post. "What are you doing?"

"Seeking aide," he said, while Daegny gracefully slid off her horse and tied it next to Quoran's mount. To Maeya's eyes, the alley was dark and empty.

"But we don't know—"

"It is the first friendly offer we've had," Daegny said, laying a hand on Darvo's forehead. He was quite pale.

"How are we going to—"

But Quoran was already leading Spiker and the travois into the alley.

Daegny shook her head disdainfully at Maeya. "You spend a lot of time in the back for a leader."

Maeya did not want to follow them; she did not want to enter the dark alley following blindly to an unknown destination, nor did she want to leave three valuable horses unattended. But if the shadow was leading them to an apothecary, or even an herbalist, Quoran would need money to get treatment for Darvo. And if the shadow was leading them to danger, Maeya needed to offer what little help and protection she could.

She pulled the ever-resisting Lark over to the post and tied her with the other horses, hoping that being left with familiar traveling companions would calm all three.

The alley was much cooler, and Maeya found herself wishing for a cloak. She ran quickly but quietly, keeping alert to her surroundings. She still did not trust the little shadow that had offered help. The voice had sounded friendly enough, but—

Abruptly, the alley open onto a bright courtyard, and Maeya stopped short. The dusty wooden buildings on either side were just as sad and tired looking as the rest of the town, but there was a lush garden with a fountain gurgling in the middle. Flowers in every color of the Storm Arc bloomed, and greens of every shade climbed trellises and windowsills. Directly opposite of the alley was a stone building painted bright white. The door was closed, and the small black shadow stood there, waiting.

Maeya waited uncertainly in the darkness of the alley. There was no sign of her friends or Spiker, but there was no other place that they could be.

The little shadow curved her arm up toward her in a "come here" gesture. Slowly Maeya took a step into the light. A white smile lit up the little girl's face, and Maeya couldn't help but smile in return. She hurried across the courtyard.

Just before Maeya reached her, the little girl slipped in through the door, though Maeya did not remember seeing her actually open it. Hesitant again, she gingerly pushed the door the rest of the way open.

An array of colors as bright and beautiful as the flowers met Maeya's eyes. Fabrics of every kind draped the walls and were piled on multiple tables. Pre-made dresses, tunics, trousers, and cloaks were stacked and, in a few cases, displayed on life-sized, headless dolls. Maeya had never been in a store that had such obvious wealth for the frivolous. The dresses and trousers were of fine material that could not possibly be worn while tending livestock or reaping crops. She felt sorely out of place and was grateful that the store appeared empty.

A jingling sound made her spin to the right. An enormous woman was coming through a doorway partially concealed by rows of cleverly hung bells. The woman was as black as the little girl Maeya had followed, and wearing a very unique dress.

The cut and style of the dress was unremarkable, other than enormous size. But the material was unlike anything Maeya had ever seen. A small red circle at the woman's navel had colors spiraling out from it, cascading up over the woman's shoulders and down her waist to a long skirt, but from what Maeya could tell there was no stitching—it was all one piece. The material itself changed colors in a deliberate pattern. It brought to mind the beautiful garden out front.

Instead of smiling as the little girl had done, however, this woman scowled, and her whole body looked angry.

"You do not have money," she declared, and though Maeya understood her, the accent made it difficult. "No money, no sale. No sale, no business in my store."

"Your pardon," Maeya said. "I was—"

"You are foreign. You do not belong. Leave."

The little shadow appeared at the woman's elbow. She was no bigger than the woman's left arm, yet she showed no fear. This close, Maeya could see that the girl's eyes were a luminescent purple. "She is the one!"

The huge woman looked down at the little girl, and her anger seemed to melt. "You brought her here?"

"Aye. She is the one!"

"How do you know?" The woman's voice was a deep rumble, and each word seemed to lilt up in the beginning of a laugh. "Did she tell you her name is The One?"

"She is a Rider!"

"I was just—" Maeya turned to leave. She did not want to know how the little girl knew she was a Rider, and she certainly did not want to be whatever "the one" was. She had more than enough going on.

"Sit!" The large woman said.

Maeya sat. Fortunately, there was a bench right behind her, else she would have simply sat on the floor.

"Who are you?"

"Who are you?" Maeya countered.

The woman crossed her arms under her massive bosom and planted her bare feet as if she were bracing for an attack. "I am the modiste," her deep voice rolled and filled the shop, but the hint of laughter she had when addressing the young girl was gone. "I am the second daughter of the third son of the eldest son of the ninth Lady Jululo. I am the protector of children, flowers, and goats. I am the good wife of Ridwan, who died too young. I am Usbarula Laureano."

With difficulty, Maeya kept her mouth closed.

The little girl giggled, and covered her mouth. Usbarula Laureano looked down at her, and the little girl stood up, straightened her shoulders, and crossed her arms over her flat chest. "I am a player of games and lover of shadows. I am a learner of Lore and Myth. I enjoy the protection of Usbarula Laureano. I am a seeker of the one who will help us all. I am Eirenya."

Usbarula Laureano nodded at Eirenya and Maeya thought she even smiled, but it was gone so quickly that Maeya was not quite sure. Then Usbarula was staring at Maeya again. "Who are you?"

"Maeya."

Eirenya burst out laughing so hard she was almost braying. Usbarula Laureano turned her glare on Eirenya, but the little girl was too far gone in her amusement to even notice. It only took Usbarula Laureano three quick strides to cross the distance between her and Maeya. She grabbed Maeya's arm and yanked her up.

"Clearly, you have not been taught. When you introduce yourself, you stand. You stand with your feet apart, to show you have no fear of where you've been or where you're going; you are balanced. You cross your arms—" Usbarula Laureano crossed Maeya's arms for her, "to show that you are female. You tell us who you *are*, not just your name. Tell who you are from, where you are going, what you have done. Introduce yourself." Usbarula Laureano took four steps backward to get back to Eirenya's side, and by then, the child had stopped laughing.

"I am Maeya Daceae."

Maeya must have blinked, for suddenly Usbarula Laureano's nose was nearly touching hers. "You are not from Sundee, Diar, or any of the Iriid towns, that much is obvious. Here in Sundee, the traditions are observed. Children are taught from a young age, and when they do not learn, they are beaten. Though you are old to be taught, you can still learn. If you choose not learn, do not doubt that I will beat you. Now. Introduce yourself. Do it properly." Usbarula Laureano once again backed up, never taking her eyes off Maeya, even though Eirenya tugged at her elbow.

"I am Maeya Daceae," she said again.

Usbarula Laureano's lips compressed into a thin line, hiding the white teeth that stood out so vividly when she spoke.

Eirenya grabbed Usbarula Laureano's elbow with both hands. "But she is the one!"

Usbarula Laureano shook little Eirenya off like she was a pebble caught between her toes. "She must be taught," she rumbled, dropping her chin like a bull and starting toward Maeya once again.

"I cannot tell you more, for I do not know more," Maeya said, fighting to keep her voice from trembling. "I know not where I go, and so much has happened that I do not truly understand where I have been. I am Maeya, and I am a Rider, and that is all."

Usbarula Laureano had taken the three steps to get in front of Maeya, and all Maeya could see were her dark eyes. She stared into Maeya's eyes, but she was searching, not challenging. Suddenly, the dark piercing eyes sparkled, and the edges crinkled up.

"Aye, *Rider* Maeya. That is all. And that is everything."

Usbarula Laureano smiled, and Maeya would later tell Quoran it seemed that someone must have lit several lamps in the store at the same time. Even when Usbarula Laureano enveloped Maeya in a hug, momentarily squashing her in the great bosom of flesh, the room around Maeya seemed much lighter.

Eirenya was jumping up and down, clapping her hands. "I told you! She's the one! She's here!" Suddenly she stopped and once again covered her mouth. "By the Power That Is, I must go pack!" And she was gone, her small frame slipping through the hanging bells so that only two or three rang.

"I must be going—"

"Sit."

Maeya felt her knees buckle, but she stopped herself before she actually sat. "Pardon, Usbarula Laureano, but I must find my companions. We are on a journey and—"

"And Eirenya will be joining you."

Maeya blinked. "She is a child."

"She will be joining you."

"We don't know where—"

"She has been waiting for you. I have tried to discourage her. Eirenya began talking of the coming Rider before she even told me her name. I am not sure she wasn't left here to become a page. But Sundee stopped being part of the page searches the awakening season before I found her. We have broken all ties with Riders and Dragons. It is not wise to mention either in this town. It is not safe to mention either in all of Iriid."

"We don't have—"

"Do you know what your name means?"

"We haven't—I don't—what?"

Usbarula Laureano sat down on the bench, and it groaned in protest but held her weight. "Do you know what your name means?"

Maeya shrugged. "My Nani always said it meant trouble."

Usbarula Laureano laughed. "Every child's name means trouble for their Nani."

"My name means peaceful," Eirenya's light voice warbled from the doorway. Her knapsack more than doubled her size, and the bells jingled merrily as she came back into the room.

"So you say," Usbarula Laureano said, "Yet there has been little enough peace in my life since you appeared on my doorstep."

"And you wouldn't have it any other way," Eirenya said serenly. She dropped her knapsack by the front door.

"What, exactly, do you have in that bag, O peaceful one?"

"My clothes, my hopes, and my future."

"And?"

"And a few loaves of bread, some dried rabbit, my sleeping blanket, and a bowl."

"And?"

Eirenya looked at the ground. "And my three pieces."

"And Ibaceta?"

"Is out front."

"Ah."

She squirmed, and Usbarula Laureano seemed content to let her wrestle with her own guilt.

Uncomfortable, Maeya cleared her throat. "I really must go."

Usbarula Laureano opened her arms, and Eirenya disappeared in the massive hug. "Be a good girl," Usbarula Laureano rumbled. "You may not be my daughter by blood, but you have more of my heart than I meant to give you." She looked up at Maeya. "Do not let anything happen to her."

"Usbarula Laureano, I cannot make that vow."

"I know," she said. She dropped a kiss on top of Eirenya's head. "But I cannot make her stay, and you cannot stop her from going with you. O, you could try," she said, as if Maeya had spoken, "but this child—" she set Eirenya away from her, "is stronger and more driven than you know. And if you do not include her in your traveling group, then she will merely follow you, and that will be more dangerous. So I ask that you let her travel with you, and that you keep her as safe as you can. The Power That Is will have to do the rest."

"The Power That Is will bring you to me soon," Eirenya said confidently.

"O, child, I have told you, I must stay," Usbarula Laureano replied in the tones of one whose nerves were sorely tried.

"I have told you, you will come. Everyone will."

Maeya couldn't help herself. "What do you mean?"

Eirenya looked up at her, violet eyes shining. "You are the one for me, but there are three of you. And together, the three Riders and their Dragons will lead us to peace."

"How—"

"We will have time to talk later; your friends are waiting now."

"Aye," Maeya said, "and I don't even know where—"

"I took them to the healer," Eirenya said.

"When?"

But Eirenya only smiled and Usbarula Laureano shrugged. "The girl moves in unusual ways. It will be best to let her travel with you."

Maeya nodded. "I'm beginning to see that."

Eirenya threw herself in Usbarula Laureano's arms again, and planted a loud kiss on her cheek. "Until I see you again," she began.

"May the Power That Is keep you safe," Usbarula Laureano finished with her. "Now go, before Zlatanian decides to take his healer's fee in blood."

"What?" Maeya tried not to squeak.

"She is joking," Eirenya said, slipping her hand into Maeya's and leading her to the front door. "Zlatanian is very kind and will not harm your friends."

Although Maeya had resolved to make sure that Eirenya knew how hard traveling was going to be, she found herself reaching for the little girl's knapsack.

"Nay, Rider," Usbarula Laureano said, "Eirenya will carry her own weight—and her own bag."

Eirenya's actions matched Usbarula Laureano's words, and she hefted the pack that doubled her size without any visible struggle. "Aye, Rider, for I am stronger than I look. I will not slow you down, nor increase your responsibilities."

"How many sleeping seasons have you seen?"

"Six," Eirenya said.

"We think," Usbarula Laureano added. "She may have seen one or two when she was left here—she has ever been small as a sprite."

"Six, seven, or eight, makes little difference. If she will be traveling with me, she will be adding to my responsibilities."

"How many sleeping seasons have *you* seen?" Usbarula Laureano asked.

"Fourteen," Maeya said, lifting her chin.

"Young to bear the responsibility of a child, yet as a Rider, you will have to bear many more responsibilities. And I think you will find that Eirenya will help more often than she will hinder you."

Maeya opened the front door, but Eirenya dropped her bag and flew back to Usbarula Laureano, getting another suffocating hug. With difficulty, Maeya did not sigh and roll her eyes. "Are you sure you won't travel with us?" she asked the modiste.

Over the top of Eirenya's head, Usbarula Laureano rolled her eyes instead. "Do I look like one who is ready to begin a long journey? My store is one of the few in Sundee that is still doing well—no, Eirenya, you will not criticize it now. You will tell Rider Maeya about it later—and my days of traveling many miles by foot or horseback and sleeping on the hard ground were long ago. Go, my heart, quickly now, you promised not to slow the Rider down."

Eirenya had just reached Maeya's side when suddenly Usbarula Laureano said, "Wait!"

Maeya groaned and thumped her head against the door.

Usbarula Laureano was pawing through a pile of vibrant fabric. "What does your name mean, Rider?"

"Truly, I do not know."

"Eirenya, do you know the meaning of Maeya?"

"Nay, Usbarula. It is not a name I've heard before."

"It has several spellings," the large woman said, "But all of them simply mean dream."

"O."

"And your family name? Do you know its meaning?"

"Declining wealth and privilege," Maeya said, parroting what her mother always claimed.

Usbarula Laureano made a tsking sound. "Wealth and privilege should only come with hard work. What does your last name mean?"

"It means my children will have the right to ride Dragons."

Usbarula Laureano tsked again, then said, "Ah!" She pulled out a bolt of fabric and moved toward them.

"I do not know what Daceae means, other than a family of Riders and an impoverished estate," Maeya said. "Do you know what it means?"

"I do," Usbarula Laureano, said, placing fabric in Maeya's hands. It was bright yellow, silky and fine, shot through with threads of gold. Maeya knew the cost of the fabric was probably equivalent to what it cost to feed all the peep at the Daceae Estate. She almost missed what Usbarula Laureano said next. "Your name means daffodil."

"Daffodil?"

"Aye. Now, you must go. I do not have time to make you a dress, but—"

"I will have time," Eirenya piped up.

"Aye," Usbarula Laureano said, smiling down at the little girl. She tugged gently on a lock of her hair. "And Eirenya has been well taught in the skills of stitching. She will make you a dress worthy of the Daffodil Rider."

"Many thanks," Maeya said, feeling overwhelmed.

"Now go. Your friends await."

Maeya and Eirenya stepped outside. It was still sunny and warm in the courtyard, but the flowers seemed pale and washed out in comparison to the rich colors that had filled the store.

Abruptly Maeya stopped and turned back to Usbarula Laureano. "How do you know the meaning of my name?"

The large black woman winked at her. "I dreamt it." She blew one more kiss to Eirenya, and then stepped back into her shop, closing the door.

"This way," Eirenya said, cutting diagonally across the courtyard from the fountain. There was another alley going from the corner, partially hidden by a large flowering tree. Eirenya skipped on ahead, forcing Maeya to jog to keep up. Once again she found herself thinking of the girl as a shadow: dark, quick, lithe, and silent.

The shadow opened a door that Maeya would not have seen, and melted into the building. Maeya followed. Darvo was lying on a raised platform; Quoran, Daegny, and an old bearded man were standing around him. As Maeya closed the door behind her, she looked carefully for Eirenya. Even knowing the girl was in the room, Maeya had to look three times before locating her sitting in the corner of room.

"You must be Maeya," the bearded man said.

"Maeya!" Quoran exclaimed, visibly anxious. "Where have you been?"

Daegny did not look up from her brother's face. Darvo's eyes were still closed, but his face was not as pale as it had been and did not seem to have the tight, pinched look anymore.

"How is Darvo?"

"Much better now, Maeya," Quoran said, confirming her observation. "The healer has done well, *Maeya*."

Maeya didn't have time to sort out why Quoran was stressing her name so. "Has he woken?"

"Nay," Daegny whispered, "but he will soon."

"His sister speaks true," the bearded man said. "It is lucky that he had young Quoran with him. He has been well-trained. I find it hard to believe that he is not an apprentice to a healer or a Tare."

"Ha!" Quoran shot a quick look at Maeya.

"Have you also gotten our necessary herbs?" Maeya asked.

"Some," Quoran said, "But Zlatanian has told me where we may buy the rest."

"And what do we owe Zlatanian?"

The bearded man bowed slightly, his eyes bright in contrast to the gray frizzled hair and heavy wrinkles that lined his face. They searched Maeya as carefully as Usbarula Laureano's eyes had, but without the kindness.

"Times are hard, young miss, and prices are high."

"Aye. What do we owe?"

"Five pieces of silver."

Maeya heard Daegny's sharp intake of breath, and she tried not to smile. If Zlatanian had heard the gasp as well, then he would be ready for her to haggle, and haggle hard.

"Maeya, we have other needs as well—" Quoran began.

"He has saved my brother's life! And he has already tended to him!"

"I rendered care to him in good faith," Zlatanian stated.

"I fear I only have one piece," Maeya said quietly. She waited and made sure she had Zlatanian's full attention. "It is gold, and I will gladly give it to you for all that you have done for my friends, but I must ask for one more thing."

"Aye?" Zlatanian was not a fool; he recognized that the extra payment was going to require something extra of him.

"Your confidence. Your *complete* confidence."

Zlatanian lowered his head ever so slightly. "It was a slow day, like so many of my days have been. I spent much of my morning cleaning and counting my stock. I believe I will soon need more Japon and Gyphanna root."

Quoran began nodding, and Daegny did not seem to be listening at all. But Maeya asked, "And who brought the beat up nag to your door?" For though she trusted that Quoran had brought the travois inside, she knew that Spiker was waiting patiently out the front door as sure as she knew that Pharla and the hatchling were still curled up near the bush, and that Tare Igny was busy seeking fresh fruit near their camp.

"Nag? He may be done with his high stepping days, but he is not a nag. I recall a widow and her young child stopped by on their way to Tiburn—" Daegny jerked suddenly; she was more aware of the conversation than Maeya had thought, "—seeking a bit of moss to ease the child's sad case of Orb fire skin."

Maeya smiled and flipped him the piece of gold. He caught it neatly and it disappeared into one of the many folds of his cloak

"Is he ready to travel?"

Zlatanian hesitated. "I would advise against it, Maeya, but I sense it does not matter. You seem to need to make distance. He should be able to travel horseback when the Orb rises again."

Maeya released the breath she had not realized she was holding. She had not hoped to hear such good news. "Daegny—"

"I'm not leaving him!"

"Will you please stay here until Quoran and I return?" Maeya thought she had done a good job of keeping her tone polite, but Quoran's look said otherwise. "And watch Eirenya, too," she added as an afterthought.

"Who?" Quoran asked while Daegny only said, "Aye, I'll stay."

"Where is the herbalist?"

"Eirenya can show you," Zlatanian began. Maeya merely raised her eyebrows. He sighed. "Out the front door, to your left. It is the only two-story building on this side of the street."

As Maeya and Quoran moved toward the front door, Eirenya stood up. Quoran flinched, and Maeya smiled. The little shadow was good. "Wait here," she said, putting her hand on Eirenya's tight black curls. "We will not be gone long."

"I'm coming with you."

"Wait here," Maeya repeated, and she didn't look back as she and Quoran stepped out the door.

"My apologies, Rider," Quoran said immediately in a hushed tone, "I have meant no disrespect." He pulled the scarf up over his scarred face. "But this town—"

"Is not friendly toward Dragons and Riders."

"Aye. Fortunately, Daegny warned me before I said anything to the healer, but you were not around to hear."

"Did Zlatanian say anything specific?"

"Nay, not specific, but....he asked a few questions that made me uncomfortable."

"You have done well, Quoran, as usual. Now, how much will we need at the herbalist's?"

As Quoran went through his list of needs and then began on his list of wants, Maeya kept a watchful eye on the street. Again, the emptiness made her uneasy. A town this size should be bustling, should at least have a mother shopping or a couple of friends going for a drink or children running errands. Yet, apart from Quoran's voice and their footsteps, the streets were quiet.

"How much will this cost?" Maeya asked.

"I do not—"

"You're best guess, Quoran."

"Less than one piece," he said with a fleeting grin. "Do you have silver? It may make things easier."

"Aye. Here," she loosened the drawstring and pulled out four pieces of silver. "This is your budget for today."

"I will not spend it all," he said, slipping the silver into a pocket.

"Spend it quickly," Maeya said.

Quoran shot Maeya a look. "What's wrong?"

"A sense—" Maeya shook her head. "I do not know, exactly. But something is not right."

"Here? Or at camp?"

Maeya tried to actively throw her mind to Pharla and met sleepy resistance. "Here. It feels…."

"Tense."

"Aye."

"Like we're being watched."

"Aye."

Stepping into the herbalists small store initially made Maeya feel a bit claustrophobic, but soon the aroma from all the drying herbs helped soothe her. Quoran was quick, the herbalist had good supplies and few questions, and the prices were easily agreed to. It was not long before they were stepping back into the street.

As her foot touched the dusty road, Maeya felt the tension spring back up around her.

A shadow separated from the side of the building. Maeya and Quoran both moved to protect the other and as a result bounced off each other.

"Eirenya!" Maeya said in frustration. "I told you to stay at Zlatanian's!"

Eirenya grinned without remorse. "I told you I was coming with you."

"Maeya?" Quoran's voice was pitched low. "Be ready."

"There is not much I can do," Maeya said, matching his low tone but not giving any other indication that she had heard. "I have no weapon."

"There is no problem," Eirenya said, slipping one hand into Maeya's and the other into Quoran's. She raised her voice and nodded, "Clalue, it is good to see you."

"Eirenya, why aren't you helping Usbarula Laureano?" Maeya looked up to see five men spread out across the street, and it was the one farthest from them that spoke. He was also the only one without a full beard.

"I am helping her," she replied cheerfully. "They have purchased their cloth, and they asked for the herbalist. Usbarula Laureano bid me show them."

"And who are they?" The man in the middle asked. He had the most grey in his beard of any of them, but he still looked strong.

Maeya knew she must speak quickly, before Quoran inadvertently gave them away. She let go of Eirenya's hand, crossed her arms over her chest, and took a wide stance. "I am the only daughter of the second son of the fourth son of Daceae. I am a dreamer and a believer and a lover of herbs and flowers. I will travel far and go without fear. I am Maeya Daceae."

The man gave a curt nod and looked at Quoran. Maeya did too, and saw him try to tug his hand out of Eirenya's grasp, but she wouldn't let go, so he merely copied Maeya's wider stance. "I am the only son of the only son of the last son of Bergin. I am a drifter and have traveled far. I am Quoran Bergin."

"And why do you hide from us, Quoran Bergin?"

"'Tis how I was taught to dress as a child. Though I have drifted far across the land, I have stayed close in my mind."

"And who are you?" Maeya asked.

"So you will be drifting through our fair town of Sundee as well?"

"Aye," Quoran said after a quick glance at Maeya.

"See to it that you drift quickly."

"That was our intent."

"Usbarula Laureano told me to help them," Eirenya repeated. "Do you not trust me, Clalue?"

The older man nodded and then turned to leave. The others turned as well, though the beardless one smiled at Maeya before he left, and looked back over his shoulder twice before disappearing after the others into a building.

"Come," Eirenya said, taking Maeya's hand again, "Let us make haste."

"I feel we're still being watched," Quoran said.

"O, we are," Eirenya agreed, smiling and swinging her hands between the two of them. "But you are with me, so it is all right."

"And how is that?" Quoran asked.

"Because I am Sundee's favorite orphan."

"I am an orphan, too."

Eirenya stopped short and stared up at Quoran with wide eyes. "Truly?"

"Aye."

"I have never met another real orphan before."

"You know, orphans are lucky."

Eirenya looked askance at Quoran. "How can we be lucky? We have no family."

"We've used all our bad luck already; the rest will all be good."

It was on the tip of Maeya's tongue to point out that Quoran's life had hardly gotten easier since the Power That Is had taken his father; to observe that, in fact, as they had been traveling together, they seemed to have had more than their share of bad luck, but she did not. Quoran was reaching out to Eirenya in the way he knew how, and she would leave him to it.

Eirenya was watching Quoran, clearly trying to determine if he was serious. "Then we have Dragon's Luck," she said finally, "and I am tired of the extremes."

"Aye. Me, too."

Maeya nodded. Clearly Eirenya was an astute little shadow. She was going to be a good addition to their group.

Maeya had hoped Darvo would have woken by the time the got back to Zlatanian's, but he had not. Daegny, however, was much calmer.

They got Darvo back on the travois and Quoran tucked his bundles of herbs alongside him. Eirenya gave Zlatanian a hug, and he slipped her something round and shiny that earned him a giggle and another hug. When he waved farewell from the doorway, his smile was small but Maeya felt it was sincere. Though the gold piece would help keep their confidence, it was his true affection for Eirenya that would ensure it.

It wasn't until they were on horseback, with Eirenya riding pillion with Maeya, that Daegny said anything.

"Who are you?"

Maeya felt Eirenya shift behind her and imagined the little girl preparing to cross her arms and launch into her litany. She was surprised when the girl only said, "I'm Eirenya."

Daegny tossed her head. "How many strays are you going to collect?" she asked Maeya.

"You all seem to find me," Maeya said mildly. "I don't go looking for you."

They were quiet for the rest of the ride back.

CHAPTER FOURTEEN

Because of the travois, they did not travel fast, but Maeya pushed for as much speed as she dared. So she was surprised when Pharla suddenly spoke in her mind. *Wait.*

Maeya pulled up sharply on Lark's reins, causing the mare to dance and toss her head. Eirenya flailed behind her, grabbing madly at Maeya's waist.

"What's amiss?" Quoran asked.

Pharla?

The hatchling's gone, Pharla's thought was coated with disgust.

What? You lost Darvo's Dragon?

No. She is coming your way. Watch the horses.

Aye. Aloud Maeya said, "Use caution. Darvo's young Dragon is too impatient and is seeking him. Eirenya, time to get down." Maeya reached back to help her, but the girl jumped down nimbly.

Quoran was already dismounted and reaching for Lark's reins as Maeya slid off.

Eirenya was looking around. "Where is the Dragon?"

"I don't know yet. But the horses don't like the Dragons, so we must be careful." Maeya turned to put her hand on Lark's neck, trying to settle the mare. She was dancing on her hooves; the hatchling must be close. "Eirenya, stay back, but not too far. I don't want you to lose sight of us."

"The girl is gone," Quoran said, taking the reins from Daegny as well.

"What?"

"She is—"

"Find her!" Maeya interrupted.

"But Rider—" Quoran held up the four sets of reins. Lark took that moment to rear and yank Quoran off his feet. He dropped Spiker's and Daegny's mount's reins. He held on to Lark's reins, however, and Maeya was able to grab them as well and add her weight to getting the horse under control.

"Let go!" Maeya snapped, and he did, and she was able to quickly turn Lark in a tight circle away from Spiker and the travois. Maeya worked Lark in two more circles, going slightly farther away from Spiker, and finally got the mare under better control.

She looked over her shoulder and saw Daegny leaning over Darvo, her hand over his forehead, oblivious to everything. Quoran was slowly getting to his feet, his horse straining against the reins. Of Eirenya there was no sign.

"Quan dung," Maeya swore. "Quoran, take our mounts and go to camp. I will follow with Spiker."

"What about—"

"Eirenya will be fine," Maeya said shortly, and though she barely knew the girl, she was sure it must be true. "At least until I get a hold of her."

Quoran came to get Lark and then led the horses away. Maeya hurried over to pick up Spiker's reins from the ground, relieved that he had not tried to bolt. She took a quick look around, but did not see the hatchling's light green anywhere. As she began to lead Spiker in Quoran's wake, she looked up and saw him disappearing in the trees. She realized with a pang that Quoran was limping.

Spiker gave her a push in her back. Maeya turned toward him. He lowered his head, and she scratched his forehead as he bobbed his head up and down. "I know," she said. "You're the best horse we've got and you don't understand why I wasn't riding you. But it wasn't really my choice."

Tare Igny was hurrying toward them. "Greetings, Rider. Quoran says the trip to Sundee was successful."

"Aye. Darvo should be ready to travel when the Orb comes up."

"Good."

"Will you take Spiker?"

"Aye."

Maeya handed him the reins and then paused the few moments until Daegny and the travois were even with her and fell in step with them. "How is he?"

"He is getting better."

"Truly?"

"I can feel it," Daegny said fiercely.

Maeya hoped Darvo knew better than to disappoint his sister. "Good. Once you and Tare get to the camp, please help Quoran settle the horses. They will need your touch." Daegny opened her mouth and Maeya knew she was going to argue. "Zlatanian said Darvo would be better when the Orb rose. Until then, we need to let him rest. You cannot help him rest. You *can* help soothe the horses."

Daegny glared at Maeya but gave a curt nod. "Where are you going?" she asked as Maeya turned off the path.

"To Pharla." And just saying the words lifted Maeya's spirit. She did not hesitate as she wound through the trees and crossed a small brook.

You're getting better, Pharla observed as she approached the small overhang where the Dragon was basking in the fading light of the Orb.

I think you're opening to me more, Maeya countered. She sat next to Pharla and leaned back against her, sighing in contentment. Pharla wrapped her tail around Maeya and snaked her head around on the other side, effectively encircling her. Maeya could feel the last lingering stress and fear lift away, and she knew it was Pharla's doing. And yet—

"What worries you?"

The hatchling. There is something….

"Wrong?" Maeya still feared that the yellowish scales meant sickness or perhaps a fatal weakness.

Different. There was a change, a quick change, and suddenly….We had been resting in the shade of the Trident tree when she jumped up and left. Pharla's thoughts grew sheepish. *I had not realized how close you were until she was gone and I was trying to find her. I found you first.*

"So you're not sure she went looking for Darvo."

She is closer now; she is with him.

"As long as we haven't lost her."

She has a Rider. She will not leave him.

Maeya had been staring absently out at the clearing, but suddenly she registered that they were not alone.

The wolves have been around, Pharla thought with her eyes half-closed. *They have kept their distance, but they are staying with us.*

This is not a wolf, Maeya thought.

Pharla lifted her head quickly and bared her teeth. *What is it?* Fear flooded through Maeya so fast that for a moment all she could see were strange and threatening shapes in every tree and rock. She took a deep breath and pushed against Pharla's fear, trying to push it down, not back into Pharla.

"Eirenya," Maeya ground out, finding it difficult to speak clearly. "Come meet Pharla."

The little girl detached herself from the boulder's shadow she had been part of and seemed to glide across the clearing to them. She stopped well away from them, however, and though she had a small smile, her violet eyes reflected her apprehension.

"Rider Maeya," she said in her lilting voice, "and great Pharla." She bowed low, nearly bringing her forehead down to her knees.

I like her.

You would, Maeya thought, pushing Pharla's head before she

stood. Eirenya remained essentially bent in half, waiting to be released. After her earlier disappearance, Maeya was tempted to leave her bowed down.

But that—

Would not be right, Maeya thought. I know.

"Eirenya, we must talk."

"Aye?" her voice was muffled by her knees.

"Please stand."

"Pardon, Rider, not yet."

Maeya was only slightly mollified to feel the same confusion coming from Pharla that she felt. "Why not?"

Instead of answering, the girl collapsed into a small ball on the ground. Maeya immediately moved toward her, not quite sure if she was going to comfort her or simply yank her to her feet. But Maeya never got to her side.

A huge charcoal wolf was suddenly standing over the small girl. It was only later, when Maeya had time to replay the scene that she realized the wolf had been on the small cliff face directly above her and Pharla, and had jumped down on top of Eirenya.

Dark green scales abruptly blocked Maeya's view, and she was never sure how Pharla managed to get in between her and the wolf so quickly. Even looking back on it later, it would seem that Pharla was lying behind her and then standing in front of her in the next instant. Again, Pharla's fear threatened to overwhelm Maeya, but this time there was an underlying anger as well, and Maeya reached for it.

"Pharla, hold!"

The Dragon's hiss and the wolf's growl were unnaturally loud to Maeya's ears; she could feel the reverberation deep in her rib cage.

"Ibaceta, down!"

Maeya put her hand on Pharla's side, and she was not surprised to find it hot to the touch. The initial fear was gone and the anger that pulsed through both of them was white-hot. Over Pharla's back, Maeya could see that Eirenya was standing again, and appeared to have the wolf in a bear hug.

Pharla, Maeya tried with her mind, *the wolves are on our side.*

This one is new to us. And threatening you.

Protecting Eirenya, as you are protecting me. Maeya could not help but smile as she had the thought.

Pharla suddenly swung her head around so they were eye to eye. *What are you so pleased about?*

You are my Dragon, Maeya said simply.

Pharla's amber eyes glowed. *This child is trouble.*

Aye. Maeya reached up and traced a line between Pharla's eyes to the center of her nose. *But we will straighten her out.*

Pharla exhaled sharply, flaring out her nostrils, and moved around Maeya. *And the wolf?*

We will trust her to keep it in line, Maeya thought, though as she watched the beast, she wondered if that was really possible. Even sitting, the wolf's head was above Eirenya's.

"Your pardon, Rider," Eirenya said contritely. "That was not how I planned to introduce you to Ibaceta."

"O? You had a plan?"

"I was going to have her bring us evening meal."

"Ibaceta cooks?"

Eirenya giggled. "She will bring me rabbits when I ask. I was going to have her bring me a rabbit."

"I can see how that could be helpful, but one rabbit will hardly feed our group."

"It would be better than nothing."

"True. How did you and...Ibaceta become such good friends?"

"I found her last awakening season. An orphan, just like me."

"And Usbarula Laureano took her in, too?"

"She has a thing for orphans."

Maeya merely watched Eirenya for a few moments, and soon the girl began to squirm. "Usbarula Laureano didn't know I had her until the beginning of sleeping season. She tried to get rid of her."

"But at that point she was a little too big," Maeya guessed.

"Aye."

"Do you do anything anyone tells you?"

Once again Eirenya squirmed. "I try," she said, and she sounded honestly distressed, "But so often what I'm told to do goes against what I know should be done."

Set her straight.

Maeya sighed. "Eirenya, when we travel, we must trust each other. That means that when I or Quoran or Tare Igny tell you—"

"There's a Tare?" she broke in excitedly, looking around.

"—tell you something, we must trust that you will do it. Not only for your well being, but also for the well being of the rest of us. When you disappeared, we were worried for you. We—"

"I was fine!"

"—were distracted looking for you, so Quoran got hurt."

"Quoran got hurt?"

"Aye."

"Because of me?"

"Aye."

"O. My apologies."

"Your apologies need to be given to Quoran."

"Aye."

"Along with a promise to do what you are told, when you are told."

Eirenya opened her mouth to argue, and the wolf whined. She closed her mouth and looked at Ibaceta. "Aye, Rider. We will be good."

Maeya sensed Pharla shifting behind her, looking more carefully at the girl and the wolf. *There's something there.*

Can you hear its thoughts?

Nay. It's something different, but—no. I cannot read its thoughts. The wolf suddenly turned her head toward Pharla and barked. *But I can send it some of mine!*

"Does the wolf talk to you?"

"Nay, Rider," Eirenya said, but she was petting Ibaceta and did not meet Maeya's eyes.

"Come," Maeya said. "Let's go to the fire. You and Daegny have much to talk about."

Eirenya wrinkled her nose. "Daegny does not like me."

"Daegny does not like anybody," Maeya muttered.

"What?"

Louder, Maeya said, "You have much in common. I think you will be surprised. Come." Maeya held her hand out.

Eirenya took a step toward her and then hesitated.

Ibaceta will stay here with me.

Aye? Maeya looked at Pharla in surprise.

Aye, Pharla said calmly. And sure enough, the wolf trotted toward the green Dragon. She stopped just out of the Dragon's reach and extended one forefoot in front of the other and lowered her head.

"Did she just bow?"

"I think she did," Eirenya said, and her voice reflected the wonder Maeya felt.

You are right, Maeya. The wolves are on our side.

And you are right, Pharla, Maeya thought as Eirenya took her hand. *Things are teetering.*

*** ******** ***

Tare Igny was preparing the evening meal when Maeya and Eirenya arrived, and at first that pleased Maeya. But when she saw Daegny at her brother's side, and Quoran with the horses, familiar anger bubbled up.

She let go of Eirenya's hand and stormed over to Quoran. "Go," she said. "Go tend to your foot. I will finish here."

"My foot is fine, Rider," Quoran began.

"Your leg, then, or what ever is causing you pain."

"At the moment, it is your doubt."

"Quoran—"

"I did twist my leg a bit when I fell, but it hardly needs tending. I am nearly done with the horses. Let me do my job."

"Let me help," Eirenya said, bowing at Maeya's elbow. "Your pardon, Quoran, for not listening earlier. I wasn't—" she broke off abruptly.

Maeya shook her head. "Eirenya, it is not polite to stare." Quoran had removed the scarf from his face, and Orb's fading hues cast the scars in unusual light.

"Pardon," Eirenya said faintly.

"Go," Maeya said, taking Spiker's lead from Quoran with one hand and pushing him lightly in the back with the other. "Eirenya and I will tend to the horses while I attempt to teach her basic courtesies."

Quoran bent down so his face was level with Eirenya's. "Take a good look. Get over the shock and the fear. Don't try to memorize it, for there are too many to recognize at once."

"Does it hurt?" Eirenya asked, reaching up. She seemed to realize what she was about to do and grabbed her own hand with the other

"Nay. Go ahead and touch it. It feels strange, aye?"

"Aye," Eirenya whispered, running both hands over the striated crevices. "What happened?"

By the time Quoran had finished telling Eirenya his story, Maeya had hobbled all of the horses. They returned to the fire and Tare Igny.

"'Tis simple fare, but 'tis good," he said, handing bowls first to Maeya and then to Quoran. He picked up another bowl and then looked at Eirenya. "I would welcome you to our fire, but I do not know your name."

She straightened her shoulders, took a wide stance, and crossed her arms over her chest. "I am a lover of shadows and eager traveler. I am a learner of Lore and Myth. I give and seek protection for Ibaceta. I am friend to Rider Maeya and Pharla. I am Eirenya."

Tare Igny set the bowl down. He took a wide stance and put his hands on his hips. "I am the first son of the first son of the first son of the first son of the only daughter of the Dane of Hamdanie. I was Rider of Palth, may the Power That Is continue to let him soar. I seek justice and vengeance. I am Tare Igny."

"May the Power That Is grant you safe travels, empty glasses, and full dishes," Eirenya said. Tare Igny gave Eirenya a strange look while she continued, "Why do you seek vengeance?"

Maeya was pleased, for that was the very question she wished to ask. But before Tare Igny opened his mouth, there was an unusual trill from the other side of the fire.

Darvo was still in his travois, and it was propped up against a tree fairly close to the fire. Daegny, of course, was sitting on a log next to him. She was staring at the lowest branch.

The hatchling was clinging to the branch and had wings spread wide, the Orb's farewell and the firelight dancing across her pale green scales. She trilled again, loudly, but it wasn't until the third time that Maeya realized that the hatchling was trilling the same pattern again and again, almost as if it were trying to say something.

She is.

Where are you?

Here.

But before Maeya could ask for more specific details, someone else spoke.

"Could I get some water?"

Daegny shrieked. "Darvo! You're awake!"

Darvo winced. "Aye. And thirsty," he rasped.

Daegny nearly collided with Quoran as she spun to get water for her brother, but Quoran did not spill much from the cup he held out to her. She took it without a word of thanks and helped Darvo drink.

"Easy, Daegny. Do not let him have too much," Tare Igny warned.

They had all gathered around Darvo, exclaiming how happy they were to see him awake again.

Where are you? Maeya thought at Pharla again.

Here, she said, sending an image of a brambleberry bush. Maeya glanced around, and from under the third-farthest bush she could see a dark green tail. *It scratches my wings nicely.*

"Are you hungry?" Quoran asked. "You should be."

"Aye. How long have I been gone?"

"This is the second time the Orb has passed without you enjoying it," Daegny told him as she took the bowl from Quoran.

"Remember what Zlatanian said!" Quoran scolded. "Small bites. Not too much to start."

"I know," Daegny snapped. Then she smiled at Darvo. "We've all been worried about you."

"You needn't have worried. I was fine. Truly, sister, I can feed myself."

"Not yet," she said, happily sticking the spoon in his mouth. "You need to regain your strength."

Darvo made a face but chewed and swallowed quickly. He opened his mouth to speak, but found the spoon inserted instead. He glared at his sister. "Slow down!"

"Don't talk with your mouth full."

She raised another spoonful while he chewed, but he batted it away.

"Hiama is the Dragon for Lore."

"Who is?"

"Hiama. My Dragon."

Tare Igny sat down hard. "She told you her name?"

"Aye." Darvo was watching Tare Igny and Daegny shoved another spoonful into his mouth.

About time, Pharla groused.

You knew the hatchling's name? Maeya thought in surprise.

Of course.

Why didn't you tell me?

She is his Dragon; it is her name to tell.

O. Maeya looked up at the hatchling. Hiama was curled up in the crook of the branch and the tree trunk, one foreleg dangling down. I'm surprised she's not curled up on top of him.

Forced to be apart while you took him to town was good for her; now she knows that being close can be enough.

"Quit it, Daegny!" Darvo complained as soon as he had finished swallowing. "Just give me the bowl!"

"No!"

Igny reached into his tunic for something and seemed surprised when he drew out his empty hand. "Much is changing. And it is changing too fast. I have never known a Rider to hear their Dragon's name until they have seen a full set of seasons or more together. Hiama has barely seen all the faces of the Sister Orb."

I have not seen all the seasons yet, Pharla said.

Don't be jealous, Maeya thought to her. Tare Igny already knows how remarkable you are.

"But she is a special Dragon," Darvo insisted, head turned aside to avoid the spoon.

"The Dragon of Lore," Maeya repeated doubtfully.

"Dragon *for* Lore," Darvo corrected. "She knows all of it, all of the Lore we have forgotten."

"How do you know?"

"I just do."

Daegny snorted but Maeya understood. There were some things about your Dragon that simply were.

"Lore from Eleena and Naria?" Quoran asked excitedly.

Darvo nodded. "And before."

Now it was Quoran who sat. "Before?" he whispered in awe. "Lore from the time we have forgot?"

"Aye, but—" Darvo was cut off when Daegny got another spoonful in. "Quan dung!" he shouted, spraying the stew everywhere. "Enough! I'm not an invalid! I can feed myself!"

"Fine!" She yelled at him, practically tossing the stew bowl at him and turning to run from the camp.

There was no way Darvo could catch the bowl; he was going to end up with stew all over. But two small black hands reached out and deftly caught the bowl and the spoon, and only the smallest amount of stew spilled over the edge onto Darvo.

Maeya did not blame Darvo for flinching back so sharply that he fell out of the travois. She was merely grateful that he fell on the side where Tare Igny had sat so that the Tare broke his fall. Eirenya had been sitting so quietly in the shadow of the travois, and they had been so focused on talking to Darvo, that none of them had introduced her to him.

In truth, Maeya was not sure that any of them had really noticed that the little girl had been sitting there. Maeya hadn't been startled to see Eirenya grab the bowl, but until she saw the girl's hands move, she hadn't made a conscious note of her presence. It wasn't so much that Eirenya hid as it was that she had a way of blending in and avoiding attention. Until she smiled. Her smile was so bright and full of energy, it immediately drew every eye.

Quoran was scrambling to help, but as soon as he was at their side it became evident that he did not know who to help first: the injured Rider or the Tare.

"Get Darvo!" Maeya commanded, mostly because Darvo had Tare Igny well pinned.

Eirenya, meaning well, also tried to assist Darvo, but he pulled back sharply and almost landed on the ground again, in spite of Quoran's helping hand.

"Eirenya, help Tare Igny," Maeya said. "Darvo, do you want to sit?"

"Aye," he said, still staring at the little girl.

Maeya inclined her head to the fire, and Quoran led him to a log and helped him sit. Maeya brought him the bowl of stew and cup of water. What little color he had gotten back while talking about Hiama had disappeared.

"I think he needs something stronger than water. Do we have some mead?" she asked Quoran.

"Nay, Rider, no ale, mead, or wine," Tare Igny said quickly.

"Zlatanian said water and milk only for the rest of Sister Orb's cycle," Quoran said. "The injury needs time to heal inside as well."

There was a scuffling sound, and Quoran, Maeya, and Tare Igny immediately turned toward it. Both Maeya and Quoran drew their short blades.

Hiama was crawling toward them, having been left alone in the tree. Maeya's initial dismay at Hiama's awkward progress was quickly replaced with admiration.

"She's dragging a squirrel!"

"Aye." Darvo was smiling.

"Is it her first kill?"

"O....nay. She did not hunt. Tare Igny gave it to her."

"O," Maeya tried to recover. "But she's bringing it with her."

"She's getting stronger," Darvo said as the hatchling finally got to the log he was sitting on. The journey had sapped her energy and she lay down behind the log.

"Eirenya," Maeya said, trying to keep the question out of her voice. She knew the girl had helped Tare Igny to his seat across from the fire, and she knew she was nearby, but without staring she could not see where the girl had gone. "Come introduce yourself to Rider Darvo."

The girl appeared at her side, and Maeya refused to look to see where she had come from. She stood tall, widened her stance, and crossed her arms. "I am a friend of shadows and eager to travel with Dragons. I am a learner of Lore. I am friend to Rider Maeya and Pharla and Ibaceta. I am Eirenya."

Darvo blinked and then looked to Maeya. "What?"

"Apparently, that is the proper way to introduce yourself in the towns of Iriid. Were you not taught?"

"If you did that in Tiburn, you'd be run out before the Orb could warm your skin."

"Ahem," Eirenya said, lifting her chin. "It is very rude not to introduce yourself."

Darvo looked again at Maeya, who shrugged. "'Tis true," she said.

Darvo set the bowl on the log and stood. He crossed his arms, which set Eirenya off in giggles. Tare Igny coughed sharply and put his hands on his hips, and Darvo quickly mimicked him. "I am first born of....the...last born to Taormina. Twin to Daegny and Rider of Hiama... friend of Maeya. I am Darvo Hoart."

"Tiburn does not follow the introductions?" Tare Igny asked.

"Nay," Darvo said as he sat back down.

"Who is Icebeta?" Quoran asked.

"Ibaceta is my friend."

"Eirenya," Maeya warned.

"Ibaceta is my wolf."

Tare Igny dropped his spoon and bowl with a clatter. "Your what?"

"My wolf," Eirenya repeated calmly.

"Rider, I do not think it is a good idea to travel with a wolf," Tare Igny said, trying to look all around the campsite at once.

"Do you not remember how they helped in the fight?" Maeya asked.

"Aye, but that…that was—"

"Unusual," Darvo supplied.

"Aye," Tare Igny agreed.

"Like we are," Darvo added, earning a frown from the Tare.

"Several wolves have been traveling with us for a while," Maeya said. "I see little harm in having one that is already named."

"Several wolves? Truly?" Eirenya asked.

"Truly."

"I hope they'll be nice to Ibaceta."

"Icebeta?" Quoran said doubtfully.

"Ibaceta," Eirenya pronounced slowly.

"See? You do it too." At his blank look, Maeya said, "Zenlupra?"

"Lenzupra! And it's not the same thing at all! She's part of our clan Lore! This is just some wolf—" He broke off as 'some wolf' came padding up next to Eirenya and sat down. "Ibaceta. Ibaceta."

Darvo picked up his bowl and then set it back down. "Where do you suppose my sister has gone?"

Quoran stood. "I'll go get her."

"Perhaps I should go."

"If she sees you walking alone, she may kill you. If she had her way, she would wrap you in a blanket and feed you for two or three cycles of the Sister Orb, just to make sure that you are not going to die."

"Good point. Tell her…" Darvo trailed off and shook his head.

"I'll tell her," Quoran said with a smile, "But I'm sure she already knows."

***   *******   ***

They broke camp the next morning, and did so quickly. Young Eirenya was everywhere at once, her hands deftly packing things away, soothing nervous horses, filling empty water skins. Fortunately, Ibaceta wasn't anywhere. Eirenya cheerfully told Maeya that the wolf would follow them to the next camp and not to worry about her.

Daegny seemed happy enough to return to caring for the horses, though she sneered when Maeya mentioned letting Eirenya ride one of the pack animals. "I can't just throw the child on any horse. Storm has never taken a rider and Jingle is slightly lame in the left fore."

Maeya thought it best not to ask what the difference was between putting a small girl or a load of supplies on their back. Darvo, however, didn't hesitate.

"After all, either way Jingle is walking with us and carrying something," he pointed out.

"Maybe I should have just let you die!"

"I wasn't going to die, Daegny," he said, "and all I'm saying—"

"You take care of them, then, if you know so much!" And she dropped the halters in a pile in the dirt and stalked off.

Eirenya handed one of the halters to Darvo. "Is Storm the roan?" He nodded. "I bet no one's ever asked him if they could ride," she said. She walked up to the horse, and Maeya felt her breath catch. Eirenya was so tiny compared to those big hooves! "Storm, would you mind if I ride you for a while?"

The horse snorted, but then lowered his head, and Eirenya clipped the halter on. "Now what?" she asked.

"This way," Darvo said, "We'll find a good rock for you to stand on, and I'll teach you to saddle and bridle—"

"O, go tend to your Dragon," Daegny said crossly, taking the lead from Eirenya. "I'll teach her."

"Thank you, sister," Darvo said, sketching a bow.

Eirenya followed Daegny, but she looked back at Maeya twice as she went, and the apprehension on her face was clear.

Trying to make sense of Daegny's behavior made Maeya's head hurt.

"Come, Maeya, let's find our Dragons," Darvo said, leading her away from the horses and his sister.

When they set out, Quoran scouting ahead, Tare Igny in the lead, and Eirenya right behind him on the big roan, Maeya felt much better. Daegny was next, riding Lark and leading Jingle who was now their last packhorse, and many paces back, Darvo followed on Spiker. Not only did Spiker not object to the Dragon on his back, Maeya would swear to the Power That Is that he had pranced until he got too tired. Hiama was stretched across Darvo's shoulders much like she had been on the branch, hindquarters on one side and forequarters on the other, tail trailing lazily down his back.

Maeya was on foot, walking next to Pharla, which meant they would not make it to Camp Lythe for at least two more passes of the Orb.

In many ways, Maeya wished it would take even longer. They were going to a Clan with different customs than she and Quoran were used to. Tare Igny could tutor all of them in etiquette for Uture Clan, but he didn't know Panir tradition any better than they did. And it would be hard enough joining a new group of people whom she didn't know if she also didn't know her companions better. One of the most important things about life at Spike Cave had been knowing who to trust, who to turn to for help.

She would trust Quoran with her life, or anyone else's except, perhaps, his own. He seemed to value others too much and himself not enough.

She trusted Tare Igny as much as she trusted any of the Tares and Cyrs from her Cave. They were responsible adults, but not friends, not people she could talk to. She did not think he would harm her, but she did not think he would go out of his way to save her, either. She was, after all, just another Rider to him.

Maeya had trusted Darvo, but after Hiama hatched, there had been a shift in his attitude toward her that she didn't quite understand. And Daegny only confused her.

Eirenya could absolutely be trusted to do only what Eirenya wanted to do. Maeya just had to figure out what that really was.

Aye, she wished they would not be getting to Camp Lythe so fast.

***   ********   ***

At their second camp after leaving Sundee, Tare Igny seemed to be a bit jumpy. Maeya thought she had been the only one to notice, until Darvo pulled her aside.

"Is Igny ill?"

Startled that Darvo had the same observation, in spite of his preoccupation with Hiama, Maeya looked at him with new respect. "I do not think so."

Darvo shook his head. "Something is amiss."

"Do you sense something?" Maeya asked, wondering if he felt illness in peep in the same way he felt it in animals.

"Nay," he said. "'Tis his behavior. He is not being.... Igny."

"Tare Igny," Quoran corrected in a whisper as he materialized at her shoulder. "When will you learn to show respect? He is a Tare!"

"My apologies," Darvo said insincerely.

"He is nervous," Quoran went on, ignoring Darvo completely and talking only to Maeya.

"Aren't pages supposed to show respect for all Riders?" Darvo asked her. "Not just their own?"

Maeya tried not to roll her eyes. She had been hoping that after Darvo's injury, they would learn to get along together better. Instead, Darvo and Quoran had been shooting barbs at each other with increasing frequency. "What is Tare Igny nervous about?" Maeya asked.

"I do not know," Quoran said as he melted into the dark again, heading for his sleeping blankets. "But he bears watching."

Aye, Pharla said. *They all do.*

CHAPTER FIFTEEN

The next morning, they found out what was bothering the Tare. He cleared his throat nervously several times as they broke camp, then finally said, "We shall be at Camp Lythe before the Orb sinks again."

Maeya glanced around. No one seemed to be rejoicing to hear the news, but no one seemed upset either. Except, perhaps, Tare Igny. He cleared his throat yet again.

"I cannot prepare you for what we will see, for I do not know. Camp Lythe may be thriving. Or it may be…" he hesitated and Maeya suddenly realized why he was so nervous. He had seen all of Meadow Spear's Dragons wiped out. "It may be gone."

The grim potential hit Maeya harder than she thought possible. If Spike Cave, Meadow Spear Cave, and Camp Lythe—representatives from three of the four Clans—had all been destroyed, where would they go? Would they continue searching for an intact Cave? What if the Wyzards had successfully destroyed all of the Dragons? What if Pharla and Hiama and the pitch Dragon were all that was left?

We're not.

How do you know? Maeya asked her, Can you sense other Dragons?

Nay. But I do not sense emptiness, either.

Maeya wasn't convinced that meant anything. If Pharla did not feel Dragons far away, then how could she believe that they were out there?

They were all rather quiet when they began that day's traveling. Even Eirenya, who had become quite chatty with Daegny, was subdued. Maeya was sure the others had picked up on the same worry she had, but they didn't have Dragons who could try to reassure them.

By unspoken agreement, Darvo and Maeya walked together up the last hill, leading Spiker behind them. Darvo was cradling his hatchling with one arm, swinging her ever so slightly.

They crested the top of a hill, and Camp Lythe was spread out in front of them. Maeya had to stop in order to absorb what she saw.

Although the hill they had just climbed had a gentle incline to it, the other side dropped away as if the hill had cracked in half. While they had walked up the hill in a group, they would have to walk single file down the switch back trail that led down into the large valley.

A ring of hills, just a bit too small to be proper mountains, enclosed the valley; it was big enough to hold several villages. Three of the large hills—or small mountains—sloped down gradually. The fourth was full of small cliffs, steep ravines, and staggering precipices. But the fifth mountain looked as if the Power That Is had simply sliced it in half. From the top of the peak to the meadow below, it was a sheer rock wall. In the middle of the wall, there was a cave. In truth, the Cave looked big enough to hold two of Spike Cave.

In front of the cave, houses spread out in every direction across the valley. They were close together by the cave and gradually spread out more and more as they moved toward the edges of the valley. A town the size of Tiburn and Sundee combined seemed to be spread out in front of the cave.

If the ring of small mountains—or large hills—weren't enough protection, there was a thick perimeter forest of Trident trees. Maeya was surprised that the meadow grass was already so green, since growing season was just starting.

They carefully picked their way down the trail, till they reached the basin of the valley. Then they regrouped, Daegny, Eirenya and Quoran bunched together behind Tare Igny, Darvo and Maeya following the packhorse, keeping their Dragons well back.

When they were halfway across the valley, Tare Igny spurred his horse and moved out front, calling to one of the guards. Quoran followed him, leaving Daegny with Eirenya.

"Maeya," Darvo grabbed her hand and smiled. "All will be well."

She tried to return his smile.

He squeezed her hand. "Igny will see it right," he said, as if the words could make it true.

"Best get used to calling him Tare Igny," Maeya said, making her voice light. "At Spike Cave, if you called a Tare by his first name, you would end up with latrine or kitchen duty for a week, whether you were a Rider or page."

"My thanks for the warning. I will have to guard my tongue."

"You are not comfortable giving titles," Maeya said. The conversation took her mind from the peep who were gathered in front of the Cave, staring at them. She wanted to talk much more than she wanted to think.

And worry. Pharla moved to walk next to Maeya.

Aye. I don't want to worry, Maeya told Pharla. Pharla wasn't able to help her; her mind was such a jumble of nerves it was hard to tell where Maeya's fear ended and the Dragon's began. She ran her hand down her Dragon's back, trying to calm them both.

O, scratch, please!

Where?

There—along my wings.

Here?

Pharla whirred.

"I do not like being forced to show respect," Darvo was saying. Hiama was perched comfortably on his shoulders again, looking like a great cape. "I give respect when it is earned."

"And I have not earned your respect?" Maeya teased. When she saw the confusion on his face, she said, "You did not take long in dropping my title, and it took much from Quoran to get you to start using it in the first place."

Darvo flushed slightly. "That is not a matter of disrespect."

"Nay?"

"Nay," he said. "It is a matter of...wanting to be your equal."

"You are my equal now, yet you still do not call me Rider."

"Does it offend you that I call you by name?"

"Nay," Maeya said with a laugh. "In truth, I am more comfortable with my name than I am with the title."

"I like the sound of your name on my lips," he said.

Or she thought that was what he said. He mumbled a bit, and just as he did, there were shouts from up ahead.

Pharla's fear increased rapidly.

Maeya stroked Pharla's neck.

They are angry.

Who?

Everyone.

Maeya rested her hand on Pharla's side, watching the mob in front of the Cave.

"Are you well?" Darvo asked, squeezing her hand.

"We are nervous," Maeya said.

Darvo looked over at Pharla. "O." He let go of her hand.

As far as reassurances went, it fell short.

"We have honored our vow."

Maeya almost stumbled. Daegny and Eirenya had stopped and waited for them, but she and Darvo had been too involved to notice. Pharla, too, was still focused on the activities from the Cave. Even from here, they could hear many angry voices. "Aye," Maeya said, though she had no idea to what Daegny was referring.

"We will not falter now," she said. "Although we could."

Eirenya stared with wide eyes.

Darvo glared at his twin. "Do not threaten a Rider."

Suddenly Pharla hissed. Thin columns of smoke rose from her nostrils.

Quoran came galloping back. Although Lark had what looked like an easy gait, Quoran was bouncing and hanging on as if she were a wild runaway.

"Halt! Halt! Tare Igny asks that we wait here!" He shouted as Lark dashed past them. He was pulling on her reins, but she had her blood up and still feared the Dragons and did not want to stop.

He will never get her to stop, Pharla snorted.

They watched as he finally got Lark under control—almost at the first switchback—turned her around, and walked her back. Wisely, he dismounted well away from the group.

"Thank you, Daegny," he called as he began walking Lark back and forth, cooling her down.

Daegny smiled. Unlike her smiles of early in their journey, however, this one did not light her entire face.

She bears watching, Pharla said.

Maeya agreed, but had more important things on her mind. "Why must we wait here?" She called to her page.

Quoran grimaced. "Tare Igny's welcome was not as warm as one would like."

Darvo looked up sharply. "Why not?"

"I do not know. He went to find out what is going on. There is a lot of anger down there. Peep were yelling at a Tare," he said, eyes huge, "They were yelling, and the Tare was yelling back!"

"Did you hear what they were yelling about?" Darvo asked.

Quoran shook his head, but at the same time he said, "Something about wanting to leave or needing to stay, something about a Saeb."

Saeb, Pharla said, sounding like she was tasting the word.

"Saeb," Eirenya said, and Maeya could see her rolling the word in her mouth. Then she gave one nod, her dark curls bouncing sharply. "Aye. Saeb."

"Saeb?" Daegny asked.

But Quoran could only shrug helplessly.

Trouble comes now.

"Here they come," Darvo said, his face tight. Four cloaked men were crossing the field toward them, and a shorter fifth figure jogged just behind them, leading a horse and trying to keep up. "What shall we do?"

Leave!

"We greet them," Maeya told all of them, "And see what they want."

I want to leave!

You said I was your leader, Maeya reminded her. *You agreed to let me lead. You wanted me to find a new Cave.*

Aye, Pharla said sullenly. She took a few steps back from Maeya. The hatchling climbed down from Darvo's shoulders and followed her, scampering up on a rock near by. The contrast of Pharla's emerald green with Hiama's yellowish, early awakening season green was stark.

The four men stayed in a line, their long cloaks swaying lightly in the breeze. When they stopped in front of Maeya's group, Tare Igny came around the side, but stopped just short of adding himself to the line.

The first two men had red hair, though one wore it short and the other let it grow past his shoulders. The man on the other end of the line had blond hair like Tare Igny's, but he was very tall and lean. Between them, standing ever so slightly in front, was a gray-haired, gray-bearded, solid man. Although he was the shortest in the line, even shorter than Tare Igny, there was no doubt that he had power.

"I am FullTare Craedo," he said in a deep voice. "I represent Camp Lythe."

Quoran, Eirenya, and Maeya bowed low, and after a moment, she sensed the twins bowing as well. Maeya straightened first.

"I am the only daughter of Taena. I am Rider of Pharla and a seeker of justice. My Dragon and I are late of the Spike Cave of the Kollarian Clan." The cold stares from the Tares were not changing, and she finished in a rush, "I am Rider Maeya Daceae."

"I am the first born of the last born to Taormina. Twin to Daegny, Rider of Hiama and friend of Maeya. I am Darvo Hoart."

"I am the second born of the last born to Taormina. Twin to Darvo. I am Daegny Hoart." Maeya thought Daegny did well for her first introduction.

"I am the only son of the only son of the last son of Bergin. I am a drifter and have traveled far. I am page to Rider Maeya. I am Quoran Bergin." Maeya was not surprised that Quoran's introduction already felt like a practiced recitation.

"I am friend to Rider Maeya and Pharla and Ibaceta. I am Eirenya." Maeya was glad that Eirenya had picked up on the mood of the Tares, but she couldn't help wonder what Usbarula Laureano would have said to the girl.

Maeya waited, but none of the Tares seemed inclined to introduce themselves. She knew better than to threaten or scold them, but she still felt compelled to prod by saying, "We seek a new home with Camp Lythe, may the Power That Is see it always safe."

Beware!

The thought flashed through her head a mere breath before a person came hurtling through the trees at her.

"Maeya!" she heard as she was swept up in a fierce embrace. "Maeya, the Power That Is spared you!" the voice cried.

Maeya was released, and stared up in amazement. "Rider Ret," she gasped. "The Power That Is is kind indeed to let me see you again." Her heart was pounding as she looked at him.

An angry gash ran the side of his neck and disappeared under his tunic. His long glorious blond hair that had been full of curls was gone; he had shaved his head in mourning and the new hair was not long enough to curl yet.

Out of the corner of her eye, Maeya saw Quoran's hand sneak up to touch his own hair. They had both been so wrapped up in their adventures that they had not shaved their heads.

Ret was gaunt and tired looking, as if he had not eaten or slept since the attack on Spike Cave. And still he was incredibly handsome.

Ret turned to look at the rest of the group. A genuine smile lit up his face when he saw Quoran. "The Power That Is has made you hard to kill, indeed, Quoran Bergin. 'Tis good to see you." And he slapped Quoran on the back, hard enough to make Quoran take two steps forward in order to retain his balance. But Ret kept his arm protectively around Maeya. Darvo was staring.

Ret turned to face the FullTare. "I most humbly ask that you grant the same courtesies to my sister as you have me."

"Sister?" One of the Tares asked skeptically.

"Aye, for members of the Clans are all brothers and sisters, are we not? Brothers and sisters of the Dragons?"

"And the other Rider?" Tare Klaz pressed.

"Rider Ret does not know the Hoarts," Maeya said. "We had the good fortune to meet with them on our travels. When Quoran and I left our Cave, we carried one Dragon egg with us. We carried it for nearly two cycles of the Sister Orb. And yet the egg chose to hatch the first time that Rider Darvo laid hands on it."

The Tares and FullTare stared at Maeya with blank expressions.

"We seek to join Camp Lythe," she repeated.

"They will be a good addition," Ret said eagerly.

FullTare Craedo snorted. "We have not yet agreed to let you stay."

Ret flushed, whether from anger or embarrassment, Maeya could not be sure.

"What is your goal?" FullTare suddenly asked Maeya.

"I wish to defeat the Wyzards," she said. She could sense Quoran, Eirenya, Darvo and Daegny nodding next to her. Tare Igny, still standing just behind the FullTare and Tares of Camp Lythe, twisted his hands with worry.

"The best we can hope for is a truce," FullTare Craedo declared.

"Nay," Maeya said, ignoring Quoran's whimper. "We must fight." Ret squeezed her close with his arm.

FullTare Craedo crossed his arms and frowned. "Then you must leave."

"FullTare—" Tare Igny began.

FullTare Craedo held his hand up to Tare Igny. "Nay. Say nothing. We do not wish to encourage such troublesome thoughts. A female Rider will not be allowed in Clan Panir—"

"Then why did—" Ret began angrily, but the FullTare talked right over him.

"—nor will we allow radical Riders who will endanger their Dragons by pushing their training too fast, too hard." He glowered at Ret. "You should not be riding your Dragon yet, nor forcing him to flame by feeding him firestone. You show disrespect to the Tares and I will not tolerate that at my Camp."

Many voices started at once, and Maeya could not pick out who said what as her entire troupe began arguing with the FullTare.

"Enough!" FullTare Craedo bellowed. "Enough! We have answered your question, and the answer is no, you may not join us here at Camp Lythe. You will leave. Now."

The Tares behind the FullTare stood up straight and put their hands on their hips, just like the FullTare. They could not equal his glare, but the message was clear: they supported the FullTare.

"Aye," Maeya said loudly, and was almost surprised when all the other voices around her stopped. "Aye, FullTare Craedo, you have given us your answer and we will abide by it," she nodded her head at him and ignored the indignation she felt from Pharla. "And now, I will give you our answer."

The FullTare's eyebrows drew down in puzzlement.

What question did he ask?

"Soon—during the next full Sister Orb, or the dark Sister Orb of sleeping season, or perhaps even the half Sister of awakening, in truth I do not know when but soon—when Camp Lythe is attacked and the survivors of your Camp need help, we will be there for them."

Why?

"We will be there for *them*, Craedo," Maeya said, emphasizing the lack of title, "But we will not be there for *you*. Our new Cave will have no room for cowards."

Maeya turned, although for a moment she didn't think she'd be able to complete that simple maneuver, because Ret still had his arm around her and didn't seem to know how to either let go or move with her. Pharla's sense of awe and pride had Maeya unbalanced as well.

But then Ret did turn with her and they only stumbled on the first step before they were back in sync and moving smoothly. Maeya did not look for the rest of her troupe; she knew they would follow her as well.

Pharla uncurled herself and moved toward Maeya, whirring softly, and Maeya found she could not stop smiling.

You should be pleased.

I just insulted the FullTare of Panir Clan, Maeya told her. I should be terrified.

But you're not.

No, Maeya said, still smiling foolishly. I am not.

Darvo had only taken two steps toward his hatchling before she was jumping off the rock and scuttling to him. He looked at Maeya with concern, and she smiled. He grinned back, that lopsided grin, and trotted to catch up with Daegny, Quoran, and Eirenya.

"Is Veet here?"

Maeya blinked at Ret, who was staring around. "Nay, he went the way of Spike Cave."

"Then how is it his Dragon is here?"

Pharla took the last few steps toward her and nudged Maeya's arm with her nose. Maeya reached up and ran her hand along her neck.

As Maeya turned to answer Ret, he whispered, "You bonded with it. How did that happen?"

"Cyr Sajen sent me after her."

"And she accepted you. She's a smart Dragon—"

He's smart, Pharla thought to Maeya, *he picked up when you said she instead of it!*

"—much smarter than the other who did not hatch for you."

I think you should pick him for a mate.

"Pharla!"

"You know her name!" Ret exclaimed. "The Power That Is has given you much."

He knows our worth. A good choice for mate.

Maeya clenched her teeth to keep from yelling out loud. Pharla, stop it right now!

A familiar throat clearing sound came from right behind Maeya. "Aye, Tare Igny?" she asked over her shoulder.

"Rider Maeya, we may want to put distance between us and Camp Lythe rather quickly," he said.

"O?"

"Aye. They were riled at the Camp before, and you most certainly upset their Tares." Maeya was pleased that he did not give Craedo the power of the title. "Perhaps haste would be good for a bit."

They had reached the crest of the hill, and Maeya turned to look at the hill-ringed valley with the Cave on the other side. It was still big, still teeming with people, but it was not impressive anymore. Occasionally, the wind brought sounds of angry voices.

"What do they fight about?" Maeya wondered.

Tare Igny cleared his throat behind them again. "The Camp is divided."

"Divided? Divided how?"

"The FullTare and Tares wish to save the Dragons and avoid more conflict with the Wyzards. There are many peep, however, who wish to follow Saeb."

"Saeb?" Darvo asked.

"Aye. I did not have time," Tare Igny sounded apologetic, "to find all the truth. But from what I gather, Saeb rides the pitch Dragon of Prophecy."

"So why do they fight?" Maeya asked Tare Igny. "If the peep wish to follow the Prophecy, why don't they go? Does Craedo refuse to let them go?"

His brow furrowed, Tare Igny nodded. "Aye, that was the sense I got."

Danger!

A large shadow passed above Maeya. The horses skittered, including Spiker, and she knew without asking that Daegny was working hard to keep them somewhat under control. They pulled at their leads, and tossed their heads, but did not truly try to bolt. After one quick glance at the shadow, Quoran focused on helping Daegny.

Pharla ducked down, almost cowering. She was cowering in the corner of Maeya's mind, as well. *Beware!*

Hiama squealed. From the face Darvo made, Maeya could only guess what her claws were doing to his skin as she clung to him.

Ret looked up, a large smile lighting his face. "Teglin!"

Ret's gorgeous blue Dragon swooped down low, but then turned upward again, using powerful wings to quickly gain altitude. Teglin banked hard, turning around toward them, then glided down, landing well in front of them.

Danger!

Pharla, 'tis Ret's Dragon. Maeya tried to reassure her Dragon. Do you not recognize him?

Pharla squealed so loudly Maeya could not tell if it was only in her head or if the Dragon had made noise, but everyone in their group ducked as two more shadows passed overhead.

Suddenly Ret was running for Teglin, Darvo was running toward the nearest trees, Quoran was trying desperately to hold Lark's reins while the other horses all charged off, Eirenya and Tare Igny were running to Maeya, and Daegny crumpled in a heap on the ground.

Maeya stared as two Dragons, one green and one red, dove into clumsy turns, arcing out and away from each other. Their Riders were clinging to their necks, low against the Dragons' spines. The red Dragon was smaller, and seemed to be struggling just to carry its Rider's weight.

As the Dragons completed their turns and began to fly toward each other, a wave of panic washed over Maeya.

Danger! Danger! Danger!

From her crouching position, Maeya crawled over to Pharla, where her Dragon had almost burrowed into the ground. Pharla was beyond words, so Maeya tried to send her calming thoughts and reassurance. As nervous as Maeya was herself, she wasn't sure she was doing any good.

Maeya heard a sudden shout. She looked up just in time to see the Dragons cross too close to each other. The red Dragon's wing didn't get tucked in quickly enough, and collided with the green Dragon's chest. The red Dragon cried in pain, and next to Maeya, Pharla hissed. Then the green Dragon shifted, trying to get its balance back, but the Rider wasn't ready and tumbled off. Maeya heard the loud thud in spite of the thick grasses.

Ret left Teglin's side and ran to the fallen Rider. Teglin lumbered after him.

The red Dragon landed quickly and awkwardly, its wing extended, moaning low. Its Rider jumped off, reaching for the injured wing, and suddenly the moan turned to a cry. The green Dragon landed smoothly, but almost on top of its Rider.

The green spread its wings wide and arched its neck, hissing at Ret's approach, and Ret skidded to a stop. Teglin roared back at the Dragon from behind Ret. Shock flooded Ret's face. He spun back toward Teglin, raising his hands, imploring his blue Dragon to step back.

Maeya couldn't find her thoughts, there was so much noise in her head from Pharla. There were no clear words from her. Pharla was afraid of the new Dragons but scared that one would hurt the other and even more terrified that Maeya would leave her. Maeya kept stroking her neck, murmuring soothing sounds.

Glancing behind her, Maeya could see Tare Igny and Eirenya leaning over Daegny. She was sitting up now, but looked awfully pale. Quoran had somehow managed to keep hold of Lark throughout all, and he was leading her around the Dragons to the trees where Spiker had stopped. Of the other horses, Maeya saw no sign and could only hope that they had stopped further in the trees and were not gone for good.

Ret succeeded in getting Teglin away from the green Dragon. The green Dragon had its head lowered, and Maeya could only assume it was nudging its Rider. A shape appeared from the ash trees behind the green Dragon.

Maeya blinked as she recognized Darvo. He had made it to the trees and circled around. But where was Hiama?

She is safe. He would not let harm come to her.

The green Dragon snaked its head forward, but then suddenly pulled back. Darvo leaned forward, reaching into the grass, and the Dragon simply watched. Maeya sighed in relief. The Rider must be all right.

A shout from Tare Igny made her wrench her head back around. A small group of people was spilling over the top of the ridge that protected Camp Lythe, clustered together because of the narrow path. They were running full-tilt, and it was impossible to see individual faces, but Maeya could see numerous glints as the light of the Orb reflected off drawn swords.

Tare Igny yanked Daegny to her feet and began half-pulling her toward the perceived safety of the trees. When they were just a few paces away, he shoved her forward, and Eirenya after her, then turned, drawing his short sword as he ran back to Maeya.

Quoran released Lark and ran to Maeya as well, pulling arrows from his quiver.

Maeya reached for her bolo. She only had a few stones for ammunition, but she would defend her Dragon with all that she had, her life if necessary.

Nay. You will not give your life.

Maeya didn't look, but she was sure that Ret and Darvo were coming to join them, too. Even so, she felt this could only be their end. FullTare Craedo would not let them join his Camp Lythe, but apparently he would not let them leave, either. Maeya would have to hope that Pharla would be spared, and that Craedo would find a good Rider for her.

You are my Rider!

Maeya didn't respond. She was mesmerized by the group that had drawn closer without slowing down. They were close enough now to see there were only twelve of them—much less than she had thought at first—but all of them were armed.

I am not a pet kitten. I choose my Rider; I am not given to one.

I want to be your Rider, Pharla, Maeya thought. But the Power

That Is may choose differently for both of us.

Pharla shook herself and stood, her outstretched wings catching the Orb's light in a way that made emeralds seem pale.

I will fight for my Rider.

Before Maeya could respond, another yell drew her attention. She looked up again, and felt her stomach drop as she saw more peep coming over the ridge.

"Stand fast, stand fast!" Tare Igny said from her side.

"I am here, Rider," Quoran said from her other side. And just having them there made her feel better.

Suddenly, amazingly, the first group turned, organized themselves into rows, and yelled back at the second group, waving swords and notching arrows.

The second group skidded to a halt, well outside of arrow and spear range. An uneasy quiet fell over the meadow.

A man from the first group, the group that had aligned itself between Maeya's troupe and the one that was still halfway up the ridge, stepped forward. "There has been too much bloodshed," he yelled. He was one of the Tares, the redhead with long hair. "Let us go in peace to find a new Cave. Let us not fight each other."

"Do not look to us for help, Tare Vanec," a man in the second group yelled back. "When sleeping season is here and you have no food, do not look to us."

"So we may go?" Tare Vanec sounded surprised.

"Aye," the other man said, "You may go." As Tare Vanec's group began to lower their weapons, he added, "But the Dragons and their Riders may not."

Instantly, all of the weapons were back up, and angry shouts filled the air.

But an incredible roar that seemed to reverberate in Maeya's very bones drowned the shouts out.

Pharla had reared up on her back legs, and her neck was fully extended as she roared in fury to the Orb itself.

As her roar began to trail off, another roar began. Maeya turned and saw the red Dragon up on its hind legs, and then the other green Dragon reared back and added its voice.

A shadow swept past them, and Teglin roared down at the meadow. Maeya shaded her eyes against the brightness of the Orb, and gasped. Ret was astride Teglin.

Teglin's powerful wings moved easily as he carried Ret toward the group on the ridge. He dipped low, and landed between the two groups. Even as the second group scrambled backwards up to the ridge, Maeya clenched her teeth and appealed to the Power That Is.

Don't let his arrogance get him killed, she thought. *Make the men stay their weapons.*

Instead of swinging down from Teglin's back, Ret stood up on it. He had a spear in his hand, but he held it loosely at his side. "Dragons follow destiny," he declared, voice rolling clearly across the meadow. "Dragons work with their Riders to stand up to injustices. It will take more than a mob of cowards to take down a Dragon."

He should not insult them, Pharla said.

Hush, Maeya thought, almost missing the rest of what Ret said.

"As Tare Vanec said, we do not wish to fight. We merely wish to leave in peace."

"You and your Dragon may leave," the man from the other group yelled. "You and your Dragon are not from our Clan. But the Panir Riders and their Dragons must stay!"

The Dragons came to join us!

Ret was shaking his head. "It matters not what Clan we are from. Dragons will follow destiny, and destiny will not be found in your little Camp."

"We cannot lose more Dragons," the man now sounded desperate instead of threatening. "We must keep our Dragons. They must stay here."

They have lost Dragons?

"Then we will have bloodshed," Ret said, hefting his spear. Behind him, Tare Vanec's group once again raised their swords and bows. "Does Camp Lythe really want that? Can Camp Lythe really survive more injuries?"

Maeya held her breath. No one moved. And then, two people turned and ran back up the hillside, disappearing over the ridge. Before they were completely out of view, three more had run after them. Then the entire group turned to leave, except for the speaker.

"This is wrong," he said. "A Clan should not divide itself."

"The Clan already divided," Quoran yelled suddenly next to Maeya. His words carried strangely but clearly across the grasses, as if the wind itself wanted him heard. "The Clan divided when Rider Eleena took the great Naria to the skies! At times of destiny, the heroes and the cowards must define themselves, and form their own Clans. Ours will be a Clan of heroes!"

There was a roar of approval from the group in front of them. The other speaker shook his head, turned, and trudged back up the hill before disappearing over the ridge.

Ret jumped from Teglin's back, and moved to speak to Tare Vanec. Tare Vanec, however, was walking toward Maeya.

Bringing his right fist across his chest to tap his left shoulder, he said, "Rider Maeya, we ask permission to travel with you."

Maeya smiled. "We welcome you to our troupe, but I fear that at the moment, we do not know where we are going. We had planned to stop at Camp Lythe."

"Aye," Tare Vanec said, "But I have a suggestion."

"O?"

"Aye. I believe that the path of Sister Orb will lead us to the pitch Dragon."

A chill that was not her own ran down Maeya's spine. She looked over to Pharla, who was staring at Sister Orb, rising in the violet sky.

CHAPTER SIXTEEN

The green Dragon belonged to a Rider named Brunso; the red was Rider Scrifres'. Rider Brunso, amazingly, was only bruised. Although a little groggy, he was sitting up by the time his Dragon allowed anyone else get close to him. Rider Scrifres was more shaken by his Dragon's injury than Brunso was by his own.

The red Dragon wouldn't let anyone other than Scrifres near him. Tare Vanec was able to give advice, but no one had any of the herbs that he thought might help the red Dragon's pain. "Keep your Dragon on the ground," Tare Vanec said. "Even if it wants to fly, keep it on the ground."

"Aye, Tare, I will try," Scrifres panted as he trotted back to his Dragon. "I will try, but she does have a mind of her own."

Brunso joined Ret, Maeya and Pharla. After introducing himself and telling them Scrifres' name, he brought his fist up to his shoulder in salute. "We ask permission to join you," he said.

"Do you know where we go?" Maeya asked, at the same time that Ret said, "Of course you may join us, Rider."

Ret and Maeya looked at each other. He was clearly shocked that she had thought Brunso was addressing the question to her.

"I hope you will lead us to Rider Saeb and her Dragon," Brunso said, answering Maeya and further shocking Ret. "We would have left with her, had we been given the chance."

"What do you mean?"

Brunso looked indignant. "The FullTare convinced everyone that her Dragon was dangerous and should be destroyed. For their own safety, they fled."

"But you stayed behind?" Ret asked.

Now Brunso looked abashed. "Her sister made a wonderful mead for evening meal. Everyone had a cup, and several of us had two. I did not wake until the Orb was sinking for a second time."

"We would be happy to have you in our troupe," Maeya said, having a hard time keeping her attention on Brunso. Several paces beyond him, she could see Tares Igny and Vanec having a heated discussion. "I am glad you were not harmed in the fall."

Brunso's cheeks flamed. "I cannot believe I fell from Calla's back."

"I didn't think you were allowed to ride," Ret said.

"It was my first flight with her," Brunso admitted. He glanced at Maeya. "And Scrifres' as well. I will go see how he is doing," he said.

"I'll come too," Ret said. "I need to check on Teglin anyway."

Maeya nodded absently as Ret and Brunso both walked away. Eirenya materialized at her side. "Ibaceta is worried," she said.

"Why?"

"I do not know. She does not talk to me," Eirenya said, "But she is upset."

"Is she safe? Is she going to hurt somebody?"

"Nay," Eirenya said, though she sounded troubled.

It's the other wolves, Pharla said. *They have been getting closer to her. She doesn't know what to do with them.*

O. I don't know how to help her.

She will figure it out. Even orphans must learn to deal with our own kind.

So you will try to be nice to the other Dragons?

Pharla's presence pulled back in her mind.

"Eirenya, why don't you go find Daegny? I think she would appreciate some help with the horses." When Eirenya made a face, Maeya asked, "What?" Though they had gotten off to a rough start, once Eirenya had saddled Storm, Daegny seemed to take the young girl under her wing, constantly seeking her out. Maeya tried to tell herself that she wasn't jealous.

"Why don't I just start looking for the horses?" Eirenya suggested. "Storm and Jingle went that way," she pointed to the nearest edge of the Trident forest.

"Why don't you go get her and then go looking together? So you're not wandering the trees alone."

"Please, Rider Maeya," Eirenya said earnestly, "Let me go."

"What's wrong?"

Eirenya leaned in close. "They're looking at me funny," she whispered. "Like...like something's wrong with me."

Maeya remembered how mysterious she thought Eirenya's black skin had been when she had first seen her. "I still don't like you being alone in the forest," she began, but Eirenya was already moving away.

"Don't worry, Rider, I won't be alone!" She called over her shoulder.

Truly, Ibaceta will keep careful watch.

Then how will Eirenya get close to the horses?

There are many wolves and Dragons in the area. The horses are too distressed to pick one to focus on.

Maeya continued to watch the Tares. It was so frustrating to see two who were supposed to be leading acting so childishly. Everyone else was almost ready to go, and they were still arguing.

Maeya?

Aye, Pharla.

Have all of our horses gone?

Maeya glanced over her shoulder to where Eirenya had disappeared. *I'm sure we'll find Spiker, but I don't know about the rest,* she thought. *Hopefully we will find them. We have far too many peep for everyone to be able to ride now, but they can carry supplies for us.*

Too bad the peep did not bring their own mounts. We will travel slower now.

Aye, Maeya thought. *But before we can travel slowly, we first must get started.*

She walked over to the Tares. Neither of them saw her approaching.

"I have never heard such Quan dung!" Tare Vanec said.

"You cannot—"

"What's amiss?" She asked, interrupting Tare Igny.

Tare Vanec and Tare Igny stared at each other over her head. Maeya took a deep breath and tried not to shout. "What is amiss? Why do the two leaders stand here and argue instead of leading their groups?"

Tare Igny looked at her. "You are the leader, Rider Maeya."

"Aye," Tare Vanec agreed. "We follow you."

"And that is good," Maeya said, "But you must lead the others."

"Aye," Tare Vanec said again. "That is what I have been trying to tell Tare Igny."

"I do not deserve to be a Tare!" Tare Igny burst out. "I do not deserve to lead! I will follow, and do all that is asked of me, but let Tare Vanec lead."

Tare Vanec said, "I am much younger! I do now know enough to lead the Riders."

But Tare Igny was staring at the ground and would not look up.

"I will lead the Riders," Maeya said, "And I will seek advice from both of you. But you, Tare Vanec, must keep track of the peep who came with you. And you, Tare Igny—" she ignored the moan she heard from him, "—will continue to help our small troupe."

Tare Igny still looked down. Maeya jerked her head to the side, and Tare Vanec nodded before leaving them.

"Why do you suddenly resent being called Tare?" Maeya asked him softly.

"I do not resent it. I do not deserve it!"

"Why? Were you not Palth's Rider?"

"Aye, but...it is my fault Camp Meadow Spear is gone!"

That seems irrational, Pharla mused. *He did not attack his own Clan, did he?*

"Did you invite the Wyzards?" Maeya asked Tare Igny.

"Nay," he whispered, closing his eyes and raising his face up to the Orb. "Nay, we did not invite them. We had heard of the nearby attacks, and we were ready for them."

"What happened?"

"I had been in charge of setting the guards that day."

"And," Maeya prodded.

"And I did not set any guards."

Why ever not?

Maeya didn't echo Pharla's question; she just waited for Tare Igny to continue.

"I was too drunk to remember my duty."

"O."

Drunk?

Drinking something that makes you silly, Maeya thought to her.

He wasn't silly, Pharla shot back. *He was irresponsible.*

"You were willing to be a Tare before," Maeya said, ignoring Pharla. "You introduced yourself as a Tare."

"Aye, for a small group for a short journey."

"Your small group still needs you. What has changed now?"

"Now? Now we have a large troupe," Tare Igny opened his eyes and looked at her. "Now we have a troupe that may be the last chance against the Wyzards. Now we have another Tare. And you need a responsible Tare."

"You will be a responsible Tare," Maeya told him. "Because you will not drink."

Tare Igny dropped his head again. "I wish it were that easy," he said. "You need a strong Tare to lead your group."

"This is why you would not go into Sundee!"

"Aye. I cannot control myself around temptation. And now..." he gestured around helplessly.

It is time to be moving.

Maeya glanced around. Everyone had wandered in their direction, but no one had wanted to interrupt them, so they had a ring of people a few paces wide.

"I am Rider Maeya," she said, raising her voice for all to hear, "Rider of Pharla." The Dragon whirred in Maeya's head. "We do not know how far we will have to go, but we seek the Dragon of prophecy and others who will join us in the fight against the Wyzards. Tare Vanec and Tare Igny will lead us along the way, teaching us what we need to know. What they cannot teach us, we will teach them. And the first lesson we will all learn is to work together."

Maeya took a breath. "Tare Igny needs our help. We will all help him stay away from mead and ales."

When Maeya paused and several peep muttered to themselves, Daegny raised her voice. "I need your help. We had six horses that bolted because of the Dragons, and we will need to find them."

Now peep nodded their heads and many raised their hands.

"I need your help," Tare Vanec said. "I need to find Japon roots, to help the red Dragon heal faster."

"I need your help," Darvo said, "For my Dragon is small and I cannot take her hunting with me."

"I need your help," Ret said, "For I wish to make distance in our travels."

Maeya smiled. "Aye. We need to begin with distance. And we begin now."

***   *******   ***

Maeya was having a hard time remembering a time when she hadn't been traveling, when she wasn't spending each night at a different fire, in a new clearing, by a new cliff or a new creek.

The troupe was spread out, but not in a bad way. From her position, Maeya could see the peep walking out front, just reaching another creek. Behind them were Tare Igny, Tare Vanec, Eirenya and Daegny, all on horseback. Eirenya had found the runaway horses in a ravine on the other side of the first hill they climbed. Daegny had swept the girl up in an effusive embrace and complimented her skills.

Brunso and Scrifres walked ahead of Maeya, both of them having refused the offer of a horse. Their Dragons walked just behind them. Ret, Darvo, Quoran and Maeya were in the very back. Teglin and Pharla walked in front of them, but behind the other Dragons. There seemed to be a cautious truce between the four larger Dragons.

Pharla cautiously began to talk to the other Dragons. Maeya had mixed feelings about this because Pharla had a hard time keeping her thoughts meant for the Dragon's out of Maeya's head. It was disconcerting to hear Pharla ask Teglin if he thought Ret liked Maeya; but it was reassuring to hear Pharla defend Maeya's plan to Calla.

Darvo carried Hiama, and Maeya knew he would soon need a rest. His hatchling was growing, but not nearly as fast as Pharla seemed to. Maeya frowned, wondering how they were all going to make it so far on foot.

"All will be well," Ret said, picking up on her worry.

"How did you escape?" Maeya asked him. "Where were you in the Cave?"

"I wasn't. Teglin and I had gone out for an early ride," he said.

"Before first meal?" Quoran asked skeptically.

"I do not sleep well," Ret said. Dark shadows under his eyes supported this claim, yet Maeya had never noticed them when we were at the Training Cave. He smiled at her and she forgot about his tired eyes. "I'm glad you were able to bond with Pharla."

"I only wish we hadn't lost our Cave."

Ret's face fell. "It was awful. By the time Teglin and I were close to the Cave, all we could hear were screams of pain. There was nothing we could do."

"So you didn't even try?" Darvo asked indignantly.

"One Rider and Dragon against many Wyzards and their Faithful? You would have me sacrifice Teglin and myself? I chose to rally other Caves to fight the Wyzards."

"How many Caves have you rallied?" Darvo challenged.

"None so far, but I have been to three."

"O?" Maeya asked.

"Cave Meadow Spear, Arc Side Cave, and Camp Lythe. Arc Side and, obviously, Camp Lythe turned me away. I was too late to warn Meadow Spear."

Imagining several Caves looking destroyed like Spike Cave, Maeya felt cold inside and involuntarily shuddered. Ret put his arm around her again.

Ret had never paid her any mind at the Cave; she could not understand why he was holding her close now, why he was so happy to see her.

You were a page at the Cave.

And a Rider!

In training, Pharla thought dismissively.

Other Riders would say hello to me.

Perhaps he was too busy.

Too arrogant.

I believe he has learned humility, Pharla observed. *A severe loss in battle can do that.*

"I would have fought," Darvo muttered.

"O? You would have led your Dragon to her death?" Ret said scornfully.

Darvo scowled. "Of course not—"

"It was not an easy choice," Ret cut in. "I thought I had lost all but Teglin." Ret squeezed Maeya again. "I have never been so happy as when I saw Maeya and Quoran. Together we will rebuild Spike Cave."

Ah, Maeya thought at the same time Pharla thought, *He sees you as useful.*

Aye. Maeya shrugged out of his arm on the pretext of getting a drink from her water skin. When she was done, she stayed just out of his reach.

"How is your headache?" Darvo asked.

Ret turned to her. "Are you ill?"

"Nay," Maeya said, as Darvo said, "She has been suffering headaches for many days now."

Maeya glared at him. At least he hadn't mentioned the Japon root but, "I'm fine, Darvo. If I need help, I will ask."

He nodded but he did not seem upset that Maeya had snapped at him.

"Perhaps some of the peep from Camp Lythe have something that could help," Ret suggested.

Darvo grinned. "Why don't you go ask them?"

Ret looked from Maeya to him and back to her again. "Aye, that I will." He nodded to Maeya, clearly not including Darvo, and then strode off toward Teglin.

Ripples of amusement came from Pharla as she watched them take off, but whether that was from Ret's words or something Teglin had said to her, she would not tell Maeya.

"Maeya—"

"Rider Maeya," Quoran corrected. "Why can you not learn?"

"I am a Rider, too," Darvo shot back.

"Then call her Leader," Quoran snapped. "She is still above you!"

"Peace," Maeya said. "This is too much."

"Apologies Rider," Quoran said instantly, bowing as he walked next to her.

"I need to speak to Tare Vanec and Tare Igny," she said.

"I will fetch them—"

"Nay," Maeya interrupted. "I will catch up with them and ask Daegny to ride rear guard with you. You should find out what's amiss."

"I'm sure that she's just—"

"Aye," Maeya said, nodding. "Exactly." Quoran stared at her for a moment before grinning.

"I should be the one to talk to my sister," Darvo objected.

"Nay," Maeya said, "You should talk to Brunso and Scrifres. If we are forming a new Cave or Clan, we need to learn about the Riders."

Darvo bobbed his head in acceptance.

Well done, Leader Maeya, Pharla said. *You got rid of all the problems very neatly.*

Then why, Maeya asked as she patted her side and hurried past the Dragons to catch up with Tare Vanec and Tare Igny, do I feel our problems are just getting started?

*** ******* ***

Surprisingly, Daegny did not argue when Maeya asked her to drop back and ride guard with Quoran. She simply slid off Jingle and handed Maeya her reins.

"It's a sidesaddle," she said tartly. "Take care not to fall off."

Tare Vanec looked shocked but Tare Igny just shook his head and tried to hide a smile.

"I'll come with you," Eirenya said. "Do you want to ride double?"

"Nay," Daegny said as they dropped back. "It feels good to be out of the saddle for a bit."

"How is Pharla?" Tare Igny asked.

"Fine, except her wings are bothering her," Maeya said, once she was settled in the uncomfortable saddle.

"Bothering her?" Tare Vanec asked.

"They itch a lot."

"Ah," he said with a smile, "That's good."

"Why is that good?"

"It means that she is getting ready to fly."

Pharla's presence in her mind got suddenly cold.

"We are making good time," Maeya observed. "How long do you think we can keep this pace?"

Tare Vanec shook his head. "The peep in front know we need distance. If the Sister Orb passes without an attack, we will go much slower tomorrow."

"Aye," Tare Igny agreed. "With so many on foot, we must slow down."

"Do you know how far we will have to go to find this Saeb?"

They both shook their heads. "We do not even know where she was headed," Tare Vanec said. "There were children in her group, but they also took horses, so I don't know how fast they will travel."

"Tare Vanec, will you tell me the prophecy? I know you plan to tell it to everyone tonight," Maeya hurried on as he opened his mouth, "And I hate to make you say it twice, but I think I should hear it now. So that I will know what's coming."

You have heard it before.

We have the Lore from our Clan; I would hear it from another.

Rider Maeya, you deserve to be Leader. It was the first time Maeya heard genuine admiration from her Dragon.

Tare Vanec sighed deeply. "Aye, perhaps the leader should hear it first."

Maeya waited as he gathered his thoughts and then she listened to the story of the great Naria and her Rider Eleena told in a slightly new way. Tare Vanec said it was Elmrond who died, not Brind; Tinom was a page and Matew was Naria's Rider; there were eight Tares instead of four; and several other small changes that did not affect the heart of the Lore. Maeya could sense Pharla, not quite tucked in the back of her mind but trying to stay out of the way as she also heard the story from Tare Vanec.

"...The white Dragon that hatched from the damaged egg for Eleena only lived long enough to give a message to her," Tare Vanec said. He paused again before reciting the Prophecy:

> "In time of need and time of fire
> You protected your heart's desire.
> In the coming years of woe
> All will fall 'neath evil glow.
> But in the future lies our dreams
> Of power once ripped at seams
> By descendent true of witch
> And a Dragon dark as pitch.

"And the pitch Dragon has hatched?" Maeya asked.

"Aye," Tare Vanec averred. "I have seen him myself. Beautiful in a terrifying way. He is pitch black, except for the golden mark on his chest and a silver scar."

"Silver scar?"

"He was attacked during his first cycle of Sister Orb, and the scales that grew back are silver."

"What would dare attack a Dragon?"

"'Twas either a wolf or an owl. The story I heard was unclear."

We need to watch for owls, Pharla said.

Aye, and be wary of new wolves as well. It was strange to think that Maeya would recognize the wolves who had been traveling with them, yet she was sure she would be able to.

Things are teetering, Pharla said.

Aye, Maeya said. I am not Eleena.

And I am not Naria.

But many things are the same.

Too many, she agreed, and Maeya could sense her unease overlapping her own.

After a few moments of silence, Maeya turned again to Tare Vanec. "You speak of a white Dragon and a black one in this prophecy. I have never heard of either."

"It is the only mention of either color," Tare Vanec agreed. "But unusual things are occurring everywhere. The Wyzards are attacking openly. We have a pitch Dragon, and a gold one—"

"Gold?" Golden Dragons were rare; only one in every four or five generations.

"Aye, Landin's gold Dragon hatched over two years ago, and is a very good size. You will see for yourself, if we find Saeb. I feel certain Landin went with her."

"Is there mention of a yellow-green Dragon?"

Tare Vanec hesitated, and Maeya could tell he was weighing his words. "That hatchling may not be well," he said finally, "But only the Power That Is will determine how many seasons it will live to see."

What is wrong with Darvo's hatchling? Maeya asked Pharla.

I do not know. She sounded troubled.

"Will you go speak with Darvo?" Maeya asked Tare Vanec. "Perhaps get a better look at the hatchling?"

Tare Vanec shifted uncomfortably in his saddle, looking at Tare Igny. But Igny simply swayed with the rhythm of his mount, staring off to something else. Maeya was not sure he had listened to any of the prophecy. Tare Vance must have come to the same conclusion. "Aye," he said, "I will go talk to Rider Darvo."

He turned to go. After the sound of horse hooves faded, Tare Igny burst out, "Rider Maeya, I am afraid."

"Tare Igny, we will all help you—"

He waved his hand, cutting her off. "We all have much more important things to worry about than me."

"I don't—"

"Everything is teetering, don't you feel it?" Maeya flinched so hard at the word 'teetering' that she nearly fell off the sidesaddle. Tare Igny, however, didn't notice. He was babbling, and Maeya wasn't sure he was really talking to her or to himself. "The Clans, which have been separated for generations, must now find a way to unite. And it looks like we're going to be uniting behind girls—female Riders! The Panir Clan hasn't allowed a female Rider in memory! Yet there's no denying you're powerful—your Dragons are already bonding with you, communicating their names, sharing their thoughts. And one of the Dragons is black! And the other—well, it's been generations since Clan Uture had a successful re-bonding for a Dragon who had lost its Rider. Not to mention the wolves! What are the wolves doing? Our world, Maeya, our world is changing, changing too fast! I am afraid! I am afraid it is—" After rambling so fast, Tare Igny cut off with a frightening abruptness.

"Tare?" Maeya asked cautiously. "What is it you are afraid of?"

Everything, from the sounds of it, Pharla said, but her tone was frightened as well.

"Hiama is sickly. While she has already told Darvo her name, she has hardly grown in size since the day she hatched. He may be a Dragon Rider, but he will never Ride her. When things move so fast, they crash. I fear we are moving to the end of the Dragons."

"Tare?" Maeya could not have heard him correctly.

Pharla was quiet, which only increased Maeya's distress.

"How could the coming of the Prophecy mean the end of the Dragons?" she demanded. "It says 'But in the future lies our dreams/Of power once ripped at seams.' Our dreams are here, and we're going to sew the power back together, we're going to rebuild the Clans into one Clan the way it was meant to be."

O. O, yes, we will put the power back together.

"Did you not just rip Clan Uture further apart? You told Craedo he could not come, but the rest of Camp Lythe could."

"Aye, but that was—"

Tare Igny was shaking his head. "The power has been ripped, and is only barely holding together. It will rip apart now, and our dreams will be covered with the evil glow, for it is 'By descendent true of witch/And a Dragon dark as pitch' that our world is being made to change. May the Power That Is see us through it." He wheeled his horse and rode away from the group.

I like your explanation better.

Me too. We're going to make it happen our way, no matter what this Saeb and her pitch Dragon say.

***   ********   ***

Maeya wasn't sure when Tare Igny returned to the group; he avoided her and she was not interested in seeking him out.

Brunso and Scrifres' Dragons found a rocky overhang near the camp, but Pharla and Hiama stayed with their Riders in the campsite. Eirenya found Maeya as soon as they made camp and stayed at her side. The girl was nervous and clearly felt the stares from every direction. It was the quietest Maeya had ever seen her.

"Would you like me to say something at the meeting tonight?"

Eirenya shook her head frantically. "Nay, Rider, please do not. They will get used to seeing me in time."

"Aye," Maeya agreed with forced cheerfulness. Most of the Riders and all of the Tares had certainly accepted Quoran for who he was. Peep at Spike Cave, however, may have gotten used to seeing Quoran's scarred face, but there were still several who never liked to be near him, simply because he looked different. Eirenya was different from head to toe—and could make herself hard to see, too. She would be talked about with hushed voices after Sister Orb rose.

Several of the peep from Camp Lythe began cooking as soon as they stopped for camp, and soon everyone was gathered around four fires in close proximity. Food and drink was shared easily, and members of Maeya's small group were sought for conversation.

Eirenya sat between Daegny and Maeya when they began eating. Soon, Maeya was in a lively discussion with Scrifres and Brunso, and the next time she looked, the little shadow was gone. But Ret was trying to catch her eye, and Darvo actually came up and wedged himself between her and Brunso, and then Tare Vanec came to introduce Daena, a healer who had talked with a healer who had traveled with the pitch Dragon, and had ideas how to help Scrifres' Dragon, and Maeya could only worry about Eirenya.

She is fine.
Where is she?
With me.
And Ibaceta?
Of course.
You like the wolf.
Aye.

"—more of the Trident root, Maeya?"

"Pardon," Maeya said, feeling her face get hot. "I'm afraid I wasn't listening."

"Of course," Daena said, giving her a strained smile. "We are all weary from the traveling. Perhaps now is not the time to talk about the well-being of someone else's Dragon."

"Aye. Thank you for understanding." Maeya nodded her head as Daena moved gracefully away. "Perhaps you should begin, Tare," Maeya said, "So that we may get our rest. We have more traveling before us."

"Aye," Tare Vanec nodded. "But you should call the meeting."

Maeya stared at him, mouth open. "But—but—but Tare, you're—"

"Traveling with you," he said, "As is everyone else. Riders Brunso and Scrifres did not talk to me until they had your permission."

"I would rather…"

Tare Vanec took a small step away from her. "You are our leader, Rider Maeya, in the search for Rider Saeb and Galanth. It will not always be easy. And if this is the most difficult thing you have to do, then the Power That Is favors you greatly."

He is right.

I know. But I do not even know how to start.

As you mean to go on.

She stood and swallowed hard. "Peep of Camp Lythe," Maeya began.

Pssshtt. I can barely hear you and I'm listening to your thoughts.

"Peep of Camp Lythe," Maeya called, "We thank you for traveling with us. We thank you for sharing your meal with us." Eirenya appeared by her side, smiled up at her, and took her hand. "We believe that the Power That Is will help us to find Rider Saeb and her Dragon soon. Tare Vanec has offered to tell all of us the Prophecy, to help us understand why we are traveling together."

Tare Vanec told the prophecy to the troupe, but this time he used his formidable gift of storytelling. Everyone was enthralled in the drama of Wysleck, Eleena, and Naria as it unfolded around the fire, but Maeya's small group was truly awed to hear of Saeb and Galanth. The peep of Camp Lythe had seen them, and some added their own details. When Tare Vanec explained that FullTare had condemned Saeb and Galanth to death, and Brunso and Scrifres explained their escape, the crowd became rightfully agitated.

Then they all looked back to Maeya.

"O. Um. Many…O. Many things are changing. And, O. We must… must be ready to change. We must be ready to…to look at things differently, to try new things. Rider Saeb already seems to recognize this. I look forward to meeting her, and I'm sure that she will welcome hard workers. But first we must find her, and to do that, we will travel. We may travel far, so I ask you all to get rest whenever you may. Continue to help each other, for that is why we travel together and not alone. May the Power That Is give you all good rest."

Most of the peep from Camp Lythe seemed content to stay near the main fire, talking in groups of two or three. Eirenya and Maeya, however, immediately walked over where Quoran had set out their small camp.

"I'm going to check Ibaceta," Eirenya said.

"Does she want to come into camp?"

"Too many peep," Eirenya said. "I may sleep under the trees, too."

"Eirenya—"

The little girl sighed. "You are more protective than Usbarula Laureano!"

"You may return to her…" Maeya said with a smile.

"I will be back soon," Eirenya grumbled, disappearing into the darkness.

Maeya went slightly past her camp, to the evergreen bush that Pharla had chosen for the night's shelter. "Why don't you want to be with the other Dragons?"

I am. She moved her tail slightly, revealing Hiama tucked in along her side, looking up with dark green eyes.

"You know what I mean."

I like it here.

"Should I bring my blankets over?"

Nay, Pharla said, dropping her head to her forelegs. Her head was almost bigger than Hiama's body. *We will be fine.* Both Dragons closed their eyes.

Darvo knows where she is? Maeya thought.

Of course.

Sleep well.

And you.

Maeya returned to the camp, sat on her sleeping blankets and leaned back against a log, pulling off her shoes. She took a long deep breath and closed her eyes. Perhaps she would have a few moments to herself.

"Rider Maeya, may I sit with you?"

"Welcome, Darvo," she said, opening her eyes and making herself smile.

He seated himself on the ground next to her instead of on the log across the fire. Quoran had shown off his skills as Maeya's page, setting everything up for them, arranging their two pallets, and setting a small, almost flat rock with their limited selection of plates and cups. She wasn't sure when he had found the time to stitch together another bag to carry Maeya's clothes, though he continued to cram his own in with their camp supplies.

"How are you?" Maeya asked Darvo. After mid-day meal, he had ridden Spiker, his hatchling nestled against his chest.

Darvo shrugged. "Worried," he said frankly.

"Hiama?"

"Aye."

"What did the Tare say?"

"Tare Vanec said that all Dragons hatch with lighter scales than their adult color, but that the yellow hint in her scales—" he cleared his throat and looked away, blinking rapidly, "—indicates a fatal weakness."

Maeya frowned. "Wouldn't you sense that?" she asked him.

"I don't sense the other Dragons at all!" Taking a deep breath, Darvo spread his hands out then clasped them together again, looking utterly hopeless. "It makes sense, doesn't it?"

"What?"

He said, "All this time, I thought I was able to sense the weak and injured animals. Perhaps, in truth, they were drawn to me. Perhaps that's why she hatched for me."

"Nay," Maeya said. "She hatched for you because you have the qualities of a Rider that she was waiting for."

He looked doubtful, but gratified.

"Rider Maeya, you look comfortable!" Ret strode into their firelight, grinning broadly. "I'm happy to see that you can find time to rest after an arduous day of leading our Troupe."

"I am—" Maeya began, but before she could say anything else, he grabbed her ankles, lifted her legs, and sat down on the ground next to her, setting her legs across his lap. Maeya's mouth dried up as he began to rub her bare feet.

Maeya cleared her throat and with difficulty formed a question. "Where were you at midday meal?"

"Teglin was edgy," he said. "We went for a long ride, to help him calm down."

"How old is Teglin?" Darvo asked.

Ret frowned slightly, concentrating. "I have been a Rider for four years," he said.

Darvo looked like he wanted to ask something else, but he closed his mouth and looked down at his hands again.

"How hard was it to find Pharla?" Ret asked Maeya.

"It took several days to find her," Maeya said, trying to relax but finding it difficult while his hands were on her skin. "And several more to get her to accept me at all." Maeya paused, and then said, "I'm still not sure she has accepted me."

"O, she has," Ret said confidently. "You would know if she hadn't."

"But she's...difficult."

Ret smirked. "She's an intelligent being of her own. It's not like having a spirited horse."

"I know, but...well, how often does Teglin argue with you?"

"Pharla can't talk to you yet—can she?"

"Aye, she most certainly can," Maeya said glumly.

You should be pleased.

Maeya groaned. "Pharla, I am pleased when you are—"

"Are you talking to her now?" Ret looked astounded.

When will you learn to think instead of speak?

"Aye."

"Maeya, that's...that's amazing!" Ret shook his head. "Teglin does not often talk to me, unless we are together!"

"I can't get Pharla to stop," Maeya was whining, but she didn't care.

If I left, the Dragon began.

I couldn't bear it, Maeya thought to her. You are a part of me, I know.

Then stop thinking of me as a bellyache. Maeya giggled, and Ret and Darvo both looked at her oddly.

"You tickled me," Maeya said, trying to pull her feet away from Ret.

He captured her ankles and grinned. "I'll try not to do that again," he said, "At least for now."

His blue eyes were almost hypnotic. Maeya couldn't look away.

"My Dragon has not yet seen all the faces of Sister Orb, and I feel that she is already a part of me."

"Aye," Ret said, answering Darvo but not taking his eyes off Maeya. "The bond with a hatchling is strong and immediate. And soon she will send you images to communicate. But when she begins using words, it will be something all together wonderful."

"Hiama speaks to me often," Darvo said.

"You don't name your Dragon," Ret began.

"I didn't! She told me her name!"

Ret finally broke eye contact with Maeya and turned to face Darvo. "But she...she can't even walk yet!"

"She can too!"

Ret made a dismissive gesture. "You have to carry her. Is she in her second Sister Orb yet?"

"Nay."

A strange look crossed Ret's face. "But you think she told you her name?"

"I know she did."

The two boys stared at each other. Tension was in the air, but Maeya wasn't sure why. She leaned toward Ret. "How do you know when the Dragon is ready to fly?"

He looked at her, and they were close enough for her to see that he had an amber speck in his left eye, "You don't," he whispered. "They tell you!"

Maeya smiled. "I look forward to hearing Pharla say that!"

Ret turned to look at Darvo. "I don't mean to be rude, but I would like to talk to Rider Maeya alone."

Darvo flushed and stood. He nodded stiffly, and took two steps away from the fire. Then he wheeled about, almost bounded back, and swooped down to kiss Maeya. He missed her lips—not by much—but he didn't linger. Just as fast as he was at her side, he was gone, dust rising from his heels.

Ret looked at her, and with difficulty Maeya closed her mouth.

"I think that was a hint," Ret said, sounding tense.

Maeya just stared in the direction, which Darvo had disappeared.

"Maeya, you could have told me that—"

"I didn't know," Maeya blurted, although looking back it was clear and she was chagrined that she hadn't picked up on it earlier. She buried her face in her hands. "O, Darvo," she sighed.

"I will go find him," Ret said tersely, "And send him back to you. I apologize for—"

"Wait!" Maeya said, suddenly realizing what Ret thought. "Nay, that's not…I can't…it won't…" Ret stared at her patiently while she tried to collect the right words. "Darvo is my friend," Maeya said finally. "That is all he can be." She closed her eyes and sighed again. "I will have to find a way to tell him that, but not right now."

Ret smiled again, relaxing. "Not right now," he agreed. "So how did your conversation with Tare Vanec go?"

Maeya shrugged. "If I knew what I was supposed to do—"

"If you don't want to lead, don't," Ret said. "No one can make you. Let someone with more experience do it. Let one of the Tares or me take lead."

Maeya arched her eyebrows at him. "Did I say I didn't want to lead?"

Not to him and not in so many words—

Hush, Pharla.

"I meant no offense, Maeya. It's just…."

Maeya waited, watching his expression go from simply uncomfortable to very embarrassed. "It's only that you're so young. Peep will respect older leaders."

"I did not see you giving FullTare Craedo much respect."

"He was an old fool—"

"And you think I am a young one?"

Maeya heard a strange noise from Pharla's part of her mind. It sounded like she was choking. Are you all right? Maeya asked her.

Fine.

"I don't think you a fool, Maeya. A fool would not recognize that she was overwhelmed."

"I have sought advice and help when needed," she said tartly. "I do not feel overwhelmed."

There is a difference between feeling overwhelmed and acting overwhelmed.

"Not yet, perhaps, but—"

"Rider Ret, I am leader of this troupe. If you find problem with that, you may seek appropriate leadership elsewhere. Do not think to take it from me here."

"Maeya, you have yet to ride your Dragon. You cannot lead Riders who touch the sky."

"Pharla and I will touch the sky." Maeya felt Pharla twitch in the back of her mind. "Until then, I look for advisors to help me. Not schemers who would take over."

"I think I'm insulted."

It took all her will power not to apologize to him.

He does not warrant an apology.

Ret blew out his breath and began rubbing her feet again. "So you're open to advisors. We will need much help. Getting Brunso, Scrifres, Vanec and the peep was good, but Camp Lythe is a very conservative Clan. I am surprised that so many were willing to stand up to the FullTare in the end." Dropping his voice, he added, "I do not think we have heard the last of them."

"I agree," Maeya said. "And that is why I said that we would welcome them when the time comes."

"All except the Tares? Isn't that what you said?"

"Aye."

"And you will stand by that?"

"Aye." Maeya watched his hands tracing over her feet, pulling gently on her toes. "Why do you say they are a conservative Clan?"

"Brunso's Dragon has seen all of the seasons twice, yet he wasn't allowed to ride."

"Wasn't allowed?"

"The Tares oversaw every step of their training, and refuse to let the Riders ride or do anything else with the Dragons."

"What is the point of that?"

"They believe they're keeping the Dragons safe," he said. "They do not see that they are killing the Dragon's spirits. And the Riders', too," he added. "Brunso is so bottled up, it's a wonder he hasn't done someone damage."

Maeya frowned. "My training needs to start soon."

"Aye. But you and I can train together. If we use care."

Maeya nodded as she looked at him. The thought of private training sessions with Ret made her stomach tighten again.

"And when Darvo's Dragon is big enough," he began.

"They say that the hatchling is sickly," Maeya said.

"Who does?"

"Tare Vanec says she's sick."

Ret frowned. "We need healthy Dragons," he said with what she thought was a great lack of sympathy for Darvo's situation.

"Apologies, Rider, for taking so long," Quoran said, hustling towards them with a heavy tray. "It took me a while to—" he broke off when he saw Ret. "Pardon, Riders," he said, turning red. "I didn't realize—"

"It's all right, Quoran," Ret said. "It is time for me to eat as well." He gently lifted Maeya's legs off his lap and stood, stretching.

"Take good care of her," he told Quoran before slipping into the growing darkness, "She…carries much of our hope."

CHAPTER SEVENTEEN

Two days after they left Camp Lythe, they decided it would be better to send scouts out ahead and not worry about a rear guard. They didn't want to travel right past Saeb's group and not know it. Part of the theory was that the Dragons traveling at the back of the troupe were acting as guard anyway.

Brunso and Ret were valuable scouts, able to go far and wide in much less time than the horseback scouts. They had not found anyone. Their troupe, however, was ambushed while the Riders ranged ahead.

Maeya was walking next to Scrifres, listening to his story of Galanth. The more she heard of the black beast, the more nervous Maeya became. According to Scrifres, Galanth was near the same age as Pharla, yet he was much larger. He flew with speed and grace. And he had killed a Rider and a page, though both deaths were reported as a combination of accident and self-defense.

It was hard to tell, though where her nervousness ended and Pharla's began. Pharla was skittish around the other Dragons—Teglin especially—and she simply would not talk to Maeya about Galanth. She listened, though. O yes, she listened.

Pharla kept slowing down. When Maeya tried to encourage her to pick up the pace, the Dragon snapped at her. When Quoran walked with them, she snapped at Maeya for neglecting her. When Scrifres moved ahead to walk with his Dragon, all Maeya sensed from her was relief. So they walked in slow silence, and Maeya watched the rest of her troupe pull away.

Maeya tried not to think of what might be around the next river bend or behind the next hill, but images of a fierce fiery black beast permeated everything. Maeya tried instead to think of what it would feel like to soar in the sky and scatter the clouds behind them. Pharla refused to watch Teglin and Calla take off or fly.

Maeya switched her thoughts to Darvo. He was actively avoiding her. He, Daegny, and Eirenya had started camping apart. Eirenya had looked longingly at Maeya and Quoran, but Daegny kept the girl by her side as much as possible.

She had tried talking to Darvo three times since he had kissed her, and each time he skittered away like a frightened squirrel. Maeya understood how uncomfortable he felt, though; the urge to flee when she saw Ret approaching her fireside at camp was great. She wasn't afraid of Ret as much as she was confused by the change in his personality.

Tare Igny's change was almost as bad. He needed approval from either Tare Vanec or Maeya before he would send someone out to hunt or suggest Brunso or Ret go scouting. He had gone from being a confident Tare to a scared old man.

All of the changing group dynamics made traveling difficult.

At least the end of growing season was here. The Orb kept them warm and the rains of harvest were ahead of them. But it was still chilly when Sister Orb appeared. The creek that tripped along beside them teemed with fish. Pharla had stopped for a swim, and when she refused to listen to Maeya's reasons to keep up with the group, Maeya had gone up river for a bit of fishing, sending Quoran on with the group.

"Wait!"

Maeya spun as a strange raspy voice spoke nearly in her ear. Two boys her age were within arms reach.

Pharla hissed, but under her anger Maeya sensed anxiety. Pharla had no more heard their approach than Maeya.

"Rider, what Cave do you pledge?" the first boy asked. He was handsome enough, but he looked like he was nearly choking on his own fear.

"The Cave I pledged to is gone," Maeya replied. "We seek another."

"Which Cave do you seek?" For one who looked so scared, he sounded imperious.

"We do not seek a Cave so much as we seek Saeb and the Dragon of Prophecy."

The boy closed his eyes briefly, and when he opened them again, his smile was radiant. "The Power That Is put you in our path. We are returning to Speare Clan."

Pharla curled up on the riverbank, showing a supreme lack of interest in the conversation or rejoining the troupe.

"Speare Clan?"

"Aye, the new Clan that Rider Saeb has started. I'm Paben and this is Dirk. We're pages to Rider Saeb."

"Pages to Saeb?"

He seemed not to hear her. "How many in your group?" His lack of interest in Pharla confirmed that they were pages very used to seeing Dragons.

"How do I know that you're with Rider Saeb?"

Paben blinked. "I can only give you my word."

"Do you have horses?" Dirk asked. "We need pack horses!"

Paben glared at Dirk and Dirk turned bright red. "Your pardon, Rider," Paben said while still pinning Dirk with a glare. "Dirk has not been a page long and he forgets his manners."

Maeya nodded and continued, "We have horses, but only six. I suppose we can pull one of the scouts to let you have a pack horse, but—"

"I'll go get Noss!" Dirk exclaimed, turning to run.

Paben's hand shot out and grabbed Dirk's shoulder, yanking him back. "You have much to learn." Dirk hung his head. "Who is your leader? Is it a Tare?" Paben asked Maeya.

"Who is Noss?" she countered.

Dirk continued to hang his head until Paben shook his shoulder. "Noss travels with us as well," he mumbled.

"Is he also Saeb's page?"

"Rider Saeb gave Noss her honor," Paben said, emphasizing the title in a way that reminded Maeya of Quoran. "But all pages at Clan Speare will serve her."

"Where is Noss?"

"Guarding the—" Paben shook Dirk again, so violently Maeya feared Dirk would have a headache as fierce as hers had been.

Paben would exercise caution. You should do the same.

"Is there a Tare? Someone in charge?" Paben asked.

"Do you wish to speak to Tare Igny or to the leader of this Troupe?"

"Isn't the Tare in charge?" Paben didn't sound surprised.

Before Maeya could shake her head, a shadow passed over them. Maeya didn't look up, because Pharla told her it was Teglin and Ret, soaring in to rescue them. Dirk flinched, wrenched away from Paben and ducked behind a tree. Paben barely glanced up before looking back at Maeya. "Is the Tare leading, or does a Rider lead?"

Something in his tone made her smile. "A Rider leads."

He smiled back and brought his right fist to his left shoulder. "We ask to travel with you, Rider…"

"Maeya," Maeya said, smiling even more. He was a stickler for rules like Quoran, and he had just realized how improper this conversation had been.

"Rider Maeya," he agreed. "We ask to travel with you. Speare Clan is easy to find, if you know the way, and we can guide you. We have precious items that need safe passage."

"Maeya?" Ret had dismounted from Teglin on the other side of the creek but was still too far to hear the conversation. Pharla didn't move as Teglin approached her.

"Precious items?"

"Aye. We have a dozen eggs."

Maeya could not stop the near choking sound from escaping her lips. "A dozen?"

Eggs, Pharla muttered. *Always this fascination with eggs.*

"We did not expect to find so many. Our travels back have been slow. We meant to go to several Caves, but we only went to two. There were three eggs at River Reed, and nine at Sister Orb Cave."

"Where is Noss?"

Paben pointed across the river, away from where the troupe was heading.

"And Saeb sent you?" Maeya asked.

"Aye," he bobbed his head as Ret came to her side. "She sent Noss and me. Dirk volunteered himself."

Saeb should have stopped that one.

"Ret, go stop the others. We will camp here tonight."

"It is early yet, Maeya. We can travel much farther before the Orb sinks."

"Ret," Maeya began.

O, he still wants to lead!

"Apologies, Leader," he said abruptly, bringing his fist to his shoulder and thumping it soundly. "As you command." He turned on his heel and strode back to Teglin.

Maeya expected to see Paben laughing at her. Instead, his gaze was almost sympathetic as he kept his own counsel.

"Send Tare Vanec back to me!" Maeya hollered at Ret as he climbed on Teglin's back.

"Aye, Leader!" He yelled.

"Tare Vanec? He left Camp Lythe?"

"Aye."

"Any other Tares?"

Maeya shook her head. "Tare Igny travels with us as well, but he is from Meadow Spear Cave."

I liked Igny better when he was sure of himself.

"Did anyone else come with Tare Vanec?"

"Riders Brunso and Scrifres."

Paben grinned. "Two good Riders."

"What's wrong with Dirk?" Maeya asked Paben in an undertone. Dirk was still behind the tree.

Paben snorted. "He is a Spark who decided to become a page. He did not know pages work hard."

"Is Noss a new page as well?"

"Nay. He was a page at the Training Cave, and came to Camp Lythe with Saeb."

"You are not surprised to find that I'm the leader."

Paben's lips quirked up in a smile. "You do not look like Saeb—other than the red hair—but there is something about you that is very much the same."

"O?"

"'Tis the way you carry yourself," Dirk said, stepping out from the tree. When Paben arched an eyebrow at him, he shrugged. "As Sparks, we travel a lot from town to village to Cave to city. There are mannerisms that some people share. You and Saeb are similar in speech and gestures."

"Aye," Paben said, looking stern, "*Rider* Maeya and *Rider* Saeb use similar gestures."

"That is why she reminds us of Saeb," Dirk said amiably.

Maeya turned her head to hide her smile as Paben rolled his eyes. Dirk was oblivious as he continued, "The Power That Is makes the same changes all around. It must all be part of the same Prophecy."

"Page Dirk," Paben said firmly. "Please go to page Noss. Let him know that Rider Maeya has agreed to help us."

"Aye," Dirk said. "And I'll tell him to bring the eggs."

Dirk turned and began jogging away before he saw Paben open and then snap his mouth shut. "It will take several trips to bring the eggs," he muttered, "And we cannot leave them unattended."

"Page Noss knows this?"

"Aye."

"Then perhaps Dirk will spend a lot of time traveling between his location and here."

"Aye," Paben said again. Then he looked at Maeya and smiled. "Aye, he will spend a lot of time running back and forth!"

It did not take Tare Vanec long to find them, and Tare Igny was with him. During that time, Maeya learned a little more from Paben, including the fact that there were also two Tares with Rider Saeb's new Clan, and that one of them had bonded with a different Dragon.

"That's never happened before!" she exclaimed. "Has it?"

"Nay—at least, not that any in our Clan have heard of."

How could a Tare bond with another Dragon?

Things are changing.

Don't tell Igny!

Maeya acknowledged that telling Tare Igny might do more harm than good, as nervous as he was about all of the changes.

As soon as Tare Vanec and Tare Igny arrived, Maeya introduced them and explained the pages' task.

"Which Caves had the eggs?" Tare Vanec asked Paben.

"We went to River Reed and Sister Orb Caves."

Who cares about the eggs? Pharla grumbled.

"Those were the only ones with eggs?" Tare Vanec asked, sounding doubtful.

"They were the only ones we made it to," Paben said. "It was pointless to continue to look for more eggs when we could not carry all the ones we had already found."

"Of course," Tare Igny said. "How have the three of you been carrying the eggs?"

"Slowly," Paben said, "And in relays. We can only carry two eggs at a time, with our gear. So we end up playing hopfrog, two of us carrying eggs to a place ahead of us, then one of us going back and forth between the old camp and the new, until all the eggs were together at the new location. And then," he said with a big sigh, "We repeat the whole process. We would have been back to Clan Speare three days ago, had we been able to travel straight through. Instead, we are still two days out."

"Perhaps we should send peep out to the other Caves," Tare Vanec said to Maeya. "If Rider Saeb is interested in eggs and we are able to bring her more…"

They could serve a purpose as a gift, Pharla mused.

"You will be welcome at Clan Speare," Paben assured Tare Vanec. "We have room, and in truth are in need of more peep who can work and support the Clan."

"I believe there are more eggs at Camp Lythe," Tare Vanec continued.

"We would never get them from the FullTare," Maeya objected. "That would be a waste of time and effort."

"There are probably more eggs at Meadow Spear, too."

"Aye," Igny confirmed. "We had at least five that were kept in a back room."

"Why didn't you tell me?" Maeya demanded. "We were almost there!"

"I didn't know you were interested in more eggs. Besides, those eggs haven't hatched in years. The Cave was a blue inferno—they could not have survived." But his voice betrayed his own doubt.

Dragon eggs are very difficult to destroy.

Wyzard flame can do it, though.

Aye, Pharla sniffed. *Why are the Wyzards so determined now?*

But that was something Maeya would have to think about later. Pharla stood and began walking away. *Where are you going?*

To find a squirrel or rabbit, and then a comfortable place to sleep.

"There will be time to send more runners to look for eggs," Paben said. "What we are bringing back is more than we had hoped to find at six Caves, and we only went to two."

Tare Vanec and Tare Igny continued to regard Maeya steadily, waiting for her answer.

She gritted her teeth at the way that Vanec and Igny were ignoring Paben. "We will journey to Speare Clan as a whole troupe," Maeya said, "And with Paben to guide us, we will get there faster."

He smiled at her acknowledgment of him.

Other members of their group were coming back to them.

"Tare Vanec, could you send a few peep to help bring the eggs? That way Noss and Dirk will get some rest."

Both the Tares and the page looked at Maeya with horror. Tare Igny recovered first. "Maeya, these are Dragon eggs. Only Tares, Riders, and in extreme situations, pages, may handle the eggs."

"I think this is more than an extreme situation."

"We have pages and Riders."

"We do not have enough Riders and pages to spare."

"I will send Quoran," Tare Igny said, "And Brunso and Ret. That will be enough."

"Aye," Paben said, "We will each carry two back to your camp. And you said you have pack horses?"

"Aye," Tare Vanec replied. "That sounds—"

"Brunso and Ret will not come," Maeya interrupted. "They are flying with their Dragons. And Quoran is helping Daena tend to Scrifres' Dragon. Darvo, I'm sure, will already be hunting."

"Then we will run our relays," Paben said. "It will take a little longer, but—"

"There are three of us here," Maeya said. "If we help the Speare pages now, we will get it done."

Tare Igny grew pale. "Rider Maeya, I—"

"Will do what needs to be done," Maeya said firmly. "And right now, we need to bring the eggs into camp. Paben, please lead the way."

They encountered Dirk along the way, carrying a single egg.

"Dirk, where is the other egg?" Paben demanded.

"Noss told me to just take one," he said.

Paben crossed his arms and stared at Dirk. "I don't believe you."

Instead of responding, Dirk looked at Maeya. "Which way to your camp?"

"You're coming back with us," Paben said. "To get another egg."

"But—"

"We can each carry two eggs; we cannot carry three. If you only carry one egg, that means that someone will have to go back!"

"I can help," a voice said by Maeya's elbow. She shouldn't have been surprised to see Eirenya at her side, but she was. Maeya was glad Pharla was sleeping; she could only imagine the snide comment the Dragon would have.

"Nay—" Tare Vanec began.

"Aye," Maeya said.

"Rider Maeya—"

"Things are changing, Tare Vanec," Tare Igny said hoarsely. "And we must accept that."

"This dark orphan is not worthy of a Dragon's egg!"

"Eirenya has offered to help," Maeya snapped. "And we will accept it gratefully."

"Truly Tare, I will not hurt the egg," Eirenya said. "And once it is safely at camp, I will turn it over to the Riders and pages who have been trained to care for it."

Tare Vanec frowned.

"We must move forward," Tare Igny said.

"Lead on, Paben," Maeya said.

"That wasn't what I meant—"

"I know," replied Maeya, "But we must move forward in more ways than one."

"Which way to your camp, Rider Maeya?" Dirk asked again.

"You're coming with us," Paben said in exasperation.

"The dark girl is going with you, so you don't need me. I'll meet you at the camp."

"Dirk—"

"I'm tired, Paben!" The page looked like he was on the verge of crying. "I am so tired!"

"That's what it means to be a page," Paben said. "We tried to warn you—"

"Wait here for us," Maeya cut in. "We'll get you on the way back."

"Aye," the boy said. He looked around. "That Trident tree. I'll be right there."

Maeya looked back at Paben and nodded. She fell in next to him as they started off.

"I will talk to him when we get back to Camp Speare. He is not cut out to be a page."

"It was a difficult transition when I made it," Maeya said.

Paben should his head. "Aye, but he thinks its all going to be glory and Dragons. He does not recognize the everyday chores as being important, or caring for others as part of the job."

"Maybe you won't have to talk to him. He seemed pretty upset; he may have already decided he's done being a page."

"Perhaps." He sighed.

"What else?"

"We've been running the hopfrog pattern, moving the eggs, yet he always seems to have the egg that he carries now."

"How can you tell?"

Paben made a face. "Spend enough time with the eggs, and you notice where the spots or lines fall on them. The one he has now has a very unique double whorl."

"O."

"I wish we had not left him alone like that."

"You think I made a bad call."

Paben hesitated. "Your pardon, Rider, but aye. I believe it was a mistake."

"Thank you for your honesty. I appreciate it. But we have more important things to deal with right now."

She could tell that he was disappointed, but she didn't have time to worry about it. She could feel time—the shortness of it—pressing down upon her, even though she didn't know why.

They followed Paben to Noss, and introductions were quickly made. They picked up the eggs and hurried back to where they had left Dirk and the egg with double whorls.

They were gone.

Paben looked at her, but didn't say anything.

*** ******* ***

Back at camp, things happened quickly. Quoran took charge of Paben, Noss, and two peep from Camp Lythe to begin working on harness slings to carry the Dragon eggs. Tare Vanec dispatched four peep to search for Dirk.

"Make sure they're back when the Orb sinks," Maeya said.

"They may not find him by then."

"They still need to be back," Maeya insisted. "They need to be well rested. We will leave with first light and press hard."

"But—"

"Tare Vanec, you did ask to travel with me, didn't you?"

"Aye, Rider. But I think that finding this page may be important."

"Aye, but not more important than getting to Saeb."

"They can catch up—"

Maeya shook her head. "I don't think so."

"Why not?"

"I think, once we find Saeb, we'll still be traveling."

Noss snorted. "Rider Pedso certainly hopes so."

"What do you mean?" Maeya asked at the same time that Tare

Vanec said, "Don't you mean Tare Pedso?"

"Tare Pedso bonded with Wintre's Dragon," Noss said, "And he has been riding out almost daily, hoping to find a better place to make camp. He is not—"

"Tare Pedso bonded with another Dragon?" Tare Vanec interrupted. "How?"

Noss shrugged. "Only the Power That Is knows, Tare. Tare Adonso was just as surprised, and in truth, I think Pedso was even more so. But they have bonded, and bonded well, as far as this page can tell."

"It is not possible for a Tare to bond with another Dragon," Tare Vanec insisted. "It's never happened before."

"Things are changing, Tare," Maeya said.

"But—"

"'Tis no use to argue against it. Best learn to change with it."

Maeya went to find Pharla. She hadn't found a bush, so instead she was in a small hollow on the lee side of a hill. Quoran had set their sleeping blankets nearby.

Scratch?

"Of course," Maeya said, rubbing the emerald scales. "Your wings itch a lot!"

Aye. The eggs are being cared for?

Aye, Maeya thought cautiously as she sat down next to Pharla.

That is good.

Maeya listened, but she didn't hear any of the hostility that Pharla had always seemed to have when talking about Hiama's egg.

These eggs need to be protected. They may be the last.

"What?"

Tare Igny thinks—

"But we don't agree with him!"

We don't want to, Pharla agreed. *But we can't ignore that he may be right.*

"Where are the other Dragons?"

In a small cave further ahead. They are very fond of being inside.

And you don't like it at all, Maeya thought. Were you inside when the Wyzards attacked?

Pharla didn't move, but her mind shuddered so hard that Maeya almost thought the ground had moved beneath them.

Nothing that was inside survived that day. You know that!

Maeya reached out to rub Pharla's neck, trying to soothe her. I was not sure if—

Veet was inside. Wilad was inside. The Tares were inside, having a meeting—

A meeting? About what?

Pharla snorted. *I do not know. I was at the river.*

I wish we knew where Cyr Sajen went, Maeya thought.

He was not in the meeting with them.

But he might know what the meeting was about.

Perhaps we will find him with Saeb and the black Dragon. Everyone seems to be flocking to them.

"We will be with them soon, too," Maeya traced down to Pharla's wings, scratching at their base. Pharla didn't whirr. "The Tares say your wings itch because you're ready to fly."

Pharla said nothing. Maeya sensed her withdrawing.

"What is wrong?"

I am tired, Pharla said, turning her head away.

"Pharla. Tell me."

The Dragon lifted her head and looked steadily at Maeya. *I am telling you the truth. I am tired.* Two shadows passed over them, and they both looked up to see Teglin and Calla fly by. *And I am afraid.*

Of what?

That you deserve a better Dragon.

Maeya laughed; she couldn't help it. O, Pharla, she thought, turning Pharla's head so they were forehead to forehead. There is no better Dragon, she thought with all her heart.

I am afraid to fly, Pharla whispered in the corner of Maeya's mind, so lightly that Maeya wasn't sure she heard her at all.

Maeya kissed her between the eyes. I know.

Pharla's surprise would have been funny if it hadn't been followed by immediate indignation. *You knew? How long have you known? How did you know? Why don't you hate me? Why are you laughing at me?*

"You are part of me; I know when you're afraid. I may not always know *why* you're afraid, but since you get scared every time someone mentions flying, or flies overhead—"

I do not!

"—or get angry," Maeya continued, "it was pretty easy to put that together."

A Dragon shouldn't be afraid to fly. Pharla fretted.

"We're all afraid of the unknown," Maeya said. "But that's what we have each other for."

Are you going to exchange me for one of the eggs?

"Nay, Pharla. You are everything I want and need in a Dragon. And in a friend."

CHAPTER EIGHTEEN

There was a renewed sense of energy when they broke camp. The day's journey would not be a guess; Paben and Noss were going to lead them to Speare Camp. Daegny wasn't even complaining as she helped load Dragon eggs into sling carriers on Jingle's sidesaddle. Spiker and Storm were each carrying four eggs; Jingle had the last three. Pages Paben, Noss, and Quoran, of course, were going to lead the horses. Noss was eager, trying to get everyone moving faster than they already were. He had been especially upset that Dirk and the missing egg had not been found, but the Orb's early light seemed to focus him on getting the eleven eggs they did have to a safe location.

"May I walk with you, Maeya?"

"Of course, Eirenya."

"How is Ret?"

Maeya lifted her brows. "Why do you ask?"

"He seems to be spending a lot of time with you."

"He is from Spike Cave. I've known him a long time." It was only a slight exaggeration; she had known Ret for three years. But she had spent more time with him in the last four days than in all those years.

"O."

"How is Daegny? You seem to be spending a lot of time with her."

Eirenya gave Maeya a push. Maeya held her arms out for balance, and the little girl grabbed her hand as they began walking, Pharla behind them.

"She has gotten a little nicer. She's still a little hedgie, but—"

"Hedgie?"

"Prickly like a hedge hog."

"O," Maeya laughed.

"But she can be really nice when she wants to be."

"Or when she wants something."

"Aye. But that doesn't mean I have to give it to her."

"What did she want?" Maeya asked, looking down at Eirenya as they swung their hands back and forth.

"Your dress."

"My what?" Maeya didn't even own a dress.

"But I told her no. One, it's not hers, and two, it's not even done yet."

"What dress?"

"The one Usbarula Laureano bid me make you."

"I don't—wait. You've made it?"

"I just said it's not finished yet!"

"But it looks like a dress?"

Eirenya rolled her eyes. "Of course! Usbarula Laureano taught me as a modiste. I would not let her down."

"When have you had time to work on it?"

"Here and there."

"Aye, we've been here, there, and everywhere—but we haven't been anywhere long enough for you to make me a dress."

"I told you—"

"It's not done yet, I know. But the fact that Daegny knows it's a dress means you've been getting a lot done on it. You haven't been neglecting Ibaceta, have you?"

"Of course not!"

"How many other wolves travel with us?" Maeya still found it strange to see wolf tracks around Pharla's bedding area, but it was beginning to be a comfort as well. No one else in the group had mentioned it, however. Maeya didn't know if that meant the wolves were only protecting her Dragon, or if the others were not observant enough to see the signs when they broke camp.

Eirenya frowned. "Always three. Sometimes six. Once eight."

Maeya blinked. "Ibaceta and the other two are always the same? Or is Ibaceta the only one who is always here and there are different ones who make up the groups of two, six, or eight?"

"Ibaceta and the other two. I think they are friends now."

"That's good," Maeya said absently. "We all need friends. But we'll need to be careful when we get to the Speare Clan."

Eirenya bobbed her head. "I know. Ibaceta will have to stay away from most of the peep, just like she did at Sundee. She's good that way."

"Aye," Maeya said, rubbing her face. "But what about the others?"

Eirenya looked up at Maeya, her mouth forming a little o. "I don't know! What are we going to do?"

"I don't know," Maeya said. "Maybe we'll get lucky and they'll listen to Ibaceta."

"Maybe," Eirenya sounded doubtful. She was quiet for a few moments, then she asked, "Don't you like Darvo?"

"What?"

"I like Darvo. He's nice."

"Aye, he's very nice."

"And cute, too," Eirenya said.

"What are you after, little shadow?"

Eirenya cocked her head at Maeya. "Did Usbarula Laureano tell you to call me that?"

"Nay."

"Hmmm." Eirenya shrugged. "I just don't know why you don't like Darvo, that's all."

"Did Darvo ask you to talk to me?"

"Nay."

"Truly?"

Eirenya squirmed.

"It's all right, Eirenya. I do like Darvo. He's a good friend."

"That's what I told him!"

Maeya laughed again. "And I'm sure that's part of the problem." She shook her head. "I have been trying to talk to Darvo, but he's hiding from me. How is Hiama?"

"Good. When will she get big like Pharla?"

"Soon," Maeya said, hoping she was right.

*** ******** ***

They traveled harder and faster than they had before, yet not fast enough for Noss' taste. Maeya finally insisted that they stop for end of the day meal and make camp. Tare Vanec, Ret, Noss, and Paben all wanted to press on.

Why? There's a great bush here by the river.

Go ahead and settle in, Maeya though to Pharla. I'll be right there.

There's also a small cave for the other Dragons.

"This is a good place to stop," Maeya said out loud. "Plenty of room for us and the Dragons to all be comfortable. We'll continue tomorrow."

"The Sister Orb is half full," Noss said. "We can keep traveling."

"I don't want to show up in the dark," Maeya objected.

"It will be fine," Paben assured her. "Rider Saeb will not mind."

"I will," she retorted. "It's fine for you, Noss, and Tare Vanec, but I have never met her, have never seen her Camp. I'm not sneaking in under cover of darkness."

"It's only bad to sneak *out* under cover of darkness, Maeya," Ret observed.

Maeya rolled her eyes.

"Rider Maeya is right," Tare Igny said, "We should arrive with the Orb. We all want to see the pitch Dragon; he will be hard to see in the dark."

"Ride there with me now," Ret said, turning to Maeya. "You, Brunso, and I and our Dragons can go ahead. The rest may follow tomorrow."

"The Riders should all arrive together," Darvo said. He was holding Hiama just on the outside of the circle, opposite Maeya.

"'Tis not our fault that you and Scrifres cannot ride right now."

"I cannot ride yet, either," Maeya pointed out. "We will camp here."

"Rider Maeya—" Five voices rose in protest.

She cut over all of them. "Pharla and I will camp here tonight. The rest of you, do what you will."

"We will camp here," Tare Igny said.

"Aye," agreed Darvo.

"We will continue," Tare Vanec said. "We will get the eggs to safety and will let Rider Saeb know that you are coming."

Noss frowned. "Splitting up does not seem wise."

Tare Vanec shrugged. "We were traveling together for convenience; it is not convenient for us to stay when we are so close."

Maeya tried not to show how much his words hurt. "You will, of course, leave our horses with us, for it is more convenient for us to ride horseback than walk the rest of the way."

He smirked. "The horses come with us."

"They are ours!"

"They belong to the Clan, and as a Tare—"

"You are not my Tare!" Maeya flared, "And I'm not in your Clan! My six horses stay with me!"

"You do not—"

"She is right," Noss said. "Pardon, Maeya. I asked for your help, and it is wrong of me to not offer help when I may. I will stay with you and lead you to Rider Saeb when the Orb rises."

"Thank you," Maeya said.

"There is no reason to stop now, not when we are so close!" Tare Vanec argued.

"So go! No one here will stop you."

"Unless you try to take the horses," Darvo muttered.

Tare Vanec glared at him. "Watch how you talk to a Tare."

Hiama hissed from the safety of Darvo's arms.

The Tare turned and walked away. "I'm leaving. I'm sure Tare Adonso has Rider Saeb in line, but he'll probably need some help with the rest of you."

"Vanec—" Tare Igny said, trotting after him.

"Let's go unpack the horses," Noss said to Paben.

"Aye," they both saluted to Maeya before leaving.

"You can go with Vanec, too," Darvo said to Ret, "I'm sure you'd like to try to start impressing Rider Saeb."

Ret tilted his head and grinned. "Thanks, but I know my place. I'll go tell Brunso and Scrifres we're camping here." He looked at Maeya. "Your pardon, Maeya. I'll see you after I get Teglin settled." He strolled away.

"Darvo—"

But Darvo was already striding off into the trees, and he did not look back.

"He'll be all right."

"You think so?" Maeya didn't need to glance down; she knew it was Eirenya standing at her side.

"Aye. And so will you."

Glowing eyes appeared in the darkness of the trees.

"How is Ibaceta?"

At the sound of her name, the wolf bounded forward. Maeya flinched in spite of herself. Eirenya, however, giggled as the wolf nuzzled her side.

"She is well."

Maeya heard a slight hesitation in Eirenya's answer. "But?"

"But she is...acting...differently."

"How?"

Eirenya pulled on Ibaceta's ear. "She is much more...social than she was. She didn't used to hang out with me so much. And we're...." She trailed off.

"We're almost at the Speare Clan," Maeya said. "And we're going to have make sure she behaves."

"Aye," Eirenya smiled up at Maeya.

"She has met others in our group, aye? She has not caused problems for them."

"She seems to avoid most of the peep, but she likes Quoran and Darvo."

"We will ask Rider Saeb."

"We plan to ask Rider Saeb many things," Eirenya said. "I hope she has the answers."

"She won't," Tare Igny said.

Seeing Tare Igny and realizing that he hadn't left with Tare Vanec made Maeya smile before what he had said had registered.

"Why not?" Eirenya asked.

"Because everything is changing," he said as Ibaceta sniffed his hand and then disappeared into the forest. Maeya caught sight of three wolves that fell in step next to Ibaceta. Eirenya's wolf was easily half again as big as any of them.

"Then we will change with it," Maeya said.

*** ******* ***

When the Orb rose and painted the sky a creamy peach, Maeya was relieved to see that nearly everyone in their group was still there. Tare Vanec, apparently, had only been able to talk two of the peep into leaving with him.

While the pages got the packhorses loaded with the Dragon eggs, Daegny and Eirenya darted around everyone, getting first meal served. Darvo continued to avoid Maeya, always keeping close to Brunso, Scrifres, or Tare Igny, making it impossible for her to talk to him privately. Maeya saw an owl and frowned. It was late for the owl to be returning to nest now.

Why are you so worried about it? Pharla was walking into the river, submerging to her back spines. Maeya could feel the cold water along her skin where it touched her Dragon's scales.

Because….Maeya thought, but she couldn't get any further. Her emotions were too tangled to explain.

You are confusing.

That's because I'm confused.

I think I liked it better when it was just us.

Pharla—

We could stay here, Pharla said, swimming back up on the bank. *There's a river, and a bush, and beautiful trees….*

"Pharla," Maeya said, wading over to her. Maeya was struck by how much bigger the young Dragon was; she was nearly as tall as Spiker now. "I belong with other Riders, and you belong with other Dragons."

Pharla snorted.

"Why do you fear them?" Maeya asked, reaching up and running her hand along Pharla's neck.

I don't fear them! Maeya could almost feel Pharla's mind skitter away from hers.

"Are they mean to you?"

No. They don't talk to me.

"O. Do you talk to them?"

Pharla turned her head and looked across the river.

Maeya sighed as she shook her head. "If you don't—"

"Look out!"

Wha—

"They're coming!"

Voices were shouting everywhere: overlapping, contradicting, crying.

"They're here!"

"They've gone!"

"Keep them safe!"

A scream of pain made Maeya cringe, but when it cut off abruptly she cried out.

Rider, we must—

Maeya had already scrambled up the riverbank to her small pile of belongings and was grabbing her knife.

Rider, this way! It will be safer—

Maeya didn't waste her breath as she ran towards the commotion. *Pharla, they need our help!*

A scene of chaos had replaced the orderly packing of the camp.

Tare Igny was using a large branch effectively as a staff, knocking a man off a horse. Quoran had all three packhorse leads, and was urging them into the trees. Noss and Paben were grappling with three attackers, trying to keep them away from the packhorses. Two bodies lay still on the ground, but Maeya could not tell who they were as she ran past. Brunso was rolling on ground with another attacker. Eirenya was standing behind Ibaceta, and no one was nearing that fearsome beast.

Noss seemed to be handling his opponent, but Paben was struggling with the two who had ganged up on him. Maeya didn't check her stride as she ran full-tilt into the closest man, taking him down to the ground. She heard a terrible crunch as he struck the ground and he went limp; the Power That Is had landed his head on a large boulder, and he would not be moving again.

Maeya rolled quickly to her feet. Paben had dispatched his other attacker and was following Quoran; they would protect the eggs. Brunso was slowly standing, and though blood was trickling down the side of his face, he was the one rising and his opponent was still on the ground.

"Where's everyone else?" Maeya asked.

"They already headed out," Brunso panted, "They're up ahead."

"We must go help them," Noss said grimly, "They went in the direction these Faithful came from."

As if to prove his point, sudden shouts came from further in the forest.

Brunso and Noss began running toward the yells.

"Eirenya, stay here with Paben and Quoran!" Maeya shouted as she followed Brunso and Noss. Ibaceta licked Eirenya's face before she whirled and charged forward.

Maeya expected the wolf to sprint past her, but she loped at Maeya's side as they ran through the Trident trees. Maeya wished that the trees would move apart; it would be hard to fight at such close quarters.

She could catch glimpses of Brunso and Noss ahead of her, and the sounds of battle grew louder. A terrific roar made her stumble, but she kept going and was surprised to feel a smile on her face. Teglin was there. How could they possibly lose with Ret's big blue Dragon fighting on their side? Perhaps Scrifres' and Brunso's Dragons would be there, too. Selfishly, she found relief in knowing that Pharla was behind her and out of danger.

A suddenly blinding blue flash made her stumble again, and this time she fell, landing hard on her hands and knees. When she looked up, the path in front of her seemed to be twice as wide, and she could see people fighting hand to hand. Smoke was rising from the ground in patches, and several trees were smoldering.

Maeya pushed herself to her feet again, and was surprised to see Ibaceta still at her side. She continued forward, pushing herself even faster now. She could pick out individual voices, voices she recognized, voices that were in trouble.

As she reached the clearing where most of the fighting seemed to be, another flash of blue cracked out, and Maeya was horrified to see Scrifres drop in a lifeless heap. A roar from above told her that Ret and Teglin had seen it, too.

The blue light had come from a Wyzard on horseback. Teglin swept low over the clearing, and the horse shied sharply. The man fought to keep his seat on the horse. Maeya ran at him, raising her knife. When she plunged it into his thigh, she was shocked to feel pins and needles stream up to her elbow; she had been clutching the knife so hard for so long that she couldn't move her fingers. Fortunately she didn't drop the blade. She wrenched it out of his flesh and moved to plunge it in again.

He reached out with frightening speed and grabbed her wrist. With his other hand, he turned his small short staff in her direction. Numbly, Maeya tried to grab the stick. Before she could get her free hand up, however, a charcoal flash of fur burst past her, knocking the man off his horse. The horse bolted, leaving its rider in a pile on the ground.

"Ibaceta!" Maeya shouted, just as the wolf lunged at the man's throat. The wolf wrenched aside at the last moment, and then stood, growling, over him. The man lifted his arm and Maeya jumped on it, grimacing at the snapping sound, but she was too busy scrambling after the staff to worry about him.

She scooped up the staff and spun around, looking for the next danger.

Two shadows swept the ground, and Maeya looked up, but all she saw was Dragon silhouettes soaring away.

Beware!

Pharla? Where are you?

Here.

Maeya could feel that Pharla was near—she was upset to realize that her Dragon had gotten so close and had been blocking her—but she saw Daegny locked in a battle with another man. She ran to help, but before she got there, Daegny looped a rope around the man's neck and began pulling it tight.

"Maeya, duck!" Maeya obeyed without looking or questioning, dropping to her knees again. They throbbed in pain, but she heard the arrow whistle through the air above her.

Glancing up through her red curls, Maeya could see Brunso throwing a knife from his Dragon's back.

Darvo was struggling with another man; as far as Maeya could tell, neither of them had a weapon. She jumped up, intending to go help, when suddenly the other man turned and ran. Darvo stared after him for a moment, then gave chase.

"Darvo!" But he was already out of sight. Where was Hiama? How could he just leave her like that?

Because she is a Dragon. She is not a mouse.

Is she with you?

Of course.

"Whoa!"

Maeya turned to see Brunso's Dragon suddenly rear up, twisting violently, flinging Brunso to the ground.

Again, a brilliant blue flashed in the clearing, blinding them.

A roar louder than anything Maeya had ever heard suddenly filled every fiber of the world; it rolled through Maeya's arms and legs, it drenched the part of her mind that was Pharla, it encompassed the entire domain, and for a brief moment, Maeya thought it must have knocked the Orb from the sky.

The shadow that covered them all and blocked the light of the Orb was the pitch Dragon.

Orange flame from the pitch Dragon met blue flash and a dizzying storm arc of colors scattered over the clearing. Maeya dropped her chin to her chest, unable to bear everything.

A moment later, she heard pounding of feet and hooves as peep and animals panicked.

She forced herself to look up, to stand. She could not let herself be trampled.

The pitch Dragon was joined by a golden one. They landed, blocking Maeya's view of the rest of the clearing. There was more shouting and the Dragons were surrounded by an orange aura; then they both launched into the air.

She heard growling behind her and turned to find Pharla standing over the Wyzard Ibaceta had knocked from the horse. Maeya scrambled over to them.

Are you all right? Pharla asked.

Aye, Maeya thought, and you?

If he would just die, I'd be fine.

Pharla!

He tried to hurt you!

"Why are you here?" Maeya asked the Wyzard on the ground. "What do you want?"

The man was bruised and bleeding, and a spear was sticking out of his side, yet when he smiled he looked both intimidating and unbowed. "The end of the Dragons."

"What?"

"That is why we are here and what we want." He coughed, and blood sprayed from his lips.

"Why would you want the end of the Dragons?" Maeya asked in confusion.

"It has been foretold."

He's lying!

"By who?"

"By the one who matters."

"Who?"

But the man on the ground was gasping and making strange gurgling sounds. Maeya knew he must be in a lot of pain, but he never even grimaced. His rasping stopped.

Pharla wedged her head under Maeya's arm.

You left me.

I needed to help.

We need to be together.

We have to fight.

I know. Pharla nudged her again. *That's why I came.*

I'm glad.

The sounds of the fight were drifting and settling around them. Maeya scanned the clearing. Ibaceta was sitting a few feet away, tongue lolling, looking relaxed. But when she caught Maeya's glance, she stood.

"Eirenya?"

The wolf barked once before trotting back the way they had come.

The pitch Dragon is real. And he is close.

Are you afraid?

No.

I want to meet him, but—

There are still things to be done.

Will you wait here for me? Maeya asked.

Aye.

Brunso was kneeling next to a body. Maeya walked over to him.

"We were Riders-in-training together," he said, not looking up. "I was so jealous when his Dragon hatched first. And his Dragon was the first one to fly, too."

"The Power That Is will watch over Scrifres now," Maeya said, though the words felt inadequate.

"Aye," Brunso said. "But who will watch over his Dragon?"

"The Power That Is watches over all."

Brunso drew a ragged breath. "I don't believe it was watching well today."

Maeya put her hand on his shoulder and squeezed gently. "I know. I fear we have lost several friends."

"Rider Maeya, have you seen Darvo?" Daegny asked.

"Aye," Maeya said. "He went after one of them, that way." She could see Daegny's fear, so she quickly added, "I'm sure he is fine."

"But he is alone—"

"I am fine, sister," Darvo said behind them.

Daegny flew into her twin's arms, nearly knocking him to the ground. He was able to brace himself in time, however, and he said, "Let us help Brunso."

"With what?"

Darvo led Daegny over to Brunso's side.

"Rider Maeya, are the eggs safe?" Noss was almost as good at appearing silently at her side as Eirenya was.

"I believe so."

Noss simply stared at her.

"Are you all right, Noss?" she asked.

He half-shrugged. "The Wyzard got Scrifres. He was…fighting… right next to me…and…and then…then he wasn't."

"The Power That Is will watch over him now."

"Aye." Noss looked down at his feet.

"Noss, will you go get the rest of our friends? Bring them up here?"

"Who are we—"

"Eirenya, Quoran, Paben, and Tare Igny are all back with the pack horses."

"Aye, Rider Maeya." He saluted briefly left. And though he looked tired, his sense of mission replaced the shock and fear she had seen in his eyes.

Dimly, Maeya heard Daegny ask Noss where he was going.

"We'll go with you," Darvo said immediately, "In case there are more Wyzards or Faithful around."

"I'll come too," Brunso added. "The faster we get everyone back, the faster we can start the rites."

Maeya moved through the clearing. There were other bodies; three were Wyzard faithful, one was a follower of Tare Vanec's, but Maeya had never known his name. The last body was on the far edge of the clearing, leaning against a Trident tree. At first Maeya thought perhaps someone was only hurt. But when she drew close, she saw the arrow protruding from the chest.

It had been such a small fight, but six had died.

Seven.

Seven?

There's another one. I saw him earlier. Over here.

Maeya walked back to Pharla.

He was one of ours, Pharla said as way of warning.

Maeya took a deep breath. Where?

Back there, behind the big boulder.

Frowning, Maeya stepped under the Trident boughs, picking her way carefully to the boulder that Pharla indicated. When did the fighting come this far out of the clearing?

It didn't. This body has not seen life since Sister Orb rose.

How can you tell?

Pharla stayed quiet, but it made no difference, for Maeya had found him.

Dirk was curled up like a small child. Maeya could have believed that he was merely sleeping, except for his swollen, purple face.

Maeya closed her eyes for a moment and then reached forward, pulling his arms away from his side.

What are you doing?

Looking for the egg.

Why?

But Maeya was too busy to answer. Dirk was not curled up around the egg, protecting it as she had imagined. He was curled up against what must have been a painful stomach wound. Maeya stood up and looked around, hoping to see the egg nearby, maybe under a bush. Instead, she found footprints leading away from Dirk's body. The footprints went away from the clearing.

No.

Maeya looked over her shoulder in surprise. Pharla was on the other side of the boulder, watching her. "No what?"

You're not tracking the prints.

Maeya sighed.

We need to get back to our peep. And the pitch Dragon. Pharla turned and began walking back.

"Pharla?"

Her Dragon stopped and looked back over her shoulder.

"What happened? Why are you suddenly eager to be in battle and join the Prophecy?"

Because you are my Rider. And I will not let you leave me behind.

EPILOGUE

SAEB

Galanth and I had been out for an early flight with Treeva and Landin when we had heard the roar of a Dragon.

I do not know him, Galanth said.

"Treeva does not know that voice," Landin said, reaching for the knife he kept strapped to his back.

"You and Hord said there was another group approaching with Dragons," I pointed out.

"Aye, but—"

He broke off because there was another roar and the unmistakable sounds of battle.

Immediately, Galanth and I turned toward the blue flashes.

"Saeb, let's go get help—"

"There's no time! You may go if you'd like."

We swooped in, and I was happy to see that Landin and Treeva stayed with us instead of heading back to Speare Clan. The battle was small. At first glance, I did not see any Dragons. Perhaps they were hiding in the trees. There were only two Wyzards in the clearing and maybe three more Faithful, and one of the Wyzards was being handled by a curly red-head. Galanth and I quickly engaged the other Wyzard.

It had been a long time since we had last been attacked by Wyzards, but the lesson was still clear in my mind: we wanted the stick. But Galanth was still learning his own strength and power, and I did not scold my Dragon for incinerating our enemy.

I don't want you touching another one of those things.

You did that on purpose? I asked him as I looked at the broad swath that was now an ash pit in front of us.

Well, maybe not all of it.

We both must learn our strengths, and we must face our weaknesses, I thought to him. We must get another staff.

Why?

To understand how to defeat them, I said. We need the small staffs that throw the blue fire so we can begin to understand them, begin to find a way to defeat them.

"I will go get Tare Adonso," Landin said.

"And Frist and Tessah," I added, for it was very difficult to get one without the other. "But first let's take a quick look around; make sure that the area is secure."

"Aye."

Treeva jumped a fraction earlier than Galanth did, and the light of the Orb bounced off her golden scales blinding me. Galanth whirred.

Focus, I told him, now is not the time to admire your girlfriend.

I cannot think of a time not to.

I had to laugh. He was so fascinated by Treeva it was silly.

Together we flew in circles around the clearing, spreading further out. We saw no sign of other Wyzards.

"Where are the Dragons?" I called to Landin.

"I do not know," he said.

There are two in the trees, Galanth said.

What is wrong?

He hesitated so long I wasn't sure he was going to answer me. *One of them....*

Galanth?

He shook his head, so hard and so fast that his body twisted and I very nearly fell. I gripped the leather strap that looped around his chest and between his forelegs.

"Galanth!"

He righted himself. *Pardon, Rider.*

"Are you all right?"

There is something strange.

"Saeb?" Landin asked. "Are you all right?"

"Aye," I said, relaxing my hold but not releasing the strap.

"Treeva and I will be back shortly."

I waved my hand and our Dragons split directions; Treeva back to Speare Clan, Galanth to the scene of the battle.

Galanth's broad wings swept down twice before touching down lightly. I half-slid, half-jumped down from his back. Soon I would have to wait until he knelt to be able to get off him safely.

Which way to the Dragons? I asked him in my mind.

"Greetings, Rider, and greetings, Dragon. We thank you for your timely assistance."

I turned and saw a girl a year or two older than me standing in front of a young green Dragon. The girl had red hair with tight curls, and though she held a knife in one hand, I was pretty sure she had forgotten she had it. Her Dragon was the pretty dark green of Trident leaves during the growing season, but her eyes matched Treeva's golden scales.

"Greetings. I am Saeb. This is Galanth. We're glad we could help, though I fear we were a little late," I added, seeing the bodies.

"It was bad, but it could have been worse. We lost three. I think they lost five."

"Are you a group of warriors?" I asked, trying to lighten the mood.

"O, nay! We have been seeking you," the girl began. "I had not expected to meet you here."

I smiled. "Not much has been as expected lately."

"Nay," she agreed with a relieved grin. "Very little, in truth."

"How many Dragons are in your group?" If she thought it an odd question, she didn't show it, though Galanth was irritated with me.

She hasn't introduced herself or her Dragon yet!

She's nervous, I told him, and probably in shock from the battle.

"We have five," she said, "And eleven eggs."

"Where are—eleven eggs! Where did you get eleven eggs?"

"We met your pages along the way," and this time when the girl smiled, I could see real joy in it. "They had been very successful in your task."

"Where are they?" I asked.

"Two went back to get the eggs."

"Two?"

She bowed her curly head. "I'm afraid the Power That Is took one of your pages, Rider."

I closed my eyes. I had been warned. Tare Adonso, my mother, Frist, even Tyleen had tried to discourage me from sending the pages out alone. But I had been so sure—

"Rider Saeb!"

"Noss!" I charged across the clearing to him, spooking the horse he was leading. We tumbled in a tangle to the ground. I heard a thump and a groan. "Are you all right?"

"I was," he moaned. "What was that for?"

"You finally made it through a battle without an injury!"

"Until you tackled me," he said ruefully.

I laughed and helped him up. "I didn't hurt you that bad."

"Says who?" he demanded, twisting his arm sideways. "Now I'm bleeding!"

"It's...just a scratch," I said hopefully.

He grimace-smiled at me. "It's good to see you again, too, Rider Saeb."

I looked at the rest of the group. "Paben! You are safe as well!"

"Aye, Rider Saeb." He inclined his head to me.

"And you were successful," I said, approaching the horse he was leading. "I've never seen egg carriers like this."

"They were Quoran's design," Paben said, indicating a boy leading a dun horse. The boy had a severely scarred face, and he ducked his head at Paben's praise.

"Well met, Quoran. I am Rider Saeb."

Quoran stood straight and brought his right fist across his chest to his left shoulder. "Well met, Rider Saeb. Allow me to introduce Tare Igny, Rider Brunso, Rider Darvo, his sister Daegny, and our companion, Eirenya."

"Brunso, 'tis good to see you again."

"And you, Saeb," he said, stepping forward and clasping hands with me, "I told myself I would take you to task for leaving us, but I am too happy to see you now."

"We did not dare—"

"I know. But that did not keep Scrifres and me from following as soon as we got the chance."

I grinned. "Scrifres is here too? Where?"

"He fell this morning," Brunso said, sadly gesturing to one of the bodies.

"Where is his Dragon?" I asked.

Brunso blinked. "I do not know." He turned his head to the side, and I recognized a Rider listening for his Dragon. "Calla says—pardon," he said abruptly, running out of the clearing.

Tare Igny stepped forward. "Rider Saeb, we ask to pledge Speare Clan."

I nodded, though I noticed a strange look cross the dark girl's face. "You are welcome to come to our Clan, but we should talk more about expectations before anyone commits."

Quoran nodded; I sensed disappointment from Tare Igny and Daegny. But I was more concerned with Brunso and what his Dragon had said. I looked over my shoulder to where Galanth was. He and the green Dragon were lying down several paces from each other, staring at each other, almost trance-like. The green's Rider was sitting off to one side.

Do you know where Calla is? I asked Galanth. He didn't respond. "Galanth!"

He turned his head to look at me, crimson pinpoints reflecting in his eyes.

The other Dragons? Calla? Where are they?

He lifted his snout and looked up at the sky. I sensed sadness.

Galanth, what is wrong? I practically shouted at him in my mind.
We are in mourning.
For who? For Calla?
Nay. For the Dragon who lost her Rider. She could not take the pain.
What do you mean?
She...could not handle any more.
Any more what?
Any more any thing.
Galanth, you're not making any sense!

He turned his head back to the green Dragon. *Go find Brunso and the other Riders. They will explain. And they will appreciate the help.* He glanced briefly at me again. *And they might need some salve.*

I rolled my eyes before turning to Tare Igny. "Do you travel with a healer? Or one who knows herbs?"

"I have some herbs," Quoran said quickly.

"I fear the Dragons may be in some trouble," I said. "That's where Brunso went."

Darvo nearly jumped all the way across the clearing to the green Dragon. "Hiama! Hiama?"

Tare Igny, Noss, and Quoran moved quickly in the direction Brunso had gone. I followed.

It didn't take us long to find Brunso. He was with Calla, his green Dragon, and a blue Dragon that I almost took for Ludra, until I realized that it was much larger than Ludra was. Both Dragons were bleeding, that iridescent green and red that I had seen too much of and never wanted to see again.

Quoran fell to work quickly, but everyone else wanted to ask questions first.

"Where is Ret?"

"What happened?"

"Where is Calla?"

"Stop!" I shouted. They all turned to stare at me in surprise. "Quoran, Brunso, what do you need of us?"

That helped; between Quoran and Brunso they were able to give us direction to help Calla, but the blue's Rider was gone, and it wouldn't let us close. My heart ached for it; when Ludra lost Wintre she very nearly lost her life as well.

"I need some salve, Quoran, and if you have any Japon root, it would not go amiss."

At the sound of the new voice, the blue Dragon raised its head.

I turned to see a handsome blonde Rider walking up with Darvo. His hair was cropped short, so I presumed he was in mourning.

"Do you want help, Rider Ret?" Quoran asked as he handed him a small cup.

"If Brunso can spare you."

"Aye, Noss is doing quite well here."

"Brunso, take good care of your Dragon," Ret said passionately.

Brunso looked up in surprise.

"Had she not shown up when she did—" Ret broke off, visibly fighting for control of his emotions. He turned and stumbled to his Dragon, Quoran following.

"Rider Brunso, what happened? Did a Wyzard do this?"

Brunso shook his head, and then checked himself. "Well, in a manner of speaking, aye, I suppose he did. The Wyzard killed Scrifres. Then Scrifres' Dragon attacked Teglin."

I gasped, but neither of them noticed.

Tare Igny said, "But Scrifres' Dragon was hurt. She could not fly!"

"Believe me, she flew," Brunso said grimly.

"Why?" Noss asked. "They had not been fighting before."

Once again, Brunso shook his head. "I can only guess that Scrifres' death caused something in his Dragon to snap. I was busy fighting on the ground. Calla saw the fight and went to help Teglin and Rider Ret."

I looked up. Landin and Treeva had not come back yet; had they run into the berserk Dragon? "Which way did Scrifres' Dragon fly?"

Brunso looked at me. "She did not, Rider Saeb. She would not give nor accept mercy. The body fell behind that ridge." He pointed in the direction where Sister Orb would soon be rising.

I nodded. "It is a sad loss, but far better than losing Calla or Teglin."

I watched as each pair worked to help the Dragons, Tare Igny flitting between them. The Dragons, though obviously hurt, did not seem distraught. I feared I would be in the way, or worse, a distraction, so I slipped back through the trees to Galanth.

He and the green Dragon didn't appear to have moved. The other Rider, however, was gone.

Nay, she just went with the little girl.

Where?

Something about a dress.

A dress?

Galanth sent my confusion back to me. Paben and Daegny had tied the packhorses to a tree and were sitting on a log, talking. I started toward them, but heard giggling from the trees. It reminded me of Meegan, and I had to follow the sound.

"If anyone sees me—"

"You don't like it?"

"Eirenya, it's beautiful, but it's hardly the time to be wearing—"

"You're not really wearing it; you're just trying it on. I want to make sure I have the size right."

"I still can't believe you made it so fast!"

"I was well taught."

"Well, that I believe."

I wasn't really trying to sneak up on them, but I wasn't calling out to them, either. Their conversation sounded so much like my sisters' that it brought tears to my eyes. I heard clapping and a squeal of delight.

"O, it fits!"

"Aye, Eirenya, it does. You did your teacher proud."

"What's wrong?" I couldn't see the little girl yet, but I could hear the concern in her voice.

"It is so perfect, and beautiful—"

"But?"

There was a heavy sigh. "But when will I ever wear it? I am a Rider, Eirenya. I'm not a princess or even a lady of the estate."

O, she was a Rider who understood! I was smiling as I came around the tall Gyphanna bush.

In front of me was one of the strangest things I had ever seen. Eirenya, the little black girl, was sitting in a Trident tree. The Rider was standing in front of her, wearing a gorgeous flower-petal yellow dress. It scooped low on her chest and fell in sweeping folds all the way to the ground. Had she been standing in a ballroom, she would have been perfect.

The Rider saw me and turned bright red, all the way up to the roots of her red curls.

Eirenya swung backwards off her branch, caught her knees, and flipped neatly to the ground. She moved to stand directly between me and the girl in yellow.

"I am a lover of shadows and wolves. I am a learner of Lore and believer of Myth. I have learned much from Usbarula Laureano. I am a seeker of the Riders who will balance the world. I am Eirenya."

"Greetings, Eirenya, I am Saeb, Rider of Galanth, the Dragon of Prophecy."

The little girl's lips drew into a tight line, but she didn't say anything else.

"Pardon, Rider, but I do not know your name."

The girl in yellow had started to return to her natural color, but my comment made her flush again.

"O, my pardon, Rider! I am Maeya, Rider of Pharla."

My knees buckled under me and I sat down hard.

"Rider?" Maeya lifted her skirt and hurried to me. "Rider Saeb?"

"Maeya?" I asked. "You are Maeya?"

"Aye," she said in confusion.

I took her hand as she sank in a yellow pouf next to me. "I have been waiting for you and Pharla."

"Pardon?"

"You...you and I are going to do something together."

"What?"

I looked at her. "I was hoping you'd know."

Maeya stared at me and then we both started to laugh.

***   ********   ***

Tare Adonso, Frist, Landin and my mother arrived and quickly took charge. First we observed the death rites for those who had gone back to the Power That Is. When Maeya directed some peep where to find Dirk's body, Paben and Noss became agitated.

"What's wrong?" I asked.

Noss quickly explained that Dirk had absconded with one of the eggs two days before.

"So what happened?"

"I do not know, Rider."

"He still deserves the rites, Noss."

"Aye," he said, bobbing his head. Paben scowled but did not say anything.

As soon as the rites were finished, duties were assigned. Mom and Tare Adonso stayed with the injured Dragons and their Riders. Frist got everyone else moving toward the butte that I had claimed for Speare Clan.

"Saeb, are you coming?" Landin asked as he climbed on Treeva's back. Galanth looked over at me.

Pharla does not fly.

"I believe I will walk," I said.

"I will see you at camp," Landin said.

Galanth whirred. Then he stood and stretched and Pharla did, too. My Dragon looked like her double-sized shadow.

A tiny Dragon, one that must be a new hatchling, had been lying next to Pharla.

You really must pay closer attention to what's around you, Galanth said in a disgusted tone. *'Tis Darvo's Dragon.*

As if on cue, Darvo walked over to the Dragons. His hatchling raised its head, and though I could not hear its thoughts, I could sense its excitement. Darvo picked it up, and it curled up against his shoulder. He turned to leave.

"Darvo, you did well today," Maeya said.

He nodded, but did not say anything as he joined his sister, who was leading one of the egg-packhorses.

Maeya was watching Darvo with a strange expression on her face. "How did you get the horses to accept Dragons?" I asked.

"That's Spiker," Maeya said quickly. "He actually seems drawn to them. But he is the only horse who likes them."

"But your other horses seem much calmer around the Dragons than most I have seen."

"Daegny...has a way with animals."

"Are she and Darvo twins?"

"Aye. They are much alike." She stroked Pharla's neck. "Are we ready to go?"

As we walked to Camp Speare, Galanth and Pharla found much to talk about. Galanth was fascinated by Hiama, but found Pharla the easier Dragon to talk to, which was good, because Darvo and Hiama rode off on Spiker.

"Eirenya, where are you going?"

I looked around. I had not realized that the little black girl had joined us. Now I saw that she was just a few steps away, and seemed to be trying to drop back.

Eirenya squirmed. "I need to go check on something."

Maeya gave her a strange look, but merely said, "Don't go far."

"I won't," the little girl said.

I blinked, and the girl was gone. "Where did you find her?"

"In Sundee, though she seemed to think she found me." Maeya hesitated again, and I wondered if she would ever just tell me what she was thinking without prodding. "She didn't come alone."

"O?"

"She has a pet...sort of. More of a friend, really. Except it's a wolf."

"In truth?"

"You don't look surprised."

I laughed. "And you sound almost disappointed that I'm not surprised. We have a pet wolf, too."

Maeya tilted her head as she looked at me. "Why are you making fun of me?"

"I'm not. It's true. Although, I supposed that the truth is that Tam is more of Galanth's pet than anyone's. The pup has been most attached to him."

"We had a few other wolves that traveled with us as well," Maeya added, "They joined us in battle."

"They attacked you?"

"Nay, they fought with us."

"How many times were you attacked?"

"Twice."

"Hmmm."

"What?" Maeya asked.

"When Galanth was very small, he nearly drowned. When I pulled him out of the water, I found an owl and a wolf that had killed each other. He could not remember which had attacked him or attacked the other first. I believe, now, that the wolf was protecting him. We have seen owls—""

"Twice!" Maeya blurted out. "Each time right before we were attacked!"

"So you have seen them too?"

"Aye."

"I think it may be time to declare owls our enemy," I said.

"And Pharla declares wolves our friends," Maeya said.

"As does Galanth," I grinned at his whirr.

"This is the creek we use for water," I said, waiting for Galanth. He had gotten better about going through water, but it still bothered him.

Maeya waded in without hesitation and climbed the far bank. "Where is the camp?"

"Through the trees and on the other side of the meadow," I called. Galanth was stepping gingerly into the water, but Pharla jumped in, spraying us both.

Must you? He said in disgust.

Must I what? I thought to him.

Not you, he said to me, *I was talking to Pharla.*

"And this is the closest water?" Maeya asked, climbing back down the bank. She seemed concerned.

"Aye."

She tilted her head as she watched Pharla. The green Dragon was completely submerged; only the top of her head, from the eyes up, was visible.

"Is she all right?" I asked in concern. Though she was smaller than Galanth, there was no way we'd be able to lift her up and out of the water.

Right then, she lifted her head and blew out through her nostrils, spraying more water onto Galanth. I sensed his irritation but did not hear what he said to her.

"Aye," Maeya said, with a small smile, "She's just annoyed that she's going to have to travel so far to swim."

"Swim?" I asked. Galanth was disgusted—and a bit impressed as well.

"Aye. Pharla loves the water."

"Perhaps she can help Galanth get over his fear."

"If Galanth will help Pharla learn to fly."

I could only guess that Maeya was getting the same odd mixture of fear, indignation, and disgust from her Dragon as I was getting from Galanth.

As soon as we arrived at the butte, Maeya asked, "Where is Tare Vanec?"

"Tare Vanec? I'm sure he's still at Camp Lythe, fawning over FullTare Craedo."

Maeya shook her head. "Tare Vanec led the group of peep who left Camp Lythe," she said, "He was with us until last night."

"What happened last night?"

She shrugged. "He didn't want to wait, since Noss told us that we were so close to you."

"Why did you wait?"

"I did not want to arrive in darkness. It sounds silly now, but—"

"I understand," I assured her.

"Perhaps if we had all continued, we all would have made it here."

I looked at her sharply. "Perhaps if you had continued, the attack would have been in the darkness, and claimed even more lives."

Maeya shrugged again, and I could tell that she was unconvinced.

"And Tare Vanec was the only one who left?"

"With two peep."

"So where are they now?" I wondered aloud.

"I fear..."

"What?"

"Dirk left...with a Dragon's egg...."

"Aye?" I prompted when she stopped.

"He...did not have it...it was not with him...when I found his body. But there...there were...."

This was becoming annoying. "Maeya, what are you trying to say?"

"There were footprints leading away from the body," she said in a rush.

I just stared at her.

"I think someone—Tare Vanec—took the egg."

"Why would he do that?"

"Because of Tare—Rider Pedso."

For a moment it didn't make any sense, but then I saw what she was getting at. "O."

"I could be wrong," Maeya began.

I shook my head. "Nay, don't doubt yourself," I said. "There are too many peep here who are willing to do that for us. It makes sense, if he wants to bond with another Dragon, but—it was a Dragon in mourning that bonded with Tare Pedso, not an egg that hatched for him."

Maeya nodded. "That's what Noss said."

"And even if Tare Vanec wanted to see if the egg would hatch for him, why not just bring it here?"

"Exactly! Where did he go?"

But as to that, neither of us could find an answer.

*** ******** ***

Things became very hectic as soon we got to the butte. Suddenly I had too many things to do: talk to Frist about Dirk's death, talk to Tare Adonso about Tare Vanec's disappearance, introduce Tare Igny to Tare Adonso, introduce the Riders and their Dragons, find caves and rooms for all the new peep, find a safe place to store the eggs, and check in on my family. Maeya was whisked away by Tyleen as soon as I introduced her, and I did not see either of them again until we met at the central hearth for dinner.

"How is Pharla doing?"

"Uneasy," Maeya said, picking up a rabbit leg from the platter.

"O?"

Maeya began ticking points off on her fingers, "The creek is too far, I'm sleeping in a room too small for her, the climb up the butte is too steep, and there are too many Dragons for her comfort."

"She doesn't like Dragons?"

"She says she doesn't know how to talk to them."

I smiled. "Our Dragons seem very much alike. Galanth had a hard time talking to the Dragons when we first got to Camp Lythe, too."

"Pharla has liked talking to him, but I think she's a bit afraid of Treeva."

"I'm sure they'll be fine. And Galanth didn't like sleeping on the butte at first, either, but I'm not sure I'll ever get him to sleep in a Cave again."

Maeya laughed. "They do sound much alike. But it's hard to imagine him having any problems at all."

"He's come a long way. We both have." I noticed that Maeya was staring off into the camp. I looked, and saw Eirenya running through the field with Jaret chasing her.

"It looks like she's made friends with my brother Jaret."

"Aye. Eirenya was most happy to meet him and Tam. And it seems that Tam and Ibaceta have made friends, too."

I looked again, and could see flashes of fur in the grass. Jaret shrieked and fell under a pouncing light grey fur. I took a drink of the mulled wine, trying to slow my heart. I knew that Tam would never harm Jaret; I would have to trust that Eirenya and Ibaceta would be just as playful.

"Who is that?"

"Where?"

"Walking with Daegny."

I looked in the direction Maeya was staring. "That's Reena. My younger sister."

"Hmmm."

"What?"

"They seem to be having fun."

I looked again. Daegny and Reena were talking animatedly. Reena threw her head back and laughed so loud, I could hear it across the camp. When I looked back at Maeya, she was frowning.

"What's wrong?"

"I've never seen Daegny like that. So happy. So alive."

"Me either." Maeya looked at me funny, and I hastened to explain, "I've never seen Reena that happy and alive. She's usually so prickly."

"Hedgie," Maeya said with a wistful smile. Then she said, "Tyleen is very sweet."

"Aye," I said, looking around. "I wonder why she is not here?"

"I think she was talking to Darvo."

I shook my head. "That girl!"

"What is wrong?"

"Nothing," I said. Just because Tyleen seemed to find excuses to spend time with every cute boy she saw did not mean that she was already starting something with Darvo. Did it?

"Greetings, Rider!"

"Mom," I said in exasperation, "I've told you—"

"—and greetings, Saeb," Mom continued, arching an eyebrow at me.

I lowered my head as Maeya laughed and said, "Greetings..."

"Tessah," Mom supplied easily. "It will take time to learn everyone's name, especially as fast as Speare Clan is growing."

"Aye, that's certain. The rabbit's good," I added as Mom looked over the table.

"Does that mean you want more?"

"Of course!"

"But leave some for us, please," Landin said as he and Quoran joined us at the central hearth.

"All is well, Quoran?" Maeya asked. It was nice to finally see another Rider who seemed to care about her page as a friend.

"Aye, Rider. I have set your things out in the room Rider Saeb has given us."

"Thank you."

"Where are you and Pharla from?" Mom asked as she loaded her plate with rabbit, apple, and hard bread.

"Spike Cave of the Panir Clan."

"We heard they had been wiped out," I said, helping myself to some of Mom's rabbit.

"Aye," Quoran said.

"Is that where you found the proper girl?" Landin asked Maeya as he sat next to me.

"Proper girl?" I asked, taking a bit of bread off his plate as well.

"The little dark one. She gave me quite the lecture on the proper way to introduce myself."

"Really? Let's see it, then," I said, taking the plate from him.

He looked at me for a moment, then stood. "Ah...yes, I put my hands on my hips, to show that I am a man, like this," he demonstrated, and Quoran began choking on something. Mother tried to whack him on the back, but he waved her away.

"I am the second son of the first son of the first son of the house of Paers," Landin said, pitching his voice deeper than normal. "I am a believer of change. I am the twin brother of Lamry, may the Power That Is guide his spirit well. I am Treeva's Rider. I am Landin Paers."

I set the plate on my lap and clapped while he bowed. "Do you spend that much effort introducing yourself each time?" he asked Maeya as he sat down and tried to take his plate back from me. "I believe I would avoid meeting new peep whenever possible!"

Maeya laughed. "'Tis a tradition of the Iriid towns, but is very strictly adhered to in Sundee, where we met Eirenya. Her teacher was not best pleased with me when I did not immediately say, 'I am the only child of Taena Daceae and—'"

Mom dropped her plate of food with a clatter. "Taena?"

"Aye."

"She was your mother?"

"Aye," Maeya said again, staring at my mother with concern.

"Did she have a birthmark, here," Mom gestured to a spot on Quoran's back, "red, that looked like a Trident leaf?"

Maeya's eyes got huge. "Aye."

Mom fumbled and found a log to sit on. "Taena! After all these years!" she looked at Maeya with tears brimming in her eyes. "You look just like her. I thought maybe, but I hadn't dared to hope...I cannot wait to see her again!"

"I am sorry, Tessah, but my mother died."

"Taena died?"

"Aye."

"When?"

Maeya took a deep breath. "The Daceae estate was attacked at the beginning of awakening season. All were killed."

Tears overflowed and rolled down Mom's cheeks when she closed her eyes.

"Pardon, Tessah, but how did you know my mother?"

"She was my sister."

I felt my mouth drop open. "Your sister? My aunt?"

"Aye."

Maeya and I looked at each other. "Cousin!" we said together.

"Aye," Mom said, and there was something strange in the look she was giving us.

"How many aunts do I have?" I asked, dreading the answer. Mom opened her mouth and then snapped it shut, looking abashed. "How many?" I pressed.

"I had two sisters. I've not seen either since I was five."

"Were you the eldest?"

Wordlessly, Mom shook her head.

"Youngest?"

She shook her head again.

Maeya suddenly gasped. "You're a witch!"

"Taena, Tallah, and I were three born together," Mom said. "But that did not make us witches."

"Nay," I said with a sigh, though I couldn't help thinking that her grandmother had already done that. Later I would ask her if all three had leaf-shaped birthmarks, because I knew that Mom had a Trident leaf on her thigh. I turned to Maeya. "Well, Maeya, I was looking forward to meeting you and that was before I knew we were related."

"Aye," she said. "Me too."

"I hope you haven't eaten everything," Tare Adonso said as he and Tare Igny strode into the firelight, Darvo and Ret close behind. "I promised Tare Igny a good meal."

"The rabbit has rave reviews," Quoran said, standing, "Let me—"

"Now, now, Quoran," Tare Igny said, "The food is out. We can all serve ourselves. Finish your meal."

"I have," he said, "and I believe I will retire."

He left, but the central hearth was still feeling crowded.

Mom cleared her throat. "So your last name is Daceae?" She asked Maeya.

"Aye. And I just learned that it means daffodil."

"Saeb!" Landin exclaimed, trying to catch the plate that fell from my fingers.

"Daffodil?" I moved over to sit next to Maeya.

"Aye." She lowered her voice, though Tares Adonso and Igny were talking so loudly with Ret I don't think anyone else would hear her. "That's why Eirenya made the yellow dress for me."

I swallowed hard. "Are there many daffodils at your family home?"

"Nay. Isn't that strange? When Eirenya's teacher told me that my name means dream and my family name means daffodil, she seemed to think it was important. I didn't want to tell her that I have never seen a daffodil on our estate."

"Never?" I asked, thinking about my vision of the daffodil. "Is the estate big?"

Maeya shrugged. "It is a good-sized land, I supposed. It has not been well cared for in years, however. Many of our peep have left. And all buildings were burned down during the attack."

"So no one lives there now?" I asked excitedly.

Maeya shook her head.

"And the grounds are good for planting?"

"They used to be, but it's been a long time since—"

"How long would it take to travel there?"

"If we traveled quickly—"

"Could we be there by the beginning of sleeping season?"

"You mean to move the whole Clan?"

"Aye."

Maeya considered. "I believe so. But the land was burned, Saeb. There will be nothing to harvest. And sleeping season can be very, very harsh."

"But we could do it."

"There will not be any shelter."

"We can build it. Are there Trident trees?"

"A forest."

"Any Gyphanna bushes?"

"I think so."

"Wolves?"

Maeya gave me a crooked smile. "They will come with us."

"Aye. And so will many others." I reached out and grabbed her hand. "Let's make it the family home again." The wrap on my wrist shifted, and Maeya gasped. I tried to pull my hand away from her, but she reached out and grabbed it instead.

"Shh," I half-whispered, half-begged. Mother was the only one who had seen the strange marks that the Wyzard's staff had burned into my skin.

Instead of asking me what had happened, or if it hurt, Maeya asked me, "Do you know what it says?"

"Nay. Do you?"

"Nay. But the same thing is carved on my mother's jewel box." Maeya looked me in the eye for the first time without fear or hesitation. "It is time for us to go home."

        ***   ********   ***

Although everyone had found fault with my chosen location and had wanted us to move before, now that I had decided to move again, I had to fight all over. The argument had lasted long after Sister Orb had risen and the fires had guttered out.

What was most frustrating was that all the reasons I had given for staying were now being used by Tare Adonso and Frist for staying—and they sounded more convincing. And when I used their arguments to move on, they found counterpoints that I had never seen before.

Maeya had sat quietly for most of it, answering questions about her old home as best she could.

"Why is it suddenly so important for you to go home now?" Frist had asked.

"Because Rider Saeb wishes to," she had said. "And because I forgot something."

Tare Adonso looked at her. "What?"

"My mother's jewel box. I did not have time to get it when I left."

"Jewels," Frist snorted. "What good are jewels?"

"They are my heritage," Maeya said calmly, "And memories of my family."

"And mine," I added.

Maeya smiled.

"We cannot leave now," Stram said. "There have been too many attacks. We will be vulnerable while we travel."

"If we wait much longer, they may surround us."

"We will be able to dig in and fight."

"And then we will never be able to leave."

"We barely have enough crops to harvest now," Mom pointed out. She used a gentle tone, but I still felt let down, almost betrayed.

"We'll harvest what we can now and take it with us. And we will harvest what we find as we go."

"What do you mean?" Tare Adonso asked.

"We will travel as quickly as we can, but if we find wild berries, or grain, we can stop and everyone can harvest. We will probably end up with a larger, better harvest if we gather as we travel than if we try to just gather here."

Frist was shaking his head, but Mom positively beamed. "That's brilliant!"

"But what about—" Frist began.

But I had had enough.

"Galanth and I are leaving," I said. "We will welcome any who wish to travel with us."

"Pharla and I will travel with you," Maeya said, barely speaking up before Landin and Ret both said, "I am with you, Rider."

"Of course we're coming with you, daughter," Mom said.

"Rider, I cannot advise you if I let you go without me," Tare Adonso said.

"We will all be coming with you," Frist muttered. "For there really is no other choice."

"There is always a choice," I said. "The Power That Is grants many."

As Maeya and I left the central hearth, I was exhausted. The Orb's rays were just kissing the top of the butte when we reached it. At first glance, the Dragons were in their customary pile. But then I realized that there was one solitary lump at the far side of the butte.

"Excuse me, Rider Saeb," Maeya said, and she hurried off to the far side.

Galanth's head lifted from the large mass. *You're up early.*

Have not gone to sleep yet, I said, picking my way over to him.

He shook himself slightly, and Treeva shifted away, giving him room to stand up. He nudged Calla with his snout, and she moved, too. *Are we flying,* he asked as he met me in an open space, *or am I hiding you under a wing so you may sleep?*

"I haven't decided yet," I said. "How is Calla doing?"

Better, as is Teglin, though both were angry that they had to climb up the butte instead of flying. 'Twas good for Pharla, though.

"Why is she over there?" Maeya had reached Pharla now and I could see her scratching her Dragon's back.

It's where she wanted to be.

"Is that—"

It's fine. Hiama is with her.

"O." We began walking to the edge of the butte.

So we're leaving?

"Aye. We're going to the daffodil estate."

But you haven't seen it yet.

"It's the daffodil estate, and Maeya, my cousin, will take us there."

Aye, he said. *But how long a journey will it be?*

Long, I said, and I do not believe it will end when we get there.

O?

Do you?

Nay. I believe you have another cousin out there.

And I believe we will meet her soon.

Her?

Well, it would keep things easier.

Galanth unfurled his wings. *Somehow, I don't think that's what the Power That Is is worried about.*

No, I thought, as I watched the silhouette of Maeya, the Rider who had already survived the loss of her family and a Dragon egg, and Pharla, the Dragon who wanted to swim instead of fly, the Power That Is certainly does not care about making things easy.

Good thing you enjoy a challenge, Galanth said and he dropped off the butte's edge, plummeting before suddenly grabbing an air current and swooping upwards. The Orb was bright on the horizon.

Only when I am with you, my friend! I thought. With you, I can face Dragons, Wyzards, and anything the Power That Is wants to give me.

Aye. Together we can—and will—face anything.

DRAGON'S LORE
is the second in a projected short series. Look for
DRAGON'S LAMENT
in 2014.